GHOSTS OF NEW YORK

GHOSTS OF NEW YORK

A NOVEL

jim lewis

WEST VIRGINIA UNIVERSITY PRESS

MORGANTOWN

First edition published 2021 by West Virginia University Press
Printed in the United States of America

ISBN 978-1-949199-96-3 (paperback) / 978-1-949199-97-0 (ebook)

Library of Congress Cataloging-in-Publication Data
Names: Lewis, Jim, 1963– author.
Title: Ghosts of New York : a novel / Jim Lewis.
Description: First edition. | Morgantown : West Virginia University Press, 2021.
Identifiers: LCCN 2020051293 | ISBN 9781949199963 (paperback) |
          ISBN 9781949199970 (ebook)
Classification: LCC PS3562.E9475 G56 2021 | DDC 813/.54—dc23
LC record available at https://lccn.loc.gov/2020051293

Book and cover design by Than Saffel / WVU Press
Cover image: Saul Leiter, *Times Square, 1950s*. © Saul Leiter Foundation, courtesy
Howard Greenberg Gallery

In memory of Laura Anders
Heidi Kriz
and George Reiff

Surely a remedy might bring about its problem, a recompense its sorrow; a moment might be longer than a year, and backwards run, or twist like an opaline fish gasping in the sunlight. Star, man, beast and atom, alike are helpless before the simple mysteries of duration; and die upon an impossible rack. O pity! O Mnemosyne, a trollop you are!

—P. Garza, *Of the ticking of a clock*, 1864
(trans. Harriet Oberheim)

GHOSTS OF NEW YORK

THE NEW LOVE

This is how it's going to happen. A man is going to walk out the door of an apartment building on Hudson Street in New York City. He'll have been visiting a friend who lives there; they'll have been talking too much to each other, as friends sometimes do. They'll have had an argument, nothing final, nothing that really threatens their affections; the man will be leaving as much to get some air as out of frustration, but he'll leave nonetheless, and he won't plan on coming back soon. The man's name will be Dominic.

It will be a winter evening, a few weeks before the New Year, and he'll draw his black overcoat tighter and then stop to search his pockets for his gloves, cocking his head in annoyance when he realizes that he's left them upstairs, or perhaps lost them altogether. He'll pass a woman on a single crutch who's watching the street from just inside the door, and then he'll exit into the night.

He'll be a young man, though old enough, and he'll be of medium height, or perhaps a little taller, and have a medium build, or perhaps a little thinner. He'll have black hair, and skin so pale one might be inclined to call it unnatural, except it looks natural on him; and his eyes will be uncannily alert and his mouth set hard. He'll be dressed like a man who's preparing himself for some kind of combat, or returning from combat and making the transition back into civil society: black pants, a black long-sleeved T-shirt, a shapeless grey sweater, a black overcoat, and black shoes, or rather boots, which rise just past his ankles—not combat boots, they'll be Italian and fashionable, though somewhat scuffed, as if he's been wearing them every day, or bought them secondhand.

He'll pause just outside the door, startled and left almost breathless by a sudden cold wind, which blows for a few seconds and then just as quickly expires; and he'll turn hurriedly and start up the street, as if he's hoping that if he moves quickly the wind won't be able to find him. There will be no snow, but the sidewalks will have patches of ice on them, so that he'll have to slow down as he reaches the intersection, pick his way against a red light, and resume his pace when he reaches a more-traveled block, one lined with a grocery store, a jewelry shop, a liquor store, and a pharmacy, all of which are still open.

That night, in a bar on Seventh Avenue South, where he's gone for a drink and a look around, Dominic will encounter a man. He'll notice the other man when he enters: an older fellow, old enough to keep his clothes carefully pressed and his worries well hidden, sitting at a table with two women, well or at least expensively dressed, and an unusually pretty girl, eleven or perhaps twelve, who will be quietly listening to their conversation. Later, the older man will be leaving the bathroom just as Dominic is approaching it, and he'll hold the door for just a second, causing Dominic to hasten toward him. That will be a moment of mutual consideration, and a brief look, so quick as to be nothing if it's nothing, or something if it's more.

The same man will be standing outside the plate glass window of the bar as Dominic is leaving, with the fight he had with his friend earlier in the day on his mind: how unreasonable it was, and really, how foolish they both had been. The two women and the girl will be gone, and the older man will be standing in the middle of the sidewalk smoking a brown paper cigarette and gazing into the distance carelessly. His cigarette will smell like burning honey; he'll tap an ash onto the sidewalk. Dominic is going to stop a few feet away, reach into his jacket pocket for his own cigarettes and discover that he can't find his lighter. When he turns to the older man for a match, the older man is going to speak.

God is great, he will say.

Praise God, Dominic will reply. Do you have a light?

The older man will nod, reach into his pocket and light Dominic's cigarette. There will be that moment of silence while the act is concluded, followed by a breath-long pause as Dominic enjoys the first moments of smoke. Then, Were you over on Hudson earlier this evening? he'll ask the older man, though he'll have no reason to believe the other man was.

The older man will shake his head.

No? Dominic will say. I thought I might have seen you there.

I don't think so, the older man will say, and his uncertainty will underscore the fact that he speaks with a very slight accent, a noticeable inflection, but so faint that it's impossible to place.

No? Dominic will say again, and then: It must have been someone else.

They'll talk for a few minutes after that, discussing little things—how surprising it is, every year, when winter comes and the sun sets even before the workday is over; how the older man's long coat is light enough to wear in the daytime and warm enough to wear at night; how pleasant it is to have a drink in the quiet of an empty bar—and pleasant, too, to have a drink with friends, and talk over the affairs of the day.

Tell me, the older man will say, because I'm new to this city. He'll gesture out to the lights and traffic, the pale orange of the sodium-lit sky, the vapors collecting and dispersing like clouds. Tell me: Is it always so bright and so busy?

Yes, Dominic will say. Night after night.

I'd heard it was like this, the older man will say, but I wouldn't have believed it if I didn't see it with my own eyes. And the advertising. It's as if they're trying to sell you things all the time. At breakfast, buy a little something. In the afternoon, would you like a bottle of whiskey? After dinner, perhaps I can interest you in a new car? While you sleep, will you think about purchasing a new television? A computer? Some food for your dog?

Dominic will nod at this, and smile ruefully. It's that kind of place, he will say. You get used to it.

The older man will wave his hand modestly. Get used to it? he'll ask, and then answer himself. I don't think I could. Tell me something else: Is there as much crime here as they say? It's famous for that.

That would depend, Dominic will say, on what you consider a crime.

There will be a polite pause while the older man contemplates this answer. A crime, he'll say, is the way I've eaten tonight. How much— and here he'll briefly rest his hand on his midsection, which is none-theless noticeably trim—and how well. This food, he'll continue. The way the people eat here. So rich, and there's so much of it, so many restaurants. He'll smile to himself. Imagine, he'll say: complaining that the food is too good.

You weren't complaining, Dominic will say. You were just pointing it out.

That's right, the older man will say, nodding agreeably. I was merely pointing out that there is a great deal of it, and it's so good. And yet . . .

It can be too much, Dominic will say. I know: Most people don't realize how much stronger their appetite gets when they come here. Like bees on flowers, they just feed, feed, feed.

With that, there is going to be a long silence between them. Dominic will draw on his cigarette harder than usual, studying the orange tip as it flares briefly. The older man will turn away, look up and down the street, put his hands in the pockets of his coat and draw it more closely around him. We should go for a walk, he'll say. You and I.

Dominic won't respond right away, and the older man will fear that he's given offense, and his heart will quicken. But Dominic won't be offended, he'll be enjoying the moment, the way it dances like a bit of spume upon the ocean of night, until he nods and makes a slight gesture of deference, as if to say to the older man, Wherever you would like to go, I'll be happy to follow.

There are going to be photographs everywhere; billboards, posters, flyers taped to the light-poles, signs in stores and advertisements on the sides of taxicabs. Chilly as the night is, there will be men and women standing in doorways, just as they've always done; they'll be alone in the darkness that shifts inside to stairs, smoking cigarettes with their shoulders hunched to their ears; or there will be two of them watching a third swaying back and forth on his feet. A shoeless woman in a red dress is going to come darting out from a vestibule, look quickly up and down the street, and then dart back again—too late, the glass door will have closed and locked behind her, and she'll bang on it with the flat of her hand and then stand back on the sidewalk, hopping from one foot to the other, craning her neck up and shouting, Ian! Ian! I locked myself out! Goddamn it, Ian! I know you can hear me!

The avenues will be broad and busy, but the streets will be narrow and intimate, and each man will be able to hear his footsteps mingle with those of the other. They'll pass beneath trees tangled in the street-lights, step aside for a woman walking a large white dog; they'll go by a post office, now locked for the night, but inside the doors there are going to be canvas sacks of mail, letters, bills, magazines, notices, solicitations, all waiting to be delivered by the first light of morning.

In time, without any particular discussion or agreement, Dominic and the older man will find that they're walking toward the river: the blocks will grow broader and the buildings darker, creating unexpected vistas, unexplained stretches, where whole neighborhoods, industries, vast forms of life will have been entirely removed, driven back into the ground, it will seem, like nails that have been pounded into a piece of soft pine, the points that were their purpose now buried out of sight. It will be one of those nights, in one of those landscapes, when it's possible to believe that act and emotion are the same thing, after all. Still, Dominic and the older man won't touch, nor even brush against each other; they'll walk where their legs carry them, and talk happily into the hours.

I remember it well, the older man will be saying. Better than I remember yesterday, or the day before yesterday. The sensation, like having your hand in someone else's pocket, do you see what I mean?

And Dominic, who might, if he so chose, take such a metaphor to be suggestive or ill-mannered, will smile instead, and say, Yes, that was exactly what it was like. It was like waking up from a nap in another country, wasn't it? Drowsy, comfortable, but still exciting and strange.

Will we ever have days like that again? the older man will ask, and he'll mean it, not rhetorically, but as if he really wanted to know. When he's done asking there's going to be a pause so long that it'll feel more like a silence, a diminishing interrogative point, dwindling down to a hush.

Someone might, Dominic will say at last.

Before them the highway will be full of cars, stalled by the lights and stretched uptown to 14th Street, their bright husks shining like the glass-coats of beetles. A young Dominican woman in a tight black dress will get out of the front seat of a dark sedan and stand in the road, the car door open behind her as she stares at the traffic, a corona encircling her head. The driver of the car will honk once, twice, she'll duck her head and look inside, and then as he honks again she'll walk away, leaving the door open as she sways between the lanes, awash in the sound of horns, and then vanishes again into a neon-blue sports car.

I'm far from home, the older man will say. Back there, back then, I had everything a man could wish for. I had a small house that was all my own, and neighbors who were friendly but kept to themselves. No man was my enemy, and my friends were a pleasure that never failed. I had food in the cupboard, and coins in my pocket for a drink or two. I had cotton clothes in the summer and woolen clothes in the winter, and I made love in the daylight, if that was what I wanted. There were no policemen anywhere, because the world was kind. I couldn't say if I had died the day before, or would die the day after, and it never occurred to me to wonder.

I have no home, Dominic will say, and the older man will look at him with a touch of pity. — Oh, not like that, Dominic will add. I have an apartment, all the way uptown, by my school. He'll gesture vaguely north. It's just that I don't like to sleep there. I'd rather be out here, out anywhere.

School? the older man will ask. Well, now, you'll have to tell me what you're studying. — No. Allow me to guess. He'll take a step back and scrutinize Dominic, and it will be their first really good look at each other. The older man will pause for a moment, and then say, Poetry. Dominic will smile and shake his head. No? the older man will say. Then perhaps . . . theater?

Dominic will shake his head again and say, But you're close. Then he'll take a step back, hold his arms out in a welcoming gesture, smile wryly, and execute a flawless plié-assemblé sequence, encumbered though he is by winter clothes.

Ah, the older man will say. Of course: I can see it now. He'll nod amiably, and they'll start off again, until in time they reach the piers. Across the Hudson lights will be glowing; from time to time a party boat with dark figures arranged on the deck will slide past them on the night-water, making its way to or from the docks of the financial district, evidence of more cities built in the hollows of this one, each nestled inside the others. Here's a river, the older man will say. The river leads to the ocean, and in the ocean live all sorts of creatures: great schools of grey fish, sea serpents, octopus and giant squid. All of it just—and here he will gesture—out there.

I never think of it that way, Dominic will admit. When I'm here, all the life I can possibly want is here.

Couples will be huddled on the pier, and it will be hard to tell whether that was a man or a scrap of paper that just went by on the wind. Lights are going to fall from the sky as airplanes land off the water, again and again and again. A siren will pass behind them. The older man will take up the conversation again, saying, As for the island we stand upon—they will both turn to look at it—have you ever noticed that they don't bury their dead here?

What do you mean? Dominic will ask in return.

There are no cemeteries. None to speak of, anyway; maybe little churchyard things here and there. The rest have been banished to the outlands. It's the only city I've ever been in where there's no room for even the dead to rest.

This is how it's going to happen. Dominic will reflect on this, and then he'll say, But there are so many ghosts, aren't there? From all the fires and all the falls, the plagues and the murders, ghosts of dead mayors, police officers, priests, ghosts of prostitutes and addicts, ghosts of the very rich and the very dull, movie stars and shoeshine boys, every trader, every grocer, every secretary, every drunk in every bar. Here Dominic will appear to be growing angry, in a way that doesn't frighten the older man, nor is it meant to. It's just the way he feels, when he feels something immense. — No one dies in New York without leaving a phantom behind, he'll say. It doesn't matter where they're buried, or if they're buried at all. Everyone who was ever on this island remains here, everyone who ever came here to live, and loved or hated the place, or loved or hated anyone here.

They are everywhere, the older man will agree. Suppose we could set them free, you and I? Suppose we could bring them back, make them visible, to occupy the city side by side with the living, dressed as they would have dressed, alive as ever, so that time itself ceased to exist, and past and present mingled freely. Imagine if we could rejoin one another. He'll pause, the older man, and there will be something in his aspect, a premonition, as it were, of being understood, coupled with a very slight air of harshness, something bitter in his eyes, but not unpleasant—gratifying, in its way, like the first sip of black coffee, or a long-anticipated betrayal that at last becomes real. Dominic will catch it and he'll smile hotly. The older man will smile as well and say, Just for a moment. Just for a bit, maybe just one more time.

Dominic will stare at the older man's face, his skin smooth, his eyes bright, and he'll start to feel a joy that he hasn't felt in a long time. It'll be so warm that it will make him shiver, the naturalness of it will take him by surprise, and make his legs weak and his mouth drop open, and he'll sink slowly down to his knees, so that the lights rise and reel around him, framing his head. His face will be burning, and when he's caught his breath he'll look up at the older man and ask, Now?

And the older man will stop smiling, because a smile is not enough, and he'll say, Yes. Now.

THE BIG ROCK CANDY MOUNTAIN

Now it was dark. The plane was going to be late: They had been hours behind schedule leaving London, there were thunderstorms down in Spain and the airlines' plans were hopelessly mixed up, connections canceled, flights unable to leave because the necessary aircraft was still in transit, hundreds of miles away and thousands of feet up in the air. Stephanie had been caught in the backup, stuck inside the terminal, with its rank smell of industrial carpeting and artificial butter. And then suddenly there were dozens of arrivals, airline employees announcing updates and requests for patience over the din of people talking, finishing up their phone calls, collecting their things; and then all at once the planes were filled in a huge mad jam that resulted in her being upgraded to business class, where she found herself sitting in a wide, soft window seat with her head back and her eyes closed, while the echoless murmur of her fellow passengers washed over her, and the plane was shunted onto spurs and access roads—a pause—and then they were airborne, the entire cabin sighing, as if they had finally been freed, though of what no one could say: the airport, or the day, or the burden of gravity and the waste of motionlessness.

The pilot came on the public address system and admitted that he wouldn't be able to make up the time they had lost, and they would be arriving in New York at least two hours late. He apologized, and the man in the next seat made a soft, disapproving sound. The flight attendant came by with a glass of champagne, which Stephanie used to swallow a pill that was supposed to calm her nerves. She dozed and woke, dozed again, and came to in the darkened cabin. She looked at the man in the seat beside her, a dark-haired businessman in his mid-fifties who was still wearing his suit jacket, though she herself had settled in so completely that she was wondering where exactly her shoes were. She pulled up her feet and peered down at the floor, spotting her ankle boots upturned beneath the seat in front of her, and she touched them with her toes while she tried to decide whether or not to put them on again. How long was I asleep? she asked the businessman.

He drained the last of his drink and spoke without looking at her, though not rudely. Pretty much the whole way, he said. The captain said they were starting their initial descent, and the sound of New York was so strong in the businessman's voice that for a moment she thought he was joking. He shot his cuffs casually and looked at his watch, and then busied himself with resetting it. Staring frankly, still half-asleep, Stephanie noticed that he'd miscalculated the time difference, but she decided not to point it out. She slipped her shoes back on her feet and raised the window shade, but the only thing visible outside was the stately blinking light on the far end of the wing. The businessman pulled a briefcase from under the seat in front of him and placed it on his lap, and she shifted her gaze without moving her head, and watched him release the catches with a soft clunk, a sound she had always loved, brass freeing itself and striking leather. As he bent over it, she noticed that the back of his neck was unshaven; either he was unmarried, or he'd been away from home for a few weeks. He lifted the lid and she smiled to herself as he revealed, in place of the papers she'd expected, a set of children's toys made of brightly colored plastic: a yellow elephant, a sky blue baby rattle, a red camera. He drew out a pair of oversize white dice and held them studiously in the palm of his hand, as if he were trying to read some occult riddle. Surely the world never grew more familiar, nor other people any easier to understand.

She started to fall asleep again, but the flight attendant came through and asked her to pass up the glass that had been sitting empty on her tray table since she had fallen asleep. She was hungry, but it was too late to ask for anything; she wouldn't have a chance to eat until tomorrow. Which was when? She stretched. It was almost midnight— no it wasn't, it was almost one, the businessman had set his watch correctly after all. The plane began to sink through the atmosphere, and time went every which way: forwards as they traveled down the Connecticut coast and across Queens, backwards against the earth's rotation, up and out like a fountain, casting uncountable droplets down on the city that had cradled her.

Below there were widely scattered clumps of faint orange lights; when she looked forward she could see them thicken as the plane neared the airport and the suburbs grew denser. The flight attendant was explaining something to a woman a few rows down, and the man in the seat beside her was reading a business magazine. Out her window she could make out the towers of housing projects, that familiar landscape, shadowless and monochrome, like looking through night-vision goggles, though there was nothing much to see: empty streets and dark windows, while metal airships passed overhead, filled with otherworldly witnesses.

She hoped it wouldn't be too cold when they landed. It was only September, but you never knew. Freezing weather, one more thing she was going to experience again. London never was so cold. Somewhere down there in Queens, perhaps in one of those repeating warehouses, buildings too bland to bear any description at all, she had a few boxes of things, among them clothes for a harder winter. She had missed that: really bundling up, the layers and mixtures of fabric and fragrance— cotton, wool, breath, silk, skin, cashmere—and buttons and laces, and the unbinding upon coming indoors. One of those gratuitous complications that made life more pleasant, not a bother but a ritual. A bay passed by below, and then they were over land again, they descended quickly, here was tarmac, the lights of the airport depots streaking past, and they hit the runway with a gentle bump, stateside.

There was that bustle when the airplane pulled to a stop at the gate, three hundred people who'd been sitting for hours, all rising to their feet, stretching, reaching up for their bags, turning on their cell phones, and trucks and carts were approaching the plane, lights flashing, and beyond them, signs and more lights. The engines of the plane shut down. The businessman had already taken his carry-on down from the overhead compartment; he looked down at her briefly and smiled, while she sat patiently in her seat. — I know what you mean, he said. Sometimes I just don't want to get off the plane. She smiled a little. Coming home? he said.

Yes, she said.

I always think it's not going to be there, he said. The city. The passengers ahead of them had started shuffling toward the exit, and he looked up, shrugged, and started forward. She rose to her feet.

Her bags appeared on the carousel almost immediately, and it took only a few minutes to get through customs, and then she was passing through the doors into the terminal, pulling both bags behind her, the duffel bag resting on top of the one with wheels, and there were a thousand people waiting out there under the shabby fluorescent lights. All those faces, enamel and caramel, some of them as brown as Indians, some of them pink as Swedes, some of them black as Sudanese, including one woman with her hair dyed yellow-blond. Everyone looked tired. Beyond the barrier, limousine drivers held up signs with names written on them. Then there was a small, middle-aged woman in front of her saying, Are you Stephanie?

She had to think, but only briefly. Then, — Hi! she said. Yes!

I figured you must be, the woman said, although she didn't explain how. I'm Emily Coster, the woman said, and when Stephanie answered with a blank look: I'm Roger's wife. From the Carrier Institute?

Oh, of course, said Stephanie. I hope you got my message. I'm sorry about the delay.

Don't worry about it, the woman said. Not a bit. Come. She looked around. Let's get you a porter or something.

No need, said Stephanie, tugging slightly at the handle of her suitcase. It's all on wheels.

Can I help?

It's all right, said Stephanie. It just rolls.

Well, Roger should be close by, Emily Coster said. He's been circling and he sent me in to find you.

Oh, said Stephanie. How long has he been out there?

Not long, said Emily Coster. Not long at all. We called the airline a few hours ago and they told us you'd be late.

The woman was wrapped in a plush black overcoat that reached down almost to her ankles, the sort of extravagant thing a woman would wear only if it was either all she had or one of many. A pair of shiny black pumps encased her small, delicate feet. She was in her mid-fifties or, if she was especially fortunate or diligent, a few years older, and she was tiny, but not delicate-looking. She wore her hair cropped short, the way only youthful and mature women did, the first out of daring and the second for convenience; it was difficult to tell whether she was hanging on to the first or anticipating the last. Wealth will do that, too, Stephanie thought: all those accoutrements, they make a young woman seem older and an older woman seem young.

Outside the terminal there was a cold, dark wind blowing, and people being carried by, strung on a ragged line, piling up along the way. Limousine, limousine, radio car, a chorus like so many burly blackbirds.

A few people were standing off to one side, huddled slightly and smoking; grimy airport shuttles were idling on the approach road, along with a dozen or so town cars, and on the other side there was a concrete island, where a long line of travelers was being fed into an even longer line of yellow cabs; and then, on the other side of the island, more traffic, more limos and more shuttles, more lights, and horns, and everywhere there were the well-heeled, the cousins, the customers, and tired people wanting to get home. Emily Coster had walked to the curb and was scanning the approach road with a frown, and Stephanie followed. What are we looking for? she said.

Roger . . . the other woman said.

Yes, said Stephanie.

He's driving a . . . — Oh, said Emily Coster, I should just call him. She reached deep into the pocket of her overcoat, but before she could pull out the phone, a black BMW flashed its lights and pulled over, the driver leaning over the passenger seat with his head craned up solicitously. Ah, there he is, she said, as her husband awkwardly righted himself and waved a bit. He was a decade or so older than she was, and Stephanie immediately wondered if she was his second wife, and if so, what had happened to the first one. Who had been lucky here, and who had been unlucky?

Roger Coster stepped from the car. Welcome to New York, he said cheerfully. Welcome back, I suppose. Welcome home. Welcome here. He pushed a button on his key fob and the trunk lid rose gently. Let me help you with that, he said, as he met Stephanie at the rear of the car. He was about the same size as his wife, a half an inch taller at most, which made him shorter than Stephanie herself. She was a little bit surprised, as she was invariably surprised when successful men turned out to be small, and even more so when they proved to be as likeable as Coster was: he gazed amiably at her face, took her hand briefly, then reached for her duffel bag. Like his wife, he had uncommonly clear and soft skin, and his eyes were bright. A faint grey-white plume of breath streamed from his mouth; it, too, was luxurious and discreet, something he'd paid for in advance. There was no one in the world, she thought, better groomed than a certain class of New Yorker. However dirty and dross-covered the city may have been, they moved through it with perfect health and elegance, not a stitch out of place, sleek, clean, natural, composed. The Costers were the beneficiaries of a wealth that was less extreme but far more stable than a banker or industrialist or prince might amass. Any one of the latter might be at the mercy of a bad year, of history, of war, of courts or changes in fashion, but these two had been entrusted with the care of reason itself, they were the true heirs of the Gilded Age, the guardians of an invaluable commodity. They were well paid, no doubt, but more than that, their fortunes were wound deep around the base of a sturdy institution, which freed them to spend their days as they wished, dispensing patronage whenever they felt so moved.

Roger Coster quickly transferred the duffel bag into the trunk. Emily Coster said, Was the flight very bad?

Once we took off it was kind of pleasant, actually, said Stephanie. Now Roger Coster started for the suitcase with the wheels, hesitating when he got a sense of its mass and then hoisting it slowly. It wouldn't do for her to take it from him, though she was used to carrying it, so she settled for frowning apologetically and saying, It's very heavy . . . But by then he'd transferred it to the trunk of the car with a satisfied smile. What have you got in there? he said.

Just a lot of equipment, she said. Camera bodies, lenses, cases, a couple of lights that I never use. He was enjoying the litany, so she kept going. Let's see . . . two laptops, a few hard drives, a bunch of other storage thingies. Some boxes of prints. He laughed quickly and guided her toward the rear door while Emily Coster circled around to the passenger side. The seat was soft and Stephanie sank so far back in it that she had the sudden sensation of the world giving way beneath her, and she struggled to sit upright again, though it meant perching forward.

Roger Coster looked down at the car's shifter as if he'd never seen one before, reading the letters before putting it in drive and pulling into traffic. It must be quite difficult, getting through airports, he said.

It's not so bad, said Stephanie. She paused. There were rules to these things, scruples and codes, and she had no idea: Was she about to break one? For a moment she had a vision of her residency being rescinded before it had even started. I have a press pass, that helps. A friend works at the *Times*, the London one, she said, staring out the window as they got onto the highway. He stole a blank one and mocked it up with my name and picture. It even has the magnetic strip. I told him I'd only use it in emergencies, she said. There was a pause, and both Roger and Emily Coster laughed. I use it all the time, she admitted. It gets me into all kinds of places that I'd never be allowed into on my own.

They started onto a cloverleaf. What would happen if someone caught you? Emily Coster asked.

I don't know, said Stephanie thoughtlessly. I doubt they'd do anything, really, except confiscate it and give me a warning. There must be scores of those things floating around; it's a wonder anyone pays any attention to them at all.

But they do, apparently, said Roger Coster. I've always found the trappings of authority fascinating. Badges and identity cards and things. Credentials, certificates, scepters, wax stamps.

It's true, said Emily Coster. The first thing he did when he was appointed director was, he redesigned the IDs.

Roger Coster looked at her in the rearview mirror, his eyes compressed in a smile. I wanted to go fully biometric: chip implants or a database of retinal scans, neural images, that sort of thing. I looked into it. Amazing how many unique identifiers we have. Everything from your gait to the smell of your breath. He paused for her reaction, and she was dismayed to discover that she was trying not to exhale. Of course, he continued, everyone objected. As I wanted them to. If they hadn't, I would've had to fire them all.

He can't fire them all, said Emily Coster. Just so you know.

I should be able to, he said, but I can't. Anyway, we ended up going with something more traditional. Stephanie could hear the rhythmic thumping of the seams in the highway, the familiar lullaby of collapsing New York. — It would take a twelve-year-old about ninety seconds to forge one, he finished.

Stephanie went back to staring out the window, now with a new affection for these people, who had given her so much and asked for so little in return—only to be amused. She was still a little unclear on how they'd found her. Her phone had rung one late afternoon in London, just as she'd reached the end of Camden High Street with a bag of groceries. It was Roger Coster's assistant, asking if she could talk, and when she said she could, she was put on hold, and a moment later the man himself was on the line. She hadn't heard of him—she'd had to ask him to repeat his name—but she knew the Institute, she knew the main building, anyway, a large Beaux Arts palais, set back on a leafy campus a block from the East River. It had been established almost a century earlier to serve as a research facility of the most elegant and rarified kind, where physics was done on whiteboards, and data sets were converted into laureate economics. She'd found a bench and sat down, and listened as he explained: They had inaugurated an artists-in-residence program a few years back, perhaps she had heard of it? She made a noise that could have meant yes or could have meant no. Well, he went on, starting very recently we've been inviting artists, preferably those without any other institutional affiliation, to come spend a year with us. You'll have your own office, along with a small

18

apartment in one of our buildings, access to our libraries and so on, the company of our other Fellows, and a stipend to keep you comfortable for the year. You'd have no responsibilities, though if you like you can give a small lecture series at the end.

He moved so swiftly from describing the program to offering her a position that she almost missed it. It sounds lovely, she said. In fact it sounded not quite real, and she wondered if one of her friends was having her on.

We do our best, said Roger Coster. Will you think about it?

She didn't know what to say. Of course, she said.

Let me overnight you some materials, said Roger Coster, and now she was uncertain whether she'd just agreed to the year or not. Thank you, she said. There was a pause; she could hear him smiling. She wondered how she'd come to his attention, if a committee had recommended her or if he'd seen her work, and if he'd seen it, what had appealed to him in it. But he never mentioned it and she never asked. Moreover, she couldn't remember having officially said yes, though she must have, if not on the phone that day, then afterwards. She must have filled out the forms, she must have packed up her apartment, they must have sent her a plane ticket. She must have said goodbye, she must have wept in her hotel room, and here was New York. The car was silent. The dashboard glowed with glamorous information. You're from here, Roger Coster said. Isn't that right?

Stephanie nodded, and then when she realized they couldn't see her, she said, Yes, that's right. Upper East Side.

A Rikers bus pulled up and ran side by side with the car for a few hundred yards before curving off at an exit ramp. *Take my hand and walk me home.* When she was a child, her father sang her to sleep at bedtime, and that was her favorite song; she'd never heard it sung by anyone else. Back then we were poor as mice, her mother used to say. You probably don't remember that tiny little apartment we lived in, up there in the Bronx. And indeed, the only thing Stephanie could picture about the place was a small wooden bedside table that her father had painted navy blue. Soon after, his furniture-importing business had struck the perfect moment, they moved to Manhattan and she was in a private school. *Take my hand, little honey.* And then just as suddenly her father had died. She was twelve then, and when she was nineteen her mother had followed him. She was thirty-two when she moved away.

They were approaching Queens Boulevard. Emily Coster said, How long have you been gone?

Seven years, said Stephanie. They went by a power plant, a big bristling thing, humming silently under a wash of its own light.

Seven years! You didn't come back at all? Emily Coster asked. Not even to visit?

. . . No, said Stephanie. She waited to see if they would ask her why not, but they were merciful people. What would she have said? That she'd been too sad, she'd been too scared.

Well, we're happy to have you, Emily Coster said.

A yellow cab swooped past them, cut across two lanes and then abruptly slowed, laid up by a panel van that was poking along in the leftmost lane. Asshole, said Roger Coster.

Which one? said Emily Coster.

Both of them, he replied.

Outside a giant stadium passed, lit like a spaceship, the mist in the air above it glowing; a few minutes went by in silence, and then there out the window was Manhattan, extending southward, ragged and alight, its clusters of enormous stalagmites rising from the floor of the island like the serpent in a Chinese New Year's parade. Stephanie felt a tiny spark in her throat, glittering in and around her pulse and making her blink involuntarily, which in turn brought forth silent tears that refused to drop.

Roger Coster found the on-ramp for the Triborough Bridge, and in a minute they were heading south along the river. The city was no longer in the distance; they were inside and it was all around them, the music changed, none of them spoke; and they were off the highway and climbing toward the park, people on the sidewalks, people on the corners. Stephanie tensed and tried not to glance down the avenues; it was all too near. They had crossed Fifth Avenue and they were hurrying across the transverse, the car bouncing softly on its expensive suspension. What time is it for you? said Emily Coster.

Stephanie thought for a moment. 1981, she said, and Roger Coster laughed.

They were on Broadway, and the lights and cars were everywhere again. On one corner there was a market, floodlit like a movie set; outside, a Korean boy, no more than eleven or twelve years old, was arranging buckets of yellow and purple flowers while a matronly woman in a fur coat stood behind him, watching, her glossy black purse dangling down from the crook in her elbow. On the median that ran through the traffic, another woman was standing motionless, watching the cars go by as if she had no intention of ever taking her eyes from the sight. They pulled up to a red light at a crosswalk. Emily Coster was holding her hand contemplatively to her mouth; her husband peered through the window as the light turned green and he took a right, and then, a block later, a left on West End, finally coming to a stop in front of a large grey stone building with a coral-colored awning extending out halfway across the sidewalk. The two women stepped out of the car, and a doorman came out. Hector, can you give us a hand? He lifted Stephanie's bags out of the trunk and carried them effortlessly into the vestibule as Roger Coster pulled away from the curb and disappeared back into the traffic.

He's going to look for a parking space, Emily Coster said to Stephanie as they followed the doorman inside. I don't know why he needs a car at all. I really don't. But it makes him happy.

It was a prewar building in slight disrepair. There was linoleum tile on the floor of the lobby; it should have been replaced a few years earlier, but the walls had been recently painted, and the amber lights sat in polished fixtures. The doorman set the bags down at the far end with a slight grunt, and Emily Coster smiled gently. Moving, she said. Such an ordeal. She held the door while Stephanie carried one bag and used her foot to shove the other one into the elevator. — Roger and I have lived in this building for almost fifteen years now, Emily Coster continued, as the doors closed and they started up. It's bigger than we need, but the idea of packing everything up and schlepping it across town and unpacking it again: it's just too much. And then, of course, everything is so expensive these days. Beyond imagining. A million dollars for a studio? Incredible. She stopped herself just as they arrived at the 8th floor, aware of how unseemly her complaint must be.

Together, the two women managed to roll the suitcase down the hall to the Costers' door with the duffle bag balanced on top of it, until they were inside the apartment, where it slid to the ground.

Leave it there, said Emily Coster. You must be exhausted.

No, said Stephanie. A little . . . overwhelmed, but I slept on the plane.

Emily Coster nodded. Well, anyway, someone will come by from the Institute tomorrow and move them over to your apartment.

Really? said Stephanie. Emily Coster nodded again. Thank you, said Stephanie. And thanks so much for coming to pick me up and letting me stay here tonight.

Oh, it's our pleasure, said Emily Coster. We have people staying here all the time. We have an extra bedroom now that Matty's moved out, and it's just sitting there, doing nothing. It seems like such a waste. Matty's our son.

He's in college?

I wish, said Emily Coster. Come on in, she said, and led Stephanie into a well-appointed living room: dim, discreet lighting, framed prints on one wall, a floor-to-ceiling bookcase on another, everything well-matched, though not by obvious design: the dark green couch was relatively new, but the floor lamp beside it was decades older, and the library steps that served as a makeshift magazine rack were antique. Stephanie surveyed it quickly and sat on the couch. The air smelled slightly of neroli and pipe tobacco, though as far as she could tell, Roger Coster didn't smoke. Emily Coster went to a hutch against the far wall, drew out three highball glasses, poured an inch of bourbon into each of them, handed one to Stephanie, left one on the coffee table, and kept the third for herself. No, Matty decided about a year and a half ago to join the Marine Corps, she said, shrugging uncomfortably. I tried to talk him out of it. Not that I don't believe in service, but he had so many other options. There wasn't much I could say: his mother's brother was in the Marine Corps—his birth mother I mean, Roger's first wife. You know how boys are, young men: idealizing things, especially if they don't know them very well. And, of course, Roger couldn't stop him. She took a sip of her drink and then sat in a brown leather reading chair. She sighed and then looked at Stephanie as if she'd just remembered she was there. I worry about him, she said. I worry about him all the time.

Is he stationed somewhere?

We're not allowed to know, she said. He finished up training a year ago, and then he went through more training to become a . . . special . . . They're called Raiders. Anyway, they don't tell us where he is or what he's doing. I think Roger might know, secretly. He has connections all over. But he doesn't tell me. I'm not sure if I want to know. — Just then there was the sound of Roger returning. Do you think I ought to worry? Emily Coster said, staring straight ahead.

Stephanie said, Worrying is what mothers do, and Roger Coster stood in the living room doorframe, drew off his gloves, and said, What is?

Stephanie didn't say anything; Emily Coster said, Worrying.

Ah, said Roger Coster, and he went to hang his coat in the hall closet, returned and stood hesitantly until Emily Coster pointed to his glass, which he scooped up and carried to a large black armchair at the other side of the coffee table. I like a little bourbon at the end of the day, he said to Stephanie. It eases the transition from vespers to nocturnes. He took a sip, and for a few seconds the three of them sat silently in the half-dark room. At length, Roger Coster sighed and shifted in his seat, and Stephanie yawned, and then apologized.

You're tired, said Emily Coster. Roger, she's tired.

Roger Coster said nothing, merely gazed at Stephanie pleasantly, and Stephanie, not wanting to be rude to either of them, was unsure of how to respond. Come, said Emily Coster. Let's get you to bed. Roger Coster made a small toasting gesture with his glass to say goodnight, and Stephanie rose and thanked him, and followed her down the hall.

The bed was simple, the mattress high, and there was wallpaper on the walls, a faint blue rococo pattern on a background of pearl grey. The shades were down and the whole had an air of being untouched, a room that only the maid entered to dust every week or two. Through a door lay a tiny bathroom, and she removed what she needed from her bag, leaving the rest unpacked on the floor, where it sat, inert, untidy, looking guilty of something. It was past midnight, and the facing building was dark but for one apartment a few stories below, where a TV was playing, its light flickering through the window. The bed was broad and soft, and the night was quiet, but she didn't fall asleep until just before dawn.

SILVER AND GOLD

The way he remembered it, it was a Friday morning: a nice day, sunny and unseasonably warm, they said on the radio, a day Reggie had expected to spend driving livery around the East Side, but when he went out to start the car, the engine wouldn't turn over. He got a tester from his apartment and touched it to the engine block, and in time discovered that the alternator had stopped working. He was going to lose twelve or maybe fifteen dollars an hour. A little ways down 14th Street there was a garage: he'd been going down there for years, to pick up parts, to get advice, sometimes just to sit and watch the fellows work. As far as he knew it was called Angel's, but there was no listing in the phone book, so he couldn't call to see if they had what he needed. Instead, he walked on over, and was happy about it: by then it was coming up on noon and everybody was out on the street, the ladies in their finest next-to-nothing, and the blue sky smiling above the buildings, Frankie Crocker on the radio, and the police in their cars with the windows rolled down.

When he walked in, Angel himself was there, sitting in the metal desk in his office, the surface strewn with paper-tagged car keys and carbon-copy forms with his illegible handwriting on them, an old-fashioned adding machine, a paper calendar from the previous year, a couple of metal clipboards, and a little plaster statue of Jesus. He looked up at Reggie without recognizing him, lost, as he often was, in his world of broke-down things, as if his shop was one enormous engine which he was working on all the time. There was a greasy fingerprint on the lens of his thick eyeglasses. Where'd you come from? Angel said. One of his eyes was permanently dilated, black and unseeing.

I've got a bad alternator, Reggie replied. Thing won't even turn over, I'm pretty sure that's what it is.

You can be pretty sure it's something, Angel said, now looking at him as if he'd suddenly recognized him, finally if not forever. That's one thing I know: if something's wrong, then something's causing it.

Something's wrong, Reggie said. So what I'm wondering is if you have an alternator for a Crown Vic.

You still driving that piece of shit car? Angel said, and he rummaged in the papers on his desk, as if the part might be right there. He stopped and patted the pocket of his shirt. How many miles you got on that thing?

About 120, Reggie said. — What are you looking for?

My glasses, Angel said.

You're wearing them, Reggie pointed out. Angel reached up and touched the rims as if he'd known they were there all along. And you're telling me what to drive, Reggie said.

I didn't tell you what to drive, Angel said. I told you what you're driving right now is a piece of shit. He stood up from behind his desk, glanced at a stack of boxes in the corner, and then went out into the garage, with Reggie following. There were three or four cars sitting in the bays, and Angel stopped by the side of a silver Toyota, where a short man with a grey afro was using a dirty rag to wipe his fingers. I'm just about done here, he said, though no one had asked him.

Angel nodded. You remember where I put that alternator?

Which one?

From the Crown Vic. Last week.

The other man walked back into a dark corner of the garage and emerged a moment later with a silver, rotary-shaped thing.

It's working all right? Reggie asked.

Works fine, Angel said. We took it out of an old cop car that got banged up on the bridge. Thirty dollars. Reggie paid the man in cash and started home with the part wrapped in a sheet of newspaper.

An hour later he was working on the car, stopping every so often to sip from a beer, when a group of boys on bicycles came down 14th Street from the river. They didn't look like Project boys, not with those bikes, which were covered in chrome and streamers, and neon lights that glowed even in the sunshine, and the one in front with a drive chain that looked like it was made of solid gold. There were five or six of them, he didn't see how many, it all happened so quickly. They were slumped on the handlebars with their knees almost touching their forearms, working that attitude of perfect carelessness, with their sleeveless T-shirts and their sneakers without socks. One of them had a much younger boy, maybe four or five years old, riding on the seat behind him. They were looking around with that trouble-come-find-me gaze, nothing too dangerous, they were just boys after all, one of them smiled at a woman in a short azure skirt and a tight pink top, who miraculously smiled back; but they just kept on rolling through the noise, owners of the month of May. As they passed Reggie, he noticed that the little boy on the back was sitting with his legs underneath him, dangerously unsteady, and just then the kid who was steering slowed a little too much and had to jerk the handlebars to keep the bicycle upright, and the little boy fell off, landing on his hip on the sidewalk. There was a second during which nothing moved and the whole block went silent, the boy on the bicycle looking down at the fallen child with nothing more than faint and fleeting curiosity—and then everything started moving again, the pack rolling on, leaving the little one sprawled out on the pavement, now wailing loudly, from shock as much as pain, and from the misery of being alone as much as shock. By the time Reggie realized what had happened, the boys had disappeared around the corner, and the little one's wailing had reached a fullness that made the rest of the block hush, in awe before the sheer force of his grief.

Reggie's hands were stained with oil and he looked around for a rag, finally using the brown paper bag that had contained his beer. No one else had moved to comfort the boy, not yet; it was as if he were some wounded animal, which might become enraged by his own fear and attack anyone who touched him. But Reggie had been a little boy once, just like this one, and he tossed the bag, bent down, and said, That was a pretty hard fall you took.

The boy didn't say anything, he was still crying, but he looked up with an offended expression, as if it were Reggie who had caused him to fall. Reggie nodded, and the boy cried a little more, but without any expression, his mouth open but his eyes calm, even curious: he was running out the clock. When he stopped, Reggie said, You ready to stand up, you think?

The boy shook his head. Where's Trey? he said.

I don't know. That one of your friends?

He has my dollar, the boy said.

Hm, said Reggie. That's not right. How did he get it?

The boy sat up, now hiccupping through the last of his tears. I gave it to him to hold.

All right, Reggie said. We'll see if we can get it back. First let's make sure you're not hurt. Can you stand up?

I can stand up, the boy said angrily, as if his competence were at issue and not his well-being. He was wearing khaki shorts and a blue T-shirt, and when he got to his feet Reggie looked him over quickly: no bleeding anywhere, nothing broken, some bits of gravel stuck to his upper arm, which Reggie wiped away. He had startling jade-green eyes, and on his neck and shoulder there were a few light-coffee-colored scars, about the size of the tip of a cigarette. All right, said Reggie. All right. How old are you?

I'm five and a half, the boy said.

You look like you're at least six, maybe even seven.

I'm five and a half, the boy said again, now holding his left elbow in his right hand. How old are you?

I'll tell you what, Reggie said. Let's never mind how old I am. And we'll say you're six.

I'll be six in . . . the boy trailed off and started counting the months on his fingers, but he stopped to look around him. Where is this? he asked.

14th Street, Reggie answered. You know where that is? Down there is Second Avenue.

The boy shook his head.

Where do you live? Reggie asked.

In the white building.

What's the white building? But the boy just looked at him. You know what street it's on? No? Your mama never told you?

She's not my mom, the boy said.

All right. Who takes care of you? We'll find her in the phone book and get you right back home.

This woman, the boy said. I live with her.

You know her name?

I call her Ms. Miss, said the boy. But that's not her real name. Her real name is too long.

You know her phone number? Reggie asked, his voice rising with incredulity, and then a little more with fear, as he came to realize that it wasn't going to be easy getting this boy back to his people.

The boy shrugged. I don't talk to her very much. I don't want to make her mad at me. She gets mad a *lot*. She doesn't like having so many kids around. She said they forced her.

She said this to you?

That's what they call it: a forced-her home. Reggie allowed himself a quick smile. Everyone said it would be nicer than the group home, but it isn't. I ran away.

What about your own name?

What about it?

Do you know what it is?

The boy scowled and mumbled something.

What's that? said Reggie.

Pee Wee, the boy said, in a voice that suggested he hated his own tongue.

That's your name?

That's what everybody calls me.

Well, that doesn't make any sense, Reggie said. Look how big you are, for only five and a half. The boy smiled for the first time.

Some people call me Caruso, he said.

Because you got that great big voice, said Reggie. OK. Now we're getting somewhere. You have a last name to go with that?

No, said Caruso. He looked around. I'm thirsty.

Are you hungry?

I'm thirsty, said Caruso again.

Well, all right, then. What do you like to drink? You want a beer?

— No! Caruso said, with sudden wonderment and joy. I can't drink beer!

Why not?

Because I'm too little!

OK, then, how about a glass of brandy? It's a good brandy.

What's brandy?

It's like beer, only more so, said Reggie.

No! said Caruso.

Reggie looked around. The white lady from the beauty shop on the corner was looking at them. No brandy? he said, more softly.

No!

Shh. Reggie put on a perplexed look, and the boy grinned and got ready to yell out the same answer to the next offer. — Well, I don't know what else there is, Reggie said. If you don't drink beer and you don't drink brandy . . .

Grape! Caruso said.

What's grape? Grape what? You mean wine?

Caruso didn't understand that one, but he shouted No! again, and Reggie said, OK, shh, now. If you'll stop yelling at me, I guess we can go in the store and see if we can find you something.

Half an hour later, Caruso was sitting in the kitchen of Reggie's apartment, both his hands wrapped around a bottle of purple drink. Reggie was on the phone with Leila, turned away from the boy, tangled in the cord as he said, No, baby. She wanted him to contact the City. — I'm not going to spend the afternoon on the phone with those people, he said. You know what that's like.

I do it every day, she said. Well, she did: Leila worked for the Housing Authority. Forms and paperwork, she was good at that, and she was always getting on him to make sure he renewed his license, four hours at the DMV that he could have been out making money, but how would it look if he got in an accident and he wasn't driving legally in the first place? She was right about that.

I don't know how to talk to them, he said. Once you step into that world you might never come back, there'd be nothing left of you but a dried-to-death little man. He thought about the Crown Vic, still parked outside, the alternator now sitting in the sink, and she wasn't going to like that either. And now this boy, another kind of problem.

We could be guilty of kidnapping, she said. Little boys don't just fall out of the sky.

Why don't you call around, then? he said.

She raised her voice so loudly that the boy heard it across the room and looked up. Reggie smiled and nodded at him. Why do I have to call around? she said. This is your doing.

Because you know how that all works, he said. I'll just mess it up.

You should have called the police, did you even think of that? What if someone's looking for him?

The police? Reggie said, his voice rising to a higher register. No, thank you very much. Caruso was drawing something invisible on the tabletop. He lowered his voice again. — You want to put the boy back in the system? Send him off someplace, to people who don't want him and don't know what to do with him? There was silence on the other end, and then she sighed. Leila had a half-sister who was raised in a dozen different foster homes; she didn't like to talk about her, though she kept a photograph of the two of them as little girls in a dime-store frame on her dresser. He scratched the back of his head and whispered: This boy, Caruso: he's not a big one, you'll see. He's not tough. Those boys just left him right there on the sidewalk. They're hard. This is a hard neighborhood, with those white kids rioting down in the park and all of that. Wherever he's living it's no place for a boy, or else he wouldn't have been out on the street in the first place.

I can't leave you alone for one minute without you getting into some kind of mess. A boy? A little boy? That you found, on the street? You take him home with you, you're opening yourself up to all kinds of trouble. What if someone thinks you . . . ? But she wasn't able to say it, and Reggie was too innocent to imagine it.

Well, I couldn't just let him sit there crying, now could I? He sneaked a look over at the boy, who was sitting at the table, utterly absorbed in the last drops of his grape drink, his legs dangling down from the chair, the edge of the table almost at his neck, so that when he contemplated the plastic bottle he confronted it at eye level. He's just a little kid.

That what I'm saying, said Leila. You can't just take him because you want him.

Reggie waved his hand dismissively. He's here now. That's a fact. We can figure it out when you get home.

When she came through the door a few hours later, she was a little bit curt. Couldn't walk into her own apartment without wondering who was going to be sitting on the couch, Reggie taking in children like stray dogs. Too crazy to even think about. What was she supposed to say? Were they supposed to have a conversation about all this? With the boy sitting right there, watching cartoons on TV? She took a close look at him and he looked back at her, wearing an expression so guileless she didn't know what to make of it. Then she turned away, and he went back to the television. She gestured to Reggie to move a little closer to her, and then lowered her head. — Who could let a boy like that get away?

That's what I've been telling you, said Reggie. Now the boy was singing softly to the TV set.

What's his name? she said.

He says his name is Caruso.

That's an Italian name, she said. They don't make black boys in Italy.

I think that's just a nickname, said Reggie. You should hear his voice when he's hurting.

Look at him. With those green eyes.

I'm telling you, said Reggie.

You didn't ask him who he belongs to? Does he have a last name? I asked, said Reggie. You know I did. He doesn't know. The boy was looking at them, and Reggie spoke under his breath. He said his name is Caruso. That's all I know about that. You can ask him yourself.

Caruso, Leila said again. Oh, this is the end. This is the end.

But that night she was cooing and hovering over him like Pharaoh's daughter over the infant Moses. Look at this boy! He's nothing but skin and bones! And Caruso absorbed the attention like a prince, shrugging his shoulders softly and smiling; and then he dug into his bowl of chicken and rice with a spoon that was almost as long as his forearm, his elbow lifted to hold it, and the gravy already streaking down his chin. Leila took a kitchen towel from the side of the sink, rinsed it in warm water, and said, Come here, as she wiped his face. The boy frowned. What pretty eyes you have, she said, but you've got to eat like a human being, she said, and then, more softly, I don't know what they've been feeding you, I honestly don't. You'd think you'd never had a proper meal, and how are you going to grow up strong if you don't have something in your stomach? Reggie, she said. Honey, go out and get some bacon and eggs for breakfast tomorrow. Get some juice and some strawberry jam. And get some biscuits, some biscuit mix, I mean. In the box—oh, never mind, I'll go myself.

Over the following days she made a few phone calls, but not too insistently; and with Social Services such a mess, they'd leave her on hold for half an hour at a time, and then come back with four or five different lines of advice. There weren't any boys named Caruso in the system, and there wasn't anyone missing: she had a friend named Donna who worked in CPS and checked. Caruso slept on the couch at night and rode around with Reggie during the day, sitting in the front seat, asking questions—a lot of questions—and charming customers right down to their fingertips. One of them tipped the boy two dollars, with a wink to Reggie. It was a good week all around. Leila didn't say anything when Reggie cleaned out their tiny storage room, brought home a small bed, and made a little space for the boy. She was tired of the bureaucracy and its endless, contradictory trials, the wrong forms, the wrong office, the records that couldn't be located, and could you come back in a few weeks? The man you need to talk to is on vacation. This poor boy needs to eat and sleep, she said to herself as she watched Reggie cut up a roast. He needs to go to school. If anyone's looking for him, I would have heard, and if no one's looking for him, that's got to mean nobody cares. She sighed, Reggie heard her and met her gaze, she saw the happiness on his face, and she said, Caruso, that's not the way you hold a fork, like you're trying to spear a fish or something. Baby, show him how to hold a fork.

The days followed, with the months behind them, and the years in tow, and soon enough the boy didn't know of any other life, no. In time, he would hear the legend of how he fell down on 14th Street, but he didn't know, then or ever, whom he was born to or where he passed his earliest years, only that Reggie and Leila were his father and mother, and that's where he grew up, with them, while the clouds passed overhead like a crowd.

THE RIVER, PART ONE

Coming awake in New York City, it was always the same morning: always the noise of traffic, the sound of things being shifted around; and Stephanie had dreamed she was in love. She'd had those dreams since she was thirteen or fourteen, not often, but she didn't know anyone else who had them at all, they weren't part of the lore, anyhow. It was something you couldn't send back to the world when you were done: never once had she discussed them, they were far more private than anything else she had, these phantoms, and she woke feeling ripe and bursting. Usually the loved one was a woman, but every so often it was a man; it didn't matter, all she knew was the warmth spreading through her limbs, the taste of kisses on her mouth, and the memory of flawless desire spreading like a drop of red ink in a glass of water, curling languidly, giving off shoots in the shape of seahorses. They were never anonymous, though they were often someone she'd never met. That was part of the joy: the randomness of it, as if she were being transformed by a love so pure that it didn't matter who it landed on—though afterwards she'd find herself haunted by a newfound fondness. She would dream and love would come pouring out of her, for a shopkeeper, the friend of a friend, an actress from a TV show, and once for a senator she hadn't voted for. She would have liked to have known why these things happened when they did, and how their cast was chosen, but she was never going to.

That first night at the Costers' it had been someone especially strange, a man she hadn't seen in two decades, an ex-boyfriend of Bridget's whose name she couldn't remember—she'd only met him once or twice, maybe twenty years previously; it was one of the few things that Bridget didn't like to talk about, and she'd never really heard the whole story of their affair, just that it had lasted about a year and ended badly. She hadn't thought much of him at the time, but she came awake on the Upper West Side with that little ember burning in her belly, in a setting so unfamiliar she almost called out, though to whom she couldn't have said. She lay there for a while, listening for sounds from outside her door, but there weren't any, so she rose, slipped on a pair of sweatpants and a long-sleeved T-shirt that she'd had the foresight to pack at the top of her duffel bag, and then sat on the edge of the bed, trying to decide if it would be rude of her to walk out into the apartment barefoot or if she should put on a pair of sneakers. There was a clock on the night table: it was ten thirty. Did Emily Coster work? And there might be a maid. She stood by the door for a little while, listening carefully, and then eased it open.

There was no one in the kitchen, but a note on the counter advised her that she could find coffee in the cabinet, milk in the refrigerator, fresh bagels in a white bag on the countertop, and she should make herself at home. Nice people, thought Stephanie. Just nice, thoughtful people who knew how to live well.

An hour later she was standing on the corner of Broadway, turning her head this way and that to watch everyone pass. There were so many people out walking that the city felt like a crowd with some buildings poking up out of it, rather than buildings with pedestrians in between. A well-dressed man with ruddy cheeks was standing outside a drugstore, holding an orange prescription bottle up to examine the contents;

he kissed it and then slipped it into his coat pocket. She stepped off the curb just as a bus was trying to round the corner, stepped backwards again, then darted a few yards out into the street, where a cab stopped almost as soon as she raised her hand. She got in and gave the driver the address, and he took off before she'd closed the door; the car smelled of car freshener. It was an overcast day, the light sagging over building after building, all bleary in the rain-met morning. Mike: that was the man's name, the one she'd dreamed about; a man who'd had more time with Bridget than he had deserved.

The driver gunned the car. There were nannies with baby carriages at the entrance to the park, a couple on roller skates, someone trying to fix a bicycle, the sky brightened a bit. It was almost lunchtime already. Then they were in a sort of leafy declivity, hurrying like a carriage, sunlight breaking through the clouds and causing an unexpected dapple through the trees; and then they had landed on the other side, figures clustered on the sidewalk and sitting on the stairs of the Met as if they were pieces on a board game. The scatter of first fallen leaves, the ones that drift down while they're still green. *Autumn in New York* . . . the melody inevitably came to her. *Why does it seem so something something?* There had been a bookstore on one of these blocks, but she couldn't remember which one. They turned south on Park, broad and clean, with its quiet apartment houses and a view that raised her eyes. This grand boulevard, she thought, it was still the same, when almost everything else had been built over and rebuilt. Just then the clouds opened completely and the day became bright. The Armory sat cheerfully on its little slope. She sighed and leaned back in her seat. It was the beginning of the year, according to the calendar everyone had learned as schoolchildren: September to May—nine to five—like workday hours inflated into months, and now that she was getting older they passed just as quickly. The cabbie was trying to turn left but the oncoming traffic wouldn't let him. He began to make an impatient clicking noise with his tongue. Through the windshield she could see a man in a tailored grey suit walking with a woman in dark blue; she was laughing. The two of them, their skin so soft, their hair so full, their eyes so bright, people imitating an advertisement that was imitating them. Every block was like that: once the city had been a book to walk through, then it was a newspaper, then a magazine whose pages kept flipping, and now it was a video screen, refreshing itself over and over again. There were brand-new clothes on everyone, umbrellas outside cafés, and flags flying from the roofs of buildings that had never had flags before, all with a brightness around the edges.

As the cab headed east through the 60s, she pulled her bag onto her lap and waited, eager now to be on the sidewalk, and when they got caught at a light she decided she couldn't wait any longer, and she said, You can just stop here.

First Avenue: one more block, he said.

That's OK. I can get out here.

He shrugged and pulled quickly to the curb. The meter read $17 something, and she searched her bag for her wallet, and her wallet for some cash. How small and plain it looked, American money, and for the very first time she understood why; cash was very little to have, here, no more than a momentary illusion of prosperity. Property was something else, and wealth something else again. She gave the driver a twenty and a five because those were the first bills that she found, and she was on the sidewalk, waving at him to keep the change.

The Carrier Institute lay farther to the east, but its administrative offices were in a separate building; fellows were expected to imagine better worlds, and encouraged to do so at a remove from this one. There was something about the arrangement that agreed with her, and something, too, that offended her sense of democratic endeavor. She wasn't sure whether she was working for them or they were working for her, or if they were supposed to be working together, somehow; and here she was at the base of a tall, thin tower, with charcoal-grey tinted windows set between dark grey steel beams, the whole so seamlessly put together that it was hard to believe it had floors inside, and almost impossible to find the front door. At the bottom there was a café, though there was no one inside except a pair of waiters, both young men, who were standing next to each other, talking intimately. Whatever it was they were discussing, they both took it very seriously, and as she approached the door, she saw one of them reach down and take the other's hand in his own. The other, who had been speaking until then, abruptly stopped, and as Stephanie started through the door she saw his face, and the expression on it of mad, helpless love. It made her pause, and a woman in secretary's clothes almost bumped into her from behind, but said nothing as she rapidly circled her. Stephanie followed her inside and watched as she flashed a badge at the guard and headed toward the elevators.

As she approached the security desk, the guard looked up warily. Yes? he said.

I have an appointment at the Carrier Institute, she said. He gestured toward her bag, silently asking her if she would open it, and she complied. He studied the inside and frowned, and then pointed with a ballpoint pen. Do you mind? he said. It's a camera, she said, and she pulled it out and showed it to him, turning it over in her hands as if to demonstrate that no part of it was more dangerous than the rest. He looked up and said something she didn't understand.

I'm sorry?

You can't take pictures in here, he said sternly.

Of course not, she replied, though the truth was she would if she found something worth picturing. He looked down at the directory screen, where there appeared to be several hundred names to scroll through. — The Carrier Institute? she said again.

Career Institute, there isn't one of those.

Car-ri-er, she said, emphasizing all three syllables.

He said, Do you have the name of the person?

I can find one, she said, digging into her bag for the relevant page in the packet the Institute had sent her. I think it was Dutch. The guard typed a *D* into the directory. No, she said, not Dutch like that, I mean, — Hang on, van something. The guard said nothing and didn't move. She found the paper. Van Meer.

There followed a bit of confusion as to whether such a name would be listed under *V* or *M*. It wasn't under either of them, and she was beginning to think that maybe she'd come to the wrong building, and would have to start the whole process again next door or across the street; but no, the guard, who had been tracing his finger down a list of names, suddenly found what he was looking for. 1705, he said, with great satisfaction. She thanked him and started to walk toward the elevators. Miss, he said, and she turned around to see him gesturing to the logbook. She rolled her eyes in apologetic self-deprecation and went back and signed the book under the guard's now benevolent gaze. You have a good day now, he said.

The 17th floor was still and very bright. There was only one door, and after stepping off the elevators she stood before the frosted glass and pulled on it: it opened half an inch before stopping with an unpleasant sound, and when she pushed it, it didn't move at all. The little sign on the wall said *PLEASE PRESS TO ENTER*, so she pressed the button below, and the door buzzed, and she pushed it, pulled it, and went through. Once inside, she gave her name to the young woman at the desk and waited on a brown leather couch in the reception area, her bag on the floor beside her leg. The receptionist notified someone that Stephanie was there, and then went back to reading what appeared to be a scholarly journal of some sort.

Nana van Meer was a tall woman in a short black skirt, with straight black hair and perfectly applied oxblood lipstick. Stephanie?

she said, with a faint untraceable accent and a modest smile. She was in her late twenties, no older than that, but she had the unnatural self-possession of the international enlightened classes, a confidence that sometimes turned out to be real, and sometimes did not. Was there someone, somewhere who had broken her heart? Was there grief or doubt? Nana didn't show it, but then, neither did Stephanie, and she couldn't decide whether they understood each other instantly, or didn't understand each other at all. Welcome, the other woman said as they walked back to her office, through a course of desks and dividers upon which a nice sum had been spent: design-museum lamps, quiet computers, expensive chairs. — Come in, and they went into a small office dominated by a floor-to-ceiling window with a giddy view of the river. They sat. Two of Stephanie's books were conspicuously perched on the corner of the desk; beside them was a Klein-blue folder. Trip went OK? Nana said. Stephanie nodded. I'm sure you're anxious to get settled. So . . . she patted the folder softly, and an invisible tendril of lustrous perfume rose from her wrist. These are your orientation materials, she said. They'll explain most of what you need to know: where things are, and so on. She reached into the top drawer of her desk and took out a key card on a blue lanyard. This will get you in just about everywhere—at least, when the card readers on the doors are working. They aren't always, but if you can't get in, you can just call security. She withdrew a map from the folder and circled a building. Your office is in here. She grimaced. She had a lovely, expressive mouth. Now, it's a strange thing, she said, but when they first designed this place, Mr. Carrier was convinced that the free exchange of ideas was best served by a sort of primitive open plan. So there were no doors on any of the offices. She smiled ruefully. But that didn't work, so now there are doors, but there are no locks. It can take a little getting used to, especially for women, and especially at night. All I can tell you is that we've never had an incident, not in the ninety years we've been open.

Stephanie said, I'm sure I'll be fine.

Nana van Meer reached into her desk again, this time taking out a set of keys. For your apartment. Stephanie took them, noticing as she did that the other woman had a perfect French manicure, and a half dozen small silver bracelets on her wrist, which drew attention to her somewhat nervous hands. A tell, a giveaway. The big one opens the building, but there's a doorman twenty-four hours a day, Nana said. The smaller one opens the apartment. Here—she reached into the folder and took out a large, stiff card—is pretty much everything you need to know about the building: the address, where the closest subway stop is, restaurants that deliver, all of that. I'm told you grew up here? Stephanie nodded. You probably won't need most of this, then. She leaned back. Well, I guess that's it.

That's all?

Pretty much, said Nana. There's a schedule of seminars and talks on the Institute's website. You're welcome to attend or ignore any or all of them. You can find my number there too. If you need anything, just call me. There was a pause and then they both smiled, stood, and shook hands, the other woman's bracelets jingling for just a second, and then, very well, they were done.

On the sidewalk again, she felt like she'd been ejected into the rapids. On First Avenue, there was a girl of about fourteen standing on the sidewalk with a soda; three boys walked past, and one simply lifted the drink from her hands, took a sip, and gave it back to her without breaking his stride. At first, Stephanie thought the girl was going to burst into tears, but instead she laughed and said, Kyle, you asshole. By now the clouds had dispelled altogether, and it had become one of those impossibly clear days that seem to happen only in New York, glassy and refractive, the light bouncing cheerfully off the windows, a breeze clipping up the avenues, carrying a reminder that cold weather was coming. Everything was glimmering and swimming, awnings flapping, the limbs of the trees bobbing up and down, a spaniel went by on the end of a leash, his knees up in a short trot, celebrating his good luck. A triumphant day for animism, happy spirits swooping under the light-poles and turning cartwheels on the corners—was Bridget among them?—all sprites cheering, all the dybbuks dancing, OK OK OK. She turned upstream and started to walk, a middle-aged man with long hair walking beside her until he overtook her and disappeared into a doorway. There was a burst of multicolored hieroglyphs painted on the road, where utility companies had marked out the mains and pipes below.

When she was a child, New York had been as dappled as a human eye, all the neighborhoods flecks and striations and quickening glistening bits, gathered around a dark and featureless center. There were blocks on which her friends had lived, apartments from which she'd watched the sun come up, restaurants where her mother had taken her for birthdays and events, like the little French café on 83rd Street where they had gone on the afternoon her braces had been removed. There were corners in Tribeca that had sported the unmarked doors of secret nightclubs, which she had once thought so important to know and now could not name. But Midtown might as well have been another city, the one that wasn't full of her love and time.

Still, the Institute's apartment was very nice—small but sleek, just on the near side of comfortable, furnished like a good hotel: in the bedroom, there was an enormous bed covered with a snowy duvet and a half dozen pillows. The place smelled at once warm and empty, with the faint tang of white paint and the chemicals they'd used on the wood floors. Her bags had been delivered from the Costers' and lay beside the couch looking dirty and disheveled. The room was silent, though humming with the electricity of her things, comforts and mementos now singing little snippets of chanteys, like dead sailors at the end of a drinking binge. She was too tired to sing along, so she drew her laptop out of her luggage, opened the lid and started it up, blowing on the screen to clear it of dust and realizing, as she did, that it was London dust, after all. She remembered having learned in Hebrew school that every breath she took contained some tiny portion of the air that Moses himself had breathed. Or was it Abraham? No matter, the point was the reach of the elements in time and space. But was it Abraham or Moses? Well, presumably it was both, but it bothered her that she couldn't remember, and she stood by the window, her brow furrowed, looking out.

At the cocktail party for the incoming fellows the following night—an affair for which Stephanie was, to her mild embarrassment, significantly underdressed—Roger Coster gave a short, pleasant speech summarizing some of the Institute's more monumental achievements, among them a groundbreaking account of how encephalitis was transmitted, an explanation of the economics of scarce resources, and the resolution of certain mathematical puzzles that had contributed, in some attenuated way, to the invention of the atomic bomb. Afterwards, she spent a few minutes talking to an older woman in a bland dress, a psychologist from Oregon who was working on a book about the history of fear—or at least that's what Stephanie heard her say; she didn't want to ask again. Instead she simply nodded as the woman went on a bit, her low, monotonous voice never quite rising above the surrounding noise. She found herself looking around for the caterers, assuming that at least one of them would be attractive. Now a portly man with rheumy, hound-dog eyes was making a toast, which threatened to turn into a short speech, and Roger Coster touched her elbow and whispered. Everything all right?

Yes, said Stephanie, thank you so much.

I assumed it would be, he said. It isn't for everyone. We had an Australian physicist a few years ago. I can't remember his name . . . Anyway, he was Australian, and we were told he was quite brilliant.

Coster smiled. — Unfortunately, none of us got a chance to talk to him. I'm not sure if anyone even met him. I guess we all thought he was simply working odd hours. Physicists often do. Finally, I asked one of the administrators about him, and she said she had no idea where he was either. It took us about a week to figure it out: he'd met a woman almost as soon as he arrived, a Russian woman, I think. Ukrainian, something like that. She'd hustled him out to Brighton Beach and slowly bled him dry. It was quite a mess. The Australian Embassy had to get involved. He paused and studied her for a moment. I won't worry about you, he said, and then he touched her arm again and wandered off. The toast was ending, and she slipped out.

The next day she walked over to the Institute. Her office was two-thirds of the way down a dark hall in a building called Jessup One on the south side of a small complex, one of the first that had been built, back when twelve acres of Manhattan was a reasonable size to set aside for people to solve problems of their own devising. The campus had been put together like a New England town, the buildings close enough to one another to share a library but far enough apart to keep a secret. Jessup One was built of red brick, dusty inside, with wide, shadowy halls, linoleum floors, and doors with pebbled glass windows. There was only one electrical outlet per room, and ceiling fans distributed a very faint bit of air-conditioning, but its age was a charm. When she reached her own door, there was a brass nameplate in a slot that said THOMAS PRAEGER, and she left it there.

It was late afternoon and the office itself was cool and dark. She stood in the doorway without turning on the overhead lights. The room was narrow but quite deep, and the ceiling was high; through the window at the far end came sunlight that illuminated a slight haze in the air. In three boxes beside the desk sat her computer, monitor, and printer. There was a high-speed line leading from a socket in the wall to a coil underneath the desk. Whoever had occupied it before her—this Praeger man, apparently—had left behind some thoughtless trash: a newspaper, three months out of date, lay on one of the bookshelves, alongside a paper coffee cup and a blue felt-tip pen. A single stereo speaker trailing a few feet of wire stood on the shelf below; she looked around for its match, but there was none. The light bulb had been unscrewed from the lamp on her desk, and left beside it with a note attached that said, *This works*. She was suspicious of the endorsement, but when she screwed it back in, sure enough, the light burst on just as she was giving it its last twist. That was encouraging, so she unpacked her equipment and connected each to each, and then, feeling she'd done a day's worth of work, she sat in the chair, which tipped dangerously backwards, nearly causing her head to strike the windowsill. She righted herself just in time to see a very tall man, with shoulder-length hair where he wasn't bald, lope past her door in a distracted stoop. A physicist, she remembered meeting him at the cocktail party; he was introduced to her as Rainer, on loan from CERN. His eyes were starry spirals, and he was one of those men who could prove to be either fascinating or as dull as death, but today was not the day to find out. Today was not the day to do anything, really, so she turned on her computer and flipped randomly through her photographs until she couldn't see them anymore, then shut everything down and left, closing the lockless door behind her.

UNTO US LOWLIEST SOMETIME SWEEP

A man named Benjamin Russell stood in the middle of a walkway across a bridge: a beautiful bridge it was, and he was alone. It was just before midnight. The sky was cloudless but the air was thick, the light arriving in woozy clumps. The bridge hummed and the water moved. New York, he thought to himself, surrounded by rivers and kills: how fast this current flows, and how long it's been flowing. Long before New York was named New York, before the Dutch or the Delaware Indians had settled, long before any mistakes were made, here was the river, trying to drag this island back into the sea.

He was a cautious man and his perch made him dizzy, his senses distressed, eyes uncertain in their sockets; or perhaps it was because the previous month had been full of difficult nights, not so much sleepless as filled with waking—being drawn back to consciousness every hour or two, like a small boat on this very river, carried unhappily southwards to the ever-shores surrounding the Land of Aware. The night before, he'd woken again and again and again, each time finding himself sitting on the edge of his bed with his hands waving in the air, in a gesture that even he didn't quite understand—fending off an attacker, or describing an urgent point of argument, or bidding goodbye. That very evening he'd slept for no more than an hour, and rather than lying in bed thinking his thoughts for the rest of the night, he'd risen and dressed and found himself, just a few minutes later, standing on the sidewalk outside his apartment on Rivington Street. He started walking.

The way was all pockets and corners, stairs leading down from the street into dark dens, creatures hiding in the gutters, beasts in waiting beneath the subway gratings; he couldn't control his responses, the little jerks of fright, electric shocks left over from dreams that he hadn't finished. He had walked down Bowery and passed through Chatham Square, anonymous amid the anonymous buildings, a panel van passing, a police car parked outside a Chinese bank, now and then a solitary man flickering past him. Then he'd cut west on Worth and started down Centre Street, and there was no one around at all. The streets were clean, the walls unmarked with posters or graffiti, no shops or shoppers. How sturdy it all looked, how elegant, reasonable and fair: the soul of adjudication, unsullied by the mess of real men and women. He'd looked back at the courthouse, which sat there on its granite flanks, uncomprehending. How many lives had been changed by this old man of a building? A mad old man, a dotard, stubborn and formidable, whom no one defied although no one knew why.

He'd continued down to the corner and started up the pedestrian walkway that led onto the bridge. A young man and a young woman on bicycles raced passed him, going in the other direction, but neither so much as glanced at him. Perhaps all they saw was each other; perhaps all they saw was the road. There was no one else along the way, and midway across the river he stopped. It would be a simple matter from there to swing his legs over the side, climb onto a beam, and make his way out to the edge. — Actually, it would be quite impossible. The beam was wide enough, and if it had been painted on a sidewalk he could have strolled across it easily, but knowing that he could fall made it almost certain that he would. Perhaps he could crawl. He had never been particularly athletic, but he'd played all the games little boys played, and he'd once been a fine Latin dancer: good enough to draw a little attention even at the clubs uptown. All those places were gone. Women in red dresses and men in white silk scarves. Gone. They'd stepped into their black limousines and disappeared.

Somehow he made it to the other side of the beam, though he had no idea how. He might have walked, the Devil might have carried him, he may very well have flown. He did feel like some kind of bird, now, folded up in the night. He could hear cars passing on the level below, another rhythm that made no sense; and all around him there were streamers of light. The rivets pressed into the bottoms of his feet, the thick fibers of the cable in his hand; and there was a faint wind blowing up from the south, smelling distinctly of murky water and slippery fish—a nineteenth-century odor, the salt of poets, still lingering. Another car passed below, and he wondered how many times he himself might have crossed this bridge, oblivious to a man standing where he was now, above it all. A machine: that's what the bridge was. John A. Roebling, inventor of a device for the abbreviation of lonely hearts.

He stood on his iron plinth and thought like a monster. Love was one of those diseases that strike only once in life, strengthening your immunity if you were lucky enough to get it young, becoming more and more destructive with the age of the victim, likely killing you if you were old. He'd missed it in his early years, and he'd grown stoic in his decision not to pursue it. Well, that was all right, there was a thinness to his experience, he understood; he had other things to occupy him. But the lack of a woman had made him fussy and distant, which in turn made a woman less likely. He'd known this, but he couldn't fix it. He had always been too careful: Was that the problem? No, other men were careful. Meek, was that a better word? A handsome little boy, he had been: fair-skinned and bright, but by seventeen he had lost all confidence. Too sensitive, too conscious. He hadn't been to college, that was one thing; he had gone to an Episcopal high school, and at one time he'd even thought of becoming a minister, but the summer after graduating he'd decided the whole thing was grotesque—this life, this world, these people, and the God they thought was watching them. In time, he recovered some measure of sympathy, though never his faith; in any case, by then he was in his mid-twenties, he had been working in the men's department of Macy's, and it was too late for him to try to pursue a degree. But he went to museums on the weekends, and one afternoon in the Met he'd stumbled upon a room filled with Africana, and in it a small vitrine containing a statue of a man, carved out of wood, elongated, enchanting, an altar figure from the Ivory Coast. That had set him off on thirty-five years of buying and selling, occupying a small storefront on Lexington, then a tony little office on East 90th, and at last a showroom of his very own on Elizabeth Street.

Hey now. There was a boat on the water, some kind of barge, coming north, lights glowing on the grey deck as it glided through the waves. It was surprisingly swift against the current, and as it approached the bridge the captain blew the horn, letting loose a huge, stunning sound, a brass parabola that radiated outwards, its lip expanding, nearly knocking him to his knees, and then rippling and resounding off the buildings on either side with such force that it shook the bridge, the great cables humming in sympathy. When the noise passed it seemed to take the earth with it, leaving the bridge to hang there like an arc etched in space, and he felt the whole system turn over and over again in the emptiness.

The money had all melted away, and with it had gone his little life: the apartment, the shop. There had never been much of it, but now there was none, instead there was this burden, the monstrous weight of owing absolutely everyone. Each day the amount had grown;

each day he had been driven down a little deeper. He looked across to Manhattan; Malebolge-on-the-Hudson, and there was so much money there, millions per cubic yard, but there was none to spare for him. Months earlier he'd tried to calculate how long it would take him to become solvent again if he sold everything he had, worked very hard, spent the favors owed and nothing else. It would have taken him not quite forever, he would have been a very old man, but there had been some hope: if he lived to be eighty, he might not die in outrageous debt. Then the letter had come from the IRS, notifying him that he owed them some enormous sum, and interest on top of that, and penalties on top of that. A staggering number, when all he had was a handful of grimy coins. Since then, the lawyer he'd hired had become more difficult to reach, no doubt because he realized that there was no money left to pay him. No one even bothered to tell him what was going on anymore. One morning, the marshals had come at dawn to put a lock on the door of his shop. Then what did they have all those meetings for? He had no more assets so they made him give all of his time, and when he had no more time they took his dignity, and when his dignity was gone they began shaving away at his very existence, one sliver at a time.

He'd only been by the shop once since they'd shuttered it; he'd stood on the sidewalk and peered through the front window, while people who had once been his neighbors and friends passed behind him, staring like the figures in an Ensor painting. The inside was almost empty, except for a few small things—beautiful but worthless, and still he wasn't allowed to take them home. He was coming undone.

He felt a wind come whipping up from the Atlantic, funneling past Staten Island and quickening on the river. It blew him backwards, almost pushing him off the beam and onto the road below, and he jerked forward to counter it. What a way to go, he thought. Another botch, done in by pavement rather than midnight water, by some delivery van or bus. Overhead, the slow floating wing lights of a private plane; in another direction, there was a helicopter flying slightly sideways, its searchlight sipping at the darkness, and he could hear its blades shearing through the atmosphere again and again, a rhythm like the sound of film running through a projector. Yes? That was the beat behind the chords of the bridge and the voice of the ship's horn, which was still sounding. Still. Such confidence the river had in its own music, never to pause for a breath, its melody continually unspooling.

In the wake of the wind came the pale tendrils of a beloved ghostess—Jillian's perfume, a murmuring, rose-heavy bouquet, still lingering on his coat from the last time she'd hugged him, three months previously. If he'd known it was going to be the last time, he would have driven his hands into her flesh to hold her, bolted his wrists behind her and refused to let go. Instead she had walked away, leaving behind a scent as distinct and constant as the sound of her breathing. It had tortured him for months, but what could he do? Buy a new coat? What would that cost? And besides, the smell of her skin was the only part of her that he had left. When that was all gone it would mean she was all gone, and then he would have nothing.

Such a waste, that's what he was. A man should leave more behind than he took from the world. This bridge, for example, with its massive lace and its great tense peaks, the very pitch and image of success—the men who built it could look at it for the rest of their lives and say, *I did that* to their wives and children. And he with his little bankrupt store, Jillian gone, all his days summoning zero, and all those remaining hours to fill, without work to occupy him, without a kiss to look forward to at night, all the same slow spending on an empty draft.

He wavered back and forth on his feet, blown by the wind, though he hardly noticed. What was wind but more of nothing moving from one place to another? Then another car passed below, this one thumping with the beat of its sound system, the sound so low it rattled his sternum: *lub lub lub lub lub*, young men rolling and laughing. Then a truck: all this traffic, and he wondered if that's what the world comes to. Is it? This busyness, this movement, and why? Somewhere boxes of things were making their way from one building to another, airplanes landing, another train on another bridge. Where was he supposed to find stillness in all this? The taking and trading, the passing tumult of days battering by. There should have been more to it, but he didn't know what or how to get it.

THE LION OF STUYVESANT

Reggie's foundling grew up under the name Caruso, though no one ever did know for sure whether it was his given name or a nickname he'd acquired. He grew up right there on 14th Street, down by the East River, within view of the power plant and the projects, a skinny boy with those soft green eyes and a smile that made the girls knot their fingers together. Different but not shy, exactly: quiet, a little sensitive, his teachers said, and they said he was well liked, but the truth was that no one much knew him. A middling student, easily distracted, had a little trouble paying attention in class, but he was never a trouble, not to anyone. He could be stubborn when he wanted to be: during his freshman year in high school, he earned a place at the front of the school choir, but he quit midway through the school year because the choirmaster had suspended him for a week, for failing to bring in the songbook they were all required to carry and then claiming that he didn't need it, because he'd already learned every part. But he had, he was always singing little things to himself, and he invited—almost dared—the choirmaster to test him. Leila was proud of him for that, though she didn't say so. You have to do well in school, she told him. Everything depends on that. And if that means playing by their little rules, then that's what you're going to do.

It was around this time that Reggie left for a little while. Much as he loved the boy and thought of him as his own, he and Leila were arguing all the time, almost always about money. After a while he said to himself, A man can only give so much, and then he's got to take care of himself: and look how tired I am, my back hurting from driving that car all day, and fifty has come and gone. His own father had died at forty-one, fell asleep in front of the television and never woke up, and no one told Reggie why. It had left him feeling cursed and haunted, knowing any day could be the end, and men like him didn't go anywhere afterwards.

And Leila had a temper, which she saved for when no one else was around, so only he'd seen it: a mirror shattered by a thrown remote control, a favorite jacket torn to shreds. She would say terrible things to him, hard things, cruel things, other people didn't see that side of her. One morning, when the apartment was empty, he packed a few things into some paper bags from below the kitchen sink, and with his arms full, and shaking his head sadly, he went down to the car and threw them in the trunk, and then lowered himself slowly into the seat and drove away—disappeared, maybe he went down South or maybe he just moved to another part of the city. For a few months, Leila raised the boy on her own and loved him even more: she fed him in the morning and sent him to school, and when he came home in the evening she fussed over him and told him he was a child of God, until he came to believe it, to believe that he was a child of fortune, a ring around the moon. And then one day Reggie came back, and things were different again, different than they were when he was gone, and different than the early days too. Something had passed between him and Leila, as if they'd struck some kind of secret bargain or pact, one that they acknowledged in the most indirect ways, in undertones and glances, a touch, signals and cues, a conversation that trailed off. Caruso never knew why his father left, where he went, or why he returned.

They didn't talk about those things in front of him, but he could see the source-pools of anger and disappointment that lay between them, as well as the sudden flashes of faith, small smiles traded sidelong just when it seemed they were going to fight, Reggie leaning over to whisper in her ear as she cooked, and she paused, a ladle in her hand, to listen to him.

A few weeks later Caruso showed up on the sidewalk, just standing there all by himself, singing. He sang songs about the neighborhood, about the chips of glass embedded in the sidewalk, and the Chinese couple who ran the bagel store, the fine new bus stop, and a neighborhood dog named Boom-Boom. He sang songs in praise of warm weather, songs of rue and principle, songs for his mother and songs for his father, and what a world this is, what a course of trouble, is there anyone who understands? At the age of fifteen, he stood on the corner to coax and serenade, all by himself, frail, confident, and as far as the neighborhood was concerned, half-crazy. — Can I sing you something? Ma'am? Ma'am? Can I sing you something? I just wrote it this morning. Do you like it? Songs for the girls walking home from school, pretty things decorated with ribbons and spangles and bracelets and laughter, they never kept still. Most of them were a little older than he was, but couldn't he make them shiver. Songs for the two cops watching from their parked car, trying to decide whether it was worth making him move or whether there might be something more interesting happening around the corner; songs for the men who went with men, the healthy ones who smiled at him kindly and were the most likely to leave a dollar in the hat at his feet; and the sick ones who shuffled into the drugstore down the block; songs for the children of C-Squat, who called out for their favorites; and songs for the women in their capri pants and high heels, for the old white ladies, who shuffling down the sidewalk two by two with their wheeled shopping baskets. — Will you stop, will you listen for a second? he'd say. There was something in his expression, some offer, some plea, that made them want to stay, and when they did he said, This one, it's just for you. Then he'd bend forward a little bit, as if he hadn't quite finished writing the thing yet and he was leaning into the words to come; and then he'd straighten up and sing.

He sang like a lion, little as he was; he sang like a lover, leaning back again, smiling, looking every listener in the eye, and with a voice that resonated all the way down to his toes, a mighty thing, a blessing. Who could have suspected that such a young man could want so much, and that his will would get bigger and bigger? He had a tenor that could fill a stadium, and a confidence that could quiet the crowd while he does; when he sang, nothing was lost—not the slightest flicker of emotion, nor the merest ridge of joy, nor the smallest shadow of grief.

There was a neighborhood drunk, an ageless man with thyroid eyes named Maurice, who heckled the boy and sometimes tried to sing along, until the girls shushed him and he muttered sordid things. — I wrote that, the boy said to his audience one afternoon, after an especially bracing round of applause. There were windows open in Stuyvesant Town. The 99-cent store had strung little plastic flags from its door to the street, to announce a sale on school supplies. Do you like it?

You wrote that, did you? Maurice said, rising up from his bent-over stance, swaying on his ragged feet. What you say? You wrote that song? And the boy turned to Maurice, his long lashes slowly parting, as if he was just waking. Hey, boy, you wrote that song? He smiled; Maurice wiped his mouth.

The girls liked to say his name, drawing out the middle syllable just for fun, Caruuuuuso! Carry me around the world. — Where'd you learn to sing like that?

It just comes out of me.

And you wrote that song?

He nodded vigorously. Do you like it? he said. I've got more. Then he was sixteen, maybe seventeen years old, and he wrote songs all day long, scrawling couplets in his notebooks, humming under his breath in his homeroom class until his teacher stopped what she was saying and cocked her head at him; answering a store clerk on Third Avenue with a little sing-songy rhyme; shutting himself in his room and singing into his cupped hands to make the sound larger. He thought his songs protected him like a djinn, and one evening in July, when the afternoon rain had given way to dark and musk, he walked over to the projects by the river in search of a new audience. Graffiti on the benches, plastic bags caught in the trees. He found a spot on the footpath before one of the buildings, but he was no more than halfway through a brand-new song when two older boys from Queens came by, drunk on 7 and 7 and looking for a girl named Cherie. One laughed with his eyes downcast while the other, an angry boy, stole a sheaf of lyrics from Caruso's back pocket. — Too much cream in that coffee, the angry one said. Creamy Nigger, the laughing one said, though Caruso was only a shade or two lighter than they were themselves. Creamy Nigger! They taunted him some more, and then one of them smacked him in the mouth so hard that he fell down, in tears before he reached the ground, and when he looked up to ask them why, the angry one was laughing and the laughing one was angry.

He was hiding in his room by the time Reggie got home that evening; he didn't want his father to find out what had happened, and Leila helped him. The next morning, she told Reggie that the boy had split his lip playing basketball at school, and the true story was a secret she and Caruso shared. The secret only Caruso knew was that he hated those two boys and wished them dead, and then wished them alive again so he could kill them again. (And indeed, though he never knew it, just six months later one of the boys fell off the roof of the very tower he had been standing outside.) Afterwards, his voice hardened, just a little bit, with lust or something like it. From then on he had something to hit with, and a memory to furnish the arc of his swing.

He was famous; he had always been famous, it just took a while for anyone to find out. Your boy was at it again the other day, someone said to Reggie at the bodega one afternoon, someone he'd never even seen before. Going to go very far. Head shaking, smile wide.

I don't know where he gets it from, Reggie said. Not from me, that's for sure. I can't sing at all, man. He put his six-pack up on the counter. Not at all.

Going to be a star, the other man said. You can see it already. You won't be drinking out of those cans for long, you'll be drinking fine liquor from a heavy glass.

That's right, Reggie said. On a beach in Hawaii. He laughed loudly, but as he left the store his face was dark, because life was good right now, and as far as he was concerned it could only get worse.

Leila had dreams of Caruso collecting his degree from a good college, but he didn't even want to finish high school. Instead he began skipping classes, and then dodging entire days, and as he neared the end of eleventh grade she started getting letters, each one more stern than the last. But what could she do? What could she say? Reggie pretended to care, but he didn't: he hadn't graduated himself, and if Caruso was going to make something out of his music, why not start as soon as possible? The boy begged her to sign the papers so he could drop out. She didn't want to, but she was starting to give in: he was headstrong, he was persuasive, that was part of his talent—oh, he could charm the moon into releasing the tides. And maybe he was old enough to make these kinds of decisions for himself. He was already so tall she had to shade her eyes just to see his face, and he had wisps of hair on his jawline. Maybe he wasn't a boy at all anymore. The decade was a dream. She stood at the window and watched him walk down to the subway stop, and she felt weak. Nothing grows quicker than a young man; and she retreated from the window and sat on the couch with the photo albums she'd been keeping in a small plastic pocket binder for years, pictures of him sitting on Reggie's lap, mugging in a school portrait, on the first day of summer with those jet-black high-top sneakers that he liked so much he wore them to bed for a week, though he never seemed to notice that they were on the floor by his closet when he woke; and there he was, dressed for her cousin's wedding in a light blue suit that he'd outgrown in the month between buying it and wearing it. Beautiful boy, waving and smiling, and there he goes.

For the next year, he left the house in the morning and didn't return until late at night. Occasionally, Leila would find him at the kitchen table at breakfast, and she'd hug him from behind, each time, she thought, having to make a broader circle with her arms. Over his shoulder she could see scraps of paper arranged around his cereal bowl, some of them words to songs that she couldn't read, he had such terrible handwriting; some of them looked like the names of people. Girls? Or fellow musicians, nightclub managers, recording people, she didn't know. She saw him only briefly at the end of the night, and Reggie, who left for work earlier than she did and came home later, hardly saw him at all. Only their Sunday dinners remained as regular and full as they had been, the three of them sitting around the table, laughing and eating. She made her special Gullah stew, a dish her grandmother had taught her many years ago, Caruso's favorite, it never failed; and Reggie told stories about the fares he'd picked up, crazy things on the street, while Caruso listened bright-eyed and laughing.

Then one Sunday night Caruso came home a little bit late, rushing into the room where the table had been carefully laid. His parents stared: he was wearing a ruby cape over a white dress shirt and black linen pants, and he had kohl around his eyes like an Arab in an old movie. He sat down without taking the cape off, and Reggie, who was wearing a faded blue T-shirt, with his vaccination scar glinting like a dark purple peony on his upper left arm, couldn't hold back. Boy! he said. What the hell have you got on! His voice was so saturated with contempt that it would have curdled cream, and the shock of it silenced the table. Caruso studied his food. I think he looks very fine, Leila said. I think he looks the fool, Reggie answered. She reached her hand halfway to Caruso, letting it rest on the table between them. The boy was wearing his skin like a mask of grief. He stood. Where are you going? she said, and he said, I've got to be somewhere, his voice trembling terribly. When he left, he left a dirty pool of silence. Leila glared at Reggie, and Reggie said nothing, half embarrassed and half still angry, and wearing a grimace to express them both. A long moment passed, and then she said, He's still our boy. But Reggie wasn't sure he was their boy, anymore; he was beginning to think that Caruso had been no more than a visitor, a red glass egg entrusted to them, and when the shell had shattered a dragon had come out, swinging his red tail high.

How could she keep track of a seventeen-year-old boy, one as willful as he was, especially when she was working all the time? He was a good boy, she knew that. Never one to look for trouble, not much sense in him, maybe, but no malice either. Where are you going, Caruso? — Just out. If the police didn't call, that was good enough. It was months before she learned that he'd been singing at parties, sitting in at clubs, meeting people, picking up gunner's dollars, money he spent on equipment until his little room was crowded with instruments and electronics, little boxes joined by cords, every outlet stuffed with plugs. He learned to play the piano, and then the guitar, and then the drums, just like that, seeing the song and seeing how to make the song. Caruso, Caruso: he lied when people asked him how old he was, and they believed him: he had the confidence to front a dance band made up of men twice his age, hugging himself with his left arm while his right hand floated around, bringing the sound up, up again, up higher.

— Goddamn, boy, where'd you learn to shout like that? Quick and growing, and in time he eased the weaker musicians out and replaced them, ruthlessly poaching players from other bands, drawing them closer to him by allowing them to share his beat. Now a few horns to make the sound bigger, now an extra percussionist to run cross-rhythms against the grain, they had to know how to dance and they had to watch him for cues, when he made a fist and when he cocked his head, boys and girls and men and women, making his sound, the sound in his head.

Leila didn't realize that he was saving up his money to move out. Reggie knew, the way he knew the leaves fell off the trees in autumn: of course, a boy his age wanted to be on his own in the world. It was something so obvious he didn't need to mention it. But she wasn't ready and she took it hard. Caruso was eighteen then, and his mother's angry tears took him by surprise. Mama-Lee, he said, using the pet name he first settled on back when he was a boy. I'm making good money now. I thought you'd be proud of me.

Good money? Leila said, her hand on her chest as if she was having an attack. Like our money's bad? He couldn't leave her like that, so he stayed another year, but he got a room by Penn Station, blacked out the windows and soundproofed the walls, and installed all the recording equipment he could afford, and that's where he spent his time, from one blue summer through the following fall and winter, and halfway through the spring, bringing in this player and that one, putting down one part after another, redoing and redoing, sometimes staying up until dawn and only realizing as much when he put his hand to the windows and felt the vibrations of the traffic on the street, a new day beginning. Once or twice a producer or promoter stopped by, but he couldn't explain what he was doing, he could only practice and find a way to play it.

Then one very warm week in June, he finished a set of six songs, the final mix of step and croon, songs of love, about which he knew little, and sex, about which he knew even less. He sent them around to everyone he could think of, with personalized notes, and then waited impatiently for the response—which faltered in its own silence—tapping his fingers on the table, walking the floors, unable to look at anyone for a good six weeks. He had never imagined, not even for a moment, that all his work and hope would never be recovered, never amount to a man. He stopped speaking, and the days chipped away. Leila asked him if he wanted to talk to Reggie, maybe he could pick up some hours driving a second shift on the livery, but he just shook his noisy head. Then suddenly the phone rang, a club DJ named High-Hat, a label in the Bronx, a radio station, another label, and all at once the sky gathered and the dollars started pouring down, huger and harder than he'd ever expected: the rhythm, the voice and the noise, the song of the summer: Mighty Caruso, the Sound of the City, the WonderBeat, and August was his.

The boys postured and posed to the sound, and the girls all shouted. And sure, then, they came around—not just girls from the neighborhood but from all over town, and sometimes from farther away than that, from California, from Buenos Aires, from Japan. Where did they get the money? How did they end up on 14th Street? Who let them out and who was going to take them in? These were mysteries; but there they were, standing on the sidewalk, waiting for him to come home, holding copies of his records, bouquets of flowers, handmade tribute books, magazine photographs, all those things that girls collect. They came in laughing groups of three or four, or alone with that sad desirous look on their face, they fought with one another and left messages for him, love notes on cards leaned carefully against the stoop. They brought balloons in parti-colored bundles, some of which inevitably escaped, so that the treetops were decorated with them. And late at night, when everyone had gone home, Leila went downstairs, opened the door, and with a sigh and her knees cracking, she bent down, collected it all and brought it upstairs, storing the cards and notes in boxes and putting the flowers in vases of water. (Why don't you write a song about diamonds? she teased Caruso. Why don't you write a song about groceries? And he looked at her with great concern and said, Do you need grocery money? She laughed at that and kissed his forehead.)

Reggie thought the girls were funny, now that his beard had turned white. Hello, young ladies, he said when he came home in the evening. Hello, Mr. Caruso, they chorused in unison, giggling at their own voices. They didn't care what his real name was, and he didn't care to correct them. Harmless, happy stuff, until one night when a white girl, a little taller than the rest but surely no older, stopped him and asked him to hold the flowers she'd brought so she could have both hands free to put up her hair, and as he complied she took him by the back of the head and tried to kiss him. She wasn't more than fifteen or sixteen. He jumped backwards about three yards in a single hop, wide-eyed and terrified. — What the hell? The girl just looked at him, he couldn't tell at all what she was thinking, and he dashed into the house while she watched on blankly.

HONEY AND ASHES

This, too, is going to happen. A woman will stand in the wings of a theater. She'll be a West African woman, and the theater will be on the campus of a university, a university in New York City. Most of the people in the audience will be students, but some of them will be professors and support staff, and some will be people from the community, many of whom have never been on the campus before and have come on this occasion—a clear fall night—to see the woman speak.

The theater is going to be crowded, all the seats filled: there will be a dozen people standing in the back, and a few more sitting in the aisles with their coats and bags tucked around their legs. An usher will try to move the people in the aisles, but as soon as he succeeds in doing so others will take their place, and in time he'll simply give up, turning to the back of the theater with an irritated shrug and an expression on his face that says, What can I do? But there will be no one who cares enough either to chide him or excuse him.

There are going to be camera crews along the side walls: two on the right side and one on the left, and they'll have bright lights set up, which will make the atmosphere slightly tense, as it often is when everything is easily visible. A man in a heavy black V-neck sweater is going to turn to his companion, a woman in a slate grey coat, and say, Someone should tell them to turn those off. He'll pause and start to get to his feet—but just then the young woman will walk out and take her place at the podium, so he'll sit down again. The audience will quickly hush, and the woman at the podium will look out over the people gathered there and take a few breaths.

She'll be dressed in a conservative charcoal-colored suit and black shoes, and wearing a pair of small silver earrings, an outfit that will be meant to make her look formal, dignified, and perhaps more mature, though in truth it'll make her look even younger than she is—so much so that some people in the audience will assume she's not the speaker at all, not the main speaker, anyway, but a student who's been tasked with introducing her—perhaps because they're from the same country, for when the woman begins to speak, she'll have an accent, slight and charming, but unmistakable, especially when she pronounces less common words, like *amnesia*, which she'll render with four distinct syllables, or words with prominent *r*'s—*treason*, for example, or *resources* or *revival*. And soon the audience will realize that she's the one they came to see.

Her name will be Matilda, or something like that—a Western name, but an old-fashioned one: a church name, slightly ungainly, but also elegant, dignified, even comforting. She'll be a Christian woman, and she'll say so, with a plainness that seems to prove it: I am a Christian woman. My mother was a Christian, and so too was my father. And then she'll tell them about her country, the country where she was born and where she continues to live, even though she could live elsewhere if she wanted. She'll talk about the landscape, the reddish color of the dirt, and the rains, and about the way the air smells when the rain has passed. She'll talk about her father's sign-painting shop, and how she used to sit there watching him work. She'll talk about her sister, who was several years older than she was; how strong the woman was, even through all her losses; how little she spoke but how much she knew; and how many people attended her funeral, where they sang the old songs of grief.

She'll talk about punishment and she'll talk about forgiveness, and then about mercy, even for those who haven't asked for forgiveness. The audience, which will be mixed—some black, some brown, some white; some Christian, some not—will listen carefully, even with the distraction of the television cameras and the lights. They'll sit, motionless and attentive, while she describes, with a slight smile, the difference between the tears one cries when one remembers, and the tears one cries at the pain of something present and immediate. She'll say a few words about the size and shape of the world, how round it is, and its three colors: blue, green, and brown, just like the eyes of the people who populate it. She'll talk about having learned a few things along the days, specifically, about what people must have, regardless of what else they might be blessed with, like wealth or soul-sweetness or very good luck. They need the words, for example, all the words to a few valuable songs, like the old songs of grief; a place to go where they can be alone and a place to go where they're never alone; someone to admire, someone they know personally and can visit when they want to. She'll mention a saying that she once heard from a man that she herself admired: that the phrase *Thank you* is among the first that a child learns, and they should be the last words all men and women say when they close their eyes and their spirits are ready to rise, at last, away from this good, grim world. And then she'll thank the audience for coming out to see her and for listening to the things she has to say.

When she's finished, the applause will be long and very loud, and afterwards people are going to linger in the lobby, talking to each other, even after the house lights have come up, the television crews have packed their things and left, and the university employee charged with locking up has taken to making shooing gestures. Extraordinary, that such a young woman, from such a poor place, could have achieved so much. I only wish our own leaders were as courageous. — Remarks like that, not really conversations, and spoken with a certain dazedness. Then there's going to be a brief scuffle by the door, when one man accidentally steps on the back of another man's shoe.

Later that evening there will be a dinner, in a restaurant just off campus that's been rented out for the night. Matilda will be the guest of honor, though any stranger who might happen to peer through the window would find it impossible to tell that she is. There will be four identical round tables, with six seats at each table, and one long rectangular table with ten seats. The guests will arrive all at once—or not all at once, exactly, but within a few minutes of one another, having walked from the auditorium in groups of three and four, chatting pleasantly and even laughing, because however important the speech was, now was the time to celebrate having heard it. Matilda will arrive with a middle-aged man, well-dressed but startlingly ugly, with pockmarked skin and red-rimmed eyes, and what's more, walking with a slight limp, the result of a bout of polio he suffered as a child—a well-known poet from her own country, though long since exiled and writing in English. To an observer, they'll look as if they're bound to each other by their shared origin, though the truth will be more complicated and subtle than that: their conversation will be an elaborate and slightly artificial exchange, consisting largely of gestures, on his part of deference to her fame, and on her part of deference to his wisdom. He'll call her by a name that means *dearest* (or *most valuable* or *most unusual*) *one*, for example, and she'll call him by a name that means *one of the men for whom I feel almost the way I feel for my father*. Still, their respect for each other, touched though it is with real warmth and pride, will be tempered by the fact that the older man is not a Christian, and indeed, has made the imposition of Christianity in his native country one of the themes he visits and revisits in his work; and while neither of them will be offended by such a disagreement, each will assume that the other one is, and the result will be a slight awkwardness between them, manifested in exaggerated courtesies.

There's going to be a bustle at the door to the restaurant, with the maître d' checking names against a list, people stopping dazedly to gaze around the room while others pile up in the vestibule behind them, waiters coming forward with trays of hors d'oeuvres, and two or perhaps three very large men, security agents of some sort, hired by the university against Matilda's wishes, who will stand motionless just inside the door, causing the flow of people around them to become more chaotic, the way water in a stream roils around boulders. The poet will disappear without saying goodbye, and a hand will touch Matilda's back, a voice murmur in her ear, and she'll be guided through the room to the rectangular table, where she'll be seated with a city councilman on one side and a television personality on the other side; and there will be an American diplomat, a very rich man and his wife, and then, all the way around at the other side of the table, a young man, a few years younger than herself, black as a blackbird and wearing glasses so thick his eyes appear distended behind them.

The television personality sitting at her right is going to be a large man, well over six feet tall and broad. She will have been on his show that afternoon. It won't have been the first time she's been on television, but it will have been her first time doing so in this country, and she'll have been vexed by the way they stopped every few minutes for a commercial. And in fact even now, at dinner, he'll have the same sort of attention span, as if the rhythms of his television show were a direct reflection of the rhythms of his thought. — You know, you mean so much to so many people, he'll say to her. I've never seen the people who work in my office so excited to meet a guest. Honestly. Tomorrow I'm going to go in and tell them that I was sitting right next to you at dinner, and they're going to want to know everything you said and did.

Matilda is going to be taken aback by this, but she'll recover quickly enough to make fun of her own alarm, widening her eyes and raising her eyebrows, smiling and moving backwards in her seat a little bit, with her hands gripping the edge of the table as if she were on a roller coaster. The television personality will chuckle and say, Don't worry: I'm not going to tell on you. In my profession, you don't last long if you're the kind of man who gossips. He'll lean in to speak to her: They say things about me, too, you know. The newspapers. They pay people—he'll point—like that waiter, for example, to be informants, to provide information.

Matilda is going to look at the waiter. Him? she'll say, in a tone of voice somewhere between curiosity and shock, and unsure whether she's understood.

The television personality will say, Not him, necessarily. You know what I mean, he'll say, and Matilda will nod distractedly. It will have grown very loud in the restaurant, with everyone talking and the waiters moving about, and chairs being shifted slightly so that someone can speak more directly to someone else; and she'll be trying to smile at everyone who smiles at her, but she'll be thinking about her two young boys, whom she'd left at home and whom she misses terribly. The television personality will pat her hand and say, That's all right, never mind. I'm just very pleased to spend some time with you.

There's going to be a glass of wine to the right of her table setting, but she won't drink from it. Where she's from, a woman tastes wine only in church, and while part of what she'll have spoken about that very evening will have been the problems—the difficulties—the issues—besetting her culture, she is after all a woman from just that place, and its habits are not so easily left behind; and this is one phenomenon that will always disconcert her when she travels to cities like this, the alcohol with a meal, the assumption that she wants to have alcohol, and more broadly, that everyone wants to be intoxicated whenever it might be possible. She'll remember an occasion in London some years previously, when someone she needed to speak to, someone she was soliciting, at last relented and agreed to meet with her the following afternoon in a bar near her hotel. When she arrived, she found a dark, discreet room, overseen by a bartender in a grey vest; and while it was pleasant enough, no men at the bar with machetes sheathed under the waistband of their pants, no party girls tucking cash between their pressed-together breasts, still she'd felt uncomfortable there, the more so when the waiter asked her what she was having. She'd needed to search for the right words, a response that wouldn't be prudish or impolite; and she'd worried that she was resisting some fundamental gesture of hospitality, like a piece of bread, or a bit of colored cloth—the kind of thing that, in other parts of the world, would be an untenable breach of manners to refuse. But in the years since that afternoon she'll have discovered that it's easiest to allow her glass to be filled and then simply to ignore it, as she'll do that night.

Across the table, just now arriving, there's going to be a grey-haired woman, a professor from the university, and her husband, once a dean at the same institution and now retired, both of them prominent figures, the wife perhaps more so than the husband. Matilda will smile at them and wave, happy and a little bit relieved to see them, because it's the professor who will have made it possible for her to come here, who sought her out, contacted her, issued the invitation, arranged her airplane flight and her stay in one of the university's guest rooms, set up her speaking engagement, composed the guest list for this dinner, and so on. And yet the weekend will have been so busy that Matilda won't have had the time to meet with her privately, to get to know her and to thank her for this opportunity.

They will be very old, the professor and her husband: where Matilda is from, men and women that old will be very scarce, a thing to look upon with wonder and respect; but here in this city there will be a great many old people, the sidewalks will be full of them. Still, these two will be special, as if age were its own crown; it'll be evident from their bearing, in how much they give out and how much they hold back. It will show in the unhurried way they take their seats, the professor waiting patiently while her husband, who's noticeably stiff and perhaps even a little bit unsure of where he is, slowly lowers himself into his chair. When he's settled the woman will take her own seat, and only then will she look across the table and say with great warmth, Matilda! How are you holding up? And when Matilda indicates that all is well, the professor will turn and whisper something to her husband, and he'll nod and then sit back in his chair and observe the scene before him, as old people do: silent, expressionless, his eyes peering out hawklike from behind his large hooked nose, his hands folded on the tabletop.

Afterwards, Matilda, the professor, and her husband will linger on the sidewalk outside the restaurant, saying goodbye to their guests with thanks and promises, compliments, more and more handshakes and kisses, until at last they'll look around and discover that they're alone, and they'll sigh and collect themselves. Hm! the dean will say, but when Matilda turns her attention to him she'll find that he's looking across the street at nothing in particular. Come, the professor will say to her, we'll walk you back to your room.

There will be scholars on Broadway, and mothers with all of their belongings in plastic bags, Chinese men on bicycles, and scaffolding everywhere, as if the city proper ended at the first floor, above which there was only a stage set. Outside a subway station a young black man—just a boy, really—will be sitting on a small stool, drumming loudly on a little jazz kit, and the professor will stop to watch, nod approvingly, and drop a few dollars in the cardboard box at the drummer's feet. They'll pass through a narrow iron gate onto a grand, quiet campus of old stone and brick buildings topped with green copper roofs, quite a different landscape than the one they just left; for one thing, the smells of the street, of food and refuse and aging concrete, will have disappeared—but there'll be the same spring mist overhead, charged with a million particles of discarded light. Matilda will be struck by the evidence of riches around her and how suddenly it appeared, the quiet, the lovely lampposts and architecture, the students in their expensive clothes, or in tattered clothes worn as wealthy people wear them; and the three of them will slow, not to take in their surroundings, though Matilda will use the opportunity to do so, but because the dean will have grown tired and will have conveyed as much to his wife, perhaps by clutching her arm a little more tightly, or by allowing his shoes to scrape the ground a little more audibly, or by one of the many unspoken signals that couples who have been together for a long time send to each other.

Now moving quite slowly, they're going to make their way past a monumental building, its windows shining from within. — That's the library, the professor will say.

Ah, yes, I see, Matilda will say. Is it open always?

Yes, the professor will explain, stopping. Twenty-four hours a day while classes are in session.

Matilda will watch through the windows as a young man strolls swiftly down one of the inside corridors, pauses to say something flirtatious to a girl about his age, and then emerges, just a few seconds later, from the front door of the library, slowing as he nears them and glancing for a long moment at Matilda's face before his pace quickens again and he passes down the long pathway to the north end of the campus. Matilda will turn to the professor. He knew who you were, the professor will say.

No . . . Matilda will reply, not out of modesty but in genuine disbelief.

Yes, he did, the professor will say.

Matilda will laugh brightly and then change the subject, as she often does; if there is one thing she will have learned, over the years, it's how to change the subject without others noticing. Have you been here a long time? she'll ask.

Yes, the professor will say. A very long time, almost all my life. And my husband has been here even longer than I have. In fact, I was once his student. — This was quite some time ago, you know, back when he was teaching. He was young then, and I was even younger. The professor will touch Matilda's arm. — You should have seen him, she'll continue. He was so handsome and he dressed so elegantly: like a gigolo, he was.

I'm sorry? Matilda will say, tilting her head. A . . .

Oh, the professor will say, a man who hires himself out to women for sex. And Matilda, slightly shocked, will look over at the professor's husband to see if he minds the imputation, and find nothing at all in his expression to suggest that he does. Instead, he'll stop and speak to Matilda for the first time. Everybody was in love with her! he'll say. But I got her! Then he'll smile, with large yellow teeth, a smile so broad and ferocious that for a moment he'll look like a madman, and he'll nod once emphatically.

Yes, the professor will say warmly. You certainly did. And her husband will nod once more, and then they'll start walking again.

You had many suitors, Matilda will say.

I had my share, the professor will say, as if her share was a large one and no more needed to be said about that. She'll point. — This is the main administration building.

Matilda will look up and see the wide marble stairs, the heavy colonnade, and she'll wonder who paid for such a magnificent building; and who designed it; and who quarried the marble, and who lifted it into place: how many thousands of men and where they all lived—were there camps here, where the students now walk?—and who cooked for them when they came home at night.

What are you thinking? the professor will ask.

Oh, nothing, I was just looking, Matilda will say. And then: This campus, this entire city, it's all so . . . The word will escape her. — Venerable?

The professor will nod and then pause, waiting for Matilda to say more. The professor's husband, too, will be looking at her, his eyes so clear that Matilda will feel like she's looking through them, straight into the spark that animates him. Both of them will seem to be smiling, although neither of them actually will be; and Matilda is going to smile herself in phantom empathy. No, she'll say, I don't think that's the exact word. Ancient. Aboriginal. Like a civilization that's been lost for thousands of years and then reappears, yes? With its magnificent buildings appearing out of the mist, and all the people with their customs and rites, bent to their business.

The professor will nod and say, The New World. It's always been here.

Matilda won't think of this moment for many years, not until two more wars have passed in her country, and one season of very heavy rain, and one where there was no rain at all. Some diseases will have been cured, and a few new diseases will have sprung up to take their place. She'll have gone from being universally admired to being almost as universally despised, and then back to being treasured again; and then almost forgotten, until a man who had been in love with her many years earlier wrote a song about her called Honey and Ashes, with a sweet and mournful melody and the words *when we were young, and time was time for kissing,* made all the more piercing because he recorded it himself. People heard the song and remembered her as he remembered her.

By then, her husband will be long since gone, but she'll have many people whom she considers part of her family, and indeed, one of her own sons will be a professor himself. When she does think of that night in New York, she's going to remember it very well: the scent in the air, the luxury of the campus, the pride of the dean and the affection of the professor. She'll be sitting in a comfortable wooden chair, in the dooryard of her nephew's house, when it'll come back to her, all at once, in part because she's grown old and she's reflecting on her past, but mostly because she's been thinking this: They say the butterfly evolved so that its wings would resemble the petals of flowers; but what if it's the flowers that evolved to look like the butterfly's wings?

AVAILABLE NIGHT

Later, Stephanie would explain, in a short, sharp introduction to the book, that it all began because of her jet lag; or perhaps it was the noise, the sirens and horns and car alarms at night; or maybe it was the visions. She couldn't sleep. The first two nights she got up and began to circle the living room, unevenly and a little bit thoughtlessly, unpacking, carrying clothes into the bedroom, rearranging the bedside lamp, setting up the bathroom, but always returning back into the living room, where she would make a pass by the windows and look down on the street below, streaked with yellow, the traffic lights with their slightly off colors—the red wasn't quite red, and the green was half blue—changing one to the next.

Years ago a friend of hers had bought a new lens that he wanted to show off. She'd gone over to his apartment and he brought it out, a gorgeous thing to be sure, and very expensive. She did not, as a rule, have any particular feel for machinery, but lenses were different, almost like jewelry, with their perfect crystals and their interlocking parts. Isn't it pretty? her friend had said. And so it was: a beautiful thing for capturing beautiful things. But then, what was New York itself? A magnificent machine composed of miles and miles of glass, under-girded by a machinery so intricate and complicated that no one could comprehend it all—a camera feeding on its own light, built by millions of people over hundreds of years for the purpose of capturing this very life they were building. She stood by the window, stared and inhaled, taking in the scent of it, floating above all the service and retail, the smell of light, ash and concrete, mixed with the sometimes sickly sweet odor that wafted up from the rear doors of restaurants, where they had thrown out whatever they hadn't managed to sell. On the third night she got dressed before she could change her mind, took a camera, and went downstairs. She felt like she was wandering off the clockface, away from books, away from the day and its responsibilities, into a dark field unencumbered with landmarks.

She started over toward Fifth Avenue, listening to the sound of her own heels striking the pavement. She felt the usual vague fear, that dank uncertain glaze over everything, because it was nighttime and she was alone. But the camera was her protection, that was the worst and best thing about it: people were afraid of it. She stopped under a scaffolding and fired off a few quick shots of an empty doorway across the street just to make sure the exposure was set properly. Pop, pop, pop, she said to herself. If she was seeing, she was invisible: that's how it worked.

Film couldn't do this. There had never been any that was fast enough to shoot at night, not without holding the exposure for so long that anything that moved became blurred, or using a flash so powerful that every scene looked like a crime had occurred there. But these new cameras, with their apertures open wide and their hypersensitive sensors: they were owl-eyed, they could see a drizzle of photons in the dead of dark. Quite suddenly and for the very first time, the world at night had become as visible to the camera as it was to the eye, a third of the planet's rotation now available to the photographer, where it had once been too dim to see. It was a development as momentous as Muybridge, as revelatory as color, and she was greedy for it, starving.

She watched the avenues grow less busy as she got closer to the park, fewer shops and restaurants open, none at all on Fifth, nor even much traffic, so she stood in the middle of the street for a moment, shooting first downtown, then uptown, before hastening back to the sidewalk. There was a doorman watching her: she was on public property, although being so never prevented someone from trying to stop her, and in fact he came over, palm raised, and said, You can't do that here. She glanced at him; sometimes it was best to push back and sometimes it was best to implore, but it was her first night out and she just said, I'm OK, and started walking downtown. It was always useful to confuse them, and she'd collected a half dozen phrases—sheer nonsense that sounded enough like a response to hold someone off for a second or two. *Hang on, it's broken*, that usually worked. It didn't help if you pretended not to hear them, or not to understand: then they just got physical. You had to come back at them with some sort of authority, the more senseless the better. You could say almost anything if you said it with enough confidence. *The horses are almost ready. There's something wrong with those trees.*

A cab pulled over to the corner, unsolicited; she shook her head and it drove off again. A jogger passed her on the sidewalk. There was a ghost bicycle, white as bone, chained to a parking sign. If everyone was asleep, how come so many of the lights were on in the buildings overhead? Now that she'd left the doorman behind, she panned the camera across the top floors of an office building, though from street level she couldn't see anything but ceilings. She turned back east; on the other side of Madison there were men unloading cardboard boxes from the back of a van and stacking them on the sidewalk, and a woman in her twenties standing just inside the door of a bank, the machines behind her waiting patiently, sky blue and mute, for someone to come take her safely home. She met Stephanie's gaze for a second, saw the camera, and turned away. To the south, the street was spotted with little lights from the stores that were still open, or had closed but left their signs lit, and from fifteen blocks away she could see two taxis swimming northwards. She liked people, she liked stealing from people.

London wasn't the same, not at this hour. It was all so stony and antiquated; there was never the surprise of a subway letting out or police cars gunning through an intersection. At one or two in the morning, there was just the architecture, occasionally interrupted by drunken children. She had never been a Londoner. But New York at night was New York. She took pictures in bursts, mashing the button down to get five or six frames in a second, listening to the soft, swift clicking of the aperture. Her teachers would have upbraided her for failing to kill the beast with one shot, but she didn't care. She loved this feeling, of being joined to the whole world by the tip of her finger; she was profligate, promiscuous, she could surface from a single day with hundreds of images. It was time-consuming and occasionally maddening, going through them all and trying to decide which ones to keep; all she wanted was a picture, and she wasn't patient. But neither could she bear to lose a frame, no matter how banal. She might print one out of every hundred she shot and exhibit one out of every ten she printed, but the rest she kept stored, the memory cards archived, boxed up, and shelved. — Now here was a man in an expensive grey overcoat, leaning against the hood of his expensive car, smoking a cigarette and talking on a phone. He saw her faint smile and nodded to her, he didn't know that she'd taken his picture before he saw her, and that was why she'd smiled. As she passed, he turned away slightly, shoulders hunched, leaning forward over the sidewalk and saying, I'm sorry. I'm sorry. I'm sorry.

She walked a few blocks south and then over to Lexington, where she started north again, slow as an army scout getting used to the terrain, not just looking for landmarks but settling into her own gait, adjusting her eyes' saccade, glancing at the screen on the back of the camera, clocking the numbers, how much time and how much memory.

She had been no one until she discovered photography, late in college: just another New York girl with a good education and invisible manners, unsure of whom to love. The camera had taught her how to look, and looking had taught her what she wanted. She hadn't always gotten it, but she had gotten pictures of it.

She went out the next night, and almost every night thereafter. It was a demanding and disorienting schedule, she knew, but it suited her and it suited her circumstances; it was a way to return to New York, entering through the side door, unobserved. She decided that 8 p.m. was the end of the day, and she would leave the apartment just past sunset, carrying her smallest good camera, take a cab to a corner and start to walk, wandering down to Cooper Square one night, across 42nd Street from river to river the next, up one avenue and down another, walking and watching, from nightfall until the sky's first cherub-colored note of dawn. Here there were five or six restaurants on each block, extending back from sidewalks into dark and distant rooms, excavated out of solid stone. Here there were theaters, here there were lights, here there were brownstones and here there were tenements. Here there were old people, and here there were none. Here there were white people, and here there were none.

Every so often, especially in the early hours, she would run into someone she knew on the street, though it was never anyone she knew well: a man she'd met at a dinner party in a luxurious apartment on Gramercy Park, the sister of a woman she'd dated from Memorial Day to Labor Day, an editor who had once offered her a gig shooting fashion, and had kept raising the fee as Stephanie kept declining. They looked exactly as they had a decade previously, but for some tightening around the eyes; and they dressed just as they had, the only changes being an update in a line or hem here and there, finer cloth and smaller stiches. A woman she'd worked with in a gallery on West Broadway, who was pushing a softly bouncing baby stroller with twin boys inside, and who was so exhausted she could only say Hello. An elderly man who was coming up out of the 72nd Street subway station as she was going down, and asked her, quite sincerely, how she was doing, but before she could answer a flock of hurrying passengers carried him away, and it was only after he was gone that she realized he was a friend of her parents, whom she'd last seen at her mother's funeral.

She found blocks of office buildings and blocks of tenements, concert halls, docks; there were neighborhoods so quiet she could hear herself breathing, and others so noisy she came home with a headache; there were monuments and hospitals, chain-link fences in front of empty lots; there were drunken tourists, wandering groups of young women in nearly identical sheath-tight dresses, sanitation workers and drug dealers, men standing in front of all-night pizza parlors. But the people were only ornaments on the things, and she shot in her eccentric way. There was one night when she spent more than an hour documenting a construction site from the sidewalk, her eyes drifting across the foundation, the crane, the stacks of rebar, a single bare light bulb burning on the third or fourth floor. Long before she finished, she knew she wasn't going to get anything she could use. The forms were uninteresting, and while banality had its virtues, they were exceedingly refined, and she'd never quite trusted her own taste in such things. Besides, the scene had an allegorical air about it, some point that it made about Erasing History or Capital, or something like that; but she had no point to make and didn't want to be mistaken for someone who did. She looked for angles in the un-angled sky. She didn't find them but she kept shooting anyway, working the muscles, calibrating her eye, until the memory card was full.

Another night she walked the length of Columbus, passing closed cafés and shuttered newsstands, people coming alone out of bars. She stopped at a basketball court and watched four boys, no older than fourteen or fifteen, playing hard at a game at two in the morning.

She stood back from the fence and listened to the rhythm of the ball striking the pavement, holding the camera at her side with her finger twitching on the shutter release. She brought it up to her eye and tried to frame the scene as quickly as possible: she didn't want the boys, she wanted the ball, dim and orange, sailing on its inspired arc across the dark reflecting windows of a brick apartment building, and she shot the way the boys were shooting, swiftly, casually-carefully, glancing.

On yet another night she found herself on Canal and Church, having wandered down from the Village taking pictures of the trees in their dark uniforms, shops behind rolled-down grates, the backlit door to an after-hours club, which opened every few minutes to let in someone new. She crossed into Tribeca and found a pair of subway conductors sitting on the steps of a pocket park, unwrapping sandwiches. She asked if she could take their picture and the smaller one spoke in a thick Caribbean accent: What for?

She made herself plain and said, Just for me.

OK, the larger one said. Just for you. The two of them leaned back against the wrought-iron fence and smiled.

She shot four or five, and then said, Thank you.

Him not going to come out, the smaller one said, jerking his head at the other man. You'll get no picture of him. Him a demon.

The other made a mock-angry face and said, Stop that! Why you try to scare her, hm? He pushed at the smaller one's head and they both started laughing. The smaller one said something Stephanie didn't understand, but it sounded like a curse, and the two men screamed with laughter and she took their picture again. You be good now, one said as she was walking away. You make us famous.

By the time she got to Chambers, the faint pearly-pink dome of morning had just started to come down. Dawn didn't arrive here from the horizon: it descended slowly from the sky, and the city still thought it was nighttime and the streetlights were on. This was the moment of soul's first breath. She stood on the north side of the intersection and a woman emerged from down the block, paused on the sidewalk to check her handbag, then stood with one foot in the road, her ankle bisecting the curb like a lady in a Watteau. She was in her late twenties or early thirties, and she was facing away in heels and a tan raincoat, her hair expensively cut and then tied with a ribbon, and when she looked across the street, where another woman was getting into another cab, Stephanie could see her features, which were elegant if not beautiful, clear skin, a simple silk scarf at her neck. She began to shoot in deliberately overexposed bursts, hoping to get the exact moment it all came together, the controlled curve of her form, the lights fracturing behind her. A cab pulled over and she shot a few more as the woman moved into the street, bent down to ask something of the driver, one arm clenched around her waist to keep her coat closed, and then opened the door and slipped into the back seat. The cabbie watched Stephanie, but if he said anything to the woman in back she didn't notice or didn't care. When the cab started forward, Stephanie stepped back into the shadows of a doorway, and, emboldened by her great good fortune, took a few more pictures as it passed. Then she hugged her camera to her chest, happy as a child, started around the corner and hurried uptown, suddenly very tired and ready for sleep.

There came the evening when Stephanie found herself on the block where she'd grown up, scarcely knowing whether she'd deliberately steered that way or not. It came over her slowly: the streets were familiar, but the details had been redone. The trash cans were green instead of grey, there were no phone booths, no cracks in the sidewalk, no supers watching from basement railings. New York, busy being new and being New York: alone among things it got younger instead of older. Walking through the neighborhood was like meeting the son of an old friend and recognizing in him some trace of his parents, an intermittent signal, a gesture, the route his expression took from one emotion to another, the beats and breaths in his voice, the way he squinted when he thought, which together created something more subtle than an imitation: more like a condition, a syndrome. She looked up at the buildings overhead; they, at least, were still the same, they'd been there for as long as she could remember, they were the ancestors upon which this entire plot was played, and they gave the whole scene a strange-familiar feel. Here was the block where she had dawdled on the way home from middle school, stopping in her favorite dress shop to smell the perfumes and collect a piece of licorice candy from the proprietress, an elderly woman with henna-colored hair. Here was the corner where she'd bent to pet an older girl's little poodle, only to have the creature bite her on her index finger. She remembered his sweet and sour breath, and the greasy off-white curls of his coat. There was the street-level apartment where a portly and melancholy man in a wheelchair had spent one afternoon a week for nine months trying to teach her to play the piano; and here was the broken curb where her mother had confessed, one day when Stephanie was fifteen, that she couldn't remember what her father had said about the man now running for Congress, whether he was for him or against him, back when he was still a city councilman.

And here was once home. The building itself was not especially different from the others around it: twelve brick stories furnished with concrete cornices and sills, with a single decorative badge toward the top, and an arched door over which there stood a canopy, which had once been maroon and now was forest green. Many years previously—in another century, she realized with a shock—it had been a respectable address, if not quite a distinguished one. Some of the residents had taken generations to land there, moving from tenements on the Lower East Side or cramped apartments in Queens to Morningside Heights or Kips Bay, then at last to a prewar classic six in Carnegie Hill or Yorkville, where they dreamed of townhouses that they would never be able to afford. Even as a child, she'd known that there was nothing particularly glamorous about the place, though it must have been expensive. The residents dressed well and spoke well, they wore sleek wool coats in the wintertime; the men wore understated watches, the women elegant brooches. They had maids, china in the sideboard that never got used, theater tickets, unhappy marriages. The building had no name, or if it did no one ever used it. Names were another thing We Didn't Do, that was a custom for the West Side; they called it by its street address.

After her father died, she and her mother had moved into a smaller apartment in the same building. She never did remember which of the larger apartments—the end doors on each floor—had once been theirs, nor had her mother ever mentioned who had moved into it, although they knew almost everyone who lived in the building, by sight if not by name. Either the sorrow of her collapsed adulthood was a rebuke too painful to contemplate, or she was trying to spare her daughter any sense of resentment or inferiority. It didn't matter: by the time she was sixteen, Stephanie had hated the building, hated everything about it, and everything about the neighborhood, her private school with its inane rituals and ugly uniforms, where she'd felt invisibly marked, a shadow on her surname and she never talked about boys—though when her mother had offered to send her to Ramaz instead, she'd declined immediately, since the only thing worse than being different was being the same as everyone else. She hated the boutiques, the delivery vans, the little wrought iron fencing around the trees, the old ladies perched on too-high heels; the quiet at night and the emptiness on weekends, above all the fact that her father wasn't there to leaven it with his good humor, and her mother was helpless and confused, with pill bottles accumulating on her nightstand, more of them each year, mumbling on the telephone and stumbling to the door, wearing a hopeless, squinting stare. Stephanie had just started her sophomore year at Barnard when the police called. It was a night not unlike this one, brisk and scuttering:

that afternoon, her mother had walked into Central Park, taken her favorite seat on a bench by the Boathouse, and swallowed two months' worth of tranquilizers: no one knew how many, exactly, nor what she'd meant. As the sun grew low and golden, casting long, seductive shadows across the greenery, she'd fallen into a sleep that dropped deeper and deeper, and then deeper still, stopping at last when it hit the bottom. She was only fifty years old, but she seemed to belong to another age, one full of worries and things unspoken, black-and-white film clips of troops marching down the boulevard, boiled cabbages, of unbearable losses and intolerable isolation, coupled with a will to survive that turned indolent and rank when survival was no longer threatened.

That fall Stephanie discovered that she could cry in the darkened auditorium of an art history lecture without anyone knowing. The pictures would bypass her perception and pierce straight through to her grief. Almost anything might do it: a boy by Caravaggio, a Rembrandt self-portrait, a Malevich black monochrome, the spectral smudges of Rauschenberg's erased de Kooning, one of Eva Hesse's skeins of dangling rope and latex. The professor would murmur, one slide would vanish and another appear in its place, and at once she would feel hot tears on her cheeks. She wondered afterwards if that was how she'd come to associate grief with beauty and beauty with grief: not every beauty, but the ones that people made, pictures, songs, poems, dances. And not every grief, but the ones she couldn't bear, that left her astonished and skeletal, like a body from which the flesh has suddenly dropped. The work needn't be mournful or even serious, it could be playful, even joyful, antic, knotted up, sly. But if it was well-made, it made her sad, and she was always at least a little bit sad when she was making her own. She never talked about this, not with anyone: for one thing, it was buried too deep to exhume, and for another, she considered it a failing on her part, mere useless biography, an ingredient added to a recipe which left no taste, and yet there it was.

And there she was herself, back home, as if the intervening years had been blown away on a single puff of breath. The doorman, a tall, thin man in a blue uniform, stood inside the door, watching her for a few moments, and then came out to greet her. He looked like a cartoon mortician, and spoke in a low and doleful voice. Can I help you, miss?

My mother was Mrs. Teller, in 7D.

7D is Jenkins, he said.

No, this was a while ago.

Ah, said the doorman. The brass pin on his lapel said that his name was Gerald.

She peered over his shoulder into the dark lobby, the red legatee, the last in her line, trying not to show her hand. A long time ago, she said. She thought if she could see how it smelled—that mixture of perfume and medicine—she would swoon upon time's slope, and she felt simultaneously tempted and frightened. She couldn't imagine her mother being anywhere but here, and if she came upon her, a shadow on the stair, what would she ask? What would she say? Are you happy with what I've done?

Of course I am. How could I not be?

Are you disappointed to find that you'll have no grandchildren, even ones you'll never meet?

A little. But just a little.

Does it frighten you to find that I love other women?

And her mother would say, Oh, honey: but I always knew that.

The doorman had darted to the curb to help a carefully groomed woman with two small children and several brightly colored shopping bags exit a black car. That would have been the time to slip past him, but she couldn't. It was a trap, the whole thing: the draw, the difference, the obscurity inside, and by the time the doorman had reassumed his post Stephanie was gone.

BENNY RUSSELL, STANDING ON THE EDGE OF THE BROOKLYN BRIDGE, CONTEMPLATES SELF-MURDER AND REFLECTS ON THE EVENTS THAT BROUGHT HIM THERE

Jillian was not like anybody else. Not like anything or anybody. Benny's shop had only been open for a month or so, and it was empty when she came in. It was a day in late November, and she was bundled up; she undid her scarf and unbuttoned her coat and shivered. She had platinum hair, cardinal-colored lipstick, and plucked eyebrows, and she smiled at him and said, Isn't it just too cold out? She wasn't wealthy, he could tell by her accent and by her carriage; and there was something childlike about her, though she was just a few years younger than he was. She had plump white hands and pink nail polish. She glanced around and almost immediately started picking things up, so haphazardly and carelessly that it was all he could do to keep from taking them away from her; but he could tell at once that she didn't mean any harm. She was guileless in the way she moved, wanting only to be entertained and amused. From time to time, she would ask him what something was and listen carefully as he told her, and then put it back on the nearest shelf, while he trailed her, reordering things and answering her next question. Oooh, she said as she turned over a coal-colored figurine and inspected the underside. Where does this come from?

Togo, he'd replied.

Is that a real place? she said.

It's in Africa, he said. The western part. Near . . . — But she'd already picked up something else, a piece of ivory carved in the shape of a crocodile, and she wanted to know the price. Her fingers paler than the bone, her ruby tongue sliding against her upper lip. My brother Mickey would love this, she said. But crocodiles aren't white, are they?

No, he said. It's bone, you see.

I was kidding, she said. She made a mock-offended face. You must really think I'm a dummy.

Not at all, he said, but now he was flustered. She was asking something else: she wanted to know who bought such things and who had made them, and how he had gotten them, and they were all so beautiful, she wished she could afford them but she just couldn't. She'd sounded so forlorn at this admission that he'd wanted to give the crocodile to her just to change the expression on her face; and it was an expensive piece, too, and acquiring it had taken him a month of nights. — It was funny how much the neighborhood had changed, she said. There were no shops like this when she was a girl. In those days you knew everyone on the block, not that that was better, necessarily. It was nice to have some change, but she missed the way things used to be, too. She had come from regular people, she said. Her father had been a bus driver, and she and Mickey had been raised just around the corner. There was a slender silver chain around her neck, and dangling from it there was a cross, though just the very top was visible. She was bare where it hung. He started to think of her lace and elastic, but he stopped himself, wondering how he had come to be so coarse—that wasn't like him at all—and wondering, too, if she could tell, if she could see it in his eyes, as she must have seen it in men's eyes all her life. He should be better than that: he wanted to listen to her, but the mind of a man in the first stages of love's grief can hear little more than *want want want*, like the pulling sound of oars in the water.

She went on, she liked talking to him, she said, even though they had just met. She lived nearby, with Mickey, who was studying to be an accountant. My baby brother, she called him. Her father had worked until it was time to collect his pension, then he spent a few years as a security guard, and then he'd passed away. She spoke quickly when she was talking about her family, the way some people hasten through their prayers, because however important they may be, they've long since been memorized and repeated. She had lived with her father until the end, she said, and then Mickey had moved in to save money for tuition. When he gets his diploma, when he gets a good job, then at last she'd be able to stop worrying. She frowned, and he imagined she was thinking about what would happen to her, then, with no one for her to take care of; but then she smiled at him, so broadly that it was hard to imagine she'd ever been unhappy in her life. All this as the winter night came halfway down into the afternoon, and out the window tourists strolled by in their overcoats, some stopping to peer inside, framing themselves like the swells in a black-and-white movie.

But I don't know, Jillian said. I'm not a young thing anymore.

Neither am I, he replied. She faltered, and right away he knew that was the wrong thing to say, though not how he'd come to be so clumsy, and still less how to repair it. Soon afterwards she said goodbye a little wistfully and left, leaving him alone in his silent shop, the front room humid and rich with her scent. Later that night as he was preparing for bed, he looked at his face in the mirror—his own old face. Putty nose, and the same wire-rim glasses he'd been wearing for years. Grey hair, he'd had that since his early thirties; it didn't make him look aged so much as the opposite: it gave him a kind of timeless, dull quality, like pewter. He could have used a little more wear, some wrinkles, some scars and rough patches, but instead his features were smooth, unused: faded a little bit, but not from adventure. And he was too stupid to know how to compliment a woman. Fool! he said to himself, and then he butted the reflection of his forehead with his forehead so forcefully that the mirror cracked, and a small blue-and-cardinal lump appeared just above his right eye. The bruise disappeared within a week, but he never did get around to replacing the glass.

He wasn't sure if he would ever see her again: he thought he must have offended her, he was afraid he might have hurt her. But a few days later she came by again, and it was as if they'd never mentioned time and age at all; and then she began stopping in regularly. She never wore the same outfit twice, he noticed that, and there was always something extra about her, a bit of ribbon around her neck, a pair of heart-shaped silver earrings, a new shade of nail polish, a brooch above her heart. He found himself half crazy, half smashed, like the young man in a poem. Her visits became the point of his days, the hours leading up to them preparation and prologue, the time afterwards spent on reflection, analysis, correction. A day when she didn't show was almost unbearable, but she had no schedule that he could see. His own days were fixed—the store was open full time from Tuesday through Saturday, half a day on Sunday, and closed on Monday, and he felt trapped, pinned, put on display like one of his own artifacts, boxed behind glass and begging for a tender look. It doesn't seem quite fair, he said to her late one afternoon. She was sitting on a stool on the other side of his desk, watching him as he wrapped a bronze bracelet in tissue paper, boxed it and addressed it to a client in St. Louis, then put it in the pile of packages to be mailed the following day. Five o'clock, in a week or two Rivington Street would be windy and cold.

What's not fair? She looked distressed.

You can always find me right here, but I never know where you are or when you're coming in.

She didn't hesitate. Then you should take me on a date, she said, so directly and easily that at first he wasn't sure what she meant. He hadn't been on a date in more than a decade—more than two, if he was going to be honest. His last paramour had been an Argentinian woman he'd met in a hotel bar in Lima, back when he was considering expanding his stock to include pre-Columbian. It was so long ago that he couldn't even remember how it had ended, except that there had been a series of very expensive phone calls, six or seven in one day. Madness: not like this, which was true and serene. There Jillian waited, and before he knew what he was doing he cleared his throat and said, Would you like to go out to dinner one evening? He felt as if he was pronouncing the sentence phonetically, like an unhinged man eating dust balls in the belief that they were food. She touched his arm. I'd love to, she said brightly, and she looked at his expression and laughed. How about Friday? she said. I'll meet you here at the end of the day?

He recovered and said, Yes. Perfect. Then it was time for her to leave, and he went to the window, hiding a bit behind a pillar, and watched her walk down the street; and then he closed for the day, a little bit early, and strolled up the avenues of his city.

On Friday, she came over for a cocktail, eagerly exploring his apartment though there wasn't much to it. A living room with a view of a loading dock across the way, where every morning at four a.m. trucks came and picked up bales of newspapers; and a kitchenette, which he seldom used (she said, I'm a very good cook, you know); and his bedroom, the door of which he had deliberately left open, if only to show that he had no secrets. That was when she saw the mirror, and she frowned and faltered, but she didn't say anything about it.

The date had been chaste enough: dinner in a small French place in SoHo, she had ordered very little and eaten almost nothing, though he couldn't tell whether it was because she was worried about the expense or because she didn't want to show the true outlines of her appetite. She drank two glasses of red wine: he had three. At the end, he ordered an almond and chocolate tart because he knew she would have ordered it herself if she'd dared. She took a bite, with an almost concupiscent expression on her mouth. She had no coffee: it kept her from sleeping all night.

Then they walked. It was one of those nights when the city felt like a giant sports stadium, brighter than any day, with every motion, every stride, every smile six or seven times as large as life. They crossed Lafayette at Spring Street; down the block there was a burst of golden yellow, where a score of taxicabs sat waiting in the night outside a garage. A willow tree, an open firehouse, a small, dark church, a Korean grocery: he stopped in and bought a handful of ginger candy, which she chewed with an expression of perfect candor and mild disgust, then swallowed hastily. My God, she said. Who could invent such a thing?

I always found them delicious, he said, peeling the waxy paper from the powdered confection and popping it into his mouth.

That's because you're a sick, sick man, she said.

He laughed. À chacun son goût, he said.

What? What was that?

It's French for Each to his own taste. Her own taste.

Oh. Across the street, a man had laid a coconut on the curb and was striking at the shell with a hammer. Bang! And he swore: Goddamn it. Bang!

Do you speak French? Jillian said.

No, not really, he admitted. Just a few phrases.

He was afraid she'd be disappointed, but she appeared to be impressed. Will you teach me another? she said.

Another saying?

Another phrase, another saying, yes, she said.

In French?

In anything.

He thought for a bit, and then they started coming out of him. Plus ça change, plus c'est la même chose. Sans souci. Entre nous. By the time he got to La vie en rose, they were in Chinatown, the two phenomena combining to make Vietnam in 1954. And there was the Brooklyn Bridge, rising above it all.

There was an evening, not long afterwards, when she'd come by the store as he was closing up, and they'd somehow found themselves walking downtown, all the way to Wall Street, the bent, honey-colored streets already quiet, the stone buildings hanging sternly overhead. They had been talking about her grandfather's apartment in Flushing, and her grandmother's ash-grey cat. She stopped on the corner of Exchange Place and looked up. This is Wall Street? she asked.

More or less, he replied. The actual street is just back there.

Oh. There was something settled in her voice, a bump that had found its notch, and he realized that she'd never seen the financial district before, though it was no more than a few miles from where she lived. You know the city so well, she said, though the striking thing, he thought, was that she knew it so little. Or perhaps it was something more common than that; New York bred its own species of provincials, men and women who never left their borough, or their neighborhood, or their block, unless it was to take the subway to another neighborhood they knew almost as well, or to one of the airports, to fly off to some distant world and place. So he was thinking, as he studied her face, and she looked back at him with something like fear. What? she said, touching her hair with the tips of her fingers; and he said, Nothing. Just looking.

She said, I bet you hear that a lot. He didn't understand. — In your

96

store, she said. People come in, you ask if you can help them and they say, Just looking. Right?

Yes, of course. Just looking, they say that all the time.

She gave him the smile a woman gives a man the moment before he kisses her for the first time, but instead of offering her lips she put her arm through his, leaning against him slightly and shivering a bit to justify getting closer. She knew then. She must have always known, just as he'd always been too late to see.

His bed, now with double the weight on it, had ridden low on the night, like a boat in shallow water. The smell of her skin was perfumed and powdery, with just the faintest edge of agreeable rankness; the smell of her breath was like a wet animal. The night before, she'd been shy at first, saying, Don't look at me! when she emerged from the bathroom in a slip of some sort, bare-legged and plump. He'd stared at her for a second longer, and then, with considerable effort, turned away to unbutton his shirt, sat down to remove his shoes, and stood back up again to undo his pants. By then she was already in his bed and under the covers, leaving him the one who was naked and exposed, while she giggled, almost cruelly, though not at the sight of him, but just because. Her laughter was damp, as if she had already begun without him, and he was relieved because he had been wondering, more than anything, how to start. He crossed the room in his boxer shorts.

—The light? she said.

Oh, yes, sorry. He made a detour to switch off the floor lamp by the window, which immediately turned the room inside out, with the lights of the city now looking in on them. So that was what the mercury felt like in a thermometer, rising feverishly in its column of glass.

She had drawn the bedsheets over herself and he carefully eased in beside her. He was shocked when he first touched her: she was so profoundly soft. How could someone go about the world and be so pliable, as yielding as the flesh beneath a shell? Even in the darkness of the room she shined like some sea creature, pearly in the deep. So soft and so pale: he felt as if he might sink so far into her that he'd become lost in all that whiteness, his bearings gone, that he'd disappear. Her skin was hot, much hotter than his own, and she was damp but he felt dry, his skin desiccated, his eyes abrading their sockets. She reached up to him with her hand, a gesture at once tender and curious, the two entwined into a single fond motion, he expected her to touch his face, but she put her hand on the back of his neck and slowly started to draw him downward, and he felt his heart quicken and thought: it's beginning.

It was exhausting, that first night, there was so much to go through. Afterwards, he had trouble falling asleep, but she'd drifted off at once, her face against his arm, her mouth open just a touch, her leg bent and her ankle tucked between his calves. He hadn't wanted to move for fear of waking her, so he'd ended up taking a series of naps, interspersed with dreamshots in the darkness. Toward dawn he fell into a profound and seamless slumber, as restful as it was absolutely empty. The morning began with the sound of birds. When he woke again he was alone, and he wondered if he'd done something wrong, if he'd performed badly or perhaps been difficult to sleep with, if he sprawled or snored. He felt every minute keenly, the sun, the sound of the city already furiously busy, trucks on the street, a man somewhere down below singing a bit of *Turandot* in an unexpectedly good baritone. As he made the bed he noticed a lingering odor in the sheets: not his and not hers either, but some rough mix of the two of them. He drifted around the apartment for a while, head leaking out onto the floor, and he got to the store an hour late and without the bottle of mineral water that he'd put on the kitchen counter, precisely so that he wouldn't forget it.

She appeared that afternoon, just past lunch, and at first she seemed unchanged, as if she'd simply forgotten about the night before, an attitude that so threw him that he wondered if he hadn't imagined the whole thing himself, and for a moment he pretended that he had. Then she came near to him with her eyes downcast, her fingers trailing on the edge of a table, wearing a tentative smile. — When I got up this morning you were gone, he said.

I know, she said. I woke up at six, and I couldn't get back to sleep, so I just went home. I should have left you a note—I'm sorry. He apologized himself, and they had that, at least. Then there was some more fluttering, he offered her a cup of coffee, she said, No, but thank you. A pair of customers came in, both men, apparently a couple, who asked to see an Ethiopian vessel that he had in the window, and were so absorbed in considering it that they hardly noticed Jillian standing toward the back of the store, wearing an expression of mischievous impatience. By the time they bought the thing she was beaming, and when they left, with the piece carefully wrapped in white and blue tissue paper and deposited in a glossy white, flat-bottomed bag, he turned from watching them go and found her standing next to him, facing the door; and she said, Well, aren't you going to kiss me?

GHOSTS OF NEW YORK: A PARTIAL ACCOUNT

Marie Lloyd, she lived in a tenement on Grand Street and died there of tuberculosis in the spring of 1871. Emily von Hoffman, hit by a stray bullet on Astoria Boulevard, she was fourteen and will always be fourteen, and Ruth Rosen, wasted away by cancer at an advanced age, on the fifth floor of Mount Sinai, she weighed sixty-three pounds when she took her last breath, and no one was quite sure how old she really was. Charlie Willis, also cancer, aged fifty-four but his spirit is that of a much younger man. Julio Garza, nineteen, fell down an elevator shaft in the King Towers on 115th Street. Daniel Eismann, who was thirty-one in 1991 when he died at home of AIDS, and Michael Brown, his true love, who hanged himself from a pipe in the bathroom of the apartment they shared on 12th Street and University; they are together still. Chester Perkins, who wants everyone to know that it was that dirty dog, Al Jefferson, who beat him to death with a brick in the courtyard of a building on Jerome Avenue, four days after the end of the Korean War. Andrea Robinson, who leaped to her death from her Juliette balcony on West End Avenue after learning that her husband had confessed to raping an eleven-year-old girl in Riverside Park. Mitchell Rockman, who fell to the sidewalk on the corner of 47th Street and Broadway one winter's day, dead of a stroke at the age of sixty-two, who was buried beside his mother and father under the name he was born with, Morris Roth, and whose son Brian said Kaddish for him every day for the following year. Indra Vajpajan, of complications from lupus; Katherine Biggs, of complications from diabetes; and Smitty Dufresne, of complications from alcoholism. Juan Javier, one of eighty-seven people killed on March 25, 1990, in a fire at the Happy Land Social Club on Southern Boulevard in the Bronx. Amy Castro, who was diagnosed with breast cancer at the age of twenty-nine but died when she was struck on the head by a bottle that a college boy named Dave Perkins threw from the roof of a dormitory on LaGuardia Place. Joseph Levy, who ran six times for the Queens city council and never won, dead, everyone said, of sheer disappointment. Rosemarie Winter, known to the residents of East Tremont as Miss Rose, dead at the age of ninety-six in her bed, with her nurse holding her hand; and Susan Araki, who passed away from leukemia in a rented room on 35th Avenue, with her husband sitting quietly in a chair against the wall, and she still wishes someone had told her that she was dying. Anna De Lancey, the wife of financier Paul T. De Lancey: she was photographed in a Dior dress outside the first Metropolitan Opera House on the opening night of the 1955–56 season, and for more than ten years thereafter was known as one of the most fashionable women in Manhattan, until she passed away of acute nephritis on the very same day the old Met was torn down. Simon Simmons, overdosed on heroin and vodka in a penthouse apartment overlooking Madison Square, who would like to come back and try and get clean again; and Valerie Perricone, who died that same night, also of an overdose, though in her case of heroin alone, who would like to come back and have another taste. John Berman, struck by a horse-drawn wagon on Maiden Lane; Giovanni Garaglia, knifed by a man with a large port-wine birthmark on his face, who mistakenly thought Giovanni was laughing at him; Tilly Carter, eight years old, who woke one night suffering from an acute attack of asthma and never made it as far as her mother's bedroom door. William Cisco, who was on the 94th floor of the South Tower on the morning of September 11, 2001. Trey Halloway, drowned attempting to swim across Spuyten Duyvil in 1907, in order to win a bet with his brother; he has been cold ever since, and wonders why no one builds fires anymore; and Hillary Woods, who was the only colored person in the Rainbow Room on New Year's Eve, 1935, when she sang Auld Lang Syne with Skip Patterson's Band, and everyone applauded and called out for more. Gary Sykes, who died of injuries he sustained when he drove his semi into a bus on the Brooklyn-Queens Expressway, and he would like to apologize to the nine people on that bus who also died. Louise Hantagan, who insists that it was not syphilis that killed her but a broken heart. Sam Chan, of emphysema on a beautiful spring day in 1922, who wonders why his old neighborhood has changed so much. Matthew Holder, who was stabbed to death with a pencil by a prisoner at Rikers Island one week into his job as a corrections officer, and who has spent the years since trying to find out if his wife and children are safe. The O'Malley family, all of whom—fourteen in number—died during the influenza epidemic of 1918 and who, having no descendants, ask to be remembered by anyone who has a memory to spare.

JOHNNY AND BRIDGET

I am sitting in a comfortable chair in a comfortable room, with a glass of water on the table beside my laptop, a warm light on a pleasant evening, and no one who cares very much what I have to say about anything. Thousands of miles from here, Johnny is keeping up a constant stream of messages to the outside world, by way of letters written on sheets of paper that sympathetic guards smuggle in, which he then passes to Red Cross inspectors and the occasional priest or nun. He's trying very hard to explain himself, though the Johnny I knew would have considered such an effort beneath his dignity. Other forces, infinitely more powerful than myself, have surrounded him and control what he does from moment to moment: nations, security forces, diplomats from many countries, peace groups and activists, news organizations, heads of state. I watch helplessly, I might as well be on another planet. I did try to call his mother, using a number I found in an old address book. The phone rang on the other end in a pattern I'd never heard before, so I had no idea what country she was in. It went straight to her voicemail—at least I think it was hers, the outgoing message was a stock recording—and I left a message, though it was no doubt inadequate. I would have been surprised if she called me back, and she didn't.

I've read some of the excerpts from Johnny's letters, which have been posted on the internet by a British newspaper: long, rambling disquisitions on the progress of Western history, the push of money, the etiology of disease, the fathomless turns of love and time, and how they all interacted to create a universe that's both unbearably cruel and irresistibly beautiful. It was his obligation to try to untangle such a world from itself, he says. Not his calling, but his duty: he was not a messianic man, not when I knew him, not at all, and neither was he vain. We are all incomplete, he once told me, though he may have been teasing me. He often liked to cross back and forth between sincerity and sport, and challenge me to tell the difference. In these statements he's produced from his confinement he is not, of course, so blithe, but his respect for fragility and defeat is apparent there, too. His own attempt to sort things out, he admits, had been unlikely to succeed, but he'd found one loose thread and decided to start there.

I know Johnny well enough to be sure that his communiqués haven't been undertaken for publicity, at least not for its own sake: he may believe publicity will save his life, but I would be surprised if he really cared, and besides, he must know it's unlikely. He was very much a realist, even a pessimist, by temperament, experience, and philosophy. That is part of what I want to explain to you. Still, publicity has come for him, and rather than flaring and then fading, it has grown and grown. Already there are books being planned—at least two that I know about, one written by a British man, who, with the cooperation of Johnny's family, apparently has access to his papers. This is in accordance with his wishes.

But you see, Johnny and I met where the sea of history, looming and dark, meets the shore of days. We were young and we didn't know much, but we knew not to mistake the tide for the total. Still, we were students, and both of us had relied, again and again, on people who had written down everything; so I'm going to write down everything and leave it somewhere where no one can be hurt by it—for that someday littoral where I'm buried beneath the waves, along with everyone I know.

Johnny and I met at Columbia, where I'd gone to pursue a graduate degree in Classics, in part because I loved it, and in part because it was the most useless kind of accreditation I could imagine. Johnny, too, was a graduate student, but in Political Science, where he was preparing himself for a career in international relations. He and I had met early in the first semester of my second year, in a seminar on Milton, a subject well outside of either of our fields; I think the gratuitousness of the study was part of what drew us to each other—that and our shared contempt for the class itself, which was taught by a middle-aged woman on loan from Berkeley, who would place her index finger on a passage from *Paradise Lost* and drone on absently and endlessly, in a voice so soft that I could hear the air passing through the registers overhead. To be fair, my own department wasn't known for its thrills—most of my professors were odd, aged, and unkempt—but the comic futility of it was much of the point, at least to me; and besides, the faculty was known for hosting eccentrics of all kinds, so there was always the chance of some interesting scandal, usually one involving freshman boys. The Milton class was ridiculous the way television in a foreign language is ridiculous: its flaws were all I could see.

I stopped going within a few weeks, so Johnny and I must have met early in the semester, falling into conversation in the hallway outside the classroom, a wide corridor with the pleasant, nodding smell of wood polish and unfiltered cigarettes. Oh, God, I said to him. Are all graduate English classes that bad?

I honestly don't know, he said. It's not my department. He paused and pushed his glasses back up onto the bridge of his nose. — I thought it was quite interesting, actually.

For a moment, I thought I'd misjudged him, and I was just about to mutter some pleasantry and slip away, when he suddenly threw his head back a bit and burst out with a clap of laughter, so loud that the sound echoed down the hallway and students coming out of another class turned to look at us. — No, he said, turning away from the doorway to hide his mirth. You're right, it was dreadful. Of course it was. Poor Milton. Just then the professor herself shuffled out of the classroom, and we both went silent; she raised her hand in an absent sort of half-wave as she passed. Do you think she knows what a disservice she's doing? Johnny said when she was gone. To a poet she must have once admired.

To Milton? I said. I don't know if she owes anything to Milton, but her students deserve either some real teaching or some uninterrupted nap time. At this, too, Johnny laughed, albeit more softly; and so we became friends, though that was the last time I read Milton. Johnny saw the course all the way through, though according to him it never got better. In any case, we had met.

Looking back, it's hard to imagine or explain what drew us to each other. We had almost nothing in common. I was a New Yorker, born and bred, one of those small, scrappy middle children that large Irish families breed; my parents were liberal about everything, in a laissez-faire sort of way, except for education, which they took seriously enough to send me to Regis to study with the Jesuits. As for Johnny, his story was almost absurdly complicated, and it was never quite clear where he called home. He went by an English first name, but his last name was a conjunction of abutting syllables in one of the scores of Volta-Congo languages. He once challenged me to pronounce it properly and laughed as I struggled. — No, no, Yankee man, he said. You're aspirating the *n*. And the *l* is rounder than that.

He was taller than me by a good four inches, his skin was very dark, he kept his hair cropped close and his eyes were deep brown.

Sooner or later everyone asked him where he was from, I must have seen him answer twenty or thirty times, always patiently, often with amusement, and almost never with the truth. Once I watched him try to convince an undergraduate girl that he was from Queens, a ruse he might have been able to pull off if he hadn't tried to fake the accent, producing, instead, a bizarre mishmash of syllables that even the girl, who was from Oklahoma, recognized immediately as an imposture.

In time I learned that his mother's family was from West Africa, though they had detoured, for two or three generations, through the Caribbean, so he had some distant Spanish cousins whom he'd never met, and a rumored great uncle who had been an Amerindian tribal chief. His paternal grandfather had been too poor to measure and lived in some now-forgotten village on the British-controlled edge of the Gulf of Guinea, but his father had done very well in school, qualified for a scholarship at Oxford, became a geological engineer, and returned home to start a company that made storage containers for natural gas. It had made him rich, tremendously so by local standards, and he had sold the business when Johnny was a toddler, then served for some short period as the Minister of Energy under one of the country's less vile presidents—who had promptly been overthrown in a coup, sending Johnny's family into exile, first in Caracas, then in Frankfurt, and finally in London, where his father had taken a job consulting with an oil firm—which in turn assigned him to various stations around the world, usually for a year or so. He died when Johnny was twelve in somewhat mysterious circumstances: killed in a single-vehicle car crash, in broad daylight on a well-paved road outside of Kampala. There was reason to believe it was an assassination: My father made some political mistakes, Johnny once told me, though he never explained to me what they were. Afterwards, his mother, who had been quite a bit younger than her husband, surprised everyone, including herself, by moving back home and becoming a spokeswoman and an activist.

For what? I asked him, and he said, Oh, you know: justice, reform, healing, he replied.

All of this history emerged slowly and in a sidelong fashion, so while there were many things I knew about him, many basic facts remained mysterious to me. It was unclear, for example, what passport he traveled under. Though we ate together often enough, he never favored one kind of food over another, or mentioned any childhood dishes; he measured distance in kilometers, temperature in centigrade. He had grown up with a governess, who had moved with them from city to city. His father listened to BBC news on the shortwave, and it wasn't until they arrived in London that they acquired a television at all, and then just to watch BBC news on TV. His mother read to him when he was a child, and then he read to himself: Dickens and the like. His English, then, could be formal to the point of eccentricity—he was the only person I'd ever heard use the word *bosom* in conversation—his diction was immaculate, and his habits were old-school to the point of mannerism. He played cricket with his friends. — Cricket? I asked. One of the unimpeachably pleasurable byproducts of colonialism, he said. One of the very few. I think most people thought of him as British, if only for lack of an alternative. I thought of him as Johnny.

I was a heedless young man, and what I knew of the world I knew through curiosity, not experience. If you had asked me whether I really intended to spend my life teaching Latin grammar to recalcitrant freshmen, I would have said, Of course, and I may even have believed it, but the truth was that I was hiding out in academia, waiting for the sullen years of my early twenties and all their attendant police to pass me by, before I emerged again, free and still free. Johnny had much more to gain or lose. He was the only one of his mother's children to be in a position to honor the family's name, both forward to his descendants and retroactively to the reputation and renown of his ancestors. In fact his family, by his own account, scarcely distinguished between past, present, and future: it was all blended and alive, a spirit always beside him, which he treated with layer upon layer of sarcasm, amusement, affection, and gentle anger. My brother is a ne'er-do-well, he once told me—the only time he mentioned that he had a brother at all—and you know how it is with people like mine. There was a quarter-tone of self-mockery in his voice and a quarter-tone of weariness; the rest was simply factual. The family's name, the family's honor, these are all that matter, he continued. Well, that and the family's money.

But we had more in common than our differences might have suggested, and for two or three years I saw him more often, and talked to him more openly, than I did anyone else. Together, we formed a little rampart in defense against the university itself, which we regarded with a combination of skepticism and gratitude, frustration and affection. It was an impressive place, in its way, sober and scholarly, and with a history that had been polished, over the centuries, to a deep chestnut color; but it was monkish in its isolation and dedication, and like a monastery, almost proud of its irrelevance. Many of our professors had been there for decades, some had done their own graduate work in the very same rooms in which they now taught, and while they earned a modicum of respect for having the good sense to find their place and stay there, deep in their devotion to whatever chalk god they prayed to, the other students, both graduate and undergraduate, were harder to take seriously. They were almost universally callow, unworldly at best and ignorant at worst, and occupied with things that neither Johnny nor I cared about at all: good grades, career advancement, and the pressure to be loyal to the school itself, for no other reason than the fact that we were all there. — Patriotism in miniature, Johnny once called it, with his usual accuracy and vividness: all those men and women, most of them a few years younger, wearing sweatshirts branded with the school's name rendered in its distinctive stale blue; the row of fraternities on 114th Street, where every Sunday morning one would find filthy mattresses stacked up on the curbside; the young man in the apartment next to mine, whom I knew only through legend, because he spent all his time in the library, living on a diet of vending-machine pretzels that proved to be so lacking that he actually contracted scurvy, collapsed in a chemistry class, and had to be sent home; the circles of friends that formed as much out of mutual competition as genuine affection; and their helpless prostration before professors who, in another context, would have been ignored, and from whom they sought, not even the cynical dispensations of a job, but simply the assurance that they were bright and belonged. All this I found more dull than disturbing, and what was worse, inescapable; for while I had friends from high school still living in town, they had jobs, they had weekends, whereas I had a tiny stipend and an ever-replenishing stack of books that needed to be read.

Johnny had a princely air about him, a slight hauteur coupled with the tentativeness of a regent, for whom more things can go wrong than right, and who must therefore suspend his instincts indefinitely. He was worldlier than the rest of my friends: he was, for example, the only person I knew who'd done military service, an experience that told in his posture and a bit of fussiness in his dress. But he was naive in ways that were hard to predict. Manhattan was both rule-bound and enigmatic, and he couldn't quite resolve it. He often relied on me to explain things to him, and it was endlessly entertaining to do so, and touching to be asked. He didn't understand, for example, how the neighborhoods could change so quickly from block to block, nor how to find the borders—where Morningside Heights became Harlem, or Little Italy turned into the Lower East Side. Nor was he ever quite sure which was a bad block and which a better one; they all felt very much alike. He was appalled and disgusted by the presence of cockroaches in his kitchen, and shocked to discover that even rich people had them. I taught him the phrase *Las cucarachas entran, pero no pueden salir,* which amused him to no end, but when I told him that it was from a subway ad, he shuddered: he'd been told that the subway was as unsafe as a favela, and was surprised to find that I took it all the time. I never could convince him that the chances of anything happening to him were small; instead, he took cabs, which meant he was always broke, or buses, which meant he was always late. Whenever he saw a policeman, he would immediately stop whatever he was doing, no matter how innocent, a habit that led to him being questioned twice and searched once, which in turn made him more uneasy when he saw the next.

He had never seen a snowstorm before, and when the first one struck, surprising everyone midway through November, he didn't know how to react. For one thing, he had a winter coat that was warm but not weatherproof, and he had no wool socks or boots: it hadn't occurred to him that his dress shoes wouldn't be sufficient for every occasion. He tried to call me that night, but I had gone for a walk down Broadway, enjoying the sight of the buildings hung from the sky, the soft scrim of snowflakes, the antique silence interrupted only by the occasional sound of a car creeping by. — You went out? he asked me the next time I talked to him. It turned out he hadn't left his apartment in two days, and toward the end had almost fainted from hunger, because it hadn't occurred to him that restaurants would deliver in such weather.

Above all, he was bewildered by New York's women, whom he found both entrancing and impossible; though his taste, I found, could be unexpectedly common. I remember him going on about a beautiful creature he had seen the night before. She was, he insisted, extraordinarily attractive, intelligent, a true and worthy wonder. He was perfectly serious about this, and it took me a while to realize that he was talking about a lifestyles reporter on a local morning show. When I tried to explain to him that she was mostly an illusion, a bleachy sprite whose primary skills were reading from a prompter without moving her eyes and making three or four seconds of small talk in between segments, he said, That's the trouble with you, Mike. That is exactly your trouble. You have no sense of romance. Another time he took me aside to ask me what, exactly, a cheerleader was, whether that was all they did, whether they received scholarships for doing it, and who chose that path rather than, say, gymnastics.

— But I don't mean to portray him as leering and shallow. He was, in virtually every regard, more sophisticated than I was, and in most regards more self-possessed: discreet, courteous, considerate, honorable. He liked and respected women almost universally, whereas I liked some, didn't like others, and respected some portion of both. On the other hand, I enjoyed them, whereas he seemed to consider enjoyment a form of ill-treatment.

He was a brilliant student, and not just because he was intelligent but because he cared deeply about what he was studying. It wasn't merely coursework to him, it was the vantage point from which he gazed upon the world and himself in it, from an altitude so high that the air was thin and the atmosphere was completely transparent. I think even his professors found him a little bit daunting: graduate students are, for the most part, a timid bunch, a quality that usually makes them neurotic, and sometimes makes them aggressive, but rarely makes them formidable. Johnny was simply absorbed, as thoughtful and professional as any diplomat. Moreover, he was the beneficiary, and perhaps also the victim, of a rare mystique. It wasn't just a recognition of the difficulties he must have faced in the past, or those he would face in the future. It was a kind of awe; because he came across as a natural-born aristocrat—a concept he would have been the first to denounce.

By contrast, I was merely smart, a very good student but not destined to be a notable figure in my field. I was undisciplined and easily distracted: it wasn't unusual for me to write papers from beginning to end the night before they were due, or again, to finish them weeks before I was supposed to hand them in, depending on what kind of mood I was in and how interested I was in the topic. And I didn't have Johnny's evenness of manner, his poise. I was raw and blue, and had none of his filigree and finish.

He had a name to protect: I only had a reputation, which I cared little about and couldn't have managed even if I'd wanted to. I was the sort of man about whom people are willing to believe almost anything, and what they believed was equal parts real, reality misconstrued, and sheer conjecture. Perhaps I invited it, though not deliberately. Certainly I was an anomaly in my department. For one thing, I knew the city and knew how to live there cheaply, an incalculable advantage, since it meant I didn't have to rely on the sad formalities the university put in place to provide students on stipends with a social life. And the department in which I studied was an unusually delicate one, a small program, conscious of its own eccentricity and anachronism; and I was indelicate. My professors were thoughtful, deliberate, and peculiar: athlete-worshippers, middle-aged virgins, an alcoholic or two; a few would-be Caesars, stuck in a modern world that they found both vulgar and unappreciative, and within which they cleared a space to exercise palace intrigues and moments of tyranny; dreamers of poems in long-forgotten languages; grammarians for whom the exact meaning of an unusually formed verb was worth an entire volume of essays and debate. They were prone to attacks of overt contempt for anyone who disagreed with them on the slightest matter, but their aggression ended at the door to the department. One had a grand apartment on Riverside Drive that was decorated with nautical memorabilia. Another, Scottish-born and Oxford-educated, wore a bolo tie with a large turquoise stone in the center. They were smart and they could be funny, and as tender over a line of Thucydides as a dowager over her cabbage roses. They were learned, cultured, generous with their time. But, like any small group of people fastidiously and competitively engaged in an arcane task, they had elaborate codes of behavior; and they liked to gossip. They gossiped about everyone; they gossiped about me.

I remember, for example, some months before meeting Bridget, inviting a girl I knew, who was then a freshman at NYU, to a lecture on historiography delivered by a distinguished and elderly professor from Leipzig. I'd mentioned it to her because she was smart and she was curious, and it didn't matter to me that she was nineteen. She was just a friend, someone I'd met in a dilapidated club we both frequented in the East Village: I'm not sure I'd ever seen her in daylight. She came north a hundred blocks and met me in the hallway outside a classroom, dressed very much the same way she dressed at night, braless beneath her ragged black silk shirt, torn stockings, and a startling smear of crimson lipstick. She was a college girl trying to look like a child prostitute; she came off as a child prostitute trying to look like a college girl. Even the lecturer noticed her; I saw him glance her way repeatedly, and at least once he lost his place in his notes. When he was done, she raised her hand matter-of-factly, exposing a very pretty, porcelain-white armpit. The three or four other people with their hands raised immediately lowered them, leaving the distinguished scholar no choice but to call on her. I don't remember what she asked, but it was a perfectly well-formed question, one which he had some difficulty answering.

Thereafter I was fair game for any supposition, mostly unspoken, though no less obvious for that. Of the two women who worked in the department's office, for example, the elder, funnier one became more solicitous, asking me on Monday mornings how my weekend had been, and once telling me an off-color joke; the younger one became more sour, and grumbled when I asked for another copy of a handout I'd lost or permission to use the telephone. Beyond that, there were remarks made now and then, not-quite-sincere compliments on my clothes (which were poor-man's downtown black), and once, in a seminar, when I said that I considered Catullus's *venustas* a version of

Cicero's *virtus*, my professor said, almost under his breath, Well, you would, wouldn't you? Two students behind me laughed.

Yes, I would: Wasn't charm another form of leadership? Think of Alcibiades and the power he acquired, simply by causing others to fall in love with him.

At that very moment a group of undergraduate women walked by outside, and while I looked at them more briefly than my classmates, they all turned to look at me when the girls had passed, and I knew I had lost my argument.

Then I showed up in a morning seminar still reeking-drunk from the night before, a monstrously stupid thing to do; and while I acquitted myself well enough, I knew that I would thereafter be known as dissolute. A few days later, one of the younger professors took me aside in the hallway and asked me in a low voice if I knew where he could get . . . something, I'm not sure what, for he was so afraid to ask that he couldn't bring himself to name it, and assumed that I would know what he meant. I didn't, nor did I want to, and the encounter ended with the two of us, equally embarrassed, nodding and smiling as we backed away from each other, he with his leather satchel somehow undone, so that a half dozen blue exam books slid out onto the floor. He knelt to collect them and I turned away.

Johnny was unaware of all of this, at least so far as I know. Our conversations were almost always about our studies, only occasionally about life beyond them. My politics were more radical than Johnny's and certainly more naive: for while he was neither conservative nor cynical, he was very much the skeptic, and grew more so whenever the topic we were discussing—the future of the Soviet Union, which was just then on the verge of collapse; the miners' strike in Britain; the fate of Cuba—became more polarizing. I was given to enthusiasms and grand pronouncements: I remember an evening that I spent trying to convince him that we were entering an era in which out-and-out warfare would become obsolete, to be supplanted instead by various forms of economic shackling and information aggression, and that oil, which at the time was the Fist in the Pocket, would soon be supplanted by water, which would grow scarcer and scarcer. Johnny was not convinced, but more than that, he found such predictions absurd. You never know, he said, smiling a bit and shaking his head. It's easy enough to look back on history, see it as determined, and assume that one can project into the future, at least in principle. And it is determined, yes it is, but we shall never know enough to know where we are going. And then, as if to signal that the argument was over, he pushed his eyeglasses back up on his nose.

He was right, so I changed the subject. Why don't you get yourself some contact lenses? I said. You spend about half your day adjusting those glasses.

He laughed, took off the glasses altogether, and studied them thoughtfully. Because, he said, I refuse to put my finger in my eye, and more than that, I refuse to have pieces of plastic resting on my corneas. You want a prediction for the future? I'll tell you what: twenty years from now there's going to be an epidemic of blindness, brought on by the too-hasty adoption of what is clearly an unwise practice. Eye cancer—that's what will bring down the West.

There's no such thing as eye cancer, I said, though I didn't know that to be true.

There will be, said Johnny, and then you'll see. What's the saying? In the country of the blind, the one-eyed man is king? He put his glasses on with a flourish. Do you know who coined that expression? No, you don't, because you don't know anything that happened after the sack of Rome.

Erasmus, I said.

Johnny pulled his head back in surprise. Lucky guess.

Jesuit education, I said.

Yes. I always forget that about you. I suppose that's where you learned to bust my balls.

This was an expression that I had taught him, and one that he found so delightful he used it as often as he could, enunciating each syllable impeccably, and swapping *chops* for *balls* if he felt the context or the company demanded it. Brilliant language, American, he used to say. Vivid, flexible, truly democratic. Everything that's best about this country is represented in its language. Do you know what my favorite word is? I waited while he basked in anticipation, a little too long: Johnny always did have a bad sense of timing. — *Sure*, he said at last. I love this word, he said. Sure.

He had a collection of idioms, which he deployed in the midst of his more formal diction. *Kid* was one, a word I doubt he ever spoke before he arrived in New York. *Jerk* was another; and once he told me that he'd been standing in line at a pizza parlor when an undergraduate ahead of him had loudly denounced his roommate, using a word that Johnny couldn't bring himself to repeat. The man behind the counter had said, Hey! You kiss your mother with that mouth? He asked me what the question meant, I explained it to him, and he was awestruck. There isn't a culture in the world that wouldn't appreciate such a remark, he said.

He was contradictory, surprising: he could drink copiously, for example, though I only knew by counting: after five or six glasses his features softened slightly, but I never saw him lose his diction, let alone his judgment—nor, for that matter, did I ever see him with a hangover. He took no drugs at all and found the very idea peculiar. He had moved so often that he was constantly forced to restudy subjects that he'd already mastered, and had no opportunity to learn those he missed. As a result, he was unexpectedly knowledgeable about some things—architecture, for example—and shockingly ignorant of others. He was adept at numbers but hopeless at geometry, and unsure of the difference between an atom and a molecule. He could sing great swaths of opera, his right hand waving in teasing imitation of a conductor, but he couldn't recognize a Rembrandt; he could recite Hölderlin from memory but had scarcely heard of Beckett. Somewhere he had acquired a detailed knowledge of the history of avionics (he could tell me which version of a 707 was flying overhead by the sound of its engine), but couldn't distinguish between an El Dorado and a Volvo. Everything else was hit or miss. His father had worked as an adviser in Egypt under Nasser, but Johnny was unwelcome at the Western schools there and had found himself, instead, in a local private school, where classes were taught in English but students were required to memorize long suras from the Koran. He could still recite many of them, but more or less phonetically—his Arabic was poor—and he'd long since forgotten what they signified. It was an eccentric upbringing, he knew that. He once told me that he had experienced the Enlightenment in real time, as it were, that when he first studied it he reacted in much the same way as Europe had in the eighteenth century—all those hoary old metaphors, he said: a light turned on, a door opened, a road revealed. It was just like that, you see.

He was different from everyone else, black, brown, or white. I suspect anyone would seem different if they came under the kind of scrutiny Johnny is getting these days; and all friends are singular to those who knew and loved them; and time is a diopter, bringing some subjects into pin-sharp focus while leaving others blurred or lost behind a blind spot. But I hope these things I'm setting down will be useful for any future scholars who may find this whole horrific affair worth examining. — Context? Johnny would say, whenever someone accused him of lacking it. Context is overrated. Voltaire didn't emerge from a context, he would continue, using the honed diction he brought out whenever he was being purposefully contrary. He was the context.

I knew that he didn't believe this, quite; no scholar could. He was

118

simply trying to vex people whose reasoning he found sloppy. In any case, here I am, and context is all I really have to offer. I'm trying to be careful, I am trying to be useful, but I can't help but wonder if I'm doing it as well as he deserves.

The night we met Bridget, I was in the midst of ending an affair with another woman—or rather, she was ending it with me. It had been a month of angry tears, desperate coupling, rooms left behind. She was a bartender down on Houston, a small, blond, and somewhat unkempt woman who lived in a sad sterile apartment near Penn Station. From summer to November we'd been profoundly in love, and we expected to have fun forever. I don't remember why she left me, but I remember that it felt deeply unfair at the time.

Winter was coming, the weather was mean, the streets were decked with trash, the sun went down before dinner. Then it was Thanksgiving break: the holiday meant nothing to Johnny, and my parents had gone to Maine to visit their own parents, so he and I spent several days drinking together in a tiny, pitch-dark bar on Broadway and 125th Street, underneath the elevated subway tracks. It's no longer there, and I'm not sure if we knew the name of it even then. We called it Rusty's because that was the owner's name; he was a solid and slow man, Harlem born and bred, who poured shots with the parsimony of an elderly woman fishing in her change purse. Still, they only cost a dollar a throw, and we got drunk by the thimbleful, night after night. That winter it was my favorite place in the world.

Rusty was uncomfortable around Johnny; once, when I was in there alone he said, Where's your biggity friend tonight? I shrugged, and when I mentioned the remark to Johnny, he laughed, with something too close to contempt for me to laugh along with him. Thereafter, he was as likely to recommend the place as I was. It was as if he had entered into some kind of silent battle with the other man—a standoff of sorts, that had been transformed over time into a little ritual, unchanging, forever unresolved, and somewhat comforting precisely because it was slightly irritating, like a pair of shoelaces that won't stay tied. There was a trace of sadism on both sides that bothered me more than it bothered either of them.

We almost always went to Rusty's, almost always sitting in one of the booths in the back room. And since one element of Johnny's subtle torture of the other man was to walk in, say a cheerful hello, and then disappear for the rest of the night, I was usually the one who went to the bar to get the next round; and that was how I happened upon Bridget.

Her parents were divorced, and she hadn't been able to decide whether to go to her father's house or her mother's for Thanksgiving, so she had chosen neither. But she'd only arrived at school a few months earlier, an undergraduate transfer from a state school in Northern California, and she didn't have many close friends; the first few nights of the break she spent studying in her room, and then, on the Sunday before classes resumed, she decided to venture out on her own. How she found Rusty's, I don't know; it was on the very edge of the area around campus generally considered safe. Nor can I imagine the noise in her head that she must have needed to come in by herself; ordinarily, the only women who sat at the bar alone were either middle-aged alcoholics, younger drug addicts, or prostitutes of various ages; but even they had gone somewhere for the holiday. Bridget, I soon discovered, had a curious mixture of timidity and fearlessness—or rather, not a mixture, but a striation, like a cocktail: bitter girding the sweet. She could, for example, be absolutely stricken by the thought of having to go back to the store to return a defective lamp; but I once saw her approach Professor Youngerman, universally regarded as one of the most forbidding men on campus, and insist that he had completely misinterpreted a poem that he'd been teaching for nearly forty years, which had been written by a man, long since in his grave, who'd once been his mentor and had probably been his lover. — I can't believe you did that, I said to her afterwards, and she laughed and said, I can't believe it either.

When I first saw her at Rusty's, she was sitting on a stool by herself, alone as alone can be, with a glass of something-and-soda in front of her, a pack of unfiltered Lucky Strikes beside it, and her bag in her lap. She was wearing a white leather coat over a pair of blue jeans that had become slightly frayed at the waist, revealing a pale inch of flesh, and she had long eyelashes, sleek dark hair, and a slight, '60s-style overbite peeking out from between her berry-red lips. I assumed that she was waiting to meet someone, though she appeared to be settled in and wore an expression that suggested that, as far as she was concerned, nothing was going to change any time soon. I must have been looking at her with undisguised appetite, because she glanced at me, momentarily unsure whether to be flattered, amused, or annoyed, or if she should ignore me altogether. She settled for a sort of mild friendliness, ducking her head slightly to hook my gaze with a punitive smile. — My name's Bridget, she said. — I'm Mike, I replied, though apparently indistinctly.

Happy Thanksgiving, she said, raising her drink slightly and then sipping at it through the straw.

That's a great coat, I said.

Do you think so? she said. I honestly couldn't tell if she was making fun of me or not, so I nodded. She said, You're in school around here?

Tonight, I said, gesturing around Rusty's, this is my school.

You'll go far, she said, and turned away.

Then she turned toward me again and looked me up and down. — What is it? I asked her.

Nothing, she said.

I told her I was sitting in the back with a friend and invited her to join us, and she thought about it for a second and then said, I don't know anything about you.

You know my name, I said. My friend's name is Johnny; you'll like him. You'll like him more than you'll like me. She didn't answer. — Do you want me to leave you alone? She gestured to her drink and said, Let me think about it. Maybe I'll come back when I'm done with this.

I went back to the booth, where Johnny sat reading the gossip page of a tabloid newspaper he'd found abandoned on the bench beside him. I wasn't sure that Bridget was going to join us, so I didn't say anything. At length, Johnny said, What's a hoofer? A dancer, I said, and just then Bridget appeared, with a fresh drink in her hand and her bag slung over her shoulder. Johnny watched her approach with mild curiosity, and then did a take when she came up, pulled out a chair from the end of the booth, and sat down. — Hi, I'm Bridget, she said to him. I understand you're very likable.

He looked at her, he looked at me, and he looked at her again. I don't have an answer to that, he said.

Good, she said. I like you already.

We met at the bar, I said to Johnny.

I'm just a barfly, said Bridget. A floozy.

A what? said Johnny.

I like your accent, anyway, said Bridget. — A floozy. A woman of questionable character and judgment.

Floozy? said Johnny.

Johnny's vocabulary is growing by leaps and bounds tonight, I said.

It's a real word, said Bridget. I like the way you say it. Say it again.

Floozy, said Johnny obediently.

There you go, said Bridget, and Johnny stared.

Some time later, we were talking about movies and musicals, and Johnny said, Mike can sing the entire score of . . . what's the name of that movie again?

What movie? I said.

Bridget said, I thought your name was Ike.

Ike? I said, more startled than annoyed. Do I look like someone named Ike?

Yeah, actually, said Bridget. Yes, you do. Johnny laughed. Short for Isaac, she said. It's a good name, dignified. Mike? I nodded and she sighed. OK, then. Mike.

Johnny looked at Bridget with admiration. Enough about him, he said. Now to you.

What do you mean?

Now we're going to talk about you. Tell us how you wound up here tonight. Like many fundamentally kind people, Johnny had the unfortunate habit of coming across as peremptory just when he was trying his hardest to be expansive.

I don't think so, said Bridget.

No, said Johnny, now aware that he'd said something wrong, but still unsure of what. I'm sorry. I certainly don't mean to put you on the spot, I was simply wondering . . .

She gave him a cunning smile. Because a man can walk into a bar all by himself, just to have a drink, but if a woman does the same there must be something wrong with her, right? She must be crazy, or slutty, or so horrible that she has to drink alone.

Honestly, said Johnny. I didn't mean that.

There was a long, difficult pause. . . . So which one is it? I said.

Which one what? said Bridget, turning on me.

Which one are you: crazy, slutty, or horrible?

She looked directly into my eyes, the conversation had gotten combative rather than clumsy, and that was much more interesting to her. Johnny flinched slightly, as if he thought she might physically attack me, but she just said, All three.

Now Johnny was even more uncomfortable; this form of double dare was unfamiliar to him, and what's more, the lights had gone down and then up again, revealing Bridget and me on a certain stage, while

123

he was trapped in the wings. I wish I could have explained to him why that had happened, but it wouldn't have made much difference; Johnny was incapable of being anyone but Johnny, just as Bridget was incapable of being anyone but Bridget. And me? I was just incapable. I should have been the first one off the planet.

Bridget's glass was empty. There was a cherry in the bottom that she hadn't eaten. Why don't you go buy me a drink? she said to me.

I stood obligingly. West Side Story, I said softly.

What?

Is the name of the musical. — I waited until I saw her smile and then I went to the bar.

By the time I returned, the two of them were having a respectable conversation about Sacramento, and I was happy to lean back in my chair and watch them, noting that every so often Bridget would glance my way, with an expression on her face that I couldn't quite read: she might have been preparing to spit at me, or to unzip my pants, or it may just have been the way her look was made. But at the end of the night, when I realized that she lived near me, I was the one who walked her home, while Johnny, who lived on Riverside, separated from us a little ways down Broadway. As we left, his eyes flicked back and forth between Bridget and me just once, and then he looked away again, and the expression on his face registered a dismay that for a very long time I pretended not to see.

Walking home that night, Bridget and I passed through a series of Academic Zones, like climate stripes on the city: the Valley of Lawyers and Peacemaker Hill, Poetry Plaza, the Great House of Engineers, Medical Heights, Actors Row. I could feel the wind change as we came over a crest and looked down on a dormitory, inside of which were worlds within words within worlds. Bridget wanted to detour across the main campus, though it took us out of our way; the Walk was empty, as were the lawns in front of Butler; on the stairs leading up to Low Library there was a lone man huddled in a long, shabby coat, drinking from a bottle in a brown paper bag. She shivered: I gave her my scarf—cashmere, black—hardly daring to look at her face as I tied it around her thin white throat. There was something about her that made me hesitate. She had a fierceness that I didn't want to awaken; and a fragility that I didn't want to trample upon; and a capacity for judgment that made me want to surprise her, if only by failing to confirm everything she thought she already knew about me. Moreover, I was still upset over the loss of my last girlfriend, I wasn't sure if I was ready to start something new, and Bridget was not the sort of woman I would have treated carelessly.

We came to Amsterdam. She was telling me about a professor of hers, an Eastern European woman, apparently a recent refugee, who nevertheless taught a dense political theory course that promoted the very communism from which she'd run. (As I write this, I find myself surprised by the memory of communist countries: Bridget, they are gone, all gone, documents and dust.) The professor, she said, was a mystery; her students liked to speculate on her story, imagining feverish tales of tragic suffering, but no one had the temerity to ask her, nor would there have been an opportunity even if they had, for the woman had developed a peculiar lecturing style: she arrived in the hall where she taught exactly on the hour, read aloud from a prepared text for precisely sixty minutes, and then quickly scurried away; and her office, despite its posted hours, was almost always locked. Bridget had heard that she couldn't really speak English at all, that the entire exercise was a charade of sorts, that they might just as well have had one of the graduate students stand up there and read the woman's notes. I should have dropped it when I had the chance, she said. Now it's too late.

By then we'd reached the corner of Amsterdam and 110th Street, the crossroads empty, eight lanes of traffic and not a car to be seen, the light turning from yellow to red uselessly, pointlessly, and with a slightly uncanny effect; it was like walking into a dead man's house and finding the television still on. Bridget said, Ohhhh, this city really scares me sometimes. I said nothing, because I was enjoying the feeling of emptiness, the blocks abandoned but for we two; she took my silence as a rebuke and said, Sorry.

Sorry for what? I said. She didn't answer, so there we stood, both of us thinking about her, until the light turned green again and we crossed. There was a panel truck on the southwest corner of 109th Street, passing out dinners, as late as the hour was, to a small line of ragged shadows. Bridget was unhappy to see them, I could tell, but I didn't know why—because she should have been helping; because she could easily have been one of the beggars of New York and might yet be; because winter's abrasions were time-keeping on her sensitive California skin. When we reached the corner of 107th, she said, How long have you known Johnny?

About a year.

She pulled her white leather coat tighter against the cold and retied my scarf. I wouldn't have thought of the two of you as obvious friends. I shrugged: what she meant, of course, was that she was wondering if I could be redeemed. I couldn't help her there. I was exactly the man I appeared to be.

She shook her head in a gesture of wry disbelief at the way the night was carrying her along. Bridget had a kind of clairvoyance, which visited her from time to time and told her exactly what the future held for her. She could be extraordinarily impatient, temperamental, and rash, but she was touched by an implacable foresight, I'm quite sure of that. I know because she hated it, and that kind of gift is always bestowed on those who know least what to make of it, who resent it and defy it—which is how you end up in the belly of a whale, or fighting angels in the middle of the desert, or wasting away in a room at St. Vincent's, in a city that absorbs love endlessly but only gives it back as corruption. As for me, I knew very little then. You were just a baby, my wife says, and I suppose I was, though you couldn't have told me that at the time. What I saw was the tiny tilt of Bridget's head; what I didn't see was that she was listening to the prophets who followed her around, shouting: they were telling how it was going to go, perhaps not in all its details, but the hue and tone of it—enough, in any case, to make her want to walk right through me.

I asked her what she was doing the next day, and she said, I've got my job tomorrow. The placement office got it for me, arranging the archives of—and here she mentioned a name that I didn't recognize and to this day can't remember. He's a playwright, she said. Lives in that enormous apartment building down in the 70s, she said. A famous old building, what's its name . . .

The Dakota? I said. A streetlight overhead blinked off, stayed dark for a few seconds, and then blinked on again. She shook her head. Not that one, she said. The other one with the name. It's on Broadway. It's got a big gate. — Oh, you know what I'm talking about, it's a big, fancy place. It's right there, between 73rd and 74th Street. Babe Ruth used to live there. And what's his name, the opera singer . . .

The Ansonia? I said.

That's the one. He's got two apartments in there, actually, one where he lives and one where he works. He has me going through all his private papers, I don't know. A taxi pulled over at the corner, and a man in a long coat got out of the back, ran into a bodega, emerged again a few seconds later and jumped back into the cab. I thought people like that had all sorts of secrets, said Bridget. And I guess he does, but he's not trying to keep them from me.

So . . . ? I said, and when she didn't answer: Have you come across anything shocking?

She shook her head. No, that's the thing, she said. Other people's secrets, I think that's what I'm learning. They don't mean very much. She shivered, and we started walking down 107th, back toward Broadway.

We were about halfway up the block when she stopped and turned. I wasn't sure why. I'm right here, she said, pointing over her shoulder. The building with the broken window in the doorway. Where are you?

We passed it a few blocks back, I said.

You're walking me to my door. I nodded and she hesitated, trying to decide whether that made me a good man or one on the make, and in any case what the difference was and which she preferred. She cocked her head and frowned. At the top of her stoop there was a metal door with a thick pane of reinforced glass, which nevertheless had a silvery crack running through it, glowing from the gun-blue light of the fluorescent bulb in the hallway behind. It must have taken considerable force to do that kind of damage, a baseball bat or a metal pipe; I was hoping it wasn't somebody's head. There was such mystery to violence, arising suddenly and then retreating again, leaving nothing behind but something broken, and no way of knowing how it happened, no one to ask. Bridget was silent, and I turned. She was looking at me but she didn't say anything.

We're snowing, I said.

She didn't move, but she winced slightly. Say that again.

We're snowing, you and me.

We stood there, the two of us, and looked at each other, without touching, without moving; it wasn't a stare-down, exactly, there was no aggression in it, but neither was it simply curiosity. It was a kind of mutual appeal, and it seemed to last a very long time, though it might have been just a second, or less than that—a brief hold placed on the winter city, the girl with the breath of a smile on her face. Then her smile broadened, and with dazzling purity she quickly rose up on her toes, kissed my cheek, then turned and walked up the half dozen stairs into the vestibule of her apartment building, fetching her keys from her bag and vanishing through the door, leaving me alone on the street, listening to the cold noises along the block.

When I got home that night the apartment was dark, the wind was whistling through the window frames, a poltergeist had taken up in the radiator and was cheerfully banging away. I fell asleep in front of Channel 13, and woke at noon the next day with the television still on and a blue-white wind blowing all across Manhattan.

At the time I was living in a tiny two-room apartment with very high ceilings, the result of a larger apartment that had been subdivided and then subdivided again. The larger of the rooms was circumscribed at the top by a simple molding, but the walls had been painted over so many times that they had a rubbery feel to them. My roommate was a man named Dominic who was studying dance at Juilliard, and who despised his fellow students so much that he'd refused to live with any of them and had posted a notice on the Columbia campus instead. I seldom saw him: he spent ten hours a day in classes, rehearsals, and practice, and most of the night I don't know where, returning, when he returned at all, just before dawn, when he would slip quietly into his own room, leaving, as evidence that he was there, a pair of worn, ankle-high black Italian boots that he invariably positioned just inside the front door.

He didn't sleep very much, not that I saw, though he had finder's rights to the apartment's single bedroom; I slept on a convertible couch in the living room, which as often as not I kept unfolded. Every so often I would cross paths with him, usually in the evenings before he went out, and we would sit in the apartment with glasses of gin and tonic while he tried to sell me his philosophy of love, telling me stories of his encounters with other men, which he had, by design, everywhere but at home. In fact, he once told me, he'd never had sex in a bed—or maybe just not in his own, I don't remember. I couldn't, he explained. I just couldn't. All those sheets and things, all that softness, all so clean . . . Who decided that a bed, of all places, was a turn-on? Beds are for dying. A bed is just a grave above ground.

I regarded him with the same mixture of curiosity and amusement with which he regarded me. He was no better at living his life than anyone else I knew, though he was no worse, either: soon after moving to the city he had fallen in love for the first time, with the assistant in a Midtown art gallery who was older than he was by three years, to the day. We had the same birthday, he told me, with something like wonder, as if it were enough to indicate that heaven itself had lent a crystal dome to house their affair. They'd spent a perfect month together, and then the other man had panicked and decided that he wasn't gay after all, which sent Dominic into two years of misery that had just recently started to lift. Some months previously, I'd found his flyer tacked to a board on the first floor of Philosophy Hall, met him for coffee somewhere on Broadway at two in the morning, passed whatever careless test he had for roommates, and moved in.

I thought of Bridget over the following weeks. What was it? Why? She was very pretty, with her pale skin and her savage little mouth. I wanted to kiss her all the time. But we were in New York, and there were pretty girls everywhere, reading in the libraries, dancing at parties, walking through Riverside Park, sitting together at the far end of a subway car. Bridget did more than shine. There was a density to her, a gravity. She always seemed to be standing with her back to a corner, even when she wasn't, because the corner was her territory. There were girls I saw regularly on campus, bright things shuffled regularly into view by the gears of days, lovely creatures I would never meet. Such days! One evening in mid-December, the girl who'd left me called—Just to say hello, she said sadly, which led to another week of talking, fighting, and one night in bed that was prefixed by talking and suffixed by fighting. She was, I realized a bit too late, one of those women who try to elevate a perfectly amiable disposition coupled with no great character into an almost maniacal innocence, willing to admit to weakness but never to malice, and wanting only to be despoiled. It was my first encounter with that sort of thing, and the whole matter kept me too busy and too unhappy to talk to anyone else at all, so I didn't see Johnny until final exams and the Christmas break were upon us. I remember meeting him a few times during those dark and dwindling weeks, once for coffee to argue about history and once for a drink, when the semester was finally over; and then he left the country—to Paris, I believe.

It was an especially cold winter, infamously so: almost every day the tabloids ran headlines about the disruptions caused by the so-called Ontario Front: services suspended, subways iced to the tracks in dark tunnels, people who froze to death in their own apartments when the heat went out in the middle of the night. And there was the mayor, by turns clownishly posing (snow shovel, snowman, snow fort, snowshoes) and solemnly swearing that his administration was doing everything it could. The weather even put Dominic out of commission for a few weeks: it was too cold to fuck anyone, he said, so he took a Greyhound bus down to Florida (though he later told me he only made it as far as Charleston, where he met the son of a Baptist minister in a gas station bathroom). I went to my parents' home on Christmas Eve and, despite my mother's protestations, returned to my own apartment late on Christmas Day.

I'd expected to be alone, I had some research to do on Cicero's exilic years, and how better to hide from the weather? But my reading ran out at the end of the year, or anyway my interest did. I found myself unable to concentrate, and ended up alone and home, ignoring a pile of books that had frozen along with everything else. The telephone never rang. Outside, the wind blew, the sky was opaque, the sun was too weak to do more than dodder down. There were days of amazement, when the entire city was formed from a single dark crystal, all sharp cold edges and hidden crevasses; days of abandonment, almost too empty to be endured; and days of dread, for at the age of twenty-three I felt that I was growing old, and I could see the next half-century standing before me like a wall, as if the calendar, too, had seized up from the cold.

On New Year's Eve I found a party through a friend from high school, and woke up on New Year's Day with a woman named Liz, who had black bangs, blue eyes, and dimpled knuckles, and who had never before slept with a man she'd just met. She didn't tell me her last name, and she slipped out while I was in the shower, leaving nothing behind but a cherry lipstick kiss on my mirror. I never saw her again. Did she make it this far? She was the kind who would; I hope she did. She was sweet to me for a couple of hours, and I remember those things with an unfair fondness, the way a child remembers a single bestowed candy more vividly than years of nourishing meals. On my deathbed, will she come back to me and tell me who I was? She was wetter that night than any woman I'd ever encountered, and once, when I was inside her but not moving, she laughed at something I said, and I could feel her slippery walls rhythmically contracting. I hope she wasn't lonely for long, and only sad when it suited her. I hope her children have children, and stay warm and well-fed.

A few days after New Year's I saw Bridget again; it wasn't an accident. There was something I wanted from her, I couldn't easily describe what it was. I felt no special heart-quickening or desire, no sense that having her would bring any bliss or station. It wasn't sex, though it was something like it. A man leaves home because of a famine.

I came up with a few excuses to walk by her building, but it was too cold to linger outside. Classes hadn't started yet, and the campus was empty. I stopped by Rusty's one night and asked him if he'd seen the white girl in the white coat, but he had no idea who I was talking about. By January 6th I was getting frustrated: Was it really so hard to find one girl in one city? In my city? I knew where the Ansonia was, but I didn't know how often she worked there, or whether she was working at all over the break. Still, I had plenty of time, and besides, wouldn't Cicero sound sterling in a coffee shop? He was a man of the world. So for a few days I took a small stack of books to a Chock Full o' Nuts down on 74th Street, where I sat at the counter by the window, drinking coffee after coffee and looking out on the street every so often, just to see if Bridget would pass. She didn't, but everyone else did: elderly women in rich black coats and fine leather gloves, with shopping bags dripping from their fingers; academics without portfolio, middle-aged and invariably wearing eyeglasses with black plastic frames; aging beatniks twenty years out of the Village but still carrying themselves as if they half-expected to be jumped and beaten, and Spanish boys in groups of two or three who postured as if they were half-ready to jump them; beefy delivery men, ballet dancers on their way down to Lincoln Center, and once, a towering transvestite in a rainbow-dyed fake fur coat, who marched to the corner and flagged a cab with an enormous, ring-bedecked hand. Then, late one snowy afternoon on the third or fourth day, I raised my gaze just long enough to see Bridget pass, wearing a dark green suede jacket over a thick black sweater, neither hat nor gloves, nor my scarf, either, and her shoulders hunched against the wind. She always knew how to dress, but she never knew how to take care of herself.

I knocked on the window, startling the elderly man sitting a few feet down the counter from me, but by then she'd passed and she didn't hear me, so I flew to the door and dashed out onto the sidewalk in my shirtsleeves, calling her, Bridget. At first she ignored me, as if I was some street person who wanted to harass her and just happened to know her name; and then she whipped around, a scowl on her half-declined face. — What! she said, blinking angrily into the wind. It's me, it's Mike. Her expression didn't change; I pressed on. We met over Thanksgiving in a bar uptown. I walked you home. She was hopping up and down, she stopped to tuck back a lock of hair that had been dislodged, then softened. Oh, she said. Yeah. I thought . . . One thing

I hate about this city is people constantly interrupting you when you're trying to just walk down the street. She lowered her head farther into the collar of her sweater and looked at me; I had left my coat inside and I was shivering uncontrollably. Never mind. What are you doing out here, dressed like that? she said, looking over my shoulder to see where I might have come from. You're insane.

I was having a cup of coffee, I said, or tried to, anyway: I could barely get the words out, I had the jaw of a ventriloquist's dummy, dropping, clenching, clattering. Museum, I said, or something like that: whatever it was, it was a lie.

You're walking around dressed like that?

No, no, no, I said. I stopped here—I twisted on my feet to show her—to have a cup of coffee and saw you walking by.

You better get back inside, she said.

I said, Why don't you come join me? and she hesitated, but she didn't have much time to think about it, hostage to my cold suffering. OK, she said, and then turned and walked into the place ahead of me, as if she'd been waiting there for me, rather than vice versa. Later, when we were a couple and people would ask us how we met, she would say, I took pity on him.

There was that flurry before she settled, finding a place for her bag, removing her coat to reveal a sweater so threadbare that I could see a white T-shirt through its distended weave, then she looked up at the counter to see if she wanted to order something, and if so what, and then she looked around the room to see who else was there, if there was anyone she knew or anyone interesting. There wasn't: there was me. By the time she settled, her cheeks had pink rosettes from their thaw, and she was sniffling girlishly. What did you say about a museum? she said. Natural History, I said, it's just over there. But the walk back to the subway was so cold that I stopped here for a cup of coffee. Then I saw you walk by . . .

She believed me, and she seemed happy to see me. I asked her if she'd gone home for Christmas, and she said she had, but just for a few days, because the playwright had told her that he needed her and had offered to pay her airfare back. — I had no problem with that, believe me, she said. A few days is about as much as I can take out there. But this cold. I mean, God.

She'd ordered a cup of hot chocolate, but the first sip burned her tongue and she put it down. A single pane of glass divided the two of us from a harsh world; outside, everyone was the same person, because they weren't her or me. I asked her about the playwright, and she told me that she hadn't known anything when she'd first taken the job: she didn't know his work, didn't know much about theater, really, and couldn't say she cared. But she thought it would be interesting to see how rich people, successful people lived—whether it was like it was in movies, all perfumed furs and fast talk. Broadway, she said, gesturing at the street. I wanted to see what someone had made of it. She paused and giggled, flashing a glimpse of her glamorous pink tongue. But he's not at all what I expected. He's perfectly nice, she said. He's . . . very well-mannered. He's been married to the same woman for forty years. I think one of his sons has been in a mental hospital, but I'm not sure.

She was wearing a slender silver chain around her neck; she reached up and caught it in the crook of her index finger, twisting it slightly so that it tightened against the flesh of her throat.

What about his plays? I said.

What about them?

What are they like?

She looked embarrassed. I still haven't read them, she said. She shifted in her seat. Did you ever do anything like that?

Anything like what?

Anything artistic. Write poetry, paint paintings. Paint paintings, she said again. Poet poetry. Sing songs.

I shook my head. I played violin in my high school orchestra, I said. Does that count?

That counts, she said. She had resumed her hot chocolate by running her index finger along the edge of the cup and then licking the tip. Why did you stop?

I'm left-handed, I said and held up my left hand as proof. She looked at my palm as if she expected to see something written on it, and then made a questioning face. You can't really go far if you're a lefty, I said. Conductors don't like it because it destroys the symmetry; other players don't like it because you're constantly banging into them.

She was offended on my behalf. That's not fair.

I shrugged and dropped my hand to the table. Fair or not, I was out by the end of ninth grade. It was probably just as well, because starting in tenth grade you got molested by the music teacher. Outside, a gust of wind blew a parking sign so hard that the pole swayed back and forth. She was staring at the air where my hand had been. What? I said.

I'm still trying to get my head around the fact that there are high schools that have orchestras. She snorted softly. Mine had a football team, that was about it. The edge of her nostril was glistening, and she rubbed it with the wrist of her sweater. An elderly black man shuffled into the coffee shop, slowly enough that the door remained open for a few seconds, and Bridget shivered. The overcast afternoon was quickly turning into an overcast evening. A couple walking by outside glanced at us simultaneously, she from over a wool scarf, he from beneath a tall black fur hat. Bridget cocked her head at me. How old are you? she said.

Me?

You, she said.

I'm twenty-three, I said.

I'm already twenty-four. I'm older than you. Do you want to know why?

Because you were born a year before me? I said, and she glared at me briefly.

Why I'm still an undergraduate, she said. But now I'm not going to tell you.

One of the prerogatives of middle children is a cheerful ignorance about years: I've never been very good at guessing people's ages or recognizing the protocols they call for. Johnny, for example, might have been two or three years younger than me, or four years older than me. I didn't know: I still don't. But Bridget abruptly stood up and said, Let's go somewhere, little boy, and immediately I felt like just that: clumsy and uncertain. She smiled more broadly, allowing the tip of her tongue to slip between her teeth, turned happily and collected her bag from the back of her chair, and then turned back to study me. You're strange, I like that about you. Tell me what you're thinking about, right now, she said.

I was thinking about her ass; I didn't say anything, and she knew exactly what I was thinking about. She gave me a snarling kind of smile. I wanted to play with her—together with her, I mean. For a moment her face went absolutely blank, then she said, Let's go somewhere.

Where to?

Let's go downtown, she said. Or, let's go to the Plaza Hotel bar, I don't know. Anywhere that isn't the Upper West Side. I just got paid, she said. Come on.

Sex in those days was dirty and funny, and often confused and badly executed, but always with its own jalopy beauty: drunken kisses, wrong names, ringing ears, torn underthings, the honey'd middle of the night, a cigarette left so long on the edge of a bedside table that it burned a black streak into the wood before dying. It was a harmless rehearsal, though no one had any idea what the main event would be, nor how we would arrive there, whether in a chariot or barefoot. In another age, it might have taken weeks before Bridget and I grew comfortable enough with each other to sleep together, and it's possible that we never would have. Instead, she turned to me, in the bar on Avenue A where we ended up that night. She was nervous and she said, Oh, well . . . and she kissed me.

I'd like to be able to say that when we crossed the threshold into my apartment, later that night, the stars hushed in the sky and the city itself sighed in satisfaction. It wasn't so. Instead we were nervous, as one: mumbled words, inelegant moves, mismatched glances, and once she accidentally elbowed me in the throat, hard enough that I spent a minute trying to catch my breath. She was using a half-empty beer can by the side of the bed as an ashtray; there was another one, just like it, on the opposite night table, and at one point I sipped from the wrong one and choked in disgust. What saved us was a simultaneous burst of idiot laughter, brought on by the sound of my next-door neighbors having a bout of their own sex, silent but for the rhythmic thumping of their headboard against the wall we shared. Bridget rolled off me, trailing giggles; then she rubbed her nose and promptly fell asleep, with her hand over her belly, snoring softly.

When I woke, she was sitting on the edge of the bed, fully clothed, looking at me. It was the middle of the morning. I have to go, I have a class, she said. I left my number on the kitchen counter. She looked sad for a second, and then she was gone.

I could smell her on my skin all that day, on my fingers, on my lips; I could smell her hair and taste her breath, half ghost and half drug, an omnibus of flowers and resin. I called her that afternoon, and we spent the following night together and almost every night thereafter. There was no reason not to; we just wanted to be together, in bed. I was in love with her tongue. Her sweat was like a teenager's, sometimes sweet and sometimes rank, strawlike on her forehead, thin and salty at her neck, with an almost herbal, medicinal feel to it, like witch hazel; sugary on her breasts, and by the time my mouth had reached her belly, it had thickened enough to add a translucent pink sheen to her blue-white skin. Her goo—that was what she called it—was as fresh as seaweed; I liked to smooth it along the skin of her thighs, tracing the faint map of her blue veins, drawing nonsense and invisible smut. What was that? she said. — A dandelion. She turned her head, not to watch what I was doing but to look me in the eyes. What's that? — Those are my initials. — Why? — Shhh. Later, she told me that she hadn't expected me to call her at all. I thought you were one of those men, she said. I'm not one of those men, I said. — I thought you were. I thought you were one of them. I'm not, I said. I know, she said. I thought you were.

We hid inside through the blossoming spring. It was easy; no one cared. Bridget had her own friends, of course, but she didn't seem to be especially close to them. I can picture one or two of them, though I think there were five or six in their little group. They were a miscellaneous bunch, thrown together as much by circumstance as by affinity; I gathered they had all arrived at Barnard at the same time, had been put through some kind of orientation together, and may even have shared housing for a semester. On the few occasions that we all got together—dinner at a Chinese restaurant on the last day of midterms, a birthday party in someone's tiny, dim apartment, with warm beer and homemade curtains on the windows—they were polite and somewhat distant, and in retrospect they've all blurred together like background extras, but for two. One was a transfer from somewhere down South, who'd once complained to Bridget that no one on campus took her seriously because her accent was so pronounced. The other was a Jewish girl from the Upper East Side, hardworking, sensible, with an intense but placid gaze. Her name was Stephanie, and she made a point of not speaking to me, though once, for no reason that I could see, she produced a small camera out of nowhere and took my picture. I thought she was jealous, though not of Bridget: of me.

It was some time before I figured out how she ended up an undergraduate at the age of twenty-four; she was vulnerable on the subject and I never asked her directly. All I knew, at first, was that she had transferred in from a state campus in California, where she'd been so unhappy that she'd dropped out. In time, she told me that she hadn't been convinced that she needed to go to college at all, and instead spent a few years waitressing in San Diego; then she changed her mind—in fact, and typically, reversed course—and began applying to the best schools she could think of, starting with Amherst and proceeding in alphabetical order until she ran out of money for the application fees. She arrived in New York with enough credits to consider it her sophomore year, which meant that she was supposed to choose a major, but she was finding it difficult to decide on one. She had come intending to study comparative religion, but she quickly soured on that. She'd tried philosophy next, and that animated her for a little while. She found the questions it raised fascinating, but in time—and time for Bridget meant a few weeks—she grew frustrated. The classrooms were too full of argumentative young men, she said, and the professors were impossibly irascible, and spent all their time considering ludicrous beliefs, only to dismiss them for ludicrous reasons.

Despite her difficulty settling into a discipline, she thought of the university as a refuge; she'd worked hard to get there, and it served as an escape from everything that she wanted to leave behind—the parochialism of California, the anonymous concrete-and-sunshine of the school she'd attended previously, the disruptions and unhappiness in her family—her parents had been too busy, first with their affairs and then with their divorce, to pay more than perfunctory attention to her, nor had her teachers prepared her for life beyond the town she lived in. Only a small portion of the students in her high school graduating class had gone on to college, and most of those went to study business. To me, academia was familiar enough, if not entirely satisfying; and over the course of his life Johnny had attended a dozen estimable schools on two or three continents, and had become so adaptable that he treated a new campus the way he would treat a new airport: as long as he could find a decent cup of coffee, he was fine. But most of what Bridget knew she'd taught herself. In many ways her curiosity was purer than mine, but she always felt she was missing some essential foundation or set of skills. She felt clumsy and made up for it with daring, but it wasn't always enough. If she got a mediocre grade on a paper or lost her way through a reading list, she would mope about for days, while I tried to reassure her; then she would grow angry with me, either because she found it patronizing—an unpardonable sin, for which she was ever on the lookout—or because she had become comfortable with her insecurities, and resented the possibility that they might be taken from her. I preferred anger to despond, but I never did learn how to avoid one or the other.

I saw Johnny less and less frequently, not just because I was spending time with Bridget but because he'd taken a research position with a prominent economist, a significant appointment, especially for someone as young as he was, which took up as much time as he had for it. We tried to meet for coffee every Wednesday afternoon, but often enough one of us couldn't make it, because Bridget had something she wanted to do, a show in a museum, a neighborhood to explore, or because Johnny had an unexpected deadline. When we did manage to get together he was distant and distracted. He was finishing up his coursework; I had a year left, myself, and I was already beginning to lose interest in it, but I missed his company. Occasionally, Bridget and I would meet up with him together, to attend a lecture or go to a movie, and once to go downtown to a gallery opening she'd heard about. Sometimes she would come collect me from Rusty's, where he and I still went about once a month, and sit with her knee touching mine under the table while we joked about school, about politicians and criminals, and rehearsed the latest madness, fires on the subway tracks, a cornice that fell off an East Side building and killed an elderly woman who was in the back seat of a taxi below, a string of murders in the West Village, packs of wild dogs prowling around the abandoned financial district late at night. These were the companions of our conversations as the city lifted toward summer.

When the school year ended, Bridget and I decided to live together, and we found a small apartment up on Claremont Avenue. It was easy, we had very little to move, and Dominic was indifferent to whether I stayed or left. The new place was on the third floor of a walk-up on the north end of the street, where the elegant apartments for visiting professors gave way to tenements and overflowing trash cans on the sidewalk. It was June and we left the windows open, a pair of multicolored, '50s-style curtains blowing ever inward on the noise from the street outside. We didn't do much, aside from playing house. Her internship had ended, and she was picking up shifts at a Russian restaurant down on Amsterdam, one of those places that's on deathwatch from the day it opens, where half the tables are empty, the maître d' is by turns forlorn and agitated, and the liquor stock is slowly bled dry by the waiters after hours. I was working in a used bookstore on Broadway, midway between Columbia's campus and the Upper West Side. Together we made next to nothing, and spent it all on next to nothing: breakfast specials at a Cuban-Chinese place on Broadway, used cassette tapes of salsa music, paperbacks, subway tokens, forty-watt light bulbs and bottles of vermouth. One night she came home with an enormous jar of caviar that she'd stolen from the walk-in at the restaurant where she worked. — There are about a dozen of them in there, she said. No one ever orders any: they're just going to go bad. We had to raid the change we saved for laundry day to pay the electric bill, but for a month or so we had caviar with almost every meal, until we became so sick of the stuff she began to put it out in little dishes for the stray cats that lived in the basement.

I had never lived with a woman before, and Bridget had never lived with a man. Each little morsel of domesticity was a discovery: showering together, learning each other's languors, taking phone messages, brushing her hair. She had never seen a styptic pencil, found it fascinating and impressive, and immediately began using it after she'd shaved her legs. There was one night when she decided to bake a banana bread. Baking! I don't think I'd ever turned on an oven in my life, and now look: my experiences were doubling by the day. In the next room the television was tuned to a news report about an Indonesian separatist group that had hijacked an Australian cruise ship. What are we doing Sunday? she said. It was Thursday. Nothing, I said. I waited for her to explain why she asked, but instead she rapped an egg against the rim of a glass bowl, then peered in and fished out a fragment of the shell with her fingertip. She opened a drawer at her hip. Where's the whisk?

I wasn't sure what a whisk was. They're going to kill someone on that boat, I said.

On which boat? I gestured to the television, where there was a long, blurry telephoto shot of two men on the bridge of the cruise ship, waving automatic rifles in the air. What do they want? Bridget said.

Some prisoners released, I said.

In Australia?

No, I said. In Indonesia. I'm not sure if the cruise ship was just in the wrong place at the wrong time or if there's some reason Indonesians are pissed off at Australia. A silence. Johnny would know, I said. He keeps track of these things. Another silence.

He's not Indonesian, she said.

He's not? I replied, but she missed the sarcasm in my voice.

No, she said. Jesus.

I was going to point out to her that Johnny kept up, ferociously, with most of the world's injustices and injuries, that it was both his vocation and his habit to do so, and that he had no doubt seen this coming from a considerable distance. Instead I went back to watching the television and said nothing. Do we have cinnamon? she said at last. I doubt it, I said, and got up to help her look; and when it became clear we didn't, she sent me down to the bodega on the corner. In the hallway I listened to the chirp of a smoke detector with a dead battery. In the elevator I read the elevator inspection certificate for the thousandth time, and I still remember the inspector's name—T. D'Alessandro—and his signature, as familiar as Picasso's. The bodega that sold food had no cinnamon, so I tried the one that sold dope, though they had nothing in the window but a few bottles of laundry detergent and a line of botanica candles. The man behind the plexiglass was as wide as a refrigerator; his arms stuck out at his sides. He leaned back a little bit when I walked in. — I'm not a cop, I said before he had a chance to ask. I live upstairs. The shelves behind him were almost entirely bare, though there were a few cartons of cigarettes stacked on one side. He leaned back a little farther. Do you have any cinnamon? He squinted a little bit. My girlfriend is making a banana bread.

Cinnamon, he said, and I said, The spice. The actual . . . spice.

He rose from his seat and disappeared into a back room, while I wondered if he knew what I meant or if he was going to come back with a gram of coke, or a gun, or if he'd simply left me there to realize that he couldn't help me, and wouldn't have wanted to even if he could. A few moments later he was back with a little plastic bag in the meat of his hand; he studied it briefly and then pushed it through the slot; I put it in my pocket without looking at it myself. Three bucks, he said. I thought it was little enough to pay, and if I was wrong, Bridget and I could always get high, so I pushed three singles into the tray below the plexiglass, thanked him, and left, looking straight ahead as I crossed the street, possessed as I had always been by the superstition that if you don't look at anyone, no one will suspect you, and waiting to fish the baggie out and open it until I was back inside my apartment building. Collected along the seal at the bottom there were a few teaspoons of a reddish brown power: I smelled it carefully. It was cinnamon.

When I walked into the apartment, Bridget was standing in the doorway to the kitchen, cradling a yellow bowl filled with tan batter. I told her about my little adventure, holding the baggie up as if I'd brought it back from a long sea journey. She laughed in her goofy, sudden way, then she looked down at the bowl. On the television, a newscaster was saying something about a deployment of special forces from the Australian navy who had stormed the cruise ship. There were ten dead, twelve dead. She glanced at the TV for a second and then said, Vanilla.

I stared at her: she stared back at me, mirroring my question, and then her eyes widened mockingly. She dipped her index finger in the bowl of batter and held it up to me, and now I really was confused. You're an idiot, she said, and she laughed again. She was a tattered and feral kitten, scampering through the ruins of a private palace. Vanilla, not cinnamon, she said. I sent you out for vanilla.

An apostrophe on Bridget's ass, curved as all good things are. The eye seeks its isomorph in the world, and finds its deepest satisfaction when it succeeds. Cities have been built upon a dimple, and destroyed for the love of a navel. Handwriting, the smoke from a cigarette, the arc of a baseball in the blue sky; the slope of a wave, the billow of a sheet, the spring in a watch. I once knew an architect who kept a set of silver French curves in a wooden display case in his office. He claimed that they were reminders of his student days, but I always suspected, by the look in his eye whenever his gaze fell on their neat little shell-shapes and languorous bends, that they served as a kind of abstract pornography. Bridget's ass was the white disk of a full moon, the finest calligraphic *D*, a stone polished by a thousand years of river, the hollow on the bottom of a bottle of wine, the cheek of a plum. She was not a tall woman, but her butt was high; it made her look like she was up on her toes. There was a faint indentation at the very base of her spine, nestled within the muscles of her lower back; below that there was a small, flat channel, and then the flesh began to gently swell and split, forming a palmable, pink-white globe with a gentle depression on either side, and a gratuitous upward curve at the bottom, which arced inwards for a few degrees before yielding to the back of her thighs. The whole was wonderfully allusive, almost expressive: impertinent and slightly insolent, more buttock than bottom and more rump than either, a delight, an ode, a dollop, evidence of an art in her creation. I used to try and linger in bed for a few moments in the morning so I could watch her walk to the bathroom, ass in underwear if the room was cold or she was feeling modest, naked in the summer or when she was feeling careless. I would say to myself: I can touch that. It was like having a Cellini on the kitchen table.

In moments when I felt anxious, overworked, worried, or just bored, I liked to slip my hand into the rear pocket of her jeans, just to touch her there, the way children touch their stuffed animals, or Catholics their rosaries. Forward, to our apartment, forward to our bed, where I once grabbed her ass so hard that I left bruises. — Look, she said afterwards, twisting around so that we could examine the fading purplish marks together. She sulked theatrically: You did that. She met my eyes and I didn't know what to say, until she laughed wickedly. You're a brute, she said, and then she laughed again.

But we both were: beastly children, with no money but all the time in the world, living on a large and generally unmade bed. We treated each other terribly and enjoyed ourselves enormously, laughing at our own gluttony, our selfishness and cruelty. I used to stand her up against a wall and raise my knee just enough to press it between her legs, opening her up until she spilled, rain on a dirt yard. I learned to pull her hair in bed, to spank the inside of her thighs until they were red and burning. I liked to frustrate her almost as much as she liked to be frustrated. She could never mask her excitement, nor hide the aim of its ascent, and I would pull out and pull back just as she was about to come, while she grabbed at me and swore. Then we would start again, with twice the rage and ardor, and if I was feeling strong I'd deny her again, and maybe one more time, until she held her arms around me so tightly I couldn't get away, and used me to get under-over. She would bite my lip, my cheek, my neck; she didn't apologize and I didn't mind. Once, while sitting astride me, she commanded me to open my mouth, and when I complied she pursed her lips and slowly drooled onto my tongue; I think she sharpened her nails, the better to engrave my skin. I never felt it while it was happening, but one morning, I noticed that I had scratches all over: on my arms, on my neck, my torso, and what looked like a bite mark on my leg. When she came it was like the backdraft in a house fire, she sucked everything into herself: desire, rage, affection, fear, need, joy, disgust, along with that thread of knotted quicksilver that she pulled out of me. All of this she held for as long as she could, and then let it out with gritted teeth and a howl of relief that began so low in her throat that it sounded, at the beginning, like a complaint; and her eyes widened and her thighs shook, and one of her hands would wrap around the muscles in my neck and hold on tight. Her sternum would flush and she'd bend up and look down at our hips as if they were catching on fire. If we'd drunk wine, which we often had, I could smell the change on her breath as she neared it, like an extra fermentation inside her, boiling until it flashed, and I would have sworn that she gave off light—not a glow but a burst, painful and bright. I had never seen anything like it, she didn't whimper or cry out, she gave birth to a blood-red star, and when she was done she would put her weak fingers on my hip and say, Stop . . . stop . . . stop. Then we'd both laugh, as if we'd just parachuted into the ocean. Oh, we were happy, fucking angrily and fighting affectionately.

Bridget was contrary, Bridget was difficult; she was fragile and intricately made, and therefore often angry, and just as often tender. If I agreed with her on some point of art or fact she thought I was playing her; if I laughed at one of her jokes she would sometimes regard me with suspicion; if I was enthusiastic about a plan she had devised she'd often take it as a sign that we should really do something else; if I thanked her for something she would, likely as not, dismiss it as inconsequential—or worse, accuse me of being insincere. She could be undone by her menstrual cycle, which was unusually heavy and hard for her, leaving her dismayed at one moment, ferociously aroused at another, combative at another, so that we would find ourselves arguing over nothing amid sheets smeared with blood. She had fits of jealousy, during which she would constantly accuse me of planning to betray her. It was impossible to reassure her; denial didn't work, nor did exasperation, offense, or anger. And she could turn almost any compliment into an insult, sometimes with great imagination. Once, for example, with a single candle burning dangerously on the windowsill, and the sweat drying in the pit of her throat, she asked me in a whisper if I wished her boobs—her word—were bigger. I didn't: they were pale and elegant, and unusually sensitive. I told her that there was an old French maxim to the effect that a woman's breast should fit perfectly into an upended champagne glass—and she blanched and turned away from me, leaving me to stare at the downy wisps of hair on the back of her neck. I asked her what was wrong, but she wouldn't tell me. Bridget, I said. Bridget. Bridget. At last it came out that she thought I'd meant a flute, and that the whole thing was some kind of joke against her. I explained and she was embarrassed by her mistake, but she was still convinced that I'd set her up.

So you see, I never told her that I loved her: she would have assumed I was lying, and depending on the occasion, she might have been right. There were moments when I sank happily into devotion, well over my head, and long periods when I waded in its shallows, and I was always crazy about her in ways that were close enough; but I always had a sense that the dear waters could drain in a moment, leaving us both cold and exposed. She must have felt the same. She never told me she loved me either.

The grating over the window before the fire escape pushed to one side, and both windows open, ice cream truck music, a dirty day down on Tompkins Square Park, coming home on a subway that stopped in the tunnel and didn't start up again for half an hour, Five Percenters hawking pamphlets on a folding table in front of an OTB on Broadway, and beside them a man selling housewares and years-old pornographic magazines from a worn blanket. Bridget used to buy old volumes of poetry in languages neither of us could read, cocktail glasses that we never used, and old soul albums for seventy-five cents.

She was always looking for something; she might find it inside the tattered sleeve of a record; she might find it in my arms, she might find it at school. The summer made her anxious, and she thought about taking some classes, but she couldn't find anything she liked, and besides, her scholarship wouldn't cover the tuition.

She had grown up around bland California churches and hated religious people. Hypocrites, all, she thought; vain, ignorant, cruel, coarse. She could go on. My own experience had been more muted; Regis was a Catholic school, of course, but only mildly so: Christian thinkers were required readings, but belief was not a required trait. My parents took me to church on important occasions, but only then, and I had come away from it with neither animosity nor affection. This fascinated her. I remember one night, toward the very end of summer, when we were sitting in the front room of our apartment. The window was open, the fan was blowing in the smell of the city and the sound of two Puerto Rican girls laughing on a stoop across the street, and a police radio that was broadcasting loud but incomprehensible instructions, though when I went to the window to look, there were no squad cars or officers visible. The fan was spinning invisibly at my waist, its solid blades converted into mist and a dangerous low thrumming noise. Down below and across the street, the girls were leaning back lazily on the stairs, grasping brown velvet paper bags in their long-nailed hands. Both were dressed in the green plaid skirts and white blouses of the Catholic school up the block. What are you doing? Bridget said.

Just looking, I said, but she could hear the girls herself and her voice grew tense.

Who are they?

A couple of girls who live in the building across the street. I heard a noise behind me and I turned to find her standing up; I said nothing as she came and joined me, and without touching me glanced outside. When she saw the girls she calmed down: I don't know why. Do you think they're cute? One of the girls looked up and saw us there, standing in the window, me in boxer shorts and Bridget dressed in one of my T-shirts and no bottom, as if we were so poor that we had to split a full set of underwear between us—an image not so far from the truth. The girl pantomimed a loud laugh, bending down and hiding her face behind her friend, who said, What? The first girl looked up at us again and grinned and the second girl followed her gaze.

Catholic girls, said Bridget softly. Like the ones you grew up with. Is that your thing? The little gold crosses, the shoes, the uniforms?

God no, I said. I had to wear a uniform myself.

Really? she said. What was it?

Blue blazer, white shirt, nondescript tie. Every weekday for four years. I hated it, the blazer especially.

Really? Bridget said again. Now she was standing behind me. Her hand reached around to rest on my abdomen, then slowly drifted down until I could feel her fingers, first fluttering around the fly of my underwear, then rising up, pausing, and slipping under the elastic. I hissed a little and my head went back. It's definitely my thing, she said. One of the girls below was still watching, with an expression that I couldn't quite parse: wonder, disbelief, or perhaps it was nothing to her, just a couple of white folks fooling around in the window. Her friend was flipping through a magazine in her lap. Bridget was murmuring in my ear, Catholic boys in school uniforms, you just want to see what's underneath. — And now she was petting me so deftly that I almost fell to my knees. I turned, and she widened her eyes at me, took my hand and led me to the mattress, where she lay me down on my back and carefully straddled me, leaning down so that I could smell the soap on her skin, and beginning things with a sticky kiss somewhere near my mouth. Such a nice young man, she said softly. So formal, so polite. Such a soft cheek. Such a sweet boy. I couldn't tell if she really found that sort of thing exciting or if she was just trying to throw me off-balance; or maybe it was throwing me off-balance that she found exciting. Her hips levitated and then sank down again, an unexpectedly delicate and graceful move, for someone who was trying to burn me down.

As classes began again and we returned to campus, we began to see more of Johnny. He was still working in the economist's office, but at night he'd come to the library to read. It was not a happy time for him. The man was supposed to be his mentor, but he was distant and imperious; and he was advancing a thesis—it was about the economic effects of oil exploration in Nigeria—that Johnny found both mistaken and dangerous. But what am I to do? he said, smiling slightly. It was mid-September and we were drinking at Rusty's, and I could tell he'd had more than his usual share, though Bridget couldn't. One refuses these things at the peril of one's career, he continued. He looked different to me, a little thinner, a little faded and frayed, surrounded by murk, like a tropical fish that's been kept in an unclean tank. He shook his head back and forth in a long, mournful arc.

Did you try talking to him? said Bridget. I winced; Johnny settled into an exaggerated patience.

After a fashion, he said. One doesn't just . . . talk to a man like that.

A man like what? said Bridget. He's just some guy . . .

No, said Johnny. He's not just some guy.

I tried to change the subject. The movie theater down on 96th is having a festival of kung fu movies, I said. I think we should go.

Johnny, said Bridget. He stared at his fingers, which were wrapped around a short tumbler. Just tell him what you think. Or maybe you could sabotage his research, throw in some fake statistics or something.

One just . . . doesn't, he said. Politics, after all, is compromise. As are many things. Compromise is everywhere; it's one of the few constants of the human condition. He couldn't look at her as he said this, and she took that as a sign that he needed convincing. I could see that it was going to end badly, but I didn't know what to do about it, in part because it was spoiling so quickly, and in part because I didn't know quite where my loyalties lay. Ordinarily, I would have done whatever I could to protect her; she was mine, and at the time I believed that she was the more vulnerable of the two. But I had known Johnny longer, and besides, she was both wrong and insistent. Just then, I wished I didn't know either of them and even considered finding some excuse to leave them there, but my boots wouldn't move. Instead I just watched.

Come on, said Bridget, you have a choice. She didn't mean much by it, but I saw Johnny pause, one of his delicate hands gently rotating a paper napkin on the tabletop.

A choice? he said, his voice rising. Perhaps for you. For you, yes, all right, you do nothing but choose. But you don't realize . . . you take my father—here he faltered, his brow darkening, as if he wasn't sure how far to go with this. And then, for the very first time, I watched him lose his temper—not by raising his voice, but simply by saying things I'd never heard him say before. My father spent his entire life compromising. Doing things that he knew were wrong, and why? And not little things either. Why? Because otherwise his country would not have had a chance, he would not have had a chance. I wouldn't be here now if it wasn't for my father's compromises. I wouldn't be anywhere. They would have forced him to watch while they raped my mother, and then some drunken fool would have—shot him dead. Just as they did to my uncle, my mother's brother, a good man. A gentle man. A gentle-man. And he left behind nothing at all. No family. No estate. So my father lied for people who had more power than he did, and by doing so became very wealthy. And then they killed him anyway. And here I am, in your lovely country, using that wealth to study at my leisure, and helping some foolish old man perpetuate the very same kinds of lies.

Johnny, I said.

No, no, no, he said, turning to me.

I put my hands up slightly, in a gesture of mild surrender. I'm just saying . . .

You're just saying . . . what? That these are things I mustn't consider, as I sit here enjoying my drink?

No, I said.

What are you saying, then? What is it? Go on. I glanced at Bridget, her eyes were wet. Johnny wouldn't look at her at all.

I'm saying that you're among friends, I said.

Friends, he said slowly, so slowly that he began the word almost sarcastically, modulated into irony and distress, and ended it with true warmth. We waited, Bridget and I. Yes, he said at last. You are my friends. You may be my only friends. He sighed and shook his head. And here I am, yelling at you. I'm very sorry. He looked at Bridget, though now it was she who couldn't look at him. Really, he said, please. Forgive me. I was afraid that if she didn't answer he was going to start begging her, though she wasn't withholding her pardon; on the contrary, she was too embarrassed to speak.

It's all right, it's nothing, I said pointlessly, since he was still looking at Bridget, who was now openly crying.

Honestly, said Johnny. Her tears were alchemical, a stain on her face. Honestly, he said again. I apologize.

But of course she didn't want him to apologize, and she found his obtuseness and his helplessness frustrating. She'd done something wrong and needed to say so; he was robbing her of the opportunity by apologizing himself. She shook her head, and I felt a teardrop as hot as solder land on my wrist. Oh—fuck you! she said at last, pushing back, standing, snatching her bag from the back of the chair, and hurrying out of the bar and into the night.

Johnny looked down at the table, as disconsolate as I've ever seen a man. I don't know what he was thinking; I doubt it was anything more specific than misery. Don't worry about it, I said, and he replied with silence. She just . . . I said.

You should probably go after her, said Johnny, and I said, Yes, but listen . . . — He raised his hand and said, I'll be fine, go talk to her.

By the time I got out the door onto 125th Street, she had disappeared. I went home, but she wasn't there. She must have known it was the first place I'd look. I stood in the living room, feeling panicked, while the night raged and subsided in darkening waves. I wanted to throw open the casements and call to her, but instead I lay down on the bed—not to rest, to smell her. I don't think I'd ever in my life wanted so badly to find someone.

I went downstairs and started over to La Salle, and I was going to head south, stopping in whatever bars might be open at that hour to see if she was sitting alone, but instead I turned back, dog-legging over and making my way down into Riverside Park. It was a gloomy night. Overhead, the leaves were rustling in the wind, and there was no one about, no one at all. There was graffiti on the walls of Grant's Tomb, and there was Bridget, sitting at the top of the short flight of stairs, holding a tallboy in a brown paper bag and watching me as I approached. She didn't move, she didn't even acknowledge that I was near, but when I arrived at her feet, she looked up, and I could see that she'd only just stopped crying. Her eyeliner was smeared, and even in the darkness I could see that the tip of her nose was pink. She made a sarcastic toasting motion with the beer; I smiled slightly because I didn't want her to think I pitied her. Well, she said, I fucked that one up, didn't I?

I shrugged. She would have hated me if I'd lied to her. I said, He's got a lot on his mind these days. She cocked her head. Her face was shining—and then she laughed in that sudden, awkward way that's barely distinguishable from crying.

There was an ugly odor in the air, a whiff of vomit that made me wrinkle my nose involuntarily. It wasn't me, she said. Some guy came by here about five minutes ago. Didn't say a word to me. Puked over in the corner, and then left again.

Why are you sitting here?

I was waiting for you, she said. I held out my hand to her, she took it, stood, and then suddenly hugged me, as tightly as she could, her face buried into my shoulder, the sour night city decaying around us while we indulged in that binding moment that comes from shared misery, confusion, doubt, and regret.

You know, I said. You were right. She pulled back and looked at me with a fiercely skeptical expression. I said, If he thinks the professor's wrong, he should say so.

I believed this. There was an element of convention about my friend that I found disappointing. But of course that wasn't really what they had fought about: I knew that, and so did Bridget. Off in the distance, a car horn played *La Cucaracha*. Come on, she said. Let's go home. I'm tired.

Is there anything more exhausting than grief? She wasn't just tired, she was utterly expended; she could barely make it back to our apartment, I thought she might actually faint, and I had to hold her arm as we walked up the stairs. She leaned against the wall of the hallway while I unlocked the door; once inside, she sat on the edge of the bed while I went into the bathroom to wash my face. By the time I came out again she was fast asleep on top of the bedclothes, fully dressed but for her shoes, and so motionless that I stopped breathing myself; and time would have no purchase, at least for those few seconds. Then I saw her swallow, as if she was finishing off a morsel of dreaming, so I undressed her tenderly and tucked her in, and then sat in a chair across the room for a few minutes, watching her sigh in her sleep, before joining her under the warm, aromatic sheets.

Bridget was one of the very few people I knew in New York who owned a car, even my parents had never bothered, and she was certainly the only one I knew who used it. She'd driven it out from California, it was an old red Toyota, and she refused to give it up, even though keeping it was an enormous amount of work. She hated and feared the subway, especially at night: the graffiti made her queasy and the shriek of the brakes gave her a headache. She liked to read the tabloids for the latest horror, a woman pushed in front of an oncoming train by a disturbed man, rats scurrying across the tracks. When she learned that I kept a ten-dollar bill in a different pocket than I kept my wallet, so that I could still get home if I was mugged, as I had been several times over the years, she scowled and said, I don't understand how you can live like this. But she lived like that too. Within a week of getting to town, someone had broken the passenger window of her car and stolen her stereo.

I didn't have a license, myself, though it took me some time to convince her that I didn't: she found it hard to believe that someone had reached adulthood without learning how to drive, though I'd learned the rudiments while joyriding with a friend one summer on Long Island—knew enough, anyway, to put the thing in gear and circle the block a few times, looking for an empty space. It was a nuisance, that car. I can't tell you how many nighttime hours, in total, we spent searching for a legal place to park, nor how many mornings I got out of bed, threw on whatever clothes happened to be lying on the floor— including, once, a T-shirt covered in tea roses that was actually hers, and which, because I had to be in class in twenty minutes and it took me fifteen to find a free spot, I ended up wearing all day—and rushed downstairs to move the thing before it was ticketed. A ticket would have cost us a week's worth of wine.

Driving in the city made her so tense that it was painful to watch, her fists clutching the steering wheel, her head craned, the car lurching and stopping as she waited for someone to let her into a lane, the sudden discovery that the street she was looking for was one-way in the wrong direction. It was a waste of time, that car, but so was time itself. We drove everywhere, which almost always meant downtown, and it was on one of those nights that Bridget would have killed us both.

It was October, and there was a faint, fresh note of fall in the air. We had decided at the very last minute to drive down to Alphabet City. Where were we going? I don't remember, but we were late. We were always late when we went somewhere, always rushing, always dressing and dressing again, bickering and apologizing, forgetting things until we were on the sidewalk and then dashing back upstairs to fetch them, always laughing as we got lost. Evening had passed and night had fallen;

we couldn't decide whether we wanted to go at all, and then suddenly we were leaving, trying to remember where we parked the car, midnight was approaching. We can make it, she said. We'll just go fast. We stopped for cigarettes and then got on the West Side Highway. When she was nervous or excited, Bridget could smoke like a schizophrenic, desperately, compulsively, and without pleasure, impatient to finish one so that she could start another: more than once I found her alone in our living room with two cigarettes burning in an ashtray, one just an inch shorter than the other. That night, she unwrapped the pack with both hands, steering with her wrist, and then tried to light one from the car lighter, but it didn't take, and she clicked her tongue in frustration and tried to put the thing back in its socket, missed, and looked down; and then, for no reason that I could figure, she started to take the exit at 79th Street, then changed her mind and jerked the steering wheel back, causing the car to clip the concrete barrier on one side of the exit with a monstrous metallic sound . . . then swim slowly and soundlessly through the air . . . like a zeppelin, I thought . . . and then bounce violently up the curb on the other side—I heard Bridget squeak—and strike a streetlight on my side before coming to rest on the small grassy triangle that flanked the exit, somehow facing uptown.

But that's not what I mean when I say she almost killed us. We checked each other and we were both all right, or so it looked at the time. (Later I would discover a wide purple mark, almost black, running directly across my waist where the seat belt had restrained me, and by the next morning Bridget had developed a strawberry-colored contusion on the side of her forehead, origin unknown. — I had just turned to say something to you, she told me later, but now I can't remember what.) I could smell gasoline in the air, but that isn't what I mean about getting us killed either. Her door was half-opened, and she stepped out. Mine wouldn't open at all, so I followed her on her side. I hugged her, we were both shaking. Fuck, fuck, she said, her voice wet with frustration, over the lost car, the lost occasion, the entire suite of consequences that the night had conjured. That's it for my car, she said. Fuck, fuck, fuck. Someone passing must have seen the accident, because there were sirens and lights in the distance, and Bridget said, They're coming. — And then she thrust her bag at me, said, Hang on, and darted back into the car. I could hear her making distressed sounds as she struggled to open the damaged glove compartment, and when she emerged again, she was holding a small pistol in her left hand, and she grabbed the bag back from me and tucked the gun inside it just as the carnival lights of an arriving police car broke over the dark tableau. That's what I mean: if they'd arrived a few seconds earlier they would have been perfectly happy to shoot us both.

There were two cops at first, though later another car pulled up and two more joined them. Of the four, I remember that three had mustaches. They were weary and curt. Bridget said that she had been driving and had gotten distracted, and one of them asked me why I wasn't the one behind the wheel. I told him that I didn't drive, and he shined the flashlight in my face for a few long seconds. Then how do I know that you are who you say you are? he said. I gave him my university ID, while Bridget fished her driver's license out of her purse, so swiftly and elegantly that she could have been carrying a human head in there and they wouldn't have noticed. One of their radios repeatedly burst with chatter, dispatchers and beat cops chatting and joking. A pair of citizens, I heard somebody say, and someone asked if we needed an ambulance. One of the mustaches said, Negative. At the same time, another one said something that made Bridget laugh, though I was pretty sure it wasn't her real laugh. As if by magic, a tow truck appeared, its yellow lights spinning lazily in counterpoint to the police cars' red ones, and without a word to anyone the driver winched up the car and spirited it away. Later, one of the police cars took us home while we held hands in the back seat and watched the starry city pass in reverse, like a film projected backwards; and in our dark apartment, we listened to doo-wop songs on an oldies station and drank warm wine without looking at each other, musing in the sweet, silent wake of disaster. As for the gun, she said only that her father had given it to her when she told him she was coming to New York, she had no bullets for it, had no idea how to fire it, and kept it in the car only because she didn't want to have it in the apartment. The next day, we took it down to the river and threw it in.

What else can I say about her? This is a portrait in chemicals, when what I want is blood. She was warmer than I've made her out to be, less harsh. She cried very easily, at a movie, in an argument, and often enough for no reason at all that I could see. I found this so vexing that I would become inarticulate, which almost always made it worse—though sometimes, seeing how nonplussed I was, she would grin through her tears, a little deviously; and then she would be the cheerful one, and I the churlish, and she would tease me about being too moody and emotional. What else? I loved the way she dressed. I, who rarely wore anything other than jeans and a T-shirt, found this part arcane and delightful, her pants and skirts, tights and boots, her bracelets and bras. I wanted to go shopping with her, just to see how she did it—to learn what everything was called, the tiny sleeveless undershirts, the sheer black leggings that left mildly angry crenulated marks on the skin of her thighs—but she never let me. She read fashion magazines with the same combination of lust and shame that a teenaged boy would bring to a stack of pornography, though they never had any effect on what she bought or wore. Once, when I came home with the news that I'd won a small award from the Philology Society for a paper I'd written, she cheered me like I'd singlehandedly liberated Paris, and said, I'm so proud of you! Dust on the baseboards, a brownout lamp in the living room, little jam-jar glasses lined up in the drying rack next to the sink.

She was mildly superstitious, I would discover that in time. No full moon rose without her noticing, there were secret signs here and there, designed to give her a little more grasp on things: horoscopes, lucky pennies, ways of negotiating obstacles on the sidewalk, signatures I only noticed when I was with her. The world was a rebus of good news and bad, and that was how she converted belief into knowledge, how she ordered herself among fields of serenity and dread. These forces were not to be handled casually: one late night down in Little Italy we came upon a palm reader open after hours. I wanted to stop in for a psychic reading but she protested vehemently, not because I entertained the idea, but because I didn't take it seriously enough.

She once spent an hour watching a man dealing three-card monte on a cardboard box in front of a movie theater. She never placed a bet, no matter how obvious it seemed, but she never figured out how the con worked either. She read the books assigned to her ferociously and all in, and I would often hear her clucking or murmuring sympathetically or snorting with amusement as naturally as if she was in the middle of a conversation, though when I asked her what had struck her, she wouldn't tell me. She took assiduous notes, but I never saw her reread them. She could draw beautifully, but I didn't know as much until she left me a note one morning: Good morning, sweet boy, it said, and around the words she'd sketched a circle of parading elephants, each holding the tail of the one before in its trunk.

She began to hear things about me, I don't know where, and she pretended, at first, to be amused by it all. — Is it true that you had an affair with the wife of one of your professors?

I said, No. That's crazy. Have you seen my professors? Have you seen their wives?

What does that have to do with anything? she said.

When was this supposed to have happened?

Whenever it happened.

But it didn't happen, I said.

And you had a drunken fistfight in a bar. You lost a tooth.

That was years ago, I said, and it was hardly a fight. Someone hit me. I don't even know why, I'd never seen him before.

As far as she was concerned, I'd admitted some part of some rumor, however trivial, and she was almost gleeful, as if I had granted her license to indulge in her worst fears about me, like a child allowed into an R-rated horror movie. What did you say to him? she said.

I didn't say anything, he thought I was someone else. Who's telling you this? She didn't answer. I couldn't imagine where it was coming from: not Johnny, he wouldn't have, and besides, he didn't know these things. Perhaps it was one of her friends, or someone from my department. Most likely she was making at least some of them up, feeling around in the dark to see how I responded, if I would give anything away.

She kept tiny souvenirs in a wooden box on her dresser, bar matchbooks, a small stone or feather or bead, single flower petals that had almost returned to dust. Several times she came home triumphant with a houseplant, and each time it died within a fortnight. There was nothing she did but she just had to do it, and nothing she didn't but she hated it. I never once saw her mistreat anyone, except me, and perhaps Johnny.

She had elaborate bedtime rituals. She could not, for example, sleep without her own pillow; before we moved in together she would carry it over to my apartment in a brown paper supermarket bag. She brushed her teeth every night with infinite care, flossing and whatnot, while I waited impatiently in bed. She wore contact lenses, and was purblind without them, but it was only after several weeks that she would let me see her in glasses; instead she would half-intuit her way to the edge of the mattress, her eyes clouded and slightly unfocussed. She always slept on the left side of the bed, often with one leg hanging off the edge until it almost touched the floor. She occasionally spoke in her sleep, though usually incoherently; and she often had peculiar things to say in the morning as she was waking up: non sequiturs left over from her dreams, though she never told me the dreams themselves. — Don't worry, she said to me one morning as she was waking. It's just a pin: it's just a needle. Another time: Go away, you bomb. Another time she woke and immediately announced, Bees are yellow and nuts.

She was terrified of growing old, she referred to her age all the time—twenty-four, and as I write this it's been twenty years since I was twenty-four. Bridget, it's not so bad. The hardest part is missing people, and wishing you'd been better.

I told Johnny about the car crash the next time I saw him. He laughed softly and said, Well, that sounds like an adventure, and a lot of luck.

Luck? I said.

I didn't say good luck, he pointed out, laughing even more softly at his own sophistry. We were sitting over coffee in one of the graduate student lounges, at a beautiful polished wood table surrounded by three or four mismatched chairs, and some bookshelves stocked with ancient editions of academic journals, written by obscure professors long since forgotten. Through the window drifted the sound of an anti-apartheid demonstration underway on the steps leading up to Low Library, a voice demanding something over a loudspeaker, though by the time it reached us it was impossible to say what. Johnny regarded such things with a mixture of sympathy and disdain. It wasn't that he thought the matter was trivial: on the contrary, he regarded it as almost too grievous to discuss—and he was always being asked to discuss it, to join this or that cause, to speak at a rally. I never knew him to accept. That afternoon he rose to shut an open window, which made the room much quieter. Then he said, My mother is coming to town next month. What do you suppose I should do with her?

I was surprised at how casually he brought it up, and then realized, from the stillness in his demeanor, that he wasn't casual about it at all. Has she been here before?

Several times, he said. That's part of the difficulty, you see. I've already taken her to the landmarks, the museums. Oddly enough, I think she liked Chinatown the best, but I'm afraid she'll find this weather even less appealing than I do.

I guess that rules out ice-skating at Rockefeller Center, I said.

He lowered his eyes and smiled. That would be a sight, he said, wouldn't it? But no . . . my people don't ice-skate. I should suggest it to her, though, just to see the look on her face. — And by the way, she wants to meet you, if you're available.

Wants to meet me? I said.

You look alarmed, he said.

I was, a bit, and for several reasons. We were at that age when one lives in a world without parents; Bridget hadn't even met my own, though they lived ten minutes away by cab. And they would be a formidable pair, he and his mother, who were bound to have shared experiences, a culture, a language, perhaps three or four of each, that I knew nothing about. Had I thought about it, I might have realized that Johnny was familiar with just this sort of uneasiness: he was forever a stranger, not just for an hour or two of dinner but for years on end. But I was not quite wise enough to see that. Instead I said, It's just that I always thought of her as a figure from some legend. A hippogriff, or something. And this was true. There was something slightly stiff about the way Johnny had spoken of his mother in the past, for one thing using the relationship as her name: Mother wants me to send her a souvenir from the Statue of Liberty, he said to me one afternoon, by way of explaining why he was spending an afternoon making the trip. Another time we had stopped on the street to watch a television through a store window, where a Rastafarian was holding forth on a local cable access show. Mother thinks no one takes a man with long hair seriously, he said, and we started away again. His formality made her seem distant and redoubtable: The widow whose grief was too deep to be fathomed; the reformer who successfully stared down gangsters; the demanding steward of his own brilliant calling.

A hippogriff? said Johnny that afternoon, arching his eyebrows and cocking his head. Are you implying that my mother is a jungle creature?

A hipp—, I said, then stopped myself and stared at him, exasperated. He laughed. I'm implying that she's a completely imaginary jungle creature, I said.

Well, he said, she's very real, and, I might add, quite civilized, and she said she would like to meet my friend Mike.

I'd be happy to come, I said.

Over the following weeks, he proved to be uncharacteristically uneasy about his mother's visit—nervous and slightly obsessive: once we'd set up a date for dinner, he reminded me of it a half a dozen times, and even went so far as to suggest that I might want to buy some new clothes for the occasion, or at least find something decent in my closet. She has a thing about . . . comportment, he said. That stung me a little: I reminded him, not too gently, that I was quite capable of being presentable, when I wanted to be. He darkened a bit and apologized. The truth is I don't really know her that well, he said. Isn't that an odd thing? He paused, I said nothing. He was worrying his spoon and saucer, scooping up a quarter-moon of cold coffee, contemplating it for a few seconds, and then turning it over into the dish again. After my father died, she withdrew a bit. Back home, the death of a husband is an extraordinarily complicated event, full of rituals and ceremonies. I suppose that's true of most cultures, but I was a bit surprised at how readily she embraced it. She followed the traditions. You see? A full year of mourning, special clothes, special meals, prayers, a long stream of condolence calls and visits. All of it. Almost all of it. That's what I mean: I find her hard to read. My mother . . . he paused. She believes my father is still with her, watching over her from the sky, I suppose, or perhaps a spirit on the ground: she talks to him quite a lot. She likes to say that she's a Christian, and of course she is, in many ways. But you know how it is: they make it their own. I find it all very . . . what's the word? Well, the word is *primitive*. He stopped and then started again. If anyone else said that, I'd be outraged. He looked up and blinked at the light. What a thing to say of one's own family.

My people eat the body of Christ, I pointed out.

He smiled. Yes, you do.

Bridget didn't join us. Since the accident, she and I had been fighting, sometimes and then often, always over nothing, and with a viciousness that I often found shocking and disturbing, mostly for what it brought out of me. I hadn't known I could say such things: foul and despicable things, we said them to each other, almost reveling in our ability to be hurtful, best if it was no more than a sentence, a look, a sigh of frustration. Then the animosity would subside, usually as quickly as it had appeared, and we would both act as if nothing, but something, had happened. I wondered if it was the crash itself that had broken us: it felt like nothing so much as a wrecked engine, gears catching and un-catching, making a fearsome loud noise, while the carriage lurched and then settled into an uneven idle, which might stall or might not, and was therefore difficult to drive. I wondered if it was simply time-the-disease, from which all things suffered. I wondered if this was what it meant to be an adult, and if she wondered the same. The weeks went by, we fought and we stayed. We never spoke of separating.

She had made plans to take the train down to Baltimore to see some friends who were in art school there. It would be the first time she'd left the city in almost a year. — Look at this, she said, holding a clump of hair out from the side of her head like Raggedy Ann. Look at my eyes. I didn't see anything wrong with her eyes. — The skin under my eyes. Still I saw nothing wrong, but I could tell she was tired by the slow way she moved, and the fraying at the edge of her voice. Go, I said. Have a good time, it'll be good for you, and I'll see you in a couple of days. Of course, I meant that it would be good for both of us. Of course, she knew that. But when she left I felt like she'd taken one of my senses, and I worried about her all that night, woke up cold in the morning, and skipped an Ovid seminar to stay home in bed, where I wore one of her housecoats, though it stopped above my knees, listened to the traffic below, and read a paperback copy of a trashy novel that she'd bought on the street a few days earlier. As night fell, I rose at last, showered and pulled on the suit that I'd carefully dry-cleaned and set aside. I had a white shirt and a somber tie as well, but for shoes I had only a pair of scuffed-up, secondhand wing tips that I'd bought in a thrift store a few days earlier. As I was leaving the building, the Puerto Rican woman who lived on the second floor said something to me in Spanish, and when I looked back she was nodding with a half-smile on her face. I met up with Johnny at the top of the subway stairs; his hair was smoothed down and anchored with a part so sharp that one could have rolled a dime down it. We looked each other up and down, and then laughed.

We met his mother in the lobby of her hotel, a place at once intimate, grand, and slightly time-worn, which took up a full block on the East Side. Ah, the desk clerk said to Johnny as soon as we approached. You must be Madame's son. Johnny paused and then nodded. She told us you were coming, the clerk said. She's very proud of you. He reached for the phone to call her room; I turned and saw a maid standing in a far doorway, the bare white walls of a usually hidden service hall behind her, smiling broadly at Johnny and me.

Johnny's mother emerged onto the pearl-grey marble floor a

minute or so later, smiling from something the elevator operator had said to her and waving goodbye to him; and at once a sort of receiving line formed before her: bellhops, the maître d' of the hotel's restaurant, the night manager, the maid I'd seen standing in the doorway, all making a casual cordon simply for the pleasure of seeing her pass. She addressed each one by name as she went by, and introduced several of them to her son and his friend, using a name for Johnny that I couldn't quite catch, a mash of *d*'s and *n*'s that I had never heard before—a diminutive, I assumed, since he balked slightly at the sound of it, even as he greeted everyone pleasantly, while I hung back a bit and nodded a series of hellos. The whole process took several minutes and would probably have taken longer if his mother hadn't glanced at her tiny gold watch and, with a rising lilt, said, Oh, dear, we're going to be late. Well, good night. Good night. Good night. Good night.

Would Madame like a taxi? the doorman said when we bustled out the door.

She stopped, and Johnny paused apprehensively. Now, why is everyone calling me Madame? she said to the doorman with the kind of easy, elegant smile that implies the very regality it is meant to refute. You mustn't call me Madame, that is much too formal. The doorman, though uncertain about what he'd done wrong, nevertheless started to apologize; but she continued, still smiling: You must call me Matilda. Yes, ma'am, the doorman said. Can I get you a taxi? On the street, the late autumn air was cold and slightly silvery, like a freshly washed window; Johnny's mother turned and looked at him, he looked at me, and I looked at the brightly colored scarf she was wearing. Let's walk, he said. It isn't far.

We turned toward Park, the sidewalk barely wide enough to accommodate the three of us, but there weren't many people out, and those we came across readily moved aside to let us pass: Johnny's mother carried herself in a way that suggested she was used to deference: she was neither severe nor superior, but she had a glamour about her and you could see it coming. I wondered what Johnny's father was like, and whether her self-possession had come from being his wife or being his widow; or perhaps it was why he'd married her in the first place. What a man he must have been, if this woman was his partner. I remembered a story Johnny had told me, about another man, not his father, a poor singer who'd been in love with her, and had written a song called Honey and Ashes for her, which had rescued her from a period of obscurity and made her famous again. You must call me Matilda, too, she said to me, but like the doorman, I couldn't bring myself to be so familiar; instead I avoided calling her anything at all for the rest of the night. A lovely city, she said, and at first I thought she was being sarcastic: up the street there was an ambulance parked, the lights on top flashing but no siren going; a subway rumbled underfoot, passing beneath a grating and leaving in its wake a blast of train-breath. But when I looked over at her, I saw that her eyes were raised to the windows of the skyscrapers, and she was right: it was a sight, no less so for the fact that I'd been living under it all my life. I remember my first time here, she said. I asked her why she'd come, and she said, Well, I was giving a little talk at your university. Johnny never told you? But, yes, I did. The very same one you are attending. There was a professor there, and her husband, who had been a dean. They must be long gone, but they were very good to me. It was right after my husband was killed, she said. For some time thereafter, I took up his mantle, yes? It was expected of me. She laughed a bit. I was so . . . prim in those days, prim and proper, and younger than my years. I had two sons at home, you see, but I was just a schoolgirl inside. My husband had quite spoiled me. And then after he died I was expected to travel around the world, speaking for him. Not as him, you see, but for him. And this city, you know, when I first arrived I was quite overwhelmed. You can imagine, she said, though in truth it was hard for me to imagine her being overwhelmed by anything at all. But everyone was so kind to me, and very quickly I started to feel at home. I think in another life I must have been a New Yorker. And now—she took Johnny affectionately by his upper arm—I have an excuse to visit whenever I want.

Johnny had chosen a French restaurant, one of those quiet places with interchangeable names that dotted the Upper East Side: Le Quelque Chose, with starched white tablecloths and dim lighting—the kind of restaurant where they spent more effort on placing the silverware and announcing the house specialties and fussing over water glasses and butter plates than they did on the food itself, though to be sure I was no gourmet, and Johnny's mother was perfectly happy with the place. The waiter came by and asked if we wanted drinks. Not for me, thank you, said Johnny's mother. I waited to see what Johnny would do, and when he ordered a glass of red wine, I asked for the same. Ah, she said. What is the age, then? — Eighteen, said Johnny. I can never remember, she said.

I saw Johnny start, and wondered what he was about to say; possibly something about the reach of the state in modern times, its role in the delineation of societal mores; possibly just a joke about how I, being Irish, had been drinking whiskey since I was seven. In any case, he stopped himself, she either didn't notice or pretended not to, and for the following minutes she engaged me in what I recognized only later was a kind of interview, though I don't know if it was out of genuine interest, polite conversation-making, or a test to see what kind of people her son was associating with. She wanted to know what I was studying, not just the department but the details, and when I faltered over the subject of my dissertation, she graciously turned the topic. She asked me what it was like to grow up in Manhattan, whether I'd found it frightening, what I did for fun or vacation, whether I'd had dinner with my family every night; and when I was done she said, I do wish Johnny would get out more. Enjoy himself, not spend all of his time studying. Will you take him to one of these clubs? Though she had only the faintest of accents, she'd once again pronounced his name in an odd, muddled way. We both looked at Johnny; he looked back at us both. I know he's here to learn, she said, but part of learning is getting to know the people, don't you think?

I was still trying to puzzle out what she had called him when Johnny said, Mother, he doesn't know me by that name.

Well, I don't know why not, she said. It's the name your father and I gave you. She turned to me. What do you call him, then?

Johnny, I said, feeling a bit silly.

No, no, said Johnny's mother. No, Dieudonné, you see? She pronounced it again, more slowly. It means *given by God,* in French. It's a very traditional name, and I've always thought it was lovely. I don't know why he refuses to use it.

Because, said Johnny calmly, sensibly, and with I don't know what in his heart. No one here can pronounce it.

She was neither put off nor dismayed, but she was puzzled. It's a perfectly good name, she said. You should teach them.

He nodded. I got the impression that this was a common form of exchange between them, the stubborn son rehearsing his eccentric authority before his stately mother, who demonstrates her approval by the mildness of her complaints. Well, you can't expect me to call you that, she said cheerfully. She reached over and touched his hand, gently, affectionately, but also as a form of ownership, as if to say, Whoever you are, and whatever you're doing, remember that you are mine. It was a winning response, both very delicate and very powerful. I could see, then, why the dinner had been important to him, and why it had made him anxious: he was revealing to me at one and the same time his weakness and his strength, his anger and his tenderness, and I could see both in his expression.

The rest of the dinner was thankfully less fraught, made up mostly of small, generous talk. At the end of the night, as we were walking her back to her hotel, Johnny's mother took me by the arm and let me squire her down the sidewalk; and in the lobby she thanked me for coming all the way down to Midtown to have dinner and for being a friend to her Dieudonné, and I thanked her for inviting me, and hoped that I would see her again. There was a bit of business between her and Johnny as they were parting—I held back to give them some privacy—and when he came away from her and joined me his face was quite blank. I don't know what they said, but he had a twenty-dollar bill that she had given him for cab fare. We were quiet on the way home. We crossed Central Park, each of us looking out of opposite windows at the silent, skeletal trees, until we reached the lights of Columbus.

That went well, I said. He didn't respond, but when we reached 116th Street, he got out with me, and he waited until the cab had driven away before he spoke. His hands were jammed into the pockets of his jacket. I want to thank you, he said to me.

I cocked my head in curiosity. You're welcome, I said. For what?

For coming out this evening.

It was a pleasure, I said.

Was it? he said. He was looking at me intently.

Yes, I said. Of course it was.

He nodded, started to say something else, and then thought better of it. I waited a moment to see if he was sure, but he just clapped me on the shoulder and said, Good night.

There was a trio of undergraduate girls sitting on a bench on the median; one of them surreptitiously sipped from a large bottle with a red label, then handed it to the next, who hid it between her legs and glanced at me darkly as I passed. I could hear the train conductor on the platform below announcing something, I couldn't tell what. The red light on the corner seemed to be stuck, so I cut through the traffic and then turned north, choosing quiet Broadway over quieter

Claremont, stopping for a pack of cigarettes and a few cans of beer, one of which I drank shivering on the stoop, thinking about Johnny, who had so many choices and so few: the whole world was his school, but none of it was his home. He was doomed to wander, and never mind that he'd wander from one capital to another, from one splendid university to the next; that he'd be met at the airport by people he didn't know, who would shake his hand warmly and ask him thoughtful questions on the ride into town. I found it enviable; I found it horrifying. I went upstairs at around eleven, missing Bridget, and drank the second beer in the blue light of a black-and-white television, putting cigarette after cigarette out in a cereal bowl that I had left uncleaned after breakfast.

I came home from class the next day and found Bridget sitting in the hallway outside our door: she had lost her keys somewhere along the way. She scrambled to her feet when I stepped off the elevator, ran toward me in her stompy black motorcycle boots, and literally leapt into my arms, laughing hard, she took my face in her hands, her hair falling all around, I could smell her cherry chewing gum and hairspray. Did you miss me? she said, and before I could answer she kissed me, lapping at my lips like a cat. Baltimore had been so much fun, it had been so great, running around with her friends, museums and parties. It was just what she needed, she had forgotten that there was life outside the city, out past the headlines and the hustling, away from everything. She had come to understand something that she hadn't understood before, though she didn't know how to explain what it was.

On Thursday, amid bare trees and along windy sidewalks, I went to my department's holiday party. These were drab and dreary affairs, more or less obligatory, which began in the slant-light of late afternoon and ended in the sudden darkness of evening. On a table in one corner of the seminar room there was an elaborate samovar filled with tea, and a few china plates with an assortment of dry biscuits arrayed upon them in weary semicircles.

By then I was almost done with my coursework, which gave me a kind of status—the sort, anyway, that compelled a first-year student to take me aside beforehand and confess that he was having a miserable time of it. He had come from Notre Dame and he didn't belong, and he was ever falling behind on his work. He asked me if it got better and I lied to him without hesitation, until he thanked me for the reassurances and then made a quick round of the room and headed home to study.

For reasons I never could fathom, Bridget found these sorts of things more enjoyable than I did and often came along with me; by then she was well-known and well-liked, and she would often wander off on her own to chatter with whomever: the professors, their wives (they were all wives: of the two female faculty members, one was either single or very private, and the other was a widow), other students and staff. But we had argued that evening, and she'd decided to stay home.

I left the department at nightfall and stopped to buy a bottle of wine, which cost more than we could afford. She was reading in the living room. I asked her if she wanted a drink, and she said, No, without looking up. I thought she was acting sullen, but when I went to the kitchen and turned on the light, I realized that it was me. It had struck me quite suddenly, the way only the most obvious things can: I didn't like school, I hadn't liked it in some time, I wasn't sure if I'd ever really enjoyed it, and I was going to finish my coursework and then drop out. I was exhausted from the quarreling city, and tired of being broke. I sat in the kitchen and finished the bottle, neither quickly nor slowly, but with great deliberation.

Bridget, too, had lost the joy she'd felt a few days earlier, and that was the last joy she would have to spend on me. Instead, she was distracted and unhappy; she undressed for bed as if she was disrobing for a doctor, shivered once, and then crawled beneath the covers. She was wearing her favorite best underwear, the ones I'd bought for her a few months earlier, after I'd torn off two cheaper pairs on two successive nights, but she immediately presented me with her back, which I stroked softly, feeling the knuckles of her spine rising and falling under my fingertips: she didn't respond. I stopped and turned away from her, and she was up on her elbow, hovering over me. Mike. I turned my head to look at her, and she kept perfectly still, breathing shallowly. Mike. Mike. I didn't answer her: Would all of this have been different if I had? They say there's always another world. Wave if you can hear me, Bridget.

When I told her, a few days later, that I was leaving the program, she was shocked. Was I leaving her too? No, I said, not at all: but I was changing. She responded with a mistrust so profound and varied that I could hardly grasp it, let alone reassure her, and I quickly grew weary of trying. In the days that followed she presented me with a new rumor or two—one involving a tryst I was supposed to have had with an ex-girlfriend in an empty classroom in broad daylight, and another that ended with a night in the Tombs. Neither was true. Did you spend a part of your first-year fellowship on prostitutes? Girls you picked up on the street corner and paid, they would do whatever you wanted. And you put your thing in me, that had been in them.

Where are you getting this from?

People, she said. Are you lying to me?

. . .

Hookers? said Bridget. Mike?

Yes, I said sarcastically. I'm lying.

This time, at least, she told me where they'd come from: she'd run into my old roommate Dominic on the street, and they'd sat on the median for a little while and talked. A few weeks later I saw him in the supermarket and asked him what he'd said to her, and he insisted that he hadn't said anything at all, except for the bit about the fistfight, and then only because he thought it flattered me. He was quite bothered about the rest, and convincingly so, leaving me to wonder if she was making it up to try to throw me off-balance, or worse, so that she would have me to blame for whatever needed blaming, or worse still, because she believed I was so readily faithless and foolish. The earlier anthology of these transgressions of mine had given her pause, but the pause had passed with no damage left behind. These new ones, she said, upset her much more, and began to spin out into vague but powerful suspicions, based on trivial evidence: the smell of perfume in my hair just because I happened to be in an elevator in Philosophy Hall with a woman who was wearing too much, my name overheard in someone else's conversation. (There are lots of guys named Mike, I pointed out. They meant you, she said. I know they did.) It sounds like madness, but I'm not sure that it was. It was a bad time, and the days were getting dark. I was weary of defending myself, and insulted by her inability or unwillingness to take my smile as a smile. So I became cold and critical about little things, about nothing. Did she really need to lock the door after I left, even if I was just going to the corner for a pack of cigarettes? Could she decide more quickly whether she was going down to the basement to do laundry? It used to be cute when she played keep-away with her kisses, but it wasn't anymore, and I turned away. That made her angry: that made her cry. The old system was quickly breaking down, it only took a week or two, and there was no new system to take its place.

I know she went to Johnny, who listened to her with all the patience and kindness he could bear, to make up for the fact that I, the indicted one, was becoming increasingly incapable of either. She came back from each session with him calmer and more confident, if a little dazed, like a woman after a seizure, missing, slow, and with a little smile that was tinged with death. I had no idea what they talked about, or even if I was always a significant part of it. In any case, I was certain he said nothing against me. He didn't think all was fair in war, either.

The end came swiftly, and it was more sordid than ceremonial. We had taken a weekend apart; I went upstate with a high school friend to stay at his parents' country house. It was late in January, and there would be fresh snow on the hills, hard contrails in the sky, and the kind of quiet only other people could buy, but Bridget didn't want to go. She was still acclimating to her new classes, she said; there was an exhibit of Indian silks at the Met that she wanted to see. She wore the passive, defiant expression of a small child dragging in a grocery store, and I was accordingly irritated and tried to reason with her: she could read on the bus, the exhibit had just opened and would be up for weeks. — You can't make me go, she said, an assertion that allowed for no reply, since it was obviously true and obviously irrelevant. — You can't make me stay, I said, and finally I left her there, sitting on our broken couch, looking deliberately out the back window as I walked out the front door.

I took a bus upstate, and as soon as we passed the Cloisters I began to feel better. The weather was perfect, with that curious smell of burnt rubber and apples in the air. And it's true I met a woman up there, black-haired and pink as an April moon, a friend of my friend who'd decided to join us at the last minute. She had just gotten her first real job, as an assistant to an editor at a newsmagazine. We sat on the porch and drank and talked, and we walked into town together the next day, where we spent a happy hour shopping for groceries; halfway home she made me stop so she could pluck a burr from the sleeve of my jacket. If sin or infidelity consists, as the Jesuits taught me, in desire as much as deed, then perhaps I sinned; but the deed wasn't done. No touch, no kiss, I slept alone. I don't know why, it wasn't entirely virtue on my part, though I had a little of that. An equal part was simply that I didn't know who I was. The woman's telephone number wound up scrawled on the first page of a book I'd brought with me, above the copyright and under her name, but I thought of it more as a souvenir than as an invitation.

When I arrived back home, on a cool, sharp Sunday evening, Bridget was waiting for me, sitting at the kitchen table, one hand toying with the small silver bracelet on her other wrist, and a choked look on her pretty face. She didn't dissemble, she didn't even wait for me to ask. She had gone out for coffee with one of her TAs; it had turned into dinner, then drinks, and then she'd spent the night with him.

I looked around the apartment, and we had very little: a white-painted wooden table that she'd brought over from the last place she'd lived, a chest of drawers I'd found on the street, a pile of cheap shoes on the floor, some books and an old typewriter, take-out menus, yesterday's newspaper wedged into the cushions of a worn blue couch. A sticky jar of honey on the kitchen counter, a pair of ashtrays, both full, beside it. It wasn't much of a home and it wouldn't be much to leave. You would have done it if I didn't, she said. But I hadn't, and all I could manage was a shake of my head. For a long time neither of us said anything. I gave her a few more minutes to explain, to blame me or defend herself, but she was speechless: instead, she played with her bracelet a little more attentively. Her silence was more painful to me than anything she could have said, more final, in its way, than her betrayal. What do you want me to say? I asked, but she had no answer to that. What do we do now? She said nothing, I stood up, and she looked at me with tears in her eyes and a fixed, anticipatory expression, as if she was expecting me to hit her, or smash some dishes. She wasn't afraid—I think she was hoping I would, because she needed to hear the sound of something breaking; and in fact as I was leaving I heard her take something—a glass, a plate—and dash it on the kitchen floor.

I took a taxi downtown, let myself into my sleeping parents' apartment, wrote a short note that I left on the kitchen table, drank a half-bottle of my father's whiskey, and finally fell asleep in my old bedroom, fully clothed and on top of the covers. After that, I spent a few nights at a friend's apartment on the Lower East Side, drinking too much and generally making a nuisance of myself. At last I called Bridget. We started out angry, then we both cried a bit, but just a bit and on the telephone. Then she pretended to be fine, so I pretended to be fine. I'm going to find another place to live, I said. It may take me a week or two. When I do, I'll come get my things.

OK, she said softly, and she could have been wearing any expression. I don't remember going by the apartment, but I must have; I'm sure she wasn't there, and I took very little. I moved downtown, and when school finished that spring, I left the program.

Bridget and I lived in the same city for more than fifteen years after that, but I never saw her again, never spotted her on the street or ran into her at a party, on a subway platform, in a park, at a bar. Johnny and I resumed our friendship, but on a tempered and attenuated basis; once I moved, it was harder for us to get together, and when it became clear that I wasn't going to finish my degree, we had less to talk about. Only once did Bridget's name come up, the following spring. He'd taken a bus all the way downtown to meet me in a restaurant in the West Village; he was dressed in a well-cut suit and a white dress shirt open at the neck. We spoke of his mother, of his research, of an article in a policy magazine about natural resources in Nigeria; and then he said, By the way, have you heard from Bridget? I told him I hadn't, not since the previous winter. He lowered his head. I think she's having a hard time, he said. I changed the subject.

One screaming cold and whomping drunk night, nine months later, I dialed directory assistance and then called the number they gave me from a telephone booth on the corner of Houston and Bowery, and listened to the empty line ring and ring and ring.

It was Bridget herself who showed me the letters. I was in my thirties then, and living down on Barrow Street with R., the woman who is now my wife and the mother of my children. In the intervening years, my friendship with Johnny had dwindled down to an e-mail every so often; and each time I contacted him I had to find him all over again, following him through appointments, visiting professorships, and fellowships at think tanks as he moved his way up from his first job, at the American University in Cairo, to Stanford, and then to the École Normale Supérieure in Paris. He was an inverse souvenir, traveling the world while I stayed in New York.

Then there was a morning when R. came back from an errand and dropped a handful of mail on the kitchen table, including the yellow slip for a package that couldn't be delivered—as, indeed, no package ever was, because our mailbox was the size of a paperback book, and besides, all the locks had been jimmied open years before by junkies looking for Social Security checks to steal. I picked the slip up and R. shrugged. She was wearing a red-and-white striped top, and she had her hair in a ponytail that had come partly undone. I was here when the mailman came, I said. If he buzzed, I didn't hear it. She smiled ruefully. Our mailman was an overweight man with tiny eyes and grey skin, who disliked everyone and hated us.

The next morning I went up to the little post office on Hudson, only to be told that whatever it was I'd received was being held at the larger station on Varick, where I waited in line for an hour and a half before discovering that it was out for delivery again. — Did you sign the card and leave it for the mailman? the surly woman behind the counter asked me. It came just yesterday, I said. It says here that you're holding it for pickup. The woman stared at me as if I alone stood between her and contentment. You can try back tomorrow, she said. I left, passing a gulag line of penitents and beggars. Fortunately, I arrived back at my apartment just as the mailman was leaving, and when I showed him the slip, he examined it carefully, noted that I hadn't signed it, asked for my ID, and then finally turned over a small box, wrapped in floral paper, sealed tightly with transparent tape, and addressed in a handwriting that I recognized immediately. The very sight of it made me pause, puzzled, and then suddenly suspended in a solution of memories.

The package was still sitting unopened on the kitchen counter when R. came home that afternoon. What is it? she said. I don't know. It came from an old girlfriend of mine, Bridget, I told you about her.

Was she the Puerto Rican woman with the ex-husband who was a cop?

Cuban, and it was her brother, and no, I said. Bridget and I lived together for a year or so when I was in graduate school.

Well, go on and open it, she said. R. was mildly curious about my past, and occasionally surprised by it, but she never took it personally. So far as she was concerned, the real Mike had been born the moment she started loving me, and before that there had been no more than unformed clay.

The box was wrapped like a gift, and carried the same tremble of mystery and anticipation, and the faint hesitant fear that one will be disappointed. When the paper was off I found a small, glossy navy blue cardboard box, tied with a thin white ribbon. R. made a small noise, part intrigue and part concern. I felt the same, and for a second I considered the possibility that there was something terrible inside, the product of years' worth of gathered fury. I was going to suggest to R. that she step into the other room, or out of the apartment entirely, but when I looked at her she just raised her eyebrows and nodded at me to go ahead.

Inside, I found another box, this one ochre and tattered, as if it had been opened and closed many times, or carried on a long journey. Taped carefully to the top there was an unaddressed envelope, and inside that a note. I have the whole assemblage here beside me. She wrote:

> Hey, little boy, it's been a while, hasn't it? You're probably not so little anymore.
>
> It took me some time to find you. I hope you don't mind hearing from me. We had some trouble there at the end, I know. I don't think I ever told you that I was sorry, so: I'm sorry. Late, I know. I've always been late, and soon I'll be late again.
>
> I've been saving these for a long time, and now I don't know what to do with them. So I'm giving them to you, and you can keep them, or destroy them, or you can pass them on, whichever you decide. I never thought you were as bad as I pretended you were, and I'm sure you'll make the right decision.
>
> Anyway, I'm doing well and I hope you are too.
>
> Here's a couple of kisses, one for each cheek:
>
> x   x
>
> Bridget

That was all she had to say, and it wasn't true, she wasn't doing well at all, but I didn't know that. What I knew was that a time must have come for her; she would have been thinking about sending me this box, she would have written and rewritten her letter, paring it down until it said almost nothing. She would have wrapped it up and put it to one side, waiting. Anything at all might have inspired her: a death in her family, a month of remembrance, the discovery of an old photograph, a conversation with a friend, a man barely glimpsed who was wearing a black suede jacket like the one I used to wear. She didn't tell me; she never would have. I took the box to the table.

Inside there were several stacks of letters, nestled side by side, the sheets hastily folded and entangled, in contrast to the neatness of the package they had come in. There were scores, hundreds of pages; a book of love, want, honor, and grief. But who had written them? I had left her notes from time to time, mostly silly and affectionate things that I taped to the mirror in the bathroom. These weren't them, they were in postmarked envelopes mailed from New York to New York. I picked up one: it was dated the summer Bridget and I started living together, but addressed to her box in the college mailroom, where she stopped every so often to pick up administrative material and her check from the playwright. Then it was him? That elderly man whose marriage she'd once described as different but perfect? *My darling*, it began, and I stopped there, mystified. The handwriting was precise and elegant, in a way that seemed schooled and old-fashioned, and the language was slightly archaic, with the kind of ungainly formality which can be very beautiful if the heart behind it is large enough. *My love, my breath, my future.* But why would she send them to me? At the bottom of the page, it was signed *Johnny*. The planet underfoot was spinning and stopping, spinning and stopping again.

The next letter was even higher, half-mad, besotted. *I feel as if I've been forsaken all my life, and will always be forsaken.*

Well? said R.

They're love letters, I said, a banal phrase that was inadequate to the depth and strangeness of the occasion.

Yours? she said, quietly. I shook my head. Hers? said R.

They're from my friend Johnny, I said. To her. *The rose, the lily, — the orchid, the most beautiful of them all.*

Why is she sending them to you?

I don't know. I haven't seen either of them in years.

She came to the table, hugged me from behind, glanced down at the sheet in my hands, and said, I'm going to go return some phone calls. I kissed her wrist and she left.

My thoughts divided into nauseated waves. I was shocked and shame-sick. He had written to her over and over, fashioning the letters by hand and carrying them, with who knows what nervous purpose, to the blue boxes in the college mailroom, wondering, as he did, if everyone was watching him, if he was being foolish, if he was being unfair. He wrote to her helplessly, shivering and crying out, joyous in his pain. He was a prince and a mendicant, a skin mystic, part animist and part courtly lover, and mostly singular, as if he was inventing a religion for her on the spot, with all its traditions and mores. He despaired, he sang, he complained, he became lighter than air and then heavy as a stone. Each letter was a lash, and after almost every one I thought of stopping, of folding them all back up and burning them in the bathtub, but I didn't stop, not for a little while. Instead I read through, turning.

Johnny hadn't dated the letters, though for some reason he'd put the day of the week on the top right of every first page; and Bridget hadn't kept them in any order. I began to try to organize it all, looking for repeating phrases, cryptic figures, front-to-back references, even as I shuddered and flinched. *This season of lights entangled in trees* must have meant Christmas. A sentence that mentioned *a newborn baby left on the altar of a church* was probably written the following March, when just that had happened in Harlem.

Others were more difficult to date. There was a reference to *your new home*, which could have been written around the time she moved in with me, or around the time I moved out. Another, claiming *that a blood red moon is most auspicious for tests of every sort*, might have been written anytime: I remember no such phenomenon, and it's not clear whether the tests he was talking about were school exams or something more personal. Then he would be overcome again and time-travel in pieces to someplace medieval, as if conveyed by passions that struck him like blows on a drunk: he was slow to see them coming and responded by falling to his knees, only to rise in time, looking the wrong way and finding himself knocked down again from a side that he hadn't seen. *You were brought to me, like a lamb carried by an overflowing river.* He must have started soon after we all met; his early references spoke of the cold, her distance, the bitter night. At other times he was calm, even sensible, offering her unaffected advice about her classes, about where to live and how. And then he would catch fire again and become hortatory, confessional, spendthrift, blue. *Shall I pursue life through to the end without ever feeling your breath on my face? That is unbearable to me, but what can I do except bear it?* As for the end, she apparently broke off contact with him a year or so after she and I split. He responded with two notes, one by turns stern and pleading, and the other repetitive and aggrieved, asking her why she had failed to show up for an assignation one afternoon and hadn't returned his calls since. There was nothing I could positively date after that.

Did he write about me? Very little, though he would offer her comfort, forgiveness, advice. It pained me to see how much she needed all three. But he never undermined me or tore me down; and nothing in the letters suggested that either of them had ever betrayed me with so much as a kiss. He was discreet, my friend Johnny, loyal, and instinctively dignified. His protests were all positive, adoring, chaste. *I do not believe that you can possibly be right in thinking he's repulsed by you,* he wrote in one letter, in response to what I can't say; and of course I never was, and was stunned to find that she thought otherwise. And then a further surprise: *You tell me he is breaking your heart, and you ask me what to do. I suggest to you that perhaps you simply think about him too much. You tell me you can't stop, and I sympathize: I am in the same position.* — Breaking her heart? Nothing she ever did or said to me indicated that she was suffering that way. It couldn't possibly be true, and if it was true, I couldn't possibly have known; and if I had known, I couldn't possibly have fixed what she herself had broken. At last Johnny wrote: *He's one of the lucky ones; he doesn't bear the burden of the future*, and that was surely true; but I was going to bear the burden of remembering.

I was embarrassed by the carelessness of my fortune, like a naive tourist surprised by a beggar. Then I was angry at Bridget: she had been cruel to him. She could have discouraged him if she wanted to. She must have needed him, she should have let him go. Johnny should have contained himself, he should have drawn a line. As for me, I had been the cruelest of all. I should have known how he felt; I should have known how unhappy she was. God knows, I was ill-equipped to take care of her, to minister to her insecurities and soothe her anger, especially since I was usually the one who brought them out of her. Bridget! who was racy and funny, and the best company when she wasn't in the worst mood, who struggled to believe in me, who was capricious, fearless, faithless, and proud. We were very young: Was that an excuse? Did I need an excuse? Someone would love her the way she wanted, someday, I was sure of that, but my thoughts were buzzing, distorted, and then they began to feed back, just a whine at first, gradually rising to a howl that was hard to control. I found myself confusing myself: maybe I was Johnny and I'd loved her, after all; maybe these were letters I myself had written, which she was sending back to me. *When I see you in my imagination, I see your eyes, your lips, floating over the treetops.* Maybe I had gradually come to lie to myself, over the anteceding years, until it covered my grief the way burled skin grows over a wound.

No. All around me there was the set dressing of my present life, the real one: magazines stacked on a chair, magnets affixed to the refrigerator, wineglasses in a drying rack by the sink, a box of laundry detergent. R. wandered back into the room, her hair down and her T-shirt rumpled. I guess I fell asleep, she said. What time is it? I had to check. Nearly dinner, I said, and began to box the letters up again. So? said R. She stepped into the bathroom to splash water on her face. Does she want you back? she called from across the hall. — No, I said. Not at all. Good, said R., now back in the room and kissing me with wash-cold lips. She can't have you. I closed the box and put it on the shelf in the hallway closet. Why did she send them to you?

This I couldn't answer. It was one of those acts that's so far outside the boundaries of ordinary conduct that one can't tell whether it's grotesquely immoral or virtuous on a level one can't comprehend. I didn't know what she wanted me to feel: And did she expect me to respond? She hadn't included a return address, so I had no way of knowing where she was, or where she'd last been. Did she want me to look for her?

My wife has the courting letters her grandfather wrote to her grandmother during the latter years of the War. She inherited them from her grandmother herself, just before the woman died; they were the founding documents of a sixty-year marriage that had eventually led to the bed in which she was conceived. But what of all those loves that miss their mark, those that were spurned, or unrecognized, or led to a broken or brief affair? And what about the words that were never written down, the sighs on the telephone, the shouts and tears? There must be millions just like Johnny. What happens to their ardor? Love completed becomes history at the least, family at the most, but love unstarted, or undone, is as volatile as acetone: powerful when it's pouring, but when it stops, it vanishes, leaving nothing but a sharp odor in the air, which itself is soon dissipated. Bridget had those letters and no one to give them to, so she gave them to me. Even now, from the vantage of my maturity, with my oldest child old enough to have had her heart broken, with the city so changed you'd think all of us were new to it; even now I'm sorry—not for the things I did, but for the things I was too crass and callow to notice.

A puzzle, if it be too much puzzle, makes a dunce. A decade passed before I discovered that Bridget had died, just a few months after she mailed me the package; and then I learned it only because I happened upon a picture of her in a book of photographs, an artful miscellany of the days that once were, which I found in a store on Prince Street one afternoon when I was waiting for my daughter, who was then in middle school, to finish her guitar lesson. Such a bright and colorful street, then; all the black-and-white had been buried, but there was Bridget, emerging from a halftone print, a slightly leering smile on her face as she sat at the banquette of some long-forgotten restaurant, grasping both a beer bottle and a cigarette with her right hand, while her left was brushing her hair back. Underneath was her name and below that her telephone number, which struck me as a curious thing to publish—until I looked closer and saw the faint, poorly printed smudge of an initial *1*, which turned seven digits into eight, a pair of years encompassing all the time there had ever been a Bridget. Then I felt something peculiar crawling between my shoulder blades, as I realized for the first time what I now take to be an immutable law of the universe: that any two things grow farther and farther apart over time, edging away from each other while facing in opposite directions. Later still, I would meet a man at a fundraiser for a local arts organization, who had known her in her running days and who told me, not without a witless satisfaction, that he'd always known she wasn't going to last, that girls like that seldom do—though when I asked him what girls like that were like, he caught my tone, or perhaps my posture, and said, Oh, I don't know.

I have spent some time thinking about those ever-branching worlds, the ones that exist only in might-have-been, where Bridget and I had never met, or having met as we did, had felt no attraction to each other, or had felt something but had no opportunity to act on it; where she hadn't passed by the window of the coffee shop that snowy day when I sat waiting for her; or where we'd loved each other honestly and enough that we could stay together longer, even to the ends of our lives; or alternately, if she had loved Johnny instead of me; or again, if she'd disliked him enough to discourage him from wanting her so badly; again, if she had taken better care, if her immune system had been more composed and ready, if that pathogen hadn't found a home behind her glorious pale skin, slowly smothering her, leaving her wasting at the age of twenty-nine (the life spoiling, spilling, unused); if Johnny hadn't loved her still, perhaps more than ever, as a man will sometimes love a memory; if he hadn't discovered that she'd died, severing his ties with a more innocent society, one where love was the heavenly thing, leaving him cast out, with no equity in this world; if he had been in New York, where he could grieve in a city where grief had taken up residence in every building, occupying them like a shadow severed from the body that had formed it (to me he belongs to New York, and always will); if, indeed, he hadn't watched from his Paris home as the times grew so parlous and untenable in his ruinous West African home, with its madman playing President-for-Life, its frail economy, and incursions from a neighboring country perforating the border—a place he barely knew, though he had spent his life in filial obedience to it; if he hadn't fallen in with a group of young men, who together had grown angrier, more desperate, more proud; if he hadn't been charismatic enough to rise to a position of leadership—Johnny with his flawless English, his passable French, his rudimentary Arabic, and his American nickname; with his education and his military service; and his pedigree, his self-possession, his compelling intelligence, and his charm. In the course of his communiqués to the outside world, he's mentioned Bridget only once by name, but identified her as *the cause of my cause.*

He's changed considerably, or else they have him all wrong. Or perhaps it's both. I can't say. Somewhere along the line he became an American citizen, even as he reverted to his given name (the newspapers call him what his mother called him: Dieudonné) and married an Eritrean woman who waits for him now in Rome. He has a twelve-year-old son. Wife and child were left behind while he pursued his campaign, which seems to have been something between a run for office and an attempted coup: they announced his candidacy just a few days before the elections, managed to win or take over a few radio stations, had talks with a troika of generals whom they hoped might support them. The whole thing might have been heroic, had it had even a slender chance of succeeding. He was arrested on Election Day morning. His trial was the next day and lasted eighteen minutes.

I can imagine him, sitting in some dark, well-guarded jail cell, I can sense the stink of the place, the dampness of the rainy season condensing on the bars, punishments past and punishments to come squatting heavily on the air. I can imagine him calmly reading Vico, say, or perhaps a volume of Rilke, to while away the hours between beatings and the days before his execution. In the meantime, the State Department has registered a stern protest, the French have made an effort to get him freed by diplomatic means, and a consortium of supporters, composition unclear, is rumored to have raised a considerable sum to ransom him home. All have been rebuffed. I now believe our government must have needed him for something, though I don't know what. Some value had accrued to him in the years since I'd known him: rare skills, important friends. A few nights ago, when the Atlantic sky was blotted with clouds, an American Special Forces team attempted a surreptitious rescue, coming in low over the border from an airfield in the nation next door. It ended in disaster when the moon, at the very last minute, broke through, and their helicopter was shot down by local forces with shoulder-mounted missiles. Outside my window, New York trips along, parti-colored as a felted jester, the air smells of car exhaust and fresh bread, the sky overhead is decorated with snowy contrails, and my old friend is scheduled to die on Thursday.

THE LATE HOUR

One afternoon, perhaps three months after she and Benny had started dating, Jillian brought her brother Mickey into the store. It was difficult to believe they had the same parents. For one thing, he was just five feet tall, a half-foot shorter than she was and a full ten inches shorter than Benny, though it was hard to tell whether he'd suffered some sort of birth defect or simply a misfortune, which had left him small and strange, with hair that looked like a black toupee and pinched features. He had an odd sort of stuttering walk, too: he moved abruptly, a flurry of handflapping as he talked, his head bobbing from side to side. He was always in motion, it was hard to imagine him sleeping; he was always standing up, sitting down again, gesturing with his hands, touching his face as if he were trying to reassure himself that he was still there, looking this way, that way, bending down to retie the shoelaces on his small brown dress shoes. It may have been a way of keeping people from looking at him too closely, or it may have been a symptom of some misfire in his mind; or perhaps there was nothing wrong with him at all, aside from being born a bit off, his life like a game of hide-and-seek in which no one bothers to try to find the thing that's been hidden. In any case it became clear at once why Jillian loved him so much; he was a little damaged thing, a nervous creature, constantly scrabbling to hang on to whatever he could find. He must have been in his thirties, though he looked at once older and younger than that—older by the wear in his expression and a shrewdness in his eyes—younger because of the swiftness of his tics, his reflexes still fresh.

He always wore slacks and a shirt and tie, and over them a satin warm-up jacket like the ones baseball players wore. He must have owned just two or three pairs of pants, all of them black, and about as many white shirts, or perhaps he had more but they were identical; and he had two ties, one black knit and one club striped in blue and white, which he wore on alternating days. But he appeared to have an endless supply of the jackets, all in different colors: red ones and black ones, and colors known only to sports teams and car manufacturers: teal, sherbet green, canary. Some of them had writing on the back: a plumbing business in Queens, a storage company, a Catholic high school, a law firm, a chain of dermatology clinics. So far as Benny could tell, he never wore the same one twice.

Mickey had just finished up his degree at an accounting school whose campus was the eighth floor of a building down on Chambers Street. What he had been doing until then was a mystery, something Jillian could not be coaxed into discussing. There was a gap in their history, a decade or so missing, a time when they seemed to have done little more than survive; but then, Benny had been much the same, and for an even longer period of time. Indeed, the more he came to know her, to anticipate her visits, her happy entrance, her presence stretching like a narcotic fog to all the corners of the shop and hanging back for a few minutes after she left, like some drizzle of the senses, a creature unto itself, the more he came to believe that he and Jillian had this in common: that they had been asleep for decades, and were just now beginning to wake. Yes, and just like waking on any morning, it was slow and confusing and even a little bit uncomfortable; and yet they were waking.

Now that he had graduated, Mickey started coming into the store regularly, though always with Jillian, whom he squired with great pride, as if she were a movie star and he her chauffeur. If this was her boyfriend's place, well, he had to come see what it was all about, didn't he? He had to look into it. This is all African stuff?

Yes, that's right.

All this stuff? Really? Made by African people? You brought it all the way from over there?

It was sent to me, most of it, he explained. There are dealers all around the world, you see, and we trade with each other, trying to anticipate what our clients will want.

Nice, nice. You got a lot of it here. You got more in the back? He smoothed his pants with his hands.

Inventory, yes, he said.

OK if I go back there? He started toward the door to the storage area.

Mickey, said Jillian. Why don't you stay up here with us.

He turned immediately and walked back to his sister's side. What do you keep it all back there for? he asked.

Some of the artifacts aren't ready, said Benny. They need to be cleaned or restored. Repaired. Some of them are duplicates.

Artifacts, said Mickey.

Things, said Benny, and Mickey nodded.

How much is it all worth?

Mickey, said Jillian.

Oh, I don't know, Benny said. I really don't.

Jillian smiled as if this was exactly the answer she was hoping for, and Mickey raised his eyebrows in an expressive and unexpectedly intelligent way. Later that night, Jillian apologized for her brother: he had always been a good boy, smart, really smart, but no one had given him a chance. He had a hard time of it, she said. You can tell just by looking at him. She had been sitting in the blue armchair in his living room, her legs folded under her, her lipstick slightly smeared, as if her lips had left a faint trail of themselves on her mouth. And, to be honest, she said, he made a few mistakes, like anyone else.

Well, she was touched by fragile things, that was part of her beauty, and she was fragile herself. She was the kind of woman who wept furiously when a horse broke its leg in a race on TV, who cooed at other people's babies, bending down with one arm pressed against her chest, tucking her hair behind her ear, her full attention focused on the child. Once, when they were still clothed and talking on his bed past midnight, he had slowly unbuttoned her shirt, unhooked her bra, and taken her nipple in his mouth, holding it gently in his teeth while he breathed in the soft peaty scent of her perspiring breast—held it until the nub grew, like a pebble emerging from a garden, held it until she cried out softly, and by the time he'd let it drop and went to kiss her, he found her cheek wet with hot tears. He hadn't said anything: What could he say? It was late.

He wanted to know how late, exactly; he found himself calculating, unwisely but he couldn't help himself, how much longer they might have, according to this or that variable. His father had died of a heart attack in his late fifties; if he inherited that weakness, there would only be a few years left, really. Hardly a significant portion of his life. If, on the other hand, he lived to be ninety or even one hundred ... He developed a habit of jotting numbers down on a piece of paper, adding a decade because he neither smoked nor drank to excess, subtracting four or five years because he ate badly, another two because he rarely went to the doctor for a checkup, plus three for having a safe job, minus three for having a sedentary one—always revising, like a poor man with a little stock portfolio, best case, worst case; provisional numbers and counterfactual scenarios. What if he never ate sugar again, what if he drank a glass of red wine a day, if he took up some sort of exercise, or vitamins, or meditation, what if his father had died later, of something else? What if he and Jillian loved each other so much they lived forever? Once, she had come upon these morbid exercises scrawled on a sheet of paper that he'd left on his dresser. What's this? she had asked. The arithmetic of regret, he wanted to say, but instead he had told her he was trying to date a prayer bowl he'd recently acquired.

He had spent his whole life buried in dust; he'd rescued everything but himself. Look at these things, arrayed in their boxes and cases, all of them having survived their makers. Here was a Tuareg veil weight, an exquisite thing, layered in metals that must have taken lifetimes just to mine. He held it with one hand and stroked it with the other, feeling the pieces slither over his fingers, listening to the clicking sound it made, the rhythm of a people who thought that they were the whole world. Here was a mask that turned anyone who wore it into a spirit. When he'd first started collecting, twenty years previously, he'd found them merely engaging; but as he'd aged and the years had passed, first singly, then in bunches of two and three and five, he'd come to see how otherworldly and complex they were, and he considered himself fortunate to be able to spend his days surrounded by such magical stuff, getting it and letting it go. Now, suddenly, he wanted to keep everything.

Jillian didn't understand what he did all day, not at first; she was covetous of his attention and slightly confused by the idea that a man could spend so much time buying and selling what, in all innocence and without the slightest malice, she called Old Black People Things. He'd considered sitting her down and trying to teach her, but decided instead to let her work it out, and so she had. No one came to these things easily, and at first she'd been unclear about the relationship between the black people she saw every day and the various African tribes and nations; but then, most people were. Every so often kids from the East River projects would stop in, shy and curious if they were alone, laughing uncomfortably if they were in a group, glancing at him as they circled the vitrines; but the elderly Italians in the neighborhood ignored him, as did the Jewish merchants over on Orchard and the Chinese to the south, and the young white couples who drifted by. Of the millions, there were perhaps a score whose depth of knowledge and care matched his own—a Hunter College professor, a curator or two, and some collectors—and another thirty or forty who understood a little, and trusted him enough to buy from him. Jillian wanted to know, but it was difficult. He tried to explain some of the distinctions to her—what came from Ghana, what from Nigeria, the symbolic difference between wood and ivory and bronze and brass, between fetishes and bowls and jewelry. She couldn't follow all that, but she had an innate capacity for delight that was, if anything, more like the original makers' than his own feelings were. Then what had she seen in him? He should have asked her, back when he still could—asked her what she'd found when she found him.

By then they were spending four or five nights a week together, always at his apartment, where they could be alone. Just like that, a couple, and only now and then did she leave before he woke, though he never knew when, and the uncertainty made him wonder, night after night, if she would be there in the morning; and he never again slept quite as fully as he had when he slept alone, because there was an anxious tugging on his slumber. And on those occasions when morning broke and she was gone, he'd bolt from the bed as if it was cursed, dress hurriedly, and go immediately over to the store, where he'd wait for her to come back to him. Until he found her, a day meant nothing, it was a measure of nothing: he could spend a fortnight waiting for a check to show up in the mail; months for a package to arrive from a dealer in Tunis; years for a fetish or statue he coveted to appear in a catalog; but if Jillian was missing from one night to the next he could hardly tell who he was. Still, she never did offer to explain why she sometimes found it impossible to spend the night, and he didn't ask.

In the same way, she never invited him to see where she lived, or for that matter on what; he assumed it was her father's death benefits, but he didn't know for sure. She didn't work, though she once had; at least, she'd mentioned being a receptionist, somewhere, somewhen. Perhaps she found it all embarrassing, or perhaps she was frightened. It couldn't have been easy, being a single woman at her age, with little education and no apparent skills beyond her charm. He would have liked to have reassured her, but there was something in her manner that prevented him from trying—reticence, but more than reticence, perhaps a propriety, and beyond that, too, her taste for living in a spun and crystal world, as enchanted as raindrops on a spider's web, at once ductile and delicate, so that a breeze would bring it to life, but a wind would destroy it.

Jillian didn't have to ask; it was so obvious, it could hardly have been a surprise to her, but she treated it like a present, and one night, when the three of them went to dinner at the small Italian place on Mulberry Street, she wore a daring red silk blouse. He remembered the date: it was February, the night of Ash Wednesday, and she'd called him at the last minute and said, Honey, do you mind if my brother joins us? Mickey had been waiting at the bar when they came in, perched on a barstool with one leg folded up beneath him while he chattered at the bartender, an elderly man who was polishing martini glasses and pretending to listen. Naw, Mickey was saying, do you think you can make money shorting a company that big? Naw, never happen. Never happen. He had his hands jammed in the pockets of his jacket, and he was rocking back and forth so quickly that he looked like a little toy. Jillian sucked in her breath, hurried over to him and said, Mickey, what are you doing up there?

I'm talking to this man, he said. Explaining how to trade on credit. The bartender looked at the three of them with no expression at all. Come down, said Jillian.

At the table, Mickey couldn't sit still, though the motions he made were often subtle, blinking behind his glasses, twisting his napkin in his fingers, rearranging his silverware. It was contagious, it made Jillian flutter in her seat, which in turn made Mickey fuss with his table setting some more; but in time they both settled and Mickey began to talk. Are you English? he asked Benny.

No—why do you ask?

I thought you were English, Mickey said. Where are you from?

Well, I've lived here most of my life, he had replied. But I was born and raised in Arizona.

Mickey found this unlikely, somehow. — Arizona? Seriously?

That's right.

Why there?

That's where my parents lived.

Mickey found this even more improbable. What were they doing there?

My father was a schoolteacher in Phoenix, he said. — Well, actually, by the time I was born he was an administrator.

Administrator, said Mickey. That means he ran things? He rose up in his chair a bit, rearranged his legs, and settled down again.

Help to run things, yes, Benny said.

The whole city?

It wasn't much of a city, not back then, he said. It's grown quite a bit in the past decades.

So you go back there, to Arizona?

No, he said. My parents died some time ago.

Mickey nodded vehemently. That happened to me too, he said. — How did you get into all this? Did you go to Africa and everything?

I have been there, yes, but it was long after I first started selling these sorts of things.

The retail life, right? said Mickey.

That's right.

The business of America is business, right?

Right, yes.

The invisible hand writes, and then moves on. — Here Mickey appeared to have confused two separate apothegms, but they made just enough sense together that there was no need to correct him. His enthusiasm was endearing, really. Jillian was right: he brought out something protective, this strange little man-child, this sober and serious homunculus, rocking from side to side and uttering his garbled maxims with such certainty that it was hard not to hope that he would someday succeed at whatever it was he wanted. Yes, he must have had a terribly difficult time. But pity was not the proper reaction, Mickey must have experienced more pity in his lifetime than he could possibly bear; by now he deserved some kind of understanding, sympathy, some patience and even respect. He was fascinated by the store, it was the first real business he'd ever seen up close, and he had a lot of ideas. And in truth, Benny himself had never been much of a businessman—for what are the profits of days like his? He'd been worrying lately that he was going to need at least a little bit more to make Jillian feel secure, and besides, in a decade or so he would be ready to retire; perhaps they would move upstate, find a little cabin in the mountains, and he could leave the business to Mickey. Continuity, security, peace in the evening. Jillian reached under the table and put her hand on his knee. Mickey was talking about debt-to-asset ratios, emerging middle classes worldwide, tax advantages, new modes of transport and consumption. Perhaps he was some kind of financial genius: such men often appeared in the unlikeliest of disguises. All he needed was for the world to capitulate, if the world should happen to be pleased by him. He swallowed his dinner hurriedly, and then began talking again while Benny and Jillian were still starting the main course. That's the way the nation is set up, he said excitedly. Look, it goes all the way back to the very beginning. The way those guys set up interstate trade, this is what they wanted: small businesses to grow, selling things across state lines, no sales tax and so on. You get it, I can tell. You get it, right, Benny? Benny smiled and Jillian laughed; Mickey smiled slightly in return, but reflexively, as if it were a kind of mimicry; he had a habit of doing that, copying gestures and expressions from whoever he was talking to, whether out of sympathy or lack of self. What you've got there, he said. It's a great big opportunity. I can sell anything, you know.

Benny nodded, Jillian nodded and said, He can, too. I've seen him do it.

Well then, Mickey, Benny said. Why don't you come work for me?

Once he got the hang of it, Mickey sold everything. It was quite extraordinary: in person, over the phone, by mail, he charmed and he collected the checks. Clients and customers whom Benny had worked on for years would capitulate when Mickey talked to them, suggesting in subtle ways that to pass on this piece would be a regrettable mistake, performing little acts to make the deal more memorable, commissioning special boxes and bags, throwing in tiny, worthless things—a bottle of French polish and a chamois cloth, a bead from a necklace that was too damaged to sell whole. He even brought in a few new clients, young couples with money who were looking for something to spend it on, a businessman in Atlanta, an airline pilot, the sorts of people Benny himself, quite unconsciously, tended to avoid, because they didn't care enough, weren't dedicated enough, might not keep or protect what they had been fortunate enough to buy. Mickey was more democratic, that was to his credit; he could talk to anyone as an equal and engage them in a kind of double hypnosis, he and the client joined in their pleasures and fortunes. It all happened very quickly. Benny's storage room began to empty out, and he was a bit sad to see it all move so quickly, but by then he was spending both nights and days with Jillian, long luncheons, trips to museums, they were thinking of buying a car: these things made her happy, and soon enough his only job was to find and buy his inventory, explain to Mickey what each piece was, and then leave the rest in his hands.

Several months went by this way, spring into early summer. Jillian baked Italian pastries—cannoli, zeppole, struffoli, commandeering his kitchen and casting up clouds of white flour and confectioners' sugar, until they clung to her wrist and cheek like volcanic ash, his countertop was streaked with honey, and every dish he owned was in the sink. Benny's suits grew tighter; he was developing a slight belly, and this satisfied him. Pleasure, he thought, should make a man bigger. On three successive weekends that June, he and Jillian had rented a car and driven upstate, looking for a property, something modest and serene, which they could fill with furniture and books, someplace with a proper kitchen and a view from the window. On the way home they stopped in antique stores and he bought Jillian little things, a pewter vase or an antique blanket, and they would return home tired late in the afternoon and make slow love on a soft bed to the sound of church bells.

A DEAD SOLDIER

Stephanie went into the Carrier Institute once every two weeks or so, not so much because she had any business there as because it seemed rude not to. She would spend the preceding days trying to adjust her sleep patterns, taking back an hour or two here and there, until she could be out of bed by noon; then she would hurry through her morning routine and arrive at Jessup One by early afternoon, always struck by the fusty smell of the place, the antique sunlight, the echo of her shoes on the marble floors. She would bring her laptop and make a pass through the previous fortnight's photographs, shifting streams of images as if they were trains on tracks: shunting a questionable series onto a parallel path, diverting obvious mistakes out of sight and harm's way, clearing the way for the heavy cars, shiny and right, churning through image after image, tranced and unreachable. She'd found the second speaker in one of the drawers in the desk, and had hooked the pair up to her computer; music played softly and she never knew where it came from, some magic playlist from the nether regions of the internet, which a friend had found for her months previously. She always went back to it because she liked the sound, something called the WonderBeat; it was the perfect rhythm for editing, right in tune with her heart and her breath, and so continuous in its cadence that she had no idea where one song ended and another began. She chewed her fingernails, then and only then, shamelessly snapping them off with her incisors and spitting bits onto the floor.

Every so often she would see the tall, balding man walk past her door; she could tell it was him by the shape of his silhouette passing over the window. Once she noticed him hovering motionless right outside, as if he was trying to decide whether to knock or not. There was a tiny moth on her computer screen, and for a moment she felt the deepest empathy for the thing; she thought she could imagine exactly what it was like, steering this way and that as you feed on the richness of these unexpected photons, which move past your grey silent eyes, or whatever you have for eyes, telling you, Turn here, turn here.

She rose and went to the door, opening it softly so as not to disturb the other man, though when she said, You all right? he looked up, startled, and said, Yes, yes, yes. Everything's fine. I was just ... He gestured gamely at nothing and tapped his foot a few times on the floor. He was wearing a sky-blue oxford cloth shirt and pressed khakis, and a long forelock of sandy hair fell from the crown of his head. In one hand he held an empty beer bottle, which he held up for her to see. I was just looking for someplace to recycle this. There's only one trash can in my office. She introduced herself and he said, Oh, yes, I know who you are. You're the artist.

You're Rainer, right? she said. He nodded. From Switzerland?

I work in Switzerland, but I'm from Austria, he said. From Graz. She asked him what he worked on, and he held his hands out and briefly fluttered his fingers in the air. Ah, well, he said. A certain aspect of dark energy.

Me too, she said brightly, and somewhat to her surprise, he smiled disarmingly. She had underestimated him and she was embarrassed; it must have shown, because he smiled more broadly, though not unkindly.

My mother was an artist, he said. A painter. And then, before Stephanie could ask: You would not have heard of her. But perhaps you would have liked her? She was . . . goofy. He pronounced this last word tentatively, as if he'd found it at the very bottom of his store of English adjectives.

That sounds like a good kind of mother to have, she said, and he nodded agreeably.

So, are you enjoying your time here? he said. She was still standing in the doorway: there was no one in the hall to hear them. Sunlight streamed through the windows on either end, and the space had that sienna tone of still rooms on the edges of cities.

Very much, said Stephanie. Though the truth is I'm not here very often. Photography doesn't really lend itself to working at a desk. — I mean, it does, but only to go over what I've shot out on the street.

He nodded. Yes, we haven't seen much of you.

I hope nobody minds, she said.

I'm sure they don't. There are quite a few people here who I haven't seen since the first day.

She asked if he had been going to the talks, and he sighed. I should be, but I'm not, he said. I spend my days hunched over my computer. Like everyone else. Thinking. Thinking about something that may not even exist. And it is surprising: we can do anything we want. It's quite anarchy-like. Anarchic? Stephanie nodded and he nodded along with her. She wondered how old he was. Anywhere from 30 to 50; she wondered how he would react if she asked him. — Anyway, he said, I'm not even sure if they're still holding them. I no longer receive notifications about them. Or if I do, I haven't noticed them. Now that Coster is leaving, there seems to be no one running the place.

Leaving? she said. She felt stricken and slightly panicked, though she'd hardly seen him since those first few days. Where is he going?

Ah. So. You didn't hear, said Rainer. They have been very quiet about it, because of privacy, you see, but it's been in the newspapers.

I haven't read a newspaper in weeks, said Stephanie. I usually get up at sunset: Why is he leaving?

Well, he's not leaving, exactly. It's more like a sabbatical. Have you seen him lately? She had not. He doesn't look well, Rainer said. It's a terrible story. It . . . his son was killed, somewhere overseas.

His son? Matty?

Matthew, I think that was his name, yes. He was a soldier? A Marine, I think.

For a moment, Stephanie wondered if the country had gone to war without her knowing. It wouldn't be impossible, either for the country or for her. She was having trouble with this moment. — Yes, I think that's right, she said. What happened?

There was an attempted coup, said Thomas. Somewhere in West Africa, I don't remember where. A few Americans were involved and they were captured and imprisoned, and so they sent an extraction team. She frowned at the phrase, and he said, That's what they call it. Then there was some kind of helicopter accident, or else it was shot down. This is very unclear. But Roger Coster's son was killed. It was in the newspapers. He shook his head dolefully.

When did this happen?

Just a few days ago. He looked at her and tilted his head. Did you know him?

Matty? she said. No. No. I slept in his room the first night I was in town, but it was just a room. She heard the elevator start up, its gears meshing and then settling into a soft thrumming behind the walls, perfect music as the sun settled into the red portion of its arc. Thomas was gazing thoughtfully down at his feet. She thought about Emily Coster, with an *O* where her mouth used to be. A pigeon flew

205

by the window, causing an impossibly swift shadow to flit across the wall. The shock of existence, here in the Holocene: the absurdity of it, the sunshine and technology, the green fields and shiny skyscrapers, followed by the dull ache of windward days. She should have taken pictures of Matty's bedroom.

THE WINTER MARKET

After one of these wars, there are going to be some difficult years, with high inflation, random shortages of goods, rising unemployment, and the like. Things that would have been little more than inconvenient in more stable times will be calamities now, leaving people sleeping on the sidewalks and crowding emergency rooms: a heat wave, for example, or a strike by subway conductors. Many of the buildings that were built during the boom years will change hands, and some of them will be empty. Even the fanciest and most expensive parts of town will feel deserted and in disrepair: the stately old residences off of upper Fifth Avenue, the golden lobbies on Riverside, the sharp sleek towers in Tribeca. There will be torn carpets and outdated signs in the lobbies of banks, a wall will collapse in Central Park, a few tourists will be robbed, or maybe killed, and the neighborhood where they happened to be staying will gain a reputation for being especially dangerous. Many people will have a hard time getting by, and, at the other end of the scale, quite a few fortunes will be lost. But for others these will be the happiest of known days, because they're young, say, or because they come from someplace else, where things are even worse; and they will complain, because everyone complains, but they won't mean much by it.

Certain cultures will thrive: comedy, for example, which on the one hand will get very dry and recondite, and on the other hand will enjoy a depravity that would have been unimaginable just a few years earlier, with jokes about the war and the soldiers who've returned, about sex on its most daring day, about the assassinations of political leaders—those that happened, those that could have happened, those that should happen. These schools of comedy, loosely known as the Metaphysicals and the Yallers, will each have their own clubs, their own neighborhoods, their own audience, though in truth the differences between them will be exaggerated, and there will be some performers who can move freely between the two.

And a great ocean liner is going to come into the harbor, an event that will appear on the front pages of newspapers for days beforehand: people will be excited to see such a thing, because they'll like the reminder that the city is built upon a harbor, and that it was once a sophisticated and elegant place. The ship will be on its maiden run from Europe, it'll be as large as the largest building, and the people on the deck will wave and wave to the people on the shore, just like they used to do. There will be a brief vogue, after that, for naval clothing: sailor caps, white bell-bottoms, deck shoes.

Soap operas: these will do well in the new poor city, too, and the area around the studios where they're shot will host a cluster of bars and restaurants, where fans go in the hope of seeing some of their favorite stars; and the stars will go to those same restaurants, surrounded by elaborate and somewhat fanciful teams of security, with the hope of being seen by their fans. The neighborhood will be called Silhouette Town, and the bodyguards will be as broad as oxen, very well compensated, and famous in their own right. And there will be new art but not so much dance, quite a lot of music but very little writing, and much less film. Better to be a man than a woman; better to be very young or very old than anything in between; bad to be a teacher or a politician—during an I Love New York campaign, the mayor will lose the ability to say either *love* or *New York*—but the wind down Sixth Avenue will be crisp and clear, and what a wind, the birds will ride it and banners will snap.

There's going to be a place on the edge of downtown, known to many and yet still a secret. It'll be a section of the north end of Union Square: from the fountain at the bottom, along the left-most path, the one that curves westerly up toward 16th Street and then curves back again, a vague area with uncertain borders, but a place just the same. It will be known as the Winter Market, and drugs will be bought and sold there.

The drugs themselves will not be illegal, not as such, anyway: they'll be prescriptions, new medications for old diseases, some fatal and some chronic; and medications for new diseases, some so new that no one is going to know for sure how they'll progress. Many of the treatments will be experimental, and many of them won't work. The buyers will be people who can't afford the drugs on the open market, or whose doctors have refused to write for them. There will even be some doctors among the customers, either because they're sick themselves or because they're looking for treatments for their patients, substances which, because of shortages or delays in the government's approval process, they can't get by other means. They'll be an especially nervous lot, the doctors, for if they're caught they'll lose their licenses, and if they're recognized they may be beaten.

Something will have gone wrong with the way medications are invented, marketed, priced, distributed, something no one knows how to fix, how even to begin fixing. There will be a lot of arguing among public figures about what has caused it: a failure of economic planning, the avarice of the companies that make and sell the drugs, or simply the fact that there will have been so many new diseases in recent years, illness branching off of illness, each with its own means of transmission, its pathology, its resistance. That will be the year they sell wonderful mechanical bunnies on street corners, for example, which hop across a tabletop or a floor: but they'll turn out to be only half-mechanical and the other half real, and they'll pass on an especially ferocious strain of the flu to some of the people who buy them. There will be a small resurgence of polio, a fourth serotype, less devastating than the original ones and significantly harder to transmit, but it will be immune to known vaccines and treatments. Everyone will agree that the process that had served for a hundred years had stopped working when no one was paying attention.

Though the Winter Market will be a busy place, it'll be a rare night, maybe once every two weeks, that the police come through and roust everyone out, and even then they usually won't make arrests. Still, any night could be the wrong night, and both the buyers and the sellers will be tense, eager, suspicious, and there will always be the possibility that an argument will break out, or even a fight. The bigger dealers will hire small gangs of very young boys and girls to steer customers toward them and warn them if the police are coming, or if a fight has started somewhere else, or if another prominent dealer has entered the park; so the air will be filled with private signals, hisses and whistles, callouts and clapping. It'll be one of those open-but-closed places, nightclubs, homeless encampments, brothels and the like—the kind you can't look for, you just have to know where they are.

They are going to be a mixed group, the sellers. Some of them will be looking to unload something that didn't work for them, or a regimen left unused when someone died, because there will be cash in the black market, and cash is the king of the city. Others will be people who've managed to get the drugs prescribed by lying to someone, or finding a doctor who will accept a bribe. Yet others will be thieves and insiders: nurses, pharmacy assistants, people who work for shipping companies, where things get lost. A last group, so disgraceful that they really only exist in rumors, consists of those who have pilfered the drugs from living friends and relatives.

And the buyers will be, if anything, even more sundry: shopkeepers, secretaries, husbands and wives, bankers and brokers, drivers and delivery boys, managers, students, and even a politician or two. Some will look healthy and some will look sick; some will be seeking advice, and some will know exactly what they need. In this regard, the Market will reflect the character of the city, its variety and ingenuity, its endless calamities and its canny resources. Indeed, it will occupy a part of the square that's served as a trading place of one sort or another for more than a century. Produce was sold there; narcotics, for a time; books and pamphlets, many years previously; flowers back in the days when the neighborhood to the east was home to many wealthy families, who would send their servants out every morning to purchase fresh bouquets. This is going to be the common understanding, anyway, though it may not be true. The unlucky like to think that they once were lucky, the dispossessed that they once had homes, the frightened that they used to be confident, the dying that the world they fought will be remembered.

Of course, all of this will happen at night, under gloomy treetops and vaporous skies. Soon after sunset the Market will open, slowly, as these things do, almost casually, with a glance and a transaction; then another, apparently unrelated, a few yards away; then a few more, like birds settling in the trees. Exchanges will be made behind bushes, behind benches, from hand to hand without eye contact, in part out of uneasiness and in part out of that faint shame that comes with showing weakness in a public place, in a way that could be mistaken for tenderness, if it weren't for the awkwardness and the hurry. Buyers will come in from the south side—as if by instinct, there being no fixed rules—and approach the Wall, a low, freestanding brick slab that once served to mark the entrance to the subway, opposite the raised statue of George Washington on horseback (known as Rider because few passersby will have ever checked to see who is depicted). On the light posts, beneath the pale globes gone dead from austerity, there will be taped-up flyers announcing what's for sale, with the pseudonym of the dealer who has them: Superman, White Boy White, Godzilla, MVP, Nobody Johnson, names whispered out of the grey air as the buyers walk the paths: Reactrive/30 spansules/$300 —> the Speaker. Subvir/100 X 1 + needles/$650 Come see Big Baby. Drugs for trade, new treatments marked with exclamation points, and beside them, a few notices of friends and loved ones who've gone missing, and memorials to those who died; the path will be littered with sheets of paper that have come unstuck and drifted to the ground.

Hector is going to go down to the Winter Market past midnight one Thursday, still warm, though summer has recently ended. He's going to take the train in from Astoria, a half dozen other people in the car with him, but no one on the platform when he gets out except an old woman asleep on one of the benches and, on the opposite platform, two Sikhs staring exhaustedly at the tracks. It's going to be his first time shopping for medicine this way, and he's not going to know what to expect, he won't even be sure that the place exists; but he'll have heard about it, and known stranger things that were born in rumor and appeared in fact. He'll have gone home from work that evening, all the way back out to Queens from the Upper West Side, and gotten into bed with the alarm set for one and the clock nestled under his pillow, where he clutched at it in his sleep. He'll be looking for something to cure his brother, Antonio, whose disease is so new the researchers are still deciding on the name. No one will know how it's transmitted, whether it's hereditary or environmental, infectious or inert, whether it preys on the weak, the sinful, or the unlucky; and no effective treatments will exist at all, though some new drugs, each unrelated to the others and originally designed for a different illness altogether, are rumored to alleviate some of the symptoms.

He'll have five hundred dollars in cash, carefully converted into twenties, which are collected into hundred-dollar rolls, fixed with rubber bands, and placed in each of his four pants pockets, with an extra one tucked into his right sock. It will be money he's saved from his job as a doorman in a building uptown, putting his Christmas bonuses in an empty coffee jar and using his tip money to send remittances home to Ecuador. It will be as much money as he's ever carried and not a sum he's likely to see again soon, which will make him apprehensive, worried that he'll lose it or have it stolen, that he'll get arrested, taken advantage of, ripped off, and end up feeling foolish among these people who have been working this forbidden economy for so much longer than he has, and no doubt know much more than he does about which forms of treatment are worth pursuing and which are useless.

He'll be looking for something called Provix B, a drug distributed in small, oblong, bright red pills. That will be just about all he knows, the name and what they look like. He'll have little sense of how much they cost, in a pharmacy or on the black market, still less of what they do, but he'll consider it a great success if he can acquire some. Antonio will be the only family he has, now that his mother is gone: Antonio with his fencer's posture and quick smile, the wise and wised-up one, three years older than Hector, and his tutor and protector back when Hector was a chubby and clumsy and quiet boy.

He'll emerge from the subway at the south end of the park, and what he will see will bewilder and amaze him: a small society, a different economy. He's going to think, Now, who are these men and women, and what have they been through, what's going on in their heads and what do they want? As he starts north toward the center of the market he'll come across the stragglers, the margins of even this marginal world. They'll mutter names of drugs to him, cures he's never heard of, for diseases he can't imagine, so many of both. Now, how does this work? he'll ask himself. What are the rules? Can I bargain or are the prices fixed? And how am I supposed to know that what I'm getting is really what I'm paying for, rather than some aspirin wrapped in tinfoil, or worse yet, something poisonous, like the coarse white powder the super laid down for rats in the basement of the building where he worked? The previous week he'll have helped his brother to the bathroom and balanced him on the scale, weighing him at ninety-seven pounds; and his skin was painted with blue and purple streaks, both delicate and deadly. Hector will be sure that if he can get those streaks to fade, then his brother will be all right. Like unpainting a painting, and maybe that's what this drug, this Provix B can do, erase the streaks from his brother's skin and let him start over again, like an apartment wall that's had its nail holes spackled over and a fresh coat of paint applied, maybe not as good as new but better than it was. Everybody's got some holes in them, but if you can't see them then they don't count. There was an old man named Cortez, back in the neighborhood, who showed up on the block one day wearing a perfectly fitting oyster-grey suit and a spotless Panama. Nobody dies from looking too good, he said to Hector. The idea was so striking to him, and the man who voiced it such proof, that he began to believe in it, more literally than he would have admitted, certainly enough that he'll have begun to think of saving his brother as saving his brother's looks. He'll gaze up above the treetops to the surrounding office buildings, empty as mausoleums; he'll look at the lampposts, with their fluttering offers, supplications and prayers, but he'll find their numbers overwhelming.

Instead, he'll start up the path, and right away a man will approach him, tall, thin, and colorless, eyeing him, the corner of his mouth open as if he's about to say something, and Hector will open his face too broadly on him, so that the other man looks down at the sidewalk, says nothing, and retreats back under the trees. Hector will turn around to watch him go, conscious as he's doing so that it's a mistake, that it makes him look new; and yet he can't help himself, so he'll start to follow the tall man, not knowing, after all, where else to go, clinging onto this one contact and this single clue, though smart enough to make himself appear aimless as he follows the dwindling curve toward whatever lies at the end.

The tall man will be gone. Two other men will be sitting on a bench, their legs drawn up so that they face each other, quietly sorting something between them under the watchful gaze of a much larger man—enormous, really—who stands in front of them, legs slightly apart, staring at Hector as he makes his way past them, not looking, not even nodding, and then crosses an even darker region, through a curtain of hanging tree branches, and then, suddenly, out into the Market itself, a place so open and busy that for a second he'll pause, turn, and almost run, convinced that he's made a mistake, or that someone must have made a fool of him, that this place, with all of these people milling around, all doing something subtle with their hands, must be a trap, a joke, maybe a movie set, someplace he doesn't belong.

He'll stand there, unmoving and ignored, his eyes flickering across the scene: mostly men and mostly young, but there'll be a few women among them, all looking like they're trying not to look like anything—not a bright scrap of cloth on anyone, except for one man wearing a red leather cap. He'll turn his head this way and that, trying to find something on which his gaze might alight, but no one will even catch his eye, they'll be so caught up in the matter of asking and offering, passing things from hand to hand; he'll feel like he's happened on a dance in a town square in some foreign city, something where the partners change according to beats he can barely hear, within an unfamiliar music. He'll step back into the shadows and pat his front pockets. Look, now, the patterns: the sellers moving forward just a few feet from their perches and then settling back again, while the buyers traced more eccentric routes, perturbed like the planets, dawdling and reluctant until they find something they want; then they'll quicken a bit, pause, start forward hesitantly, and finally, with the transaction upon them, they'll thrust the money at the vendor, wait for it to be counted, and then hasten away. He'll find himself fascinated by the entire process, its complexity and then again its unexpected formalities, too loose to be rituals but too keen to be random. The first open look, a mild flirtation, the first exchanges with a potential partner, the quick decision whether to continue or not, even the few polite words spoken—we're good—OK, man—when it was clear the match wasn't right, to soften the rejection and make the entire process feel a little lighter, a nodding goodbye, hands up as if to say, I'm no threat to you.

A bearded man in a green army jacket is going to approach him and say, What'll it be? Provix B, Hector will reply, though he'll feel self-conscious about saying it, concerned that he's pronouncing it wrong, or that everyone but him knows that the stuff is useless, or alternately, that it's so sought-after that a newcomer like himself couldn't hope to find it, nor afford it even if it were offered to him. And sure enough, the bearded man will smile and say, You won't find any of that around here, and if you do, it'll probably be counterfeit. But I've got something else, proven in clinical trials. It's called Mirapin. Works just as good as the other, that's what my clients tell me, and they keep coming back for more. Only difference is you have to take it four times a day instead of just once.

What does it do? Hector will ask, and the other man will say, It's just what you're looking for. Provix B, Hector will say, and the man will say, This is better. That's what I'm telling you. But Hector will know that only a fool buys from the first person who's selling, and he'll say, No, no, shaking his head and backing away before turning and walking on.

After the man in the army jacket, there will be two boys, both about fourteen years old, one of whom will hold out a dirty plastic bag containing a half dozen pink football-shaped pills. Hector will ask what they are and the boy will scowl and shrug. Then he'll meet a round, sweaty man with blister packs in various pockets of his long grey wool coat; then a weary man with a trembling Adam's apple and a pink-tipped nose, who'll catch Hector's eye and approach him hesitantly, saying, Hey, man, what can we do for each other? But the weary man will turn out to be another buyer, not a seller, and he'll be so near death that there are flecks of blood in his eyes, and blood between his teeth when he tries to smile. What are you looking for? the other man will say, and Hector will pause, unsure he wants to reveal such information, especially to someone who has nothing to lose—but the other man's voice will be kind. Provix B, he'll say, and the other man will nod or, it may be, flinch, like a dog's legs jerking when you scratch its belly, nothing deliberate at all, just a tic brought on by his mashed-up nerves, and he'll say, Someone's got it. I heard someone say it.

Where?

The other man will point further into the park. Back there somewhere. I don't know. I don't know.

So he'll start back, it was like heading deeper into a hole in the side of a mountain, which opens first into a cavern and then narrows down, splits and branches, until it's impossible to go any further and the only way to proceed is to turn around and start towards the entrance again. What are you looking for, man? What do you need? We got everything, we got it all. Month's supply, and next month I'll have more. He'll have worked through about two-thirds of the market, now dizzy and near despair, when he'll come across a young woman, all by herself, sitting forward on one of the benches with her elbows on her knees and her chin propped on her hands, one of the few who says nothing as he goes by, maybe she was just sitting there because she needed someplace to sit; but when he passes her again coming back out—two men down there with nothing but painkillers—she won't have moved, she'll be sitting in the exact same position, still gazing at the same spot on the pavement a few feet in front of her, and he'll say, Excuse me. She'll look at him, a white girl in a black beret, wearing a lot of makeup, her eyes outlined, a thin girl with her throat bare, angry, sad, sick. Still, she won't say anything, and he'll think about walking on; but she won't avert her eyes, either. Are you buying or selling? The girl will stare hard at him, and then reach into the pocket of her coat and pull out an orange bottle, shaking it slightly from side to side so that he can hear the tablets inside. What is it? he'll ask.

This—, she'll say, her voice so hoarse on the first syllable that she'll stop, clear her throat, and start again. This stuff they gave me. Went on it for two months. Provix B. It didn't do anything, but I kept filling it. There's three more months in there.

Hector is going to feel a beam of moonlight go right through him, a warm-cold sensation, dilating his ventricles and shortening his breath. He'll touch the roll of bills in his right pocket. You're selling it? he'll ask.

It doesn't work for me, she'll reply. Maybe it'll work for someone. She'll look at him like a blind woman, as if maybe she had a witch's wisdom and second vision, or maybe she just couldn't see very well.

Is it for you?

He'll shake his head. My brother. Antonio.

Yeah, she'll say, and then she won't say anything more. At first he'll think that she's changed her mind, but when she finally speaks he'll see that the pause was just to gather her strength, and he'll wonder if she's going to die right in front of him. She'll swallow, shake her head in frustration, and swallow again, weak as a newborn bird. You can have it, she'll say.

How much?

She'll shake her head, No. Just take it. It doesn't matter.

He won't understand. How much do you want? he'll ask again, already reaching into his pocket.

She'll draw her hand back as if she's going to throw the bottle at him. It's free, she'll say. Just take it. A little breeze is going to come across the park, ruffling her bones.

He'll put his hands up and shake his head, as if it were a robbery— as if, by refusing to take money from him, she were taking something even more valuable. But she'll say nothing, just hold her thin arm out to him, the bottle dangling from her fingertips, nodding, Go ahead. He'll reach out slowly and take it from her, wondering if maybe this is some white girl's game, if she's going to take it back, or scream for the police, or do something with sex, whatever it might be; but she's just going to smile at him a little, revealing a slight overbite that will show how pretty she once was, and then, when the bottle is safely in his hands, lean back on the bench, a shade more ashen from the effort, breathing, breathing. He'll turn it and look at the label, which looks right enough, though the woman has scratched out the prescription number and her last name, a common practice to prevent the police from tracing contraband back to the seller, while still allowing buyers to identify their connection. Is this you? he'll ask. Are you Bridget?

She'll nod and then say, It's real. Don't worry.

He'll stand there, looking at her. Can't I help you get home? She'll shake her head. He'll feel like he has to give her something, it won't be right otherwise, so he'll kneel down on the pavement, and take the folded bills out of his sock, thrusting them at her desperately. But she won't take them, she'll just raise her eyes and look at him, her eyelids juddering, sucking on her lower lip. It's going to hurt him, that she won't take anything from him, but she'll just smile and say, Where I'm going, I won't need money.

SUR LA TABLE

It was late in March, the further edge of what had been, until then, a relatively mild winter; but that night it was cold and the sky was low. The restaurant was one of those places, there were thousands like it all over town—Goan home cooking, French-Cuban, meticulous Filipino, Patagonian, there were restaurants on every block, and they were all new and all full, all the time. It was like being in some vast hive, each cell giving way to another, and all of them furious and dripping with dark golden energy; a thousand subsocieties with elaborate rituals and routines, friendships and hierarchies, wars, gestures of dominance and submission, manners and intoxications, and all of it paid for, again and again and again. Stephanie found restaurants shocking, and this one was called Apiary. The door was discreet, no more than a blue-black opening on 19th Street between Eighth and Ninth Avenues: from fifty feet away it was all but indistinguishable from the other doorways on the block, most of which were now secured with corrugated metal gates. The street was empty and echoed softly with the low, airy humming of great turbines emitting enormous cataracts of energy, furnaces burning deep within, their exhalations streaming from the windows up above as a constant drone. Down the block a truck had taken hold of a green dumpster, hoisted it over its own back, and then dropped it again with a terrific bang, which resounded up against the faces of the buildings and then disappeared, like a sea that's been drowned in an ocean. The door to the restaurant was black glass marked only with a single yellow hexagon. She hesitated on the sidewalk. Twenty-five years previously she'd had her first drink, and not a legal one, in a bar around the corner—one of those chains, now gone and forgotten, a Blarney Stone or a White Horse; the city had been dotted with them, they'd been open since the end of Prohibition, and they were stocked with quiet old men in slightly shabby suits. Somehow, she'd decided to drink whiskey; she'd hated the taste immediately but stuck with it for fear of looking like a novice. She'd spent the later hours of that night vomiting on the edge of a vacant lot, while her best friend sat a few yards away, confessing, as much to herself as to Stephanie, that she'd lost her virginity to the father of the children she babysat for over the previous summer.

The hostess at the door to the restaurant was young, thin, and faultlessly dressed; a Slavic woman with high cheekbones, sloe eyes, tiny diamond earrings, and a dimple in her chin. She smiled, showing a set of small white teeth, and glanced briefly at Stephanie's canvas bag. There was a large man in a beautiful black coat standing between them, holding the pearl handle of a small cage covered in dark green velvet. Can you get the manager? the man was saying. Just get the manager.

We're very busy right now, the hostess said, turning her head to look back at the room. But he will tell you the same thing I'm telling you: health department regulations do not allow patrons to bring animals into the restaurant, unless they're service dogs.

It's not a dog, the man said.

Yes, said the hostess. That is the rule, the law. Unless you are blind and that is your guide dog.

But it's not a dog, the man said. It's a panda. She just ate an hour ago; she's sleeping now.

The hostess faltered. It's a what?

A giant panda, though she's not giant yet. She's a cub, a baby panda.

It is not sanitary to have live animals . . . She hesitated again. — A panda?

The man nodded. She's only ten weeks old. She sleeps all the time, she's not going to wake up. It's just too cold to leave her out in the car.

Is that legal? asked the hostess. To have one.

They're all over the place, the man said. It's not like it used to be.

The hostess looked at Stephanie, who shrugged. Do you want to see her? the man asked. Again, the hostess hesitated, as if she wasn't sure if this was some kind of trick.

I'd like to, said Stephanie, and the man turned and smiled at her gratefully.

See what I mean? he said to the hostess. It's good for business. He raised the cage up and lifted the velvet, underneath which a small black-and-white panda cub was indeed sleeping. The hostess bent down and cooed, and at once she seemed less severe and more like what, in fact, she was: a young woman far from home. The man smiled.

It's a she?

He nodded. Her name is Mei Mei. It's Mandarin for *Little Sister*.

The hostess stepped back to let Stephanie have a look. The panda was the size of a teddy bear, and smelled of sweet hay and fur. What do you feed her? the hostess said.

Oh, you know, bamboo shoots, said the man. You can pick them up in health-food stores. I'll tell you what, though, she eats a *lot*.

It is very noisy in here, though, isn't it? said the hostess, now more concerned for the cub's well-being than for the legality of the whole affair.

She'll be fine, said the man in the black suit. Once she goes to sleep, she sleeps through everything. Can I bring her in? It's cold out.

For a moment the hostess stood motionless before her podium, and then she nodded quickly, as if she was hoping no one would notice, and the man slipped past her and disappeared into the dark room. Stephanie stepped up, the next in this machine. The reservation is under Frye, she said. Probably. The hostess was looking down at a glowing screen that was nestled into her lectern; she tapped it with her index finger, made a disappointed noise, and then tapped it again.

They never enter the right information, she said, as if she and Stephanie were old friends conspiring over the want of others' courtesy. Here it is. You're the first, said the hostess, a bit apologetically. Would you like to check your coat? But before she'd even stepped out from behind her podium, Stephanie felt a hand on her arm, and there was Brian Frye, forty years old, with the skin of a thirty-year-old and the eyes of an old man. She was so happy to see him she squealed softly, got up on her toes and kissed his pink cheek. His skin smelled faintly of vanilla. Hello! he said as he unwrapped a black cashmere scarf from around his neck and then slipped off his coat. He was a big man, in a way that people noticed without noticing. Hello! Hello! The hostess started walking them back toward a four-top in a far corner. So good to see you. He stopped and looked her up and down, and the hostess walked on a few steps before she realized they weren't following. Very nice, he said. Very nice. She smiled broadly: compliments ordinarily made her uneasy, but his had always delighted her. The hostess cocked her head, and they all started forward again. The noise in the restaurant was thick and stormy; conversations rose and fell on either side of them, reverse-interrupted by brief moments of near silence, when everyone seemed to pause simultaneously to take a breath or a bite; then there would be a small clink of a single knife or fork on a plate, and it would resume again. When they reached the table, Brian offered her the seat against the wall and took the one facing it, loosening his tie and then sitting down heavily. — Oh! he said. Can you check this for me? he said to the hostess, who obligingly took his coat; Stephanie draped hers on the back of her chair and put her bag on the floor beside her, checking it out of habit to make sure everything was inside, fussing with the clasp a bit, and then patting it a few times before she looked up. Jeannie can't make it, said Brian. She wanted to, but she's stuck at work. Stephanie frowned sympathetically. She's running a theater company now, Brian continued. Something went wrong with the . . . lighting, the seating. I don't know. He looked disconsolate and then he laughed. Stephanie had known him since she was in her teens, though not at all well. Toward the middle of her twenties they discovered each other again, and found that they'd both become interested in art, each surprised to find the other at an opening because each had thought the other staid and distant. She'd been instrumental in convincing him to open his first gallery, and he, in turn, had asked her to be his first show, in a small space on Little West 12th, and had published a small chapbook to go along with it: small, stagey, bleary chromes of women she had brought down to Wall Street on the weekends to walk the otherwise empty sidewalks. It was youthful work, both unsubtle and obscure, but it had gotten around, that book, and it led to group shows, a small museum project, another show with Brian, another book. He was a man who stayed: he and Jeannie had been together since they were in college: they had the only happy marriage she'd ever seen, it was a fortune that even the most cynical in their circle smiled at, especially since the two of them presented it as a fantastic piece of luck that even they found inexplicable, rather than as their just reward.

There was a waiter in a royal blue suit standing at the table. Can I get you a drink while you're looking things over? he said. Brian ordered a bottle of wine and the waiter disappeared.

Years ago her mother had taught Stephanie how to behave in a restaurant, over a series of lunches and one final dinner at a butter-yellow Upper East Side bistro where the staff had called her Miss; to this day she sat straight-backed, napkin on lap, left hand on napkin, though every so often she caught herself and tried to stop. She looked around the room. A few tables away, there was a young woman—just a girl, really, college-aged, wearing a man's shirt unbuttoned far enough to allow the room a look at her proud plastic surgery, and Stephanie felt a familiar distress, not disgust at the girl's pandering or pity for her foolishness, those were mistakes that anyone could make, but a clench of worry at the thought of flesh and knives, the severing of thready nerves, the buttoning of aching skin. Brian was looking at the menu.

So, he said, absently. What are you having? No, wait. He looked up and studied her for a moment. When was the last time I saw you? Was it in Berlin?

Brussels, said Stephanie. At the opening of that collection, those French people.

That's right, said Brian. That's right. The tax exiles. Rich as King Farouk, and always the last to pay. Which is why they have so much money. He sighed. Your photos looked great in there, though. You had that one whole wall, and they held the whole room together. He looked at the menu again.

I'm just going to have a salad, I think, said Stephanie.

Really? he said. Come on, you've been putting me off for months, now. I must be the last person in town to see you. Have some real food with me.

She said, I've only been up for a couple of hours, so this is breakfast to me. He furrowed his brow and waited. I've been shooting at night, she said. Overnight. So I sleep from about ten in the morning to six in the afternoon—or I guess evening, this time of year—and I never see anyone.

He smiled and said, That's what you're doing?

She nodded solemnly. You can't believe what cameras can do at night, now. They pick up everything.

You've come home after all these years, and you never go out in the daytime?

Not often, she said. But you'll like what I've been getting. No one's ever seen this. And the prints are going to be beautiful. They invented this new black ink, it's gorgeous. It changes everything. It's so . . . what's the opposite of vivid? It's the purest absence of color, of reflection. And then you get all the light on the street, weaving forward and back. She widened her eyes. And of course the people, the buildings, the streets. I should have them ready in a year or so.

Edition of twelve?

That's the thing, we have to talk about that, she said. I'm thinking maybe unique, but I don't know. Is that too precious?

Brian winced. It's not precious, aesthetically. Well, maybe it is a little, but not enough to be a problem. The problem is they'll have to sell for a lot more in order for either of us to come out ahead. Which is not impossible, but it's risky.

Stephanie nodded. I thought of that. Plus, if there's only one, it's not photography anymore. It's . . . more like a monotype or something. Pictures are plural.

Brian said, OK. When you're ready I'll come by and look at some work prints, and we can decide then. — Oh, exciting. Good news. Do you want to schedule a show? I have a month open next fall.

She shook her head. That's too soon, she said.

Well, we should do a catalog, he said. A nice, big, expensive one.

The waiter came back with a basket of bread, a plate of butter and a jar of honey. When he was gone, Stephanie took a slice and nibbled it. There's a man in here with a baby panda, she said.

What do you mean?

He had a baby panda, in a cage.

I don't think that's possible, he said.

I saw it, she insisted, and as if to take back a measure of her certainty with a measure of his own, he shook his head. She twisted in her seat to look for the man but she couldn't find him.

Are you sure he wasn't one of those comedians? said Brian.

One of what comedians?

They're called the Philosophers. Something like that. The Metaphysicals. They do these little . . . actions. Not performances, really, and not jokes. More like pranks, but smaller than that. Maybe it was a stuffed toy.

It was moving around, said Stephanie, though it wasn't true. Making little panda noises. It smelled lovely, and very much alive.

OK, said Brian. Anyway, you're out all night. Where do you sleep, when you sleep?

The Institute gave me a nice little apartment on the Upper East Side, she said. Not upper Upper, sort of Lenox Hill-ish. She twisted off another little piece of bread. This is good, she said. Have some.

And what about these Carrier people? said Brian.

They've been perfectly nice, she said. I was a little suspicious. — Not suspicious, skeptical. But they gave me everything I could want and offered me more things than I could ever use, and then, God bless them, they just left me alone.

You have an office there?

She nodded. I don't use it very often, but sometimes I'll stop in there and sit for a few minutes. And there are little things—if I want to mail something, I just leave it in a box outside my door, and someone takes care of it. I have no idea who. She picked up her forked, tapped it absently on the edge of the table and then set it down again. To tell the truth, it's a little unsettling.

And what about the others? The other . . . what do they call you?

Fellows.

Fellows. Strange word. What are they like?

Well . . . she hesitated. It's just a world I don't know very well.

Scientists and economists and people doing physics, and things like that. They send me invitations to lectures, but I have no idea what any of them are about. Cybersecurity. Climate resilience. Quantum computing. Emerging diplomacy. Microfinance. Then I go out at night and take a thousand pictures of trash cans and all-night bodegas. She picked up a few bread crumbs from the tablecloth with the tip of her forefinger, and deposited them on her plate.

So how does it feel to be back? — Oh, hell, I can't ask that. He smiled at his own banality. What happened to that woman, the one you moved over there to be with? Gemma.

Stephanie shook her head. It ended, the way these things do. She thought I was . . . cold, or not cold: distant. Which I was, I suppose, but only because I was thinking. Stephanie smiled softly. She called me a sadist, like we were the dykes in a Fassbinder movie. It was difficult at the end. It's always difficult at the end. It feels like it's always the end, and it's always difficult. She was staring contemplatively at a bare patch on the tablecloth; she shook her head to clear it, and said, Well, listen to me.

I never would have thought, of everyone who was around, that you'd be the one to leave, said Brian. Gemma or no Gemma.

I thought I'd miss it here, at first, said Stephanie. And I did, I missed little things. The newspapers. The tone of voice you find in American newspapers, that accent, how seriously they take themselves, even when they're pretending not to. I missed deli food, really good, bad-for-you food on every corner. I missed the splurge, you know? The way no one ever saves anything, they either use it or they throw it out. But I think I miss it more now that I'm back.

Well, and you were in a bad way, then.

I was, said Stephanie, a note of cheerful wonder in her voice. I was a mess. I mean, I was OK, and then suddenly everything broke down.

The waiter was standing over them, brandishing a bottle of wine, but she put her hand over her glass.

No? said Brian. No wine with your breakfast?

She smiled at him and said, Just water, please, to the waiter. And a cup of coffee? — No, but it's very easy; once you've left it's very easy to stay away. When you live here, when you're in it, it's your whole world. You simply can't imagine being anywhere else. But when you're looking from a distance, New York starts to feel like another world, half-mythological but also very stupid. Filled with ghosts, which are like children, you know. They only know how to want one thing at a time. But unlike children, it's always the same thing: remember me. First it was my father, and then my mother. And then it was Bridget, and I couldn't believe, I just couldn't believe that something so terrible could happen in the world. *Terrible* isn't the word. There is no word. The word is *Run*. So I had to leave. I had to go. I had to leave. I couldn't . . . She looked around the room. Surely all of these people had lost at least a few of the many someones they had loved. That thin little woman with the high forehead and the gold bracelets. That man talking to that other man, leaning over his plate, gesturing with his fork. It was trying to talk of such quiet matters in such a noisy room. Do you think they minded? she said. That I left them all behind?

No, said Brian. Of course not. The dead are very patient.

Stephanie smiled and said, I suppose they have to be. She was well aware that she sounded silly, if not insane; and here Brian was, playing along obligingly. He had been put on the planet to make fine things happen, and he knew it and revered the role. He protected his artists, quietly but commandingly, even when they were difficult, even when they were wrong; and he carefully negotiated the machinery of commerce, with all its interlocking parts, the wheels upon which some were saved and some were crushed, collectors and consultants, critics, auction houses, other galleries, curators, museum boards. She had never seen him angry, though he could be stern, and was fearsome when he was.

Once she had danced with him, in a bar on the northern edge of Tribeca, just below Canal, a little dive where municipal workers used to go after their shifts were done: road maintenance crews, telephone repairmen, file clerks from the police headquarters. They had been with a few friends, but Jeannie wasn't there; she couldn't remember why not. They were twenty-six or so, and when they'd first walked in she'd noticed a heavy middle-aged white man in a blue and grey uniform sitting at the bar, who'd turned to the door and gazed on them with an expression that might have been resentment, or exhaustion, or drunkenness. She had stopped, and Brian had turned back to look at her. But she had suddenly seen him, the man at the bar, as completely as she'd ever seen anyone; if she were to run into him now she would recognize him immediately. Later a song had come on the jukebox, and as soon as the first lazy notes had started Brian smiled and put his hand on her arm. You hear that? he had said. That's Count Basie, it's the most beautiful song in the world. — Listen. He sang along softly, little bits of a swank melody, soulful, lazy and seductive. Then he stood up and held out his hand, and for once she knew exactly what to do. Not for nothing, those six months of Formal Dance, in the basement of the church on Lexington; and Brian was elegant and graceful, confident with his hand on her hip and a gentle smile, never too close or too far, as they whirled and glided in a clearing among the tables. When the song was over he had stepped back, smiled, and bowed modestly, and when they returned to the table there was a moment of silence among their friends, homage to what they'd done, and then the night resumed, with that perfect ruby-colored moment set inside it.

He looked the same that night in the restaurant, or nearly so, anyway. He wore the same wire-rim glasses he'd had since high school, and his face was only slightly rounder, his hair only a bit thinner. There was another bottle of wine on the table, empty plates and his crumpled napkin. It was a good red wine, something French, she could see from the inch or so of the label that was facing her.

They talked about time; how little there was in a day and yet how much had passed; and how happy Brian was with his children. My mother says hello, he said.

Your mother never liked me, Stephanie said.

That's not true, he protested.

Stephanie smiled as if nothing could make her happier than the poverty of her reputation. She thought our whole family was unstable, she said, and my mother should have found someone to marry after my father died.

Yes, he admitted. She did think that.

She didn't think our money had deep enough roots.

Yes, he said.

She thought my father was . . . coarse, even when he was alive.

She never said that to me.

Because we weren't from the East Side. We moved there.

I didn't know that.

Stephanie smiled again. Because we were Jewish.

Brian waved his hand dismissively. My mother was suspicious of everybody, he said. From Democrats to schoolteachers.

But you know, Stephanie said, now earnestly. I always liked your mother. Will you give her my best?

Out on the street it was snowing; an inch or more had already accumulated. It had come on like a drug, first a quickening in the atmosphere, and now as a faster and more violent peace. There was a man making his way up the sidewalk across the street wearing a pith helmet, the real thing, beige and hard. Spindrift blew off the parked cars, swirling upwards and mixing with the down-falling storm. They walked toward Eighth Avenue so that Brian could get a cab uptown. Are you really going to walk around photographing tonight? he said. In this weather?

It's perfect, said Stephanie.

A woman in a down coat was hurrying carefully across the street. Brian nodded toward her so that Stephanie would look. She'll never make it, he whispered, and for a moment it looked like he was right: the woman wavered a bit, like a plastic doll in the wind, but then she righted herself and stepped delicately over the curb.

From down the block came an ascending whirr of car tires slipping, followed by sudden silence as the driver gave up. The two of them turned, chins buried in their lapels, to watch. It was a cab, and from the light on top it was evident that he had no fare. He had slewed half-sideways and was blocking the lane; and now the cabdriver himself had come out of the car, leaving the door open as he shuffled uneasily to the rear, where he bent down and examined the wheels, as if by looking at them he could make the snow melt, the tires free themselves, his work resume. He wore loafers and dress socks, and he stood in the street looking miserable, impatient and bewildered, shaking out first one ankle, then the other, then stepping back and looking at the cab, stepping forward again, reaching in and taking his cell phone from a mount on the dashboard. His door was still open and snow began to stick to the front seat, soft as ashes. He dialed a number and began arguing with someone on the other end; they couldn't hear what he was saying, but it seemed to go on and on. Stephanie found it difficult to watch and looked away.

On the corner of 18th Street, two women dressed for a night out were standing under a streetlight, one of them with a cigarette in her hand. She made a quick motion to the other, as if she was signaling something, and her friend reached into her bag and took out a lighter. The first one bent her head, and there was a dim, flickering flame, which guttered and then went out. The first woman made the gesture again; the flame appeared again, and she bent again and then quickly stood up, throwing her head back with the pleasure of the first lungful of smoke.

Whores in the snow, said Brian. He gestured elegantly, with one large dark hand.

I think they're just women, Stephanie said.

You're worried about them now, aren't you? You want to go down there and get them off the street.

It's snowing, Stephanie said, and they're wearing short skirts.

I'll tell you what, said Brian. I'll give you $250 in cash, and you can go down there and get them. Bring them back to your place and take care of them. Make them soup. Take their pictures.

They watched for a minute or two. The cabdriver had freed himself, and Brian flagged him down and climbed in. $250? Stephanie said, and she bent down and kissed him on the cheek. How do you know how much it costs?

LISA

Caruso walked down Astor Place with a willful, pale, intelligent girl named Lisa, a spirit-bird on the sidewalk, not pinched by the city, wide awake and madly in love, the envy of her friends as she gladly suffered the first sharp raking of her soul. It was a chilly spring afternoon, with a wind so strong it was keeping winter. His black cotton jacket wasn't quite warm enough, nor was hers, which was made of dark green silk; so they held on to each other tightly, happy to have an excuse for a contact that they would have indulged in without an excuse. Caruso, with his glossy skin and liquid green eyes, his soft lips and hard beats, his shyness and his confidence, his face on billboards and flyers and inside all the magazines. A skinny, long-haired boy with a phone watched them from a doorway as they approached, started to bring it up to take a picture and then thought better of it. Hey, he said as they passed, as if he knew them well but hadn't seen them in a while. Lisa smiled quickly, but Caruso said nothing. He hardly noticed this sort of thing at all, he just moved through the shimmering downpour of attention without ever feeling a drop. But she had a harder time getting used to it—having to worry about the way she looked, knowing that there were girls out there who hated her just because she was with him, trying to ignore the gossip,—and ignore, too, the people who pretended she wasn't there at all. Sometimes it bothered her and sometimes it didn't; and yet that afternoon, well, that afternoon was one of the ones she wanted to keep, the world come calling with soft and splendid gifts. A block and a half went by, and she felt him sinking deeper into himself. What are you thinking? she said, and he moved his lips silently. She touched him briefly on his backside. — Mm, he said, and he paused. My queen, my queen, in colors so fair. She kissed his cheek.

Lisa was a white girl, quick and flirtatious, bright-eyed and funny, with a heart like a bottle. Sometimes she thought of him as San Francisco, because he was saintly in his way, and his weather changed so quickly; but then, she was changeable herself, not in her attentiveness to him, her patience—her devotion, even—but in her confidence that it was all going to work out, *all* meaning everything, *work out* meaning the calf would find its way to the shade of the tree.

They were on their way to visit a college friend of hers, a red-haired girl named Rosamund, who was planning a little afternoon party, mixed drinks and so on, in her tiny apartment on Bond Street. Caruso didn't drink, but Rosamund was good that way; she made him feel welcome and comfortable, she never flattered or pried. There weren't many like her: once a girl she hardly knew had asked Lisa what he was like in bed, how big he was, what they did, and Lisa had been tempted to make up wild stories, of threesomes with groupies, fetishes and unnatural sex, but she stopped herself. She had a devious and dirty mind, and it would have been fun, but there was always the risk that the girl, who dressed with studied contrariness and stared out at the world through large but inexpressive eyes, would believe her; or that even if she didn't, she might choose to pass it on.

Rosamund had lovely taste, and her apartment was stocked with pretty things, arranged in small, mixed, neat piles. Nothing expensive, just stuff she picked up here and there: little toys, old milk bottles, a manual typewriter, a few boxes of vinyl records. It was halfway between a store and an installation, though she didn't sell anything and the place was just for friends. When Lisa showed up, leading Caruso by the hand, she gave her a hug and him a kiss on the cheek, then disappeared into the kitchen, emerging a minute or two later with two tall glasses of lemonade. Even the ice cubes were special, perfectly clear cubes with little dimples on each side, as if she'd bought them in a store that specialized in such things.

Caruso sat on a bench by the window, absently tapping his foot and running his hand over a small stack of T-shirts with something glittery written on them. Next to the T-shirts there was a copy of the Book of Mormon, and next to that, an old Tibetan rice pot with a bright live pink flower planted in it. Within an hour, three more people showed up: two men, one plump and one thin, and then a young woman with freckles and translucent eyelashes. They smiled at him as if to say, Yes, we know who you are, but they didn't approach him. Lisa glanced at him from across the room. He was listening. There was music coming from a record player, it sounded ancient and he liked it; there was a strange sort of guitar part, but it sounded like it had been tuned too high, the strings pulled so taut they were about to snap; but the man playing it was slow and gentle with his hands, and he was singing softly, almost conversationally, in another language. It sounded like he had invented the guitar and made up the language, and now he was smoothing them out so he could fit them to each other, coaxing them together. Caruso sat and looked out the window; in the building across the way, a child of about ten was lighting a candle and then blowing it out, over and over again. The song had shifted, the tempo became a little harder and the man's voice stronger. He was trying to explain something, but it was turning into a question, and then into a plea, until there was a slight sobbing undertone to his voice. Caruso wasn't sure whether the man meant what he was singing or the song meant what it said. The chorus went into a breakdown, and a little phrase appeared, a series of bent notes in a sequence he'd never heard before, so startling that it was like discovering a new color, and off the lines at that, chroma tuned to some shade of fathomless sorrow, a sadness that, paradoxically, found joy in its own darkness, the melody of a bound and singing captive with otherworldly powers but nothing to spend them on. His fingers moved softly as he tried to find the beat, his hands opening and closing. The singer repeated the same line over and over again, while the band shifted behind him, a few horns dropping out, another instrument coming in, something bowed and fretless, it sounded like it had been made to be almost impossible to play, so that the player's hands had to search for each note, producing a flash of effort and a guess so fleeting as to be barely conscious, before the next note was due.

The passage ended, and the song collapsed upwards and started back into its verse. At the same time, more and more beats came in, doubling up the time and pulling it apart like a rag. There was breathing in the background, gulping and exhaling; that became the song, too. The verse was louder, pleading, not from one person to another but from soul to night. Tell me, tell me, tell me. Lisa had been in the back room, trying on Rosamund's clothes. Maybe the place was a store, after all. She came out barefoot, wearing her jeans and a sleeveless, silvery top, cut just low enough to reveal the smooth white curve at the top of her breasts. She smiled. You like? she said.

He nodded solemnly. She turned in a slow circle, trying to get him to say something: anything would do. The song was ending and he was already trying to replay it in his head. She stood there for a moment and he said, It's beautiful, but neither of them was entirely sure what he was referring to. They stared at each other for a moment, and then he took her hand in his, his fingertips stroking the inside of her wrist.

What was that song? he said.

What song?

The one that just played.

I don't know, said Lisa. Do you want me to ask Rosie? He nodded. Come with me, she said.

He stood obediently and followed her across the room. The sunlight coming through the window was being refracted through a prismatic crystal that hung on a string from the mullion, casting dapples on the painted floor that reminded him of drops of blood.

Rosie, she said, and the other girl turned and smiled at them. What are we listening to?

Rosie hesitated. I'm not sure, she said. Someone gave me a turntable a few weeks ago, so I picked up a bunch of records at Ad Astra—that store on Jane Street, you know the one I mean. The covers are beautiful. She gestured to the stereo. Go take a look.

Caruso reached the turntable first and gently lifted the vinyl, looked at the label, flipped it over, and read the other side with a puzzled look on his face. It's just a single, he said. Same song on both sides. Lisa went and stood next to him, following his gaze. It's in French, she said.

Do you know what it says?

She looked at it again. *Miel et cendres*, she said. It means . . . Honey and Ashes. I guess that's the name of the song.

Were they singing in French? Was that the language?

I don't think so, Lisa said. She looked to Rosie. OK if we play it again?

Sure, of course, Rosie said.

Caruso replaced the record, lifted the needle, and set it down at the beginning. They listened for a bit. That's not French, though, said Lisa. What they're singing in. I don't know what it is.

They listened together, but now everyone was watching, and when the little phrase reappeared all Caruso could hear was it slipping away from him. He was disappointed, and when the song ended he wanted to ask her to play it again, but he knew that would only draw more attention. He looked at Lisa pleadingly, and she took Rosie aside. When they left, half an hour later, he had the record in his hands, unsure how to carry it, or how to play it when he got home, but more convinced of its importance by the opacity of its format, the mystery of its instrumentation, the glory of the language, which he couldn't speak and didn't understand, the fields of emotion it traveled. He wanted the song—not the recording but the song itself. He was the patron hallow of End-Up City, carrying his borrowed and beloved song like a lamp.

In Lisa's apartment on 26th Street, later that night, she sat astraddle him and smiled, put her fingertips on his ribcage and then bent down to listen to his thin chest, which rose and fell from the strain of love, and the effort of breathing with her weight on his abdomen. — Is that where it all comes from? she asked him. Mr. Genius Baby.

He took his hand off her hip and pulled her hair back in a ponytail so that he could see her face. I don't know where it comes from, he said. She was a year out of college, and he was self-conscious about the fact that for all his money, and everyone asking him to sit down for a few words, or stand up and sing, and the lights and the sound, and the girls who shimmied up to him—for all of that, she knew things that he would never know. He would catch sight of the books arrayed on shelves across her room and find himself unable to imagine what was inside them, the tales and tributes, the secrets, how things were done and what they were called.

She took his hand and put it back on her hip, then slid it up her waist, using it to lightly brush her breast. He had the hands of a much older man, with strong, spatulate fingers, the tips of which were so calloused that she could feel each ridge on her nipple; she loved his hands. She rose up a few inches, making him arch a little, and then settled down again, one frame of fucking in an endless film.

They were on the fourth floor and her window was open; as late as it was, there were children playing outside the school across the street, making a sound like no other, not a conversation or the noise of a crowd, but the shouting of childhood itself, a birdy chorus of demands for attention and screams of surprise. Two more months, Lisa said lazily. She was talking about the summer. Let's have a party.

If you want, we'll have a night so fantastic we'll make the moon blush.

No . . . I don't want a party, she said. Can we go on a trip? Rome. Istanbul. Paris. She smiled, this was their game: ask for everything, change your mind, pull promises from him like toys from a closet.

I've never been to a foreign country, he said, as if he'd just realized the fact. I've never been outside New York. He stared absently at her ribcage.

Oh! she said. Paris is the most beautiful city in the world. I want to take you. Can we go?

If that's what you want, I'll give you so much Paris it'll be spilling out of your pockets, he said.

She opened her mouth in delight, dilating and dilating, her eyes all the way open. Everything would become what it should be. She turned her head and put her ear to his hairless chest. What I really want . . . she said.

What?

She paused, maybe this was part of the game, maybe it was the game coming to an end, it just came out of her; she lifted her head and looked at him. — I want to get married.

To me? he said. He could be like that sometimes, almost shockingly thoughtless: she never quite knew whether it came from insecurity or distraction, and ordinarily she would have said, No, baby, to this other guy I've been seeing. But not then, she just looked at him carefully. He cocked his head to one side, and she wasn't sure whether he was frightened, or in love, or what he was; now she was afraid to break her gaze for fear everything she cared about would change, and she would never forgive herself. Still, he didn't say anything. She wanted to take it all back, half-angry at him and half-angry at herself. Never mind, she said, and still he just looked at her. Never mind, she said again, but she didn't want to release him, because then it would all be over. As for Caruso, he was thinking about girls, he was thinking about money, and about Reggie and his mysterious unhappiness: things he'd never spoken about with Lisa, or anybody else for that matter, but he kept them with him. He couldn't imagine staying with her forever. He couldn't imagine living without her for an hour. Was that what marriage was for, then? Stay. If he would stay and she would stay, then that should be enough; but she wanted to get married, and to him. What did that mean to her? — You want to get married? he said.

She wanted to tell him not to be stupid, but that was one word she knew well enough not to use. She came from a bookish family, kind and well-schooled: her mother's mother had been a professor at Columbia, her mother's father a dean. So she was careful with her good fortune, but was he aware of his? Don't you do it, she said. Don't you dare embarrass me. Tears came to her eyes.

She was so beautiful when she was crying, the most beautiful thing Caruso had ever seen, ripening and spilling, the shine in her eyes, the droplet on her pale cheek, the thickening of her brow, the anguished arc of her lips. He couldn't help thinking that weeping was what she was made for, the fulfillment of her features, so perfect she glowed with grief. This among other things were signs of his cruelty. I'm not going to embarrass you, he said. I promise you, I promise. I promise. She looked at him through a curtain of mortification. What? Someone outside called up to the window: Caruso! Caruso! Lisa! Caruso! Neither of them moved. From the kitchen, the sound of the refrigerator motor started up, a hum like the coming summer itself.

AN AFFLICTION

When she got sick, Bridget got sick quickly, a flu that turned out to be worse than the flu; one morning she woke up hardly able to breathe, and wound up spending that night in the hospital. She was sent home the next day with an inhaler that she hated and a bill she couldn't pay. Why didn't you call me? Stephanie said, almost angry with fear. I would have come and stayed with you. Bridget just shrugged, but when, a few days later, the inhaler proved ineffective, she phoned Stephanie at work and the two of them went back to the hospital. The doctors didn't know what it was, exactly, they believed it was a rare form of interstitial lung disease, it was just starting to show up in the literature, and they were unsure how to treat it. They could expect other opportunistic infections to follow: she was a mess inside. Bridget received the news with a strange acceptance; she took it as somehow apt, something she had earned or deserved, but Stephanie was so stricken that the entire world outside the hospital stopped like a paused movie, and by the time the two of them were standing silently on the corner, they were the only living beings amid crowds of soulless puppets, who were dressed as people but without the thoughts that people had, about how strange it was to be alive. She had wanted to say something encouraging, like,

You're going to beat this, or, I bet they'll find a treatment soon; it can't be that hard, and doctors know everything now; or even, I'll take care of you forever. But Bridget would have hated all that. Her face had a blue cast, and she was stooped over just a little bit, her hands at her sides, as if she'd suddenly become very old. She just kept getting older from there.

CAPITALISM

Now Benny was a donkey, taut between two identically strong towers, made ribby and miserable. Poor bridge, stranded underneath its fanning tension cables, this sadly singing bridge, this municipal harp, its song now cresting overhead. Here came that helicopter again, cutting through the air so viciously that it made him want to weep: what damage these great machines made. Why was anything bigger than a man? And did everything have to spin? That was the way of all matter, whirling rapidly, the whole world a centrifuge that never stopped, not for a moment.

Even now it wasn't clear whether Mickey had been venal or merely stupid, or perhaps something in between the two. It began with a registered letter from a small museum in Mississippi, to which he'd sold a Bantu neck piece; they were restructuring their insurance policies, and their appraiser had requested some written documentation of its provenance and an explanation of how its price had been determined. After some research it became clear that Mickey had sold it to them for almost ten times its real value. How? What could he possibly have said to them? Benny would never know. Mickey had kept only the most cursory record of what he had done, written down on sheets of paper torn from a school notebook and stuffed into the bottom drawer of a flat file where Benny had kept printed matter. There was no way to reconstruct it all, and as Benny started making calls he found himself facing one embarrassment after another. That little man—he'd done things that were entirely incredible, impossible to ascribe to either greed or naivete; they seemed to be unmotivated, almost random, and in the space of a few months he'd caused a damage that was as difficult to describe as it would be to repair. He had let some things go for a small fraction of what they were worth; others he had sold for huge sums, in many cases to collectors who should have known better and would be mortified to discover how easily they'd been deceived. The result was the derangement of a tiny market.

There had been a small box of old vinyl LPs; they'd been used as filler in a larger shipment at least a decade previously, and when he'd first opened them he'd found that a good third of them had cracked. They were recordings of music from Mali, Senegal, some ethnographic studies, a few things that had been pressed in Paris for fly-by-night labels, and a 12-inch single in a picture sleeve with the words Honey and Ashes written on it in French. He had no use for them, so he'd left them on a bottom shelf in his storeroom, where they'd been sitting ever since. Mickey had taken them and sold them to a record store on Jane Street called Ad Astra, promoting them as a great and undiscovered cache of obscure African pop.

In another field he might have been an extraordinary asset, Mickey: there were a thousand businesses that would have been delighted to hire him. But this was a fragile trade, and the works chose their owners as much as the opposite—chose by their history and affiliations, by the nature of their passage to America, by their materials and forms. The business trafficked in objects of no obvious worth; to disrupt it as Mickey had done was to turn delicate discriminations into a joke; his colleagues would be years sorting it all out, and they would never forgive him. Still, the entire matter might have gone on for much longer if

Mickey had remitted the proper sales tax; as it was, he'd filed the letters of demand from the state Department of Taxation and Finance in the same drawer where he kept the receipts, and it was only when a notice came from the post office indicating that a registered letter was waiting at the nearest station, requiring Benny's ID and signature, that things truly began to come apart.

News spread quickly through the community of dealers and collectors, and almost immediately Benny was shut out. His phone became a useless instrument, a lump of inert plastic. Clients refused to talk to him, though the messages he left them were always polite. His e-mails to curators went unanswered. No one looked in to see him, the days went dead. Everyone had learned of his disgrace; even his suppliers in Africa had dissolved into the sun. The Dealers' Association was considering an investigation.

The museum in Mississippi would have to have its money returned, along with an apology, but there was no money. It was gone from his accounts: Mickey showed no signs of having stolen it, it had simply vanished in a whirl, like snowflakes on the hood of a running car. Then he began to get calls from various collection agencies, politely and then not so politely reminding him that he had accounts to settle; and late at night he heard other voices, darker, whistling: You owe us, you owe us, and we're going to break your back. He had to hire a lawyer to try to sort it all out, a pasty man with thinning hair and a belligerent mustache, who had the half-conscious resentment of a man who hadn't done especially well for himself, and enjoyed knowing that other people had done worse. He took great pleasure in delivering bad news. This isn't going to make you happy, the lawyer would say, barely containing his pleasure. Another lawsuit, another penalty, another dozen hours billable at an ounce of gold each. Dark news, dim news. The lawyer referred to Mickey as *your girlfriend's brother*, as if those very facts—that he would have a woman in his life, that she would have a brother, that the two of them would have some influence over his business—were signs of a foolishness so pronounced as to be culpable, as if he should have known better. Well, and he should have, but what about love? Once, upon discovering that Mickey hadn't left his signature on a single document, the lawyer had hooked his thumbs in his vest and said, Guys like you make it possible for guys like me to send our kids to college. Another time he had startled Benny by asking him, out of nowhere, if he had a will. No, Benny had replied, adding quite sincerely, Why? Am I going to die? The lawyer looked at him as if he was trying to remember his next line, a moment so awful that Benny's stomach clutched—less because he thought the man might say something terrible than because he might try to say something clever. But the lawyer just gave him a strained look and said, I'm not a doctor, I don't know anything about that.

No, Benny had replied. No—OK. There were three paper coffee cups on the cluttered desk between them, and the lawyer picked them up in turn, looking for the one that still had something in it, but none of them did. Benny said, There's mail piling up inside the door.

Mail? said the lawyer. What kind of mail?

That's just it, I don't know, he'd said. It's inside the door. I can see it on the floor inside.

You've been going by there.

Just to check on things.

But you're not going inside, right?

I can't get inside. It's all locked up.

Probably just as well, said the lawyer. Best thing you can do now is just put some distance between you and that place.

That place, he repeated dully.

Yes, said the lawyer. As much as possible, we want to make the store look like it was Mickey's. The more we can put the responsibility of this on him, the more protected we're going to be.

Can you tell me, just—please? Benny said. When will things be back to normal?

Oh, never, said the lawyer, as if it were the most obvious thing in the world, and then he stopped. You didn't think it was going to be fixable, did you? No, no, no, no: I might as well tell you right now, the best you'll get out of this is bankruptcy. And until then there'll be court dates and so on. That's a couple of years. And then reestablishing credit. It's a long process. The lawyer tapped his pen on his blotter. It was a cheap pen. I'm not going to lie to you, he said. Maybe someone else would, but I won't. We don't have much to bargain with, so all we can do is dig in our heels, and then, when the time comes, we're going to deal, deal, deal.

Benny held his hands up, palms out and capitulating. The conversation was growing more and more inane. All I want is for something to make some sense, he said. The lawyer was scrutinizing him. That's the thing about being a lawyer, he said. Nobody comes to see you when they're happy. He sighed and opened a folder on his desk, then flipped through a few sheets, paused to read something, turned over a few more pages and then stopped. Well, here's the lease, he said. It says here you have a little less than two years to go. That's not going to happen. Technically, you're responsible for the rent during that period, but I doubt very much the landlord will enforce it. Usually, in these circumstances, you stop paying for a while and a judge will let them reclaim possession. I'm sure they'll be perfectly happy to have it back. Rents around here are going up 20 percent a year. You'll be doing them a favor.

What about the art? said Benny.

The inventory? Whatever's left of it is going to be part of the claim.

I need to see it.

Not a good idea, said the lawyer. You want to stay as far removed from this process as you can, and just let things take their course.

I need to see it, Benny said again.

It could be worse, said the lawyer. You could go to prison, breach of trust, fraud, and all that. But I don't think that's going to happen. It's a very decent world you live in, you know. I think everyone just wants the matter settled. Don't you want this settled? Don't you want to move on?

Move on to where? said Benny.

The lawyer looked down at his desk and said, I've seen men in worse shape.

And then Jillian walked away. Oh, it's just too much, she said, as she gathered a few things she'd left in his apartment and stuffed them into a shopping bag from his own store. Too much, too much, her eyes in tears. All this fighting. All this anger. He had protested that he wasn't angry, but that wouldn't have been true; there had been moments when he'd been short with her. She had apologized, in her fashion, for what Mickey had done, but she didn't want to know all the details—or any of them, really—and she would tear up if he said anything against her brother. You're not a forgiving man, she said in a cold moment. She should have clawed him to death right there and then; he wouldn't have felt a thing. She should have torn him open and thrust her sharpened fingers deep in his viscera, pulled the tendon from his bones; she should have finished him and left his insides strewn about the ground. Why was his heart still in his chest, and still beating? When everything else was empty, why was he still breathing? Why was he walking, when there was nowhere to go? It was late July, the hottest summer in years. His feet never moved, but he was walking, that was just about all he did; he walked through the neighborhoods, glass, stone, steel, past cars with dark windows, newspaper boxes on the corners, over sidewalk grates and broken curbs, all of it growing brighter, then darker, then brighter again, like a time-lapse film of the days shuffling by, the clouds jerking overhead, the sun flickering to life and then extinguishing again.

Just once during all those hours walking had he seen her. He was coming down from Houston Street like a bull in a slaughter pen and there she was, standing on the corner all alone. By the time she noticed him, he was no more than a few yards away and staring at her, not threateningly, almost in disbelief; she frowned, took a step with a single faint hitch in it, and then smiled at him and said, Hello—as if he were someone she had met once or twice, and not the man who had kissed her everywhere, whose hands had been soft between her legs, who knew the sweet, almost rotten scent of her own skin, like the petals of a decadent flower. He didn't know what to say, so he walked around her on rickety legs and turned unhindered down Eldridge Street. Even if he'd wanted to stop he couldn't have: his knees kept folding and unfolding. What would she have said? Then the street had gotten strange, bright, and sorrowful. There was a restaurant a few feet in from the corner of Stanton that he'd never seen before, a new, fashionable Cuban sandwich place with tables in the window so tiny they barely had room for more than a coffee cup or two. Trapped behind the glass there were two couples in three chairs, one of the girls sitting on a man's lap with her black-clad legs crossed at her knees, and a copy of the day's newspaper held down on the floor beside them by a green bottle of mineral water. Benny reached up to his neck and found himself caressing the notch beneath his Adam's apple with the tips of two fingers, pressing on his breath. By the time he reached the Bowery he had his hand wrapped around his own throat, and his hold was strong enough that he could feel his face reddening and warming. There was a woman standing on the far corner; she was wearing a T-shirt with an American flag on it and staring at him as if he were screaming at the top of his lungs; but he wasn't making a sound. The light turned, but the woman remained still, watching him, while he stood there softly strangling himself, until the light turned again and he started back to his apartment. Goodbye to the woman, goodbye to the city.

He went home, but found himself unable to sit or lie down, or even to touch anything, as if life itself was winding round him like a whip, eager to flay him at the slightest provocation. He stood in front of the refrigerator, wondering if there was still a bottle of white wine in there. Jillian liked to indulge, just a little, at the end of the day: she thought it was sophisticated, though she rarely finished it. It was the pour she liked, the weight of the bottle, the pale yellow liquid reflecting candlelight. Inevitably, a bit of her lipstick came off on the glass, which she would rub away with the edge of her thumb, idly, familiarly, and with the same unconscious care with which she rubbed the lipstick from his cheek when she came into the store to kiss him in the morning, smiling at the act of fixing a problem that she had smilingly caused. Either the last bottle was in the refrigerator or it wasn't. He decided it was better not to know, so he went and stood in the center of the living room. The sun was going down, but it was very hot, and his shirt was stuck to his chest with sweat. It was an unpleasant room; he wouldn't be sorry to abandon it. An unpleasant city, full of barbarous strangers. He wouldn't be sorry to leave. He looked around at his shabby furniture, a shelf of books, a lamp he had picked up in Abidjan—a place too far away to ever see again.

The telephone rang, and he broke from his reverie and went to check the caller ID: Portland Services, it said, and he let it ring a few more times before the machine picked up. No message, just a few seconds of static, the sound of someone else who had given up on him. He cleared his throat as if he were about to make a formal statement, but no one was listening, and besides, he had nothing to say, so he settled for a soft hmm instead. For a second he considered trying to write something down, a pretty thought, a profound expression, but instead he found himself smiling, standing and smiling, and then it was night.

THE ORIGINAL

Stephanie had never told anyone the whole story, the true story, not from beginning to end. There had been no one to tell; but she knew every word and turn. She had met Bridget her second year at college, and they had been an improbable pair, one so quiet and the other so adventurous. She had watched as Bridget had gone through one boyfriend after another, and some of them were fine and some were not, but none were good for her: Was anyone good for her? They hadn't been close, in those days, but they'd been friends, and for some reason they'd kept up, though sometimes a month or more would pass without their seeing each other in person—longer, the year Bridget was seeing a grad student named Mike, and Stephanie herself was spending time, on and off, with a woman she'd met in a restaurant in Greenwich Village, who she later discovered was the owner's wife. But when both affairs were over they fell on each other for company and comfort, and they became much closer, talking on the telephone almost every night and even traveling up to Toronto together, a last-minute trip during the spring break before graduation. Everyone who thought about it had assumed that she was in love with Bridget, but that wasn't quite true; she'd never been the type who fell for straight girls, that just wasn't her way. — No, if anything, the romance ran in the opposite direction, though that wasn't quite romance, either, it was just a crush, even unto jealousy. After their first commiseration, Bridget had never asked her about her own affairs, and if Stephanie mentioned anyone, from a woman she had noticed to a woman she had slept with, Bridget would listen without listening, a glum, annoyed expression on her face, and then change the subject. She needed attention, which might have been tiresome, were she not so entertaining on her way to getting it. And then one very late night, in a glossy red hotel bar they'd run to in the pouring rain, she brought her face close to Stephanie's, and then closer, letting her mouth fall open a bit, until Stephanie backed away and Bridget giggled. I'm sorry, she said. I just wanted to see what it was like to be a man. Stephanie had a few things to say to that: that she needn't apologize, it was an attempt too feckless to be significant; that loving her wouldn't have been anything like being a man, anyway, it was more complicated than that, and also simpler; but then, many things were both more complicated and simpler than Bridget seemed to think, though to tell her so would surely court dismay. All these came to her simultaneously, so she didn't say anything at all, and Bridget sat back and pushed her still-wet hair out of her face, as if to point out that it was the rain, wasn't it, that had led her to this, and the illicit luxury of the hotel, the hour and the coil of the hour. You're like a cat, sometimes, Bridget said. I should call you Pussy. A man in a double-breasted suit sitting a few feet down the bar looked up at them as if he was going to say something, and the bartender immediately walked over and asked him if he wanted another drink, distracting him while Stephanie turned her chair slightly to block his view. A quizzical flicker moved across Bridget's expression, but Stephanie didn't bother to explain. That was the sort of thing Bridget needed: someone to protect her in small ways, with gestures she would never notice. That was twenty-two years old, twenty-three, twenty-four.

Stephanie had owned a camera for as long as she could remember, a little Japanese thing, mostly automatic and with a lens the size of her thumbnail. She took as many pictures as she could afford, nothing very formal: it was part of being a good girl, the one who kept a record when everyone else was just spending time. She took pictures, kept memories and sought out new ones just to take pictures of them; she used it on the city, which was as alive as anyone who lived there, with all its turns and warrens, alleys and windows, its whispers and shouts; and she used it on Bridget, whom she saw, by then, more than anyone else by far. Bridget huddled in the corner of a restaurant booth, eating french fries; putting on eyeliner in the bathroom mirror; sitting out on the fire escape with a cigarette, four floors above the sidewalk, her hands shaking as she tried to light it, and then giving up and saying, Stop taking my fucking picture already, I'm not in the mood. But when she was in the mood, and that was most of the time, she had a mysterious ability, if ability was what it was, to come alive on film, every angle of her expression and flutter of her thoughts registering on the image. Bridget, disguised as a pop song: she wasn't a self-conscious woman, or rather, she was, but not to the point of self-regard. She could be strikingly thoughtless one moment and almost motionless with doubt the next, callous to one man and solicitous to another, when neither of them deserved it. She had an admirable sense of style, but it was more a matter of the way she wore things than the things she wore. She would talk to anyone, and some of them would roll their eyes at her, but it was never clear whether she noticed and hid her hurt, or if she was already somewhere else. She just gave it away, and gave it away; and Stephanie was there to catch it, to see and see again what a person was, what a picture was, what a picture of a person was.

By then, photography had become Stephanie's work—on impulse and alone one weekday afternoon, she went up to 47th Street and spent two months' rent on a new camera, a gorgeous silver and black body, with elegant dials and an advance lever that made a pleasant snicking noise. It was as precise as a sonnet, the first perfect thing she'd ever owned, and when she got it home, opened the box and held it in her hand, tears came to her eyes. — And Bridget was proud of her for having discovered a vocation, envious because she hadn't yet found any of her own, and good enough to suffer the difference in silence. They talked on the telephone almost every night, Bridget temping down on Wall Street after hours, all alone and bored, Stephanie moving restlessly about her apartment, trailing the extra-long cord of a powder-blue Princess phone. They spoke about nothing, bits of the day, something seen or not seen, long moments when all they shared was the sound of their breathing, filling the empty prologue before something, anything began: Bridget waiting for a man to call her back, or to find out whether she got a new, better job, or for a night when she had time and money to visit a new club. At the end of every week, Stephanie would take her rolls of film down to a lab on Broadway and slide the battery-sized plastic canister across to the man behind the counter, with their coils of time inside, waiting to be reborn in full color; and then she would return a few days later to pick up her prints, scarcely able to wait until she got outside the door to riffle through the little folder of photos, just to get a taste of what she was going to remember, a glimpse of reflected time that made her scull back to the moment she'd taken the picture, often of something she'd already forgotten: Bridget laughing with the back of her hand pressed self-consciously against her mouth; the sun burning at the base of a cross street; the crumbling facade of an abandoned apartment building; a boy with bright green eyes and a gorgeous, grown man's voice, singing on the sidewalk in the East Village. I've got a new one of you, Stephanie said one night. You look like a French movie star. I want to see that, said Bridget. Let's meet up for breakfast sometime next week. She showed up at that breakfast with her hair dyed white-blond; her face was unnaturally white, her eyes seemed out of focus, her mouth was red and her tongue dark, and at first Stephanie thought she was just hungover, and she made a little joke about it. Bridget said, No, she was just getting used up. She picked nervously at the label on a bottle of ketchup. That's what it felt like. She said the city was killing her, sometimes with pleasure, but more often by some kind of long, slow drowning. She couldn't find a job that wasn't pointless and dull; she couldn't find a man she could be with, because there was always another, always another man and always another girl just like her to take her place. She couldn't find a place to live, that was a perpetual problem, this string of sublets and crazy roommates, bad neighborhoods, too far away; and every time she moved she lost something that she cared about, an old suitcase she bought in a thrift store, a pair of earrings, some books: misplaced, stolen, vanished, piece by piece. There were times when Stephanie had trouble reaching her, because she'd switched jobs or switched boyfriends, and hadn't called in with new contact information; under *B* in her little maroon address book she had almost a full page of numbers, each one carefully crossed out and a new one written below, except for one that had been crossed out and then circled, when Bridget had moved back in with a man with whom she briefly reconciled, and then crossed out again when she'd given up on him for good.

Stephanie had a small inheritance, nothing extravagant or even comfortable, but better than panic: enough to help her afford a one-bedroom apartment on Renwick Street, albeit one so small that there was hardly room for more than a bed, a dresser, a table, and a bookcase. She'd gotten a part-time job as an assistant photo editor at a company that published trade magazines, where she spent her days going through pictures of cars, vending machines, bedroom sets, farm equipment—simple nine to five. From time to time, when things were worst for Bridget, she'd come spend a chaste night, the two of them in the same bed but wearing long T-shirts, untangled, sleeping. More ardent love remained elusive, at least for Stephanie; she couldn't find it, not the way she wanted it, anyway: long, patient, subtle in its finery, more linen than silk. All the matinee tragedies of desire left her unimpressed: seduction, urgency, gossip, infidelity, betrayal. They had no part in her instinct for partnership, even as she occasionally worried that she was missing something invaluable. Do you think I'm fussy? she asked Bridget on the phone one night. Outside, a car alarm was sounding, and all the skyscrapers were standing with their shoulders thrown back, as if they were soldiers in their finest, waiting for the queen to pass by on parade. Do you think I'm cold? Do you think I'm spoiled?

What are you talking about? said Bridget. You're perfect. You just have a smaller pool to choose from. She laughed lightly. Anyway, you have work to do. — Hey, did you read this thing in the paper this morning? It said that there are more roaches in New York than there are atoms in the universe.

No, said Stephanie, smiling softly to herself.

You're wearing your tiny smile, aren't you? said Bridget.

My what?

That little smile you get when you have a . . . droll inkling rolling around inside your head. I can hear it in your voice.

Droll . . . said Stephanie.

Inkling, said Bridget.

There was a long pause while they each hovered over the other's breath, close, slow, lazy, reluctant to part. Stephanie was feeling so languid she could hardly speak. I had a dream last night, she said. I was looking in the mirror but I wasn't there. I mean, I couldn't see my reflection. I had no reflection. All I could see was the room. It was like all the rules of perspective had been suspended. Do you think that means something?

Doesn't it mean you're a vampire?

Oh, that's right, Stephanie said. I forgot about that. — In my dream, though, right? Not in real life.

Another night, a year or two later, or maybe a year or two earlier, Bridget going on about a man she was working with, a lawyer in a firm where she was temping after hours, her voice incredulous, wicked, and insistent. He was charmless and vaguely arrogant, and above all bland; he spoke heartily to his coworkers, but when he thought no one was looking his face relapsed into its entropic default, a slightly sulky blankness, his watery eyes vacantly searching the middle distance. That afternoon, he'd brought his wife in to meet his colleagues: she was young, pretty, smart, self-possessed, even cool, in her own way. How could she have married him? How could she let him fuck her every night? Was she really going to have his children? It made no sense at all, it was like some violation of the laws of nature. Bridget seemed truly outraged by the whole thing, though it was hard to tell: she could joke completely seriously, giggle through the most mournful account.

I knew a lot of girls like that, growing up, said Stephanie. Upper East Side girls, with no more imagination than a penny.

That satisfied Bridget, and she changed the subject. I bought a book for you today, she said. I saw it on a table outside a bookstore and I thought you had to have it.

What is it?

I'm not telling you, said Bridget. I'll bring it next time I see you.

What was that book? Stephanie couldn't remember it now, or even if Bridget had given it to her. It didn't matter: things flowed between them, back and forth. Books, clothes, songs, jokes, advice, encouragements, promises, pictures, sometimes returned and sometimes kept.

They had a few more years like that, she and Bridget, in the embrace of folly and superintendent days, and while she wouldn't have called them happy at the time, waiting as they both were for the starter's pistol to fire, in retrospect they were a kind of pastoral, because they were vivid, and memories obey force more than virtue.

Bridget could be exasperating, her torments repetitive and vague and largely self-made; from time to time, Stephanie would wonder why they were friends at all, given how different they were, whether there was some sense to it or whether mere accident had brought them together and shared experience kept them so. No, but there was some meaning to it, either way. They were bound together by a wild devotion, the stronger for being unreasonable.

Will you do me a favor? Bridget asked one weekend evening in May. They'd taken the subway out to Coney Island, elaborate graffiti on the outside of the train car that said PEACE and LOVE in sky-blue bubble letters, the inside as gauded with cuneiform as a Babylonian tomb. She had photos from that day, but they were different from her memories. In her mind she was the same Stephanie, Bridget was Bridget, New York was New York; but in the pictures she was another person in another time, full of odd customs, savage rites and curious folkways: silly haircuts, blue eye shadow, boxy cars, homeless people on the sidewalks, rococo crimes in the papers. The boardwalk was rotting, the trash cans were overflowing, and there were weeds growing through the ties of a decommissioned roller coaster. The wind bore the smell of sea filth, oily and acidic. Bridget, dressed in black jeans and a blue and white flannel shirt with the top three buttons undone and no bra beneath, had begun the day entranced by a pornographic paperback she'd found beneath a bench overlooking the beach. They'd spent a happy hour driving bumper cars while disco music blared from speakers in the scaffolding overhead, but by the time the afternoon was ending, she'd become sullen and morose, picking at a recent breakout on her face and staring at the ground. They'd splurged on a cab to come home, and now they were standing on the corner of Broadway and Houston, silently preparing to part, Stephanie to her apartment, and Bridget to a bed she wouldn't name. Will you do me a favor? Bridget said.

Anything, said Stephanie, and immediately she felt a sensation she had never experienced before, the chill of angels crooning in their cold heaven, as she realized that she meant just what she'd said, meant it much more than the occasion warranted. The word had drawn it out of her: she would have done anything Bridget asked of her; it was a devotion that rose straight up through her, not romance or even love, really, it was something higher and harder, a certainty beyond faith. A newspaper blew across the intersection. Satellites rang like bells overhead. Bridget just smiled.

THE RIVER, PART TWO

Caruso began by pulling the song apart at the seams, separating out the
melody from the rhythms, the inflections from the counterpoint, but
also verse from chorus, and chorus from bridge, intro, and breaks, all of
them coming apart like a toy, drums from horns, organ and whatever
that instrument was, somewhere between a guitar and a banjo. It had
taken him three weeks to find someone who could translate the lyrics,
but when he had them on paper he found them florid and inadequate.
And time was time for kissing. He knew the song was called Honey and
Ashes, and he could tell that it was about a love lost long ago. That was
all he needed and he wrote his own words, mirroring the syllables of a
language he couldn't understand by following the melody and the surface
of the singer's voice, from revelation to the first meeting, the evening
walk, and then demurral, disavowal, the passionate return and the final
disappointment, line by line and vein by vein. Lisa caught him scribbling
couplets in his notebook one night, midway through a dinner she had
cooked from scratch, and he spent the rest of the night trying to make it
up to her, even as the song was begging him to write it down.

He sat in his studio and worked on his laptop, laying out all the
pieces and trying to learn them, each by each, and then he started to
lay down scratch tracks, playing all the instruments himself, though

not all of them well: the drums were half-live and half-manufactured on the computer, and he spent three entire days standing before a timbale in his studio, trying to find the right attack. He wanted to know how much he could subtract from the song and still retain the qualities that had drawn him to it: its sweat and sweetness, the lamenting minor-key verse giving way to the thrilling major-key chorus, like the roof lifting off a prison. How much could he add without ruining it? He took the bridge and moved it to the front of the song, putting the change before the action. He modified the melody so that it was slightly different in every verse, anticipatory, then true, then shocked, and then wise. He kept offering up rhythms, pretty and plain, but none was pleasing, none captured the strange passion of the original. This troubled him: If he was not the beat, then what was he? He wanted it to slither and snap, like a snake, like a thunderstorm. Was the melody on top of the drums, or were the drums beneath the melody? Could the whole thing shudder right there, could it stop and tremble? Who could get that sound for him? He had a percussionist named Acorn, a small man with a dark, wrinkled face and rock-hard hands, not strong enough to power a band, but he could turn it up on top. For a kit drummer he'd use Tino, who was twice his age, who had been with him since the very beginning, and who never missed. Then Sabrina playing bass, if he could find her, if he could afford her, if she would come back: he had discovered her and now everyone wanted her. She had called him from LA, her voice full of joy, and told him that she'd passed an audition and joined Comet Comet, and he had been heartbroken, resentful and cold, because he would never find anyone who had her touch, who could find an unexpected harmony, double up on the hook for half a measure and then drop to its inverse underneath, no one could do rope tricks with the beat the way she could. Beautiful Sabrina, he would beg her if he had to. He'd seen an old guitarist named Chico play all by himself at a little club in Harlem one night, tall and thin and wearing a suit and tie; he picked like he was playing flamenco, with all five fingers on his knobby hand, but it didn't sound like flamenco: it sounded like eagles coming down from the sky for a kill, their claws out and their feathers burning. He wanted that, he would spend if he had to.

It was another two months before he could get his players together in one place, and even then it wasn't everyone: Chico had agreed to play and then disappeared, right off the planet, or so it seemed. The studio was a smallish space on 32nd and Eighth, and they had one rainy day in late March to get the fundamental tracks down, seven players and an engineer named Leon, working off a demo that Caruso had e-mailed out a week earlier. He arrived early and waited anxiously, bits of sound buzzing around his ears, and there was Sabrina in the anteroom, carrying two cases, one in each hand, and a gig back over her shoulder. She leaned her head and kissed his cheek, and he could smell the shea butter on her skin. No amp, right? she said. You want me to go straight into the board?

He nodded vigorously, almost childishly. Otherwise everything will bleed into everything else, he said. We can treat the sound afterwards. Do you mind? There are a few little practice amps in the control room if you want to use one.

She smiled, bright and broad as always. Don't mind one bit, she said. I can hear better through headphones anyway.

Then came Tino and Acorn, with duffel bags full of sticks and brushes, one snare drum and a pair of congas, then an all-purpose keyboard player, and two backup singers. Then the guitarist showed up, Caruso wasn't sure who he was, exactly: a friend of a friend of Tino's, he was a white man in his late twenties, modest in demeanor, disheveled in his attire, meticulous with his instruments. He was a stand-in, though no one had told him so. His part was to be a place-holder, which would be wiped from the track and replaced by Chico, when Chico was found. Damn, we've got a lot of people in here, said the keyboard player.

I want that feeling, said Caruso. Just us, together in a room.

You think you're going to need more than three octaves from me? said the keyboard player. Because I brought a smaller synth. It'll keep me from taking up too much space, unless you want the full range.

How does it sound? said Caruso.

It can do everything the big one can do, it's just missing the very bottom and the very top.

Caruso thought for a second. No, let's set up the big one. There's room, we'll make room.

That's a beautiful song, said Tino as he unrolled his stick bag. Did you write it?

Not really, said Caruso. Some of it. He didn't explain any further, and now the backup singers were warming up together, laughing as they traded absurd exercises.

It's a strange scale, said Sabrina. It's like a . . . I don't know how to explain it. I've been practicing it. It starts out in A minor and then turns into . . . F? I'm pretty sure it's F on the chorus, but it gets there through some kind of chromatic thing. Is that right?

The keyboard player, having raised his synthesizer on its stand, played out a couple of inaudible chords. Let me get plugged in here, he said. I had a little trouble with the same part.

It doesn't really matter how you get there, said Caruso. Leon began handing out headphones. Just as long as everyone gets there at the same time. But you, he said to Sabrina, are going to need to hit the root right on the first beat of the chorus. You, he said to the keyboard player, you can land on whatever inversion you want, as long as you don't lose the rhythm. The keyboard player nodded.

The guitarist wore no expression. What about me? he said.

We're going to put you in direct too, said Caruso. And you can just play the chords, just . . . you know? Play the chords. OK? Please, because we've got a lot of stuff going on down below.

Tino started hitting the kick drum, a steady thunk like a giant ax striking a petrified tree. The engineer spoke from the control room: You don't have to worry about the kick, he said. We got that last night.

It sounds pretty squishy, said Tino. You want me to tighten it up?

No, no, said Caruso. I'm going to put an electronic kick behind it. I want yours to be a little more . . . musical. You know what I mean?

It's like a marching band, Tino said, with a note of disdain. He was worried that it was going to make him sound weak.

I want your snare to crack hard, though, said Caruso. It doesn't have to be loud, but I want it to sound tight.

Honey and Ashes, said Tino.

Honey and Ashes, that's right.

The backup singers were whispering about something, the guitar player was untangling chords and fiddling with the knobs on his guitar, trying to find a tone. A little brighter, but not too bright, said Caruso, and the guitar player fiddled some more.

Presently, everyone was settled in. The room was stuffy and one of the backup singers pulled her shirt briefly off her skin, then waved her hand over her face. Acorn hadn't said a word all morning, but he had a wide smile on his face that somehow he would wear for the rest of the day, as if he couldn't play without it. All right, said Caruso. He was nervous, clutching the sheet of notebook paper on which he'd written the lyrics. Can we try it? He stepped into a soundproof booth and put on his headphones. Can you hear me? he said.

Everyone nodded, and Leon broke in to say, Loud and clear. Play something. Sabrina? The bass was in. Guitar man? The guitar was only in the left channel. OK, guitar man, keep playing. The band waited while Leon stared at his board, then punched his finger on a button, and the guitar came through on both sides.

Same tempo as the demo? said Tino. It was unclear whether he thought that was a good idea or not.

Caruso nodded vigorously and said, No. I'm not much of a drummer, so, you know, play it how you feel it. Tino said, OK. Sabrina cracked her knuckles loudly and then laughed. The guitar player was finessing his tuning, and Caruso wondered if he should have just left the guitar track open for the time being. You want to count it?

Tino nodded and counted off, and they began, Caruso's voice first, singing the word *Once*, and then everyone joining in, chasing the song like children in pursuit of butterfly. They made it halfway through the first verse and then Caruso stopped singing. Tino lifted his hands and the whole room subsided. Sorry, said Sabrina.

Too fast? said Tino, and Caruso nodded. That's about where it was on the demo.

It sounds faster with everyone playing.

Where do you want it? said Tino.

It's not . . . said Caruso. I can hear it, but I can't describe it. Like a slow heartbeat. He put his fingers on his wrist, but he couldn't feel anything. Like this. Softly, he tapped out a steady rhythm on the head of his microphone. Around there, like that. Tino nodded. But I want the drums to be faster, so I guess that's double time. Is that possible?

I can try, said Tino. Might be better if Acorn filled in, though. He can do it in double time, get right in between the beats.

Yes! said Caruso, turning to Acorn, who was already taping his fingers a little tighter. OK, good. He sang a half measure by himself. Leon? Leon? Is there something on my voice?

Leon punched in. No, he said.

No? said Caruso.

There was a pause. A little reverb, said Leon. And a little, just a touch of harmonizer.

Sabrina laughed. Leon likes his toys, she said.

Take them off, please, said Caruso. Let's do it again.

This time they got through a verse and a chorus before Caruso stopped them again. Can you start setting up the chorus a measure earlier? he said to Sabrina. You don't have to swap out the keys, but if you can find some stairs between them . . . She nodded and then bent over her bass and played a few variations, making a couple of false starts before she settled on something that sounded all right. She looked up and nodded. She said, I think Acorn is turning the beat around, right after the intro. I like it: it sounds great. Should I follow him?

Caruso said, Let me hear what you mean. Bass, percussion, and drums started again, and yes, the rhythm took a stutter-step just before the verse started, shifting emphasis from the downbeat to the backbeat. Like that, Sabrina said, and Caruso thought for a long moment. Yes, good, he said. Yes. But don't let it get too obvious, OK? Maybe you and Tino should hit all four for that section, and let Acorn bring it around by himself.

They played it through one more time, and then one more time. Sabrina and Tino found the pocket, and made it expand and contract ever so slightly as they followed the song through its cadences. Bass and drums, how could they play so intimately when they barely spoke, and Tino was older by twenty years? The song began to burnish like a piece of brass, rubbed until its contours emerged, the figures filling in, the glow slowly appearing. They went through a few more times, stopping and starting, adjusting the sound of the snare, swapping in a vintage ribbon microphone when Caruso started ad-libbing a falsetto part that came through a little screechy, slotting in the backup singers, and then they broke for lunch—reluctantly, because Caruso didn't want to lose momentum, but it was early afternoon by then and he couldn't keep them hungry. Please be back in an hour, he said, and he stayed behind to rewrite a couplet in the second verse, too focused to eat, too anxious, too young.

By midafternoon he was losing his voice, even as he was settling into the song; a soulful grain started showing up on the tracks, which worked so long as he could control it, but how long would that be? Maybe we should just get the instrumental tracks down today and save the vocals for later, Tino said, but Caruso said, No. He could see that they were enjoying themselves now, moving to it, smiling, signaling back and forth across the sound, and here and there a little wide-eyed at themselves. Twice more through, and after each there was a period of silence while he stared at the floor, trying to hear what was missing, then looked up at them all with nothing to say. The engineer brought him a cold can of grape soda. The guitar player put down one guitar and picked up another, a hollow-body. This all right? he said, and Caruso nodded.

Again, said Caruso, and they started again. Now his voice was catching on the song, and he was bobbing around the microphone like a dancer, smoothing out the pops and sibilance, alternating smooth and hot. There were tears in his eyes: he was outside the song, begging to be let in, but it sounded as if he was inside and just begging. He shut his eyes as they made their way into the second verse, took an audible breath, and let out a moan that Sabrina must have known was coming, because she put a sweet note right beneath him. Ohhhh! he said. He backed away and let them vamp and pump while he listened to the changes, striking the air at his hip with his right hand; he held out his palm to Tino and Acorn, then looked at the rest of the band and slowly lowered his eyes, and they found the next usable sustain and rode it to silence, leaving the percussion ringing the beat. He dashed out of his box and picked up a pair of claves from a chair, got back to the mic by the end of the measure and began hitting them in slight syncopation. Then he moved his mouth in again, murmured something no one could hear, and sang a long, sobbing *Please!* and wound his arm. At the top of the next measure the band came in again, and just as he crooned the first words of the last verse he heard a noise, like nothing he'd ever heard before, it surrounded the note he was singing, crossed underneath it, and then rose, as full of harmonics as a bell tower, somewhere between discord and concord, glorious and troubled; then it seemed to calve in two, not vertically but from side to side, like a river around a boulder, rejoining on the other side before suddenly dissolving into little runnels of sound. He listened to it fade and then realized he'd stopped singing; the band stopped playing, little by little, and left him standing there, helpless, the pit of his throat shining with sweat. He said, What was that?

What was what? said Tino.

That sound, he said. Someone played . . . He was having trouble telling whether what he'd heard was real, so suddenly had it appeared, so quickly had it gone, so thoroughly had it reset the resonances of the song. He looked at each of them in turn, but none of them was sure what to say. He tried to re-create it in his head, but it was like the element of a dream that snags the consciousness upon waking, not pleasant and not unpleasant but somehow authoritative, having laid low the border guards and then faded, elusive, a trickster, thief of sense, slipping away at daybreak. He called to the engineer. Leon, did you get that? Can you play that back?

A voice came back over a monitor. Got it. Do you want to hear the whole thing?

Just from about thirty seconds before we stopped, Caruso said.

Coming up.

The song picked up in mid-measure. As the transition back into the verse neared, Caruso became nervous: What if he had imagined it, what if it was gone? Soon, soon, and yes, there it was, just as strange a new heaven as he'd thought it was. It was the guitar.

He pulled his headphones off. That was you? he said to the guitar player. Did you do that on purpose?

The guitar player nodded.

White boy! said Tino gleefully.

What was it? Can you do it again?

Sure I can, the guitar player said, his hand resting on the neck of his instrument, his face expressionless.

What was it? Caruso asked again.

It was . . . the guitar player said. It's hard to explain. It's kind of an Ornette, a harmolodic thing, open tuning.

It's beautiful, it's perfect, said Caruso. He stopped again, swimming in his own thoughts. Everything had tipped up: Chico had just been fired; this modest little white man, barely noticeable and soft on his feet, had delivered the very thing he wanted. He turned to the others. Can you follow him? he asked.

The guitar player shook his head. I don't think it'll work that way. The idea is that everyone is following everyone. That's the . . . technique. It's like a round.

A round, said Caruso.

Not a round, exactly, said the guitar player.

Caruso smiled, the wide, delighted smile of an exhausted child who's just whipped the Devil. Keep the beat. We're going to have to start all over again, he said.

THE GREAT APOSTLE OF CHARITY

When they finally admitted Bridget to St. Vincent's and Bridget finally agreed to go, Stephanie visited her regularly, but she could never remember where the entrance was. She would get off the subway at 14th and Sixth, and she knew she had to go south a few blocks and then turn, but each time she came up on the building from a different angle, and each time it was the wrong one. Occasionally she could follow an ambulance to the emergency room doors, but the emergency room wasn't where she wanted to be, and she would have to get directions from a staffer on duty, who was usually busy with other things and could do little more than point. She would go back outside and walk around to the other side of the building, or another building entirely, up two floors and down the hallway to the nurses' station, which was lit in a pinched, nauseating shade of fluorescent light. She didn't understand the place, the pavilions and entrances, behind which lay a warren of halls, cul-de-sacs, stairs, partitions, and signs, and she always felt like Bridget was waiting impatiently, though in fact she rarely called ahead to say she was coming: at first Bridget liked surprises, and by the end she didn't know whether today was yesterday, or twenty years ago, or a thousand years from now, though she believed, even more than she had before, in true love, which had no beginning and no end, and she believed that Stephanie was everyone.

Each time, Stephanie came in through a different entrance, down a new set of halls, trying not to disrupt the other patients' privacy by looking in the rooms as she passed, though the truth was, it was mostly the visitors who didn't want to be seen. The patients, who were sometimes new and sometimes the same, always watched her as she went by, waiting with wide eyes set in dark faces, with thrush on their tongues and sores on their arms, for a small smile or wave, which she was barely able to give because she had to save as much of herself as she could; and she was afraid of them, not because they were sick but because they were almost all men, and it felt like they formed a sort of coven, guardians of a suffering the more enormous for being shared among them. She wanted to tell them that she was like them, in her way, and that she, too, was losing someone she loved to something no one understood, but she didn't want to assume anything, impose anything, or somehow hurt anyone who was already suffering. And she felt young, at twenty-nine, though many of the men were the same age or younger.

There was always that smell in the air—a hospital, but it wasn't simply the smell of death or decay, or the efforts made to cover them up, and she didn't find it unpleasant at all. There was the warmth of bodies in bedsheets, and something palliative, along with the smell of clean floors, cheap but freshly laundered underthings, the metal and musk smell of blood, along with scrubbed hands, the plastic bags and tubes and the latex gloves, and beneath it all something faintly sour, like the pleasant funk of a wet dog, which she found arousing: an utterly inappropriate response but too deep for her to deny. She would sit in the waiting room, wondering just how and why her reactions had become so unspeakable: little fiery imps that no one else could see, burning holes in the silk. There was a woman in sky-blue scrubs sitting alone at the front desk, who regarded her skeptically. I'm back again, Stephanie said.

Visiting hours are over.

Stephanie frowned. I thought they might be, but I couldn't remember.

It's past ten, the woman pointed out.

I guess that's right, said Stephanie. This was the only time I could come. Can I see her? The woman softened immediately and said, Sure, you can. She was small, brown-eyed, and tired, and she looked a bit sallow against her uniform. For a long time, Stephanie had assumed that the colors the staff wore had something to do with the travels and humors of the body: blue for veins and red for arteries, green for bile and pink for breath, grey for age and black for death. It was easier than trying to distinguish between residents and doctors, specialists and surgeons, various kinds of nurses, orderlies, and rehab attendants. She never remembered anyone's name, either, and she doubted very much that any of them had ever bothered to learn hers, but in time she'd come to understand that the nurses were in charge: they watched over everyone, kept them breathing and relieved their pain; they kept the information, and if she asked them in just the right way, they would tell her what was going on. Such a strange job, drifting through this warren of dark rooms, seeing over each grim play and mournful audience. Who are you here for? the nurse had asked, and when Stephanie told her, she'd checked the name against a list and then nodded toward a trio of black plastic chairs that were bolted to a nearby wall. They often told her to wait, but she was never sure why: they had stopped treating Bridget some weeks previously and now were simply keeping her pain at bay, unable to cure her and not allowed to kill her, letting nature takes its heathen course. Down the hall, outside another room, a pair of men were waiting, just like her, one seated and one standing;

the one standing was resting on a cane, both hands grasping the knob, his eyes widened in the perpetual stare of emaciation.

Then there was a man seated beside her, with an empty chair between them. He was in his sixties, and dressed in tan corduroy pants and a blue dress shirt, and he sat hunched forward, staring at his loafers. Eventually, he turned his head and looked at Stephanie. His grey hair was disheveled and an inch-long white thread dangled from one of his buttons, but he looked as if he'd lived a comfortable life, and the habit of doing so had left him with an air of health and competence. I'm sorry, he said. I heard you mention Bridget. Are you one of her friends? he said.

She nodded. From college, she said.

I thought so, he said. You look about the same age. You're close to her?

Yes, said Stephanie.

I'm her father, the man said, but Stephanie had already realized as much: Bridget had never spoken of him, but he had her glimmering eyes, her delicate chin, and the same slight California accent. I didn't even know she was sick, he said. She never told us that she was, until just recently. She sounded fine on the telephone. Why would she do that? Stephanie shook her head. As soon as I found out, as soon as I heard, I came out here. Too late to help her. Almost too late to see her. I don't understand this all . . . He paused, and Stephanie held herself perfectly still, like a tree after a rainstorm trying not to cast droplets from its leaves onto the ground. My name is Doug Greene, the man said.

I'm Stephanie.

He nodded. Have any of her other friends been to visit her?

Some, said Stephanie, though she had never seen any.

Why do you come? he asked.

To be here, she said.

Greene made a noise, it was unlike anything she'd ever heard come out of a person, a retch of grief, low and sharp. He took a few moments to compose himself, taking off his glasses, looking at them, cleaning them quickly on his shirttail and putting them back on again.

A nurse came over to them. Mr. Greene? Bridget may not make it through the night. I think you should be prepared for that. She turned to Stephanie and said, Since you're not a member of her immediate family, I'm afraid I can't allow you to see her tonight. Unless her father agrees.

Of course I agree, said Greene, reaching out and putting his hand on Stephanie's wrist. Will you come in with me? She nodded, but she had the uncanny feeling she was being led into a séance, her reverence tempered by the sense that it was all quite superstitious, these attendants, these machines, these medications—once they stopped working, they were merely rituals for people without rituals, as immaterial as a prayer. She started to flicker through some phase changes, and she said to herself, Pay attention, this is only going to happen once.

She and Greene followed the nurse down the windowless hall, listening to the soft rustle of the other woman's shoes interspersed with the tick of her own heels. She found herself wondering whether it would have been very different if Bridget were dying in the daytime—more frightening and less like sleep, or maybe less frightening because it would feel like a decision. There was nothing to be glad about, but Stephanie was grateful. By morning, if the nurse was right, Bridget would be gone, sent off with the darkness, as if it had decided to cradle her and keep her. Bridget had always liked the city at night. They got to the threshold of the room, and there she lay, a small dying creature, quite still, face up with her eyes closed, the machines beeping softly, and Stephanie thought, Oh! She's gotten so tiny. When did that happen? She was a little doll that had been left out in a radioactive rain, with Bridget's features, but distorted, half-washed away. A noise—that same bark of grief—reminded Stephanie that she wasn't alone, and she looked up to find Greene, on the opposite side of the bed, his face looking at once perfectly normal and wildly contorted, as if he was making an enormous effort to keep his features in place. He crouched down beside Bridget's bed and said her name. Bridget. Bridget. It's Daddy. He stood up and leaned over her, brushing a bit of hair from her shrunken forehead. Bridget. I'm here. It's all right. At length, he stood up straight, breathing in and in and in. Bridget's eyes opened and she looked at him sadly, and her mouth moved, though she didn't speak. He reached down and touched the back of his fingers to her forehead for a long moment, and when he drew them away her eyes were closed again. For a second Stephanie thought he had summoned the mercy to somehow kill her; but the machines were still beeping, and Bridget sighed heavily. She drew a chair from the corner of the room up to the edge of the bed, sat down carefully, and picked up Bridget's hand, a clutch of bones wrapped in paper, half-expecting her palm to be cold, but it was so hot she almost dropped it again. It was as if there were some kind of reactor churning away just below the surface; she seemed to have an enormous power running through her, animating the machines that surrounded her, even as she lay there too weak to speak; there was something working under her skin, radiating from her heart out to her tiniest capillaries, though Stephanie couldn't tell whether it was the end of life or the beginning of death. She sat for a while with Bridget's hand in hers before she spoke, and then she whispered. — Hi, she said, we're here. We're all here. Everyone is here. Without turning her head, Bridget opened her eyes and began staring at the ceiling. She spoke, loudly but to no one, her voice hoarse from disuse: No! No! I've been good, she said. I was good! I was good!

Stephanie squeezed her hand. Yes, you were, she said softly, but Bridget didn't respond. Greene said, All right, it's all right. Was she still breathing? There was a long moment, and then the room was upside-down, and Stephanie was upside-down in it, tumbling as the planet turned over and over in the darkness; she could feel her tears flying every which way, alighting on her chin, streaking the ceiling, plashing on the sheets. Surely a nurse would be arriving any moment, brisk and irritated, to right the whole thing, smooth the night so they could begin again; but it didn't happen. Bridget sighed a bit, closed her eyes again, there was a brief second of silence so complete that Stephanie could hear the keening of her own nerves, already calling for the thing they missed, that she would miss for many, many more years, a hole in her that she would carry forward. Then one of the machines starting sounding, and Stephanie carefully held Bridget's hand for a few moments longer and then looked at her father, who was still staring down as the nurses and doctors started streaming in. Goddamn this city, he said softly. Goddamn the faggots and what they do. Before she could respond, or even decide what a response might be, she was gently pushed aside by a nurse, and she was out in the hallway, looking through the window, trying to get a glimpse at the corpse of her beloved as the doctors worked in furious pantomime, making gestures over someone who was no longer there, and wondering which, after all, was the true trace of the soul, the wet throb of the heart or the hot wind of a living breath.

CASCADING FAILURE

All up and down the spine of the city there were unexplained surges and dips in the power supply, failures on the grid as the network struggled to match the throughput to the load, too many air conditioners and entertainment systems running at once, and then suddenly shutting off as the millions changed their minds, refrigerators opening and closing, extra subways added for Labor Day weekend, and the A train short-circuited when someone running from the police though the Canal Street station threw a stolen bicycle frame onto the tracks, where it fell with one end touching the third rail, causing relays to trip circuit breakers here and there. Then it came back on line, with a billow of voltage that burned through circuit boards, caused modems to power down and then start up again, servers to overheat in the carrier hotel on Hudson Street, the balance shifting and faltering like a wing walker, now saved by a brownout in Kips Bay, now threatened by a sag in Battery Park—a thrilling and perilous journey toward midnight, almost madcap, in its way.

Are you a Brodie? Are you a Brodie? There was a young man on the path below Benny, sitting astride a motionless bicycle, his sweet moon-face turned up. — That's what they're called, people like you. If you are what I think you are. Brodie was his name. That was more than a hundred years ago. He jumped. He didn't die, though: he lived, but ... You're probably going to die. If that's what you're going to do, that's what's going to happen. You know, there's going to be cops out here in about three minutes, probably. You'll hear the sirens. Someone called them, someone who drove by and saw you up there, which wasn't all of them, but there was probably at least one. I'd call myself, but I don't have a phone. It broke. I had it in my pocket and I hit a patch of grease or something, and I went down, shattered it. Fucked up my knee, too, but it's getting better. But anyway, the cops are going to come. Look how hot it is, they must be out, all over the place. People get loose in this kind of weather, they know that, so they're ready. Cops in cop cars, EMS trucks, fire trucks, there's probably going to be a helicopter. They take this stuff very seriously, they don't like to lose someone. It makes them feel bad. I've seen them before, man, they'll throw a net on you. They hit you with that thing, a Taser. I've seen them do it. They'll tie a rope to your ankle when you aren't looking, they don't care.

Benny glanced down at the man and said, Who are you?

I was just riding across and I saw you, the man said.

Riding on the bridge? said Benny.

Across it. I'm on my way to the show, there's a thing in Washington Square Park, a concert, this kid Caruso—have you heard of him? Everyone has heard of him. Anyway, but I saw you so I stopped. At first, I thought, Well, if you wanted to jump, you should jump. That's your right. You've got rights, and that's one of them.

OK, said Benny.

Only now I'm not so sure. No. I don't think you should.

Why not? said Benny.

Because I know the question, the man on the bicycle said. That question you really want to ask. And I know the answer too. I've thought about this a lot. I don't know why: it's just one of the things I think about. So you're up there, where you are, and you wonder ... Is it going to hurt? Not dying, not leaving, none of us know that. What I mean is, is it going to hurt when you hit the water. You don't even want to admit it, but that's what you're really worried about. You don't want to say so because it should be unimportant, when you consider what you're doing, when you think of the hurt that brought you up here in the first place. Physical pain, physical . . . suffering or whatever, that wasn't on your mind until you got up here, and now you see how hard the world is, all this steel and concrete. And the water is hard. Maybe it'll be over quick, and all you'll feel is the first hit, that first tremendous hit, enormous, like nothing you ever felt before, and it'll be the last thing you feel. But if that doesn't do it? — He gestured. Swimming around in that, maybe with some broken bones. Drowning like that? He smiled, and Benny didn't know what to say. If he hadn't been thinking about that before, he was thinking about it now.

The young man knew he was, and he spoke very clearly, and now with a certain sweet confidence, like an announcer on public radio: You didn't think it through, he said. There's no disgrace in that. I just wanted to suggest to you some issues that you might have neglected to consider.

Benny looked down at the water. Thank you, he said.

OK, I'll leave you alone, the young man said, and he must have ridden soundlessly away, because when Benny looked for him again, he had disappeared.

Something had changed: the city was gone. Instead there was just a long, gently curving landscape, a grey shadow against a black sky, with masses scattered among it, barely distinguishable forms, primeval, shattered and jagged, like the mountains of black ice that lie on the far side of the River of Death. It was very quiet. So it was too late, then, and perhaps the young man hadn't been real, either. And yet he'd felt no pain, no impact, so he must have died the instant he touched the water. And the great mystery was solved! He hadn't dared contemplate it, but now he knew what no man knew: every wraith was real. For surely he was thinking, and somehow he knew that he had the sense of sight, even if there was nothing to see, and he could hear, even if there was no sound. The universe was kind and he was strong. He felt strangely braced by it all, more confident, perhaps, than he had ever been before—but no, it was something beyond confidence, it was a solemn ecstasy, a slow, serene, opiate peace, half-alert, all of love. It was no wonder the universe kept this glory hidden, leaving each to ponder, speculate, and worry. If this was death, why should anyone wish to remain alive?

He felt himself exhale, inhale, exhale again,— and then he heard the sirens, just as the man on the bicycle had said he would, and he saw the police cars coming over the darkened bridge, he felt a surge of nausea and he realized at once that he wasn't dead, after all, no he wasn't. No he wasn't. No he wasn't. Living was his crime, so living was his punishment, the true one he was sentenced to.

There was a movie showing in Washington Square Park, projected digitally onto five big screens scattered here and there, synced through an elaborate wireless apparatus that was temporarily stationed on the second floor of the library on the southeast corner, a silent film, Cocteau's *Beauty and the Beast*, for which a DJ with a girl singer from the Bronx was meant to provide the soundtrack, and then afterwards, Caruso would sing his new song, just the one, before sending these children off into the night. It was August, and the heat had been working its way into the concrete for weeks: tonight it seemed to be releasing all at once, almost audibly rising and rising, hotter and damper than breath. There was no breeze. We all knew the world was coming to an end, sooner or later, but no one was sure whether this was the start or just another warning.

The show, which was open to anyone who cared to come by, was having problems: the screens had become unsynchronized and sometimes got stuck on an image, or showed failure messages from the operating system. Occasionally, they went blank altogether. The sound, too, was faltering. The mix dropped out of the singer's monitors and she couldn't hear herself; after a few minutes of this, she turned to look around with tears in her eyes but found no one sympathetic to return her expression: the DJ was hunched over his machines, and, since he was having trouble with his headphones—the left side had switched to the right, and the right side had disappeared—he hadn't noticed that she'd missed her cue. The crowd in Washington Square was unhappy, though more indolent than angry: they were uncomfortable, and many of them were very young and waiting mostly for Caruso, waiting to see him and to hear his new song, the one about honey and ashes, and unsure of why this ancient, awkward fairy tale was playing, why there was no color. They wandered this way and that in the park, some drugged, some sick, some street-flirting. A pair of pretty boys and a pretty girl sat, all three with their legs entwined, on one of the benches. There were people standing in the windows of the sleek buildings overhead, watching silently. At each of the corners of the park, two policemen on horseback were stationed, looking at once bored and stern as they sweated through their uniforms, occasionally instructing someone to stay on the sidewalk, even though the streets around the park had been closed off, or saying, Keep it moving, to no one in particular. The horses themselves were wet and martyred. On stage, the DJ missed a segue when one of his turntables started spinning too fast, and then faster, and faster still, while he switched back to the first and tried to find a beat again, throwing the singer off; the song carried on for another minute or so, and then ended with a curse, followed by the brief, amplified sound of a police dispatcher whose frequencies had somehow found their way into the PA. What's that? the dispatcher said. 10-9. 10-9. I can't hear you. What have you got?

There was an imp in the mains. On one of the screens, Josette Day as Belle was lying back in bed, looking at herself in a small mirror on her nightstand. On another, Jean Marais as La Bête was drinking from a stream. The singer left the stage, and the DJ followed. Applause here and there. The movie played on, while the students who had conceived of the show sent frantic messages back to their colleagues in the library, trying to explain what was going wrong, though they didn't know themselves what was causing it.

Caruso was in a tour bus parked on Waverly Place, just west of MacDougal, sitting hunched over on a narrow couch, wearing a sleeveless T-shirt and the wide-legged trousers from a red zoot suit, and sipping hot tea with honey. The bus had been rented just for that night, and it was idling so that the air conditioner could run, but it was still uncomfortably warm inside, and he repeatedly dabbed at his brow with a handkerchief. He was nervous. It didn't help that the door to the bus kept opening and closing, as various members of his backing band—for that night, there were ten of them, in all—grew bored with waiting and went out to stand on the sidewalk, then became uncomfortable standing outside and climbed into the bus again. The only one who wasn't restless was the keyboard player, who sat motionless in back. Caruso watched him for a bit. What do you think? he asked.

We're going to be all right, the keyboard player said.

Lisa had been out wandering through the park, in part because she was curious, in part as a kind of reconnaissance, and in part, too, as an escape. She had always felt useless when he was working, which lately had been almost all the time. She wasn't able to see him as often, and when she did, there were always other people around, musicians, promoters, new friends, someone with a video camera, and there was never enough time to introduce her to them all. It was like watching him float out with the tide, and all she could do was wait anxiously on dry ground for it to turn and bring him back again. Some of the people around him didn't think much of her; nothing they would say out loud, not to her face, anyway, but they didn't like it, her and Caruso, together. Some of them looked right through her, as if she were an apparition, as unreal as the illuminated figures on the movie screens outside; she found that unnerving. And he didn't need to sleep, he could get by on four or five hours a night, but if she didn't get a full eight hours she could hardly make it through the next day, wandering around in a heavy cloak of dumb exhaustion, mumbling and numb, forgetting to take things when she left, fumbling with her door keys when she got home. She was supposed to be working at a production company down on Varick, but she was going to be fired soon, by a woman she hated, which will set off a season of tears and sobbing, made a hundred times worse when, after a fortnight during which they'd hardly had a chance to talk, let alone make daytime love, she'll feel like she needs Caruso to know how lonely she is, how stray and blue. But she won't be able to find the right words, so instead she'll tell him that she doesn't think they should see each other anymore, and he'll just say, Maybe you're right. She'll notice the muscles on his forearms; he hadn't had them when they met. When she leaves, she'll be crying so hard she'll get hiccups, the way she did when she was a child. You'll find another, everyone will say to her, but she won't, not for quite a few years.

In the park that night, she'd run into a friend from high school, a boy named Evan, who was shirtless and so high all he could do was say her name over and over again, grinning like a moon-man. Lisa, Lisa. Lisa. He put his hands up in an attitude of prayer and shook them back and forth like a Buddhist. Lisa! Lisa. He bit down on his lower lip. Lisa Lisa. He laughed nervously.

Hi, Evan, she said patiently. Having a good time? He nodded vigorously, and she said, Good, and kept walking.

Somewhere among the treetops, La Bête was staring at his hand, which slowly began to smoke. The smoke seemed to drift off the screen and wend its way through the branches, eventually dissipating as it reached the ground. She bought a watermelon slushy from a vendor, took a sip, and frowned: it was so sweet she shuddered. She liked the idea of having a cold red tongue, but she couldn't imagine finishing it, and she looked for someplace to throw it out, finally settling for balancing it on the very top of an overflowing garbage can on the west side of the fountain, her fingers outstretched for a few seconds as she backed away, just in case it fell. La Bête had been transformed by love into a handsome young prince, and together he and Belle were ascending into the sky. She lingered on the image for a moment and then started to the bus, through a park that had grown ten times as full in the preceding ten seconds, so that she had to push her way against the crowd as they streamed in, vaguely worried that someone was going to grab her as she passed. By the time she reached the door she was soaked through, her shirt pasted to her back, her eyeliner smeared; but it wasn't much cooler inside, there must have been a dozen people crammed in there, watching Caruso as he sat in front of a makeup mirror, doing something with his hair. She went over and kissed his cheek softly, and he smiled nervously. We're almost ready, he said, and he stood so suddenly that the entire bus abruptly shifted to accommodate him. Donny, don't miss the turnaround, he said, and from somewhere in the back of the bus a man said, I got it. Can you go out and tell them we're ready? he said to his manager.

The others were standing now, one or two stretching, Tino playing a brief, quiet paradiddle on a cushioned headrest, the horn players blowing the spit from their valves, the backup singers checking each other's hair. They began to file out of the bus, and outside there was the smell of ozone, and the faint, muffled rippling in the air that comes from a waiting audience. Backstage there were cables and consoles and scaffolding, and a stage manager with a headset, and Caruso stood at the edge of the stage, surrounded by the band, while the MC pumped up the crowd; and then they were inside the lights, swiftly plugging in and walking up to the microphones. Caruso turned to catch the eye of his mixer, who was standing just offstage holding a laptop that had been loaded with clips and effects. He didn't want to speak, he just wanted to sing his song. The drummer started playing and he danced a little bit around the mic, and then stepped up and gestured to the band.

Nothing happened, and he immediately thought they'd missed their cue, but his voice was gone, too, if he was singing then he couldn't hear himself, all he heard were the drums behind him, and he turned to look at Tino, but now curiously he couldn't see him, the lights had vanished, or the dark had crept in. The drums faltered and stopped, and Caruso walked apprehensively to the lip of the stage, where the crowd stood unmoving, some staring around at the others beside them as if they were shades, some with their heads back, looking up at the sky, and behind them all, the buildings of Lower Manhattan, impossibly tall and perfectly dark, like spaceships in a primitive time. There were no lights, no lights anywhere, and he craned his neck back just like those in the audience below him, and saw a thousand sparks spattered across the pure blackness overhead, swirling dizzily, seeming to dart and fall, and then rise back up again, a terrifying beauty that he, with all his life played under city lights, had never seen before, had hardly known existed: the universe of stars, prickly and cold, all come down and swarming around his head like heaven's nocturnal crown.

Stephanie was walking down Fifth below 14th Street, the night hot enough to melt glass, students on the sidewalk, a man in kitchen whites standing outside a deli smoking a cigarette and watching passersby. She was looking up, watching a backlit man in a bedroom a few stories up lifting hand weights as he watched television, but she didn't take his picture. She was saving her sight for the park; she had wanted to find a crowd, it would be a fitting way to finish her portfolio. Her time at the Carrier Institute was coming to a close, and she still hadn't decided what she would do afterwards, but tonight's picture was to be a gift to the place. She had something softer for the Costers, but to the Institute itself she would give the population at night, the people they were all working for—and there it was: she could hear the sound of someone shouting happily over the loudspeaker, the voice echoing up the avenue until it was unintelligible. She could hear the cheers that followed. There was a slight pause, and then the drums started playing. She walked more quickly, and as she did, she lifted her camera to shoot down the avenue, but something had gone wrong and her viewfinder was dark; she panned around, looking for the edge of a building or a street light. She couldn't find anything. The drums had stopped, but there was the sound of cars honking, so she brought the camera down and everything had changed.

Two cabs heading west on 11th had pulled out into the intersection, where they'd become entangled with a car going south on Fifth, a man on a bicycle, and another man in an expensive suit who was walking a small terrier, which barked harshly over the sound of shouting. No one was hurt, but no one was quite sure what had happened, either, and she stood with a small group, watching the five or six protagonists illuminated by the harsh raking light of their headlights. The bicycle was bent under one of the cabs, the man who'd been riding it was menacing a cabdriver with the metal chain from his lock, swinging wildly while the driver of the other car tried to calm him, eyes wide, hands up. Easy, man, easy, friend. It was an accident. No one got hurt. She looked north on the sidewalk; the deli was closed, all the stores were closed, and a hundred car headlights were illuminating the scene, as if a spaceship had somehow landed in their midst, silhouetting all the humans on the street, who stood scattered and unmoving in confusion and awe. For a moment she thought she saw Bridget emerge from the crowd and slip swiftly past her, and she almost called her name. Then someone spoke, lips pressed right up to her ear, murmuring something though she couldn't tell what, and for a moment all the figures arrayed in front of her stood stock still, shadows in a snapshot, all of them thinking the same thing, mournful and supplicating: Miss me, will you miss me? Though I am nothing, will you miss me?

The stasis was interrupted by the sound of breaking glass, another accident? Or someone was angry, overhead the buildings loomed, all of them snuffed out like so many candles, tendrils of mist floating in the night sky above the wick-dark towers. The man with the terrier stood beside her, the dog panting heavily and looking up at the two of them as if they had an answer. He took a cell phone out of his pocket and dialed a number, turning away to talk, but the call didn't go through. Hello? he said. Hello? He brought the phone down and stared at the screen, which illuminated his face so starkly that he looked like he'd been singled out.

He glanced up at Stephanie and put the phone away, and then turned in a full circle, but he didn't start off, because he wasn't sure which way he was facing. He said to Stephanie, Which way is down-town? Then he looked down at the dog, who peered back up at him eagerly, waiting for instructions. — What just happened?

As far as I can tell, someone ran a red light, Stephanie said.

He shook his head. I'm just trying to get to 10th and Broadway, he said, sounding angry and frightened. Which way am I supposed to go?

At first she thought he was shaken by the accident, but when she tried to help him she found she didn't know, either. There's the church, she said, pointing across Fifth. But—what street is this? She looked to see which way the traffic was facing, but she wasn't able to read the street sign.

12th, I think, the man said.

So the traffic is going east, she said, though the traffic wasn't moving at all, and the cars were honking again, all of them, louder and more insistently, creating a terrific cacophony. A young black man in street clothes stepped into the intersection and started directing traffic, haphazardly but with great enthusiasm, dancing a bit and making elaborate gestures as he turned to address traffic from every direction. I think that's south, Stephanie said, moving her finger around like the sight of a rifle.

OK, the man said, but he didn't move. Down the avenue she could see people walking in the street, swarming around the immobile traffic like rioters with nothing in particular on their minds. What the fuck is going on? the man said.

I'm not sure.

But something is? he said.

I think so, said Stephanie. But I'm not sure. She could smell the buildings. Now a police car lit up in the middle of it all, lights whirling, siren sounding in short, uneven bursts, mixed with the blat of its radio being keyed through the speakers, though the police inside didn't say anything, and the car, like all the others, wasn't going anywhere. There was something missing, some law of nature had dissolved. Was it gravity? She felt the sidewalk firmly under her feet.

The man on the bicycle was the first to understand. He wasn't angry anymore; instead he spoke with great wonder, like a penitent at the Final Horn, speaking truth in advance of belief. The traffic lights are out, he said. All the lights are out. There are no streetlights either. There are no streetlights, there are no . . .

The buildings, Stephanie said, there's no electricity.

The man with the dog laughed in discomfort and delight. It's a blackout, he said.

THE CITY PSALMS

These are the orders, and the names of the orders, the nations and the colors of the nations, the life and the scents of life: the restaurant, the taxicab, the subway, the apartment and the window in the apartment, the trucks that deliver all things, and all the things themselves. The lights and the sound of the lights, night and the absence of the stars. These are the sayings.

To walk with your head back, so that you can see the buildings rise around you, is to reveal your throat to the world. By your throat you will show the color of your skin. And still, you change color constantly. Ask them when they come for you, What color am I now? Ask them, Am I good? Ask them, Am I free? Ask them, If this is not my home, then what is my home? And then you will lower your face and hide your throat again.

Your pockets are heavy with silver and gold, silver and gold. It slips through your fingers, no longer precious but cinders on the wind. And you think your tears are a response to the joy of prosperity, when it is only the sting of cinders in your eyes.

The old live high in the air and on the street, and the young live on the street, and in between are those who are no longer young, but not yet old. The sick live inside and the sick live outside, and not all of those who live underground have finished with their time. The wealthy, too, live high in the air, and the poor live high in the air. The poor live on the ground, and sometimes underground, and you dare not try to tell a man's station by how he lives, or where: not even his neighbors know.

Who is rich and who is poor? The buildings stretch up into the sky and multiply into the distance, and who can count them all, let alone assign to them their kings and paupers, those preferred and those forsaken? Besides, what once were palaces are now overflowing, the people stream from them like kernels from a sack of corn. Do not forget that each provides its share of nourishment. The labor of each man is a full day's labor, and each is a ministry—the nurse as much as the banker, the teacher as much as the talent, the dealer as much as the doctor, and those who do nothing but talk. Some of these are rich, and some are poor, but the city is one city. Each thinks that their city is the only city, and that all the others are pretenders, but the city is one city.

Is there no place in the city where a man cannot walk? Once there was danger on almost every road, and corners and sorties that only the most foolish or most daring would brave. Someday there will be danger again, but for now, every part of the city may be crossed. Go to the watchman and ask him, May I cross? Go to the watchman and ask him, Am I free? Am I free to go home?

If someone should say to you, Yes, you reply Yes or you reply No. But if someone should say to you, No, you do not reply. Didn't you learn silence at your mother's knee? She would teach you when to speak and when to be silent, when to get down on one knee and when to straighten your back, when to pay and when to be paid, when to steal and when to surrender.

Oh, that someone should hear me, and then come to me!

There are no children, but there are children everywhere: they appear in the afternoon and then vanish again as night falls. Where do they go? Only the children themselves know (some men say they remember, from the days when they were children themselves, and some women say they understand, but their memories are false, and their understanding is false). The children's city is their own, exile from it is permanent, and then there is only forgetting.

How many children are there, aside from none? There is never one. There are very many, more than one man could count, even if he should spend a whole year at the task, counting from a January morning to a December night. They have a thousand joys and a thousand sorrows, and in time they will forget them all, but they will remember friendship. Thus as men and women they will have friends the way children have friends. Even those who have no friends have a million friends. At night you can feel the messages arcing over the streets and buildings as they call to one another, saying, I am well or I am restless, I am happy or I am sick, I am here, and here, and here, and here. Meet me, come and find me. Then you will go in the form of a friend.

Have you a master? — Well, then, have you a servant? You say no one is your master: then who are you traveling to see? You say servitude has long since been driven out: then who is that knocking at your door? And are you free?

There are those who fall in love every day—in the period between the opening of a subway car door and its closing again, on the corner, at their windows. They have coupled everywhere: in this bed and that bed, in stairwells and the bathrooms of restaurants, in the shadows of the streets at night, in public parks, in the backs of taxicabs, on rooftops. They walk the streets and wonder, Where is my love? Who was the last, and who is now approaching?

Where is your love? You cannot find her (him), not down the streets or across the avenues, not in the squares, neither in this room nor in that, in public or in private, in the daylight or after dark. Where is my love? You have ridden the trains uptown and then downtown again, and across, and you have waited on the corner, resting, and craned your neck to gaze up at the tall buildings: you wonder if your love is there.

There is danger on the corner because men congregate there: peddlers of vice, vendors of stolen things and intoxication, and all common and uncommon practices. They lurch and whisper, they call to you with promises, they want to steer you to a doorway, behind which lies the true fulfillment of each desire. You hesitate. You wait for a sign, and the sign will come—not the lights on the streets, which are false signs, but the glory of danger, intoxication, and noise, which are the true signs, and the only ones.

Go to the corner, stand on the corner, and open your eyes. What do you see? Is not all the world walking by?

Where do you eat when you are not at your table? And are you ever at your table? Those with whom you dine are not your family, and if these are not your family, then who is your family?

The city is a wheel, and within it there are wheels within wheels: the island is a wheel, the neighborhoods are wheels, and each block is a wheel. The waters, too, are wheels—from the largest river to the swirl of a drain. There are wheels on the cars, the taxis, the buses and the trains, wheels on the bicycles and the carriages, on the clockface and within the clock. Men and women have wheels for eyes: each citizen of the city mirrors the whole, and also their neighbors, who also have eyes.

The city is a clock, and the sun travels the canyons. There are shadows in the sky overhead; they pass and some of them are clouds, and you say, But look! And some of them are birds. But will they someday be bombs? And will they break the wheels?

The city is a shatter-box, clad in glass from head to toe. Everywhere you find your reflection, the reflection of others, and even reflections of reflections. There are lights on the other side of every pane, and nothing transparent does not glow. Some are windows, some are television screens, and some are advertisements, but all of them have people inside. Look at the people inside: some are tired and some are laughing.

I wandered the streets, looking for my beloved, but could not find her (him).

There is always someone angry in the next room. There is always someone heartbroken on the television. There is always someone ruined on the street. There is always someone shouting about their hatred. But you cannot offer shelter to the unhoused, nor solace to the injured, nor justice to those who have been denied justice. Not you alone. You will glow like a filament and shimmer like leaves in the wind, but you will never feel virtuous.

City of paper, of contracts and news, flyers and receipts, wrapping, tickets, bags and boxes, bills and ribbons. Every thought and intention, every agreement and charge. The birds carry them all away.

City of numbers, calculus city, postal codes and streets, the buildings on the streets, the floors in the elevator, the rooms along the hall,

all are named with numbers. — Arithmetical city, where prices are divided by discounts, multiplied by tips and taxes, summed in barrooms and entered into registers. So you are quick, like electricity.

You city of remembering and forgetting. Everything will change: beloved buildings will be torn down and new ones built in their place, and parks will be planted anew. Politicians will resign in disgrace, museums will move, money will come and go. What once was gorgeous will come to seem tawdry and fake; great beauties will be buried, famous men will have their names erased. Everything will change: People will vanish, and those that stay will grow old.

But you will not change.